"The etchings," declared Sy. "There they are. Do you see? Château Lafitte 1787. Th. J. for Thomas Jefferson. And the crescent. Pichard's secret code—his message to the future, his time capsule. This wine should be a treasure for the ages. And it's for you and me. And nobody else."

He spoke the last words with such force that there could be no doubt about his meaning. Now Sy picked up the corkscrew. The wine was like an old friend, and for a brief moment, he felt guilty about violating it. But all friends served a purpose, and this one was no exception.

With every eye in the room on him, Sy cut away his replacement capsule. Ever so gently, he pointed the corkscrew into the old cork, slowly coaxing it up. At first, the cork didn't want to leave its housing, but finally the top half came free and slid out soundlessly. Sy set it on the table. Tipping the bottle slightly, he edged the corkscrew back in to detach the remaining bit of cork. He got part of it out, but the rest dropped back into the bottle. Sy lifted the bottle to his nose and breathed. The luscious aroma of earth, chocolate, fruit, and smoke was dizzying. Sheer, unadulterated desire overtook him, and his entire body grew weak.

"Tripp, would you?" asked Sy, indicating the crystal rod and decanter.

"Of course," the waiter answe

Sy handed him the bottle.

PANDORA'S
BOTTLE

A novel by

JOANNE SYDNEY LESSNER

FLINT MINE PRESS

SINGIN' IN THE RAIN (from "Singin' in the Rain")
Music by NACIO HERB BROWN Lyric by ARTHUR FREED
© 1929 (Renewed) METRO-GOLDWYN-MAYER INC.
All Rights Controlled by EMI ROBBINS CATALOG INC. (Publishing)
and ALFRED MUSIC PUBLISHING CO., INC. (Print). All Rights Reserved.
Used by Permission of ALFRED PUBLISHING CO., INC.

I COULD HAVE DANCED ALL NIGHT (from "My Fair Lady")
Lyrics by ALAN JAY LERNER Music by FREDERICK LOEWE
© 1956 (Renewed) ALAN JAY LERNER and FREDERICK LOEWE
All Rights Administered by CHAPPELL & CO., INC. All Rights Reserved.
Used by Permission of ALFRED PUBLISHING CO., INC.

JUST ONE OF THOSE THINGS (from "High Society")
Words and Music by COLE PORTER
© 1935 (Renewed) WB MUSIC CORP. All Rights Reserved.
Used by Permission of ALFRED PUBLISHING CO., INC.

OLD FRIENDS (from "Merrily We Roll Along")
Words and Music by Stephen Sondheim
© 1981 RILTING MUSIC, INC.
All Rights Administered by WB MUSIC CORP.
All Rights Reserved. Used by Permission.
Reprinted by permission of Hal Leonard Corporation.

ISBN 978-0-9825208-2-6
Library of Congress Control Number: 2010925352

Printed and bound in the United States of America.
Cover design by Linda Pierro

Published by Flint Mine Press
PO Box 353, Coxsackie, NY 12051
Visit our website at www.flintminepress.com

For Joshie

ACKNOWLEDGMENTS

THIS BOOK WOULD NOT HAVE SEEN THE LIGHT of day without the help of my cousin, Debbie Lessner Gioquindo, aka the Hudson Valley Wine Goddess. She jump-started my wine education, reminded me about our family's winemaking heritage in Tapolca, Hungary, and facilitated much of my research. Most important, she introduced me to Bob Bedford and Linda Pierro of Flint Mine Press, who have proven to be the perfect collaborators for this project in every way. Michael Migliore, proprietor of Whitecliff Vineyard, gave me a thorough lesson in winemaking past and present, while Yancey Stanforth-Migliore provided a delicious impromptu omelet to complement the wines I tasted. Kristop Brown, former winemaker at Benmarl Winery, graciously uncorked his oldest bottles for me. Thanks to Debbie's children, Michael and Melanie, and husband, Paul, for the babysitting that made our winery visits possible. I owe a significant debt of gratitude to Sylvia Schoenbaum for introducing me to Sally Pope, Ralf Kuettel, Erin Ward, and the staff of Trestle on Tenth. They welcomed me into "the family" for a day, tossing delicacies my way as I absorbed the kitchen hubbub, and, thankfully, didn't make me do anything more difficult than peel apples.

I am fortunate to have a cadre of supportive and knowledgeable friends upon whose expertise I continually draw. In particular, I must thank Tim Peierls for additional oeno-insights and for splurging on the questionable Haut-Brion, as well as fellow novelists Rick Hamlin, Jonathan Rabb, and Helen Faye Rosenblum for their keen advice and constant encouragement. *Un grand merci* to Catherine Marquet Elliott and Claudine Marquet, who de-Americanized my

French, and Patrick Delisle Crevier (via Rob Tate), who then Canadianized it. Thanks also to Deborah Chapnick and Jason Baruch for their wise counsel, Claudia Cross for early stewardship, and Janet Bushor, Cornelia Iredell, Cristiane Young, Laurie Dodge, Owen Blicksilver, and especially Win Rutherfurd for corroborative detail.

I will forever be deeply grateful to my parents, Helen and Alford Lessner, and my sister, Kathy Lessner Yellen, for their endless cheerleading and unconditional love and support. To my remarkable and unfailingly entertaining children, Julian and Phoebe, I send a giant thank-you squeeze for their patience and newfound enthusiasm for wine—even though they think it all tastes the same. Finally, I float an ocean of gratitude toward my husband, Josh Rosenblum, for everything always, and for being what my great-aunt Lucy perspicaciously described—after knowing him for only five minutes—as "the other half of the nut."

in vino veritas
(In wine, there is truth.)

—Latin proverb

"What's in a name?"

—William Shakespeare

PANDORA'S
BOTTLE

ANYONE WATCHING SY HAMPTON would think he had never been to a wine auction before. Sweat was beading on his high, rounded forehead, and he was having difficulty keeping the fingernails of his right hand from drumming a steady tattoo up and down the white plastic paddle that rested on his knee. The catalog he clutched in his left hand was so crumpled and shiny that it looked like it had spent a night or two under his pillow, which, he would have been forced to admit, it had. In fact, he had been carrying the glossy book with him everywhere, ever since he first learned the bottle had come up for sale.

An involuntary groan escaped Sy's lips, causing the elderly woman sitting next to him to look over. Quickly disguising the outburst as a cough, Sy smiled apologetically, at the same time taking in the woman's salmon bouclé Escada suit, multi-carat diamond earrings, and heavy necklace of what were either garnets or exquisite dark rubies. From the way she inclined her head toward him with an indulgent smile, he could tell she was dismissing him as any threat to her plans. He glanced down at the page to which her pristine catalog lay open, and his heart gave a tiny jolt as he realized that her plans were identical to his.

In truth, Sy Hampton attended Shoreham's wine auctions regularly. In the twenty years since the auction house opened its International Fine and Rare Wines Department, he'd come to prefer it to Sotheby's or Christie's. The two larger houses often fought so hard over coveted bottles that sellers got fed up and turned to Shoreham's, which had slowly and steadily built up its name and reputation almost before the other houses knew what was happening. So while Sy still visited Sotheby's and Christie's when something really spectacular came up, it was the tuxedoed waiters at Shoreham's handing out complimentary glasses of champagne who knew him by name. He was only surprised he'd never spotted the old woman before. On any other day, at any other auction, he would have relished giving her a run for her money, but there was too much riding on this particular event—on this particular lot— for him to savor the thrill of competitive bidding. He hadn't felt this internally agitated since his first big leveraged buyout, twenty years ago. The sangfroid he had developed in the ensuing years staring down recalcitrant CEOs and cajoling millions out of frigid bankers was in frustratingly short supply today.

It occurred to him that he might press this maddening breach of composure to his advantage. Let the dowager underestimate him. Let her take him for a nervous novice who couldn't possibly have enough money to compete with her. Let her drop her guard so that when he moved in for the kill, she'd be so blindsided that she'd forget to raise her paddle. His partner, Warren Sage, was an expert at sucker punch negotiating, and Sy liked to think he was still capable of learning from those around him.

With a sudden move, he took up his catalog, which fell open easily, as the binding had long since broken. He gave an ostentatious shiver that wasn't entirely faked as his fingers caressed the color photograph of the 1787 Château Lafite, reputed to have been part of Thomas Jefferson's private collection. He traced the small golden crescent on the top right-hand side of the label and imagined that he could see the telltale initials Th. J. etched in the dark opaque glass underneath it. Two ex-wives and the spiraling markets had taken a bite out of Sy's fortune, but he still had millions at his disposal, and if the old woman forced him to drop one on the Lafite, he would. Money was meant to be spent, wine was meant to be drunk, and he had never—*ever*—wanted a bottle of wine as much as he wanted this one.

Sy Hampton was an oenophile, and while he didn't flatter himself that his was a remarkable palate, he had listened, smelled, tasted, and learned. For almost as long as he'd known anything about wine, he'd known about—and fantasized about—this legendary bottle. He'd learned of its existence from François, the elderly sommelier who had served him the first bottle of wine he'd ever ordered. It was 1983, and Sy, fresh out of Columbia Business School, had landed his first job at Randall Ventures, a coup he had accomplished by waylaying Sumner Randall at a cocktail party and refusing to let the financier through to the bar until he'd been promised employment.

Sy had taken himself out to a fancy little restaurant on the Upper East Side called L'Étoile to celebrate. He had never ordered a bottle of wine before. As the eldest child of a hardware store manager and a substitute teacher, simply dining out had been enough of a treat; a luxury like wine was off the table, so to speak. Buoyed by his good fortune and envisioning a moneyed future, Sy had admitted to François that he was ignorant about wine, and the sommelier had happily responded by giving him a primer. Sy repaid the sommelier's kindness by returning frequently to L'Étoile until the restaurant closed several years later. As Sy's palate became stimulated and his spending power increased, he purchased, with François's advice, increasingly expensive and adventurous wines.

On his third or fourth visit to L'Étoile, the sommelier had told him the story of the fabled Pichard Lafites. Legend had it that among the wines Jefferson purchased on a voyage to Bordeaux in 1787 was a single bottle that had been the subject of an experiment by the famous winemaker Nicolas Pierre de Pichard, owner of Château Lafite, or Lafitte, as it was spelled at the time. Lafite, derived from the Gascon *la hite,* or "small hill," had already become one of the most important wine-producing estates in Pauillac, the greatest wine-growing region of Bordeaux. The 1787 vintage was an exceptional one, and Pichard selected the best barrel to experiment with. Using a process called extended maceration, Pichard kept the skins, seeds, and stems in with the fermenting wine for a biblical forty days, rather than the customary seven to fourteen. The added exposure to the adjunct parts of the grape increased the level of tannins and phenols, the antioxidants that act as a preservative in wine. It would take many decades for the harsh chemicals to polymerize and precipitate out, but the result would be a smooth, well-integrated wine that Pichard intended to last into the next century and beyond. A later discovery of writings by Pichard referred to *la chose secrète*—some additional secret ingredient he added to the wine—which only fanned the frenzied imaginations of oenophiles the world over.

True or not, Pichard's claims to viticultural immortality were not looked upon kindly by the Republicans, whose mission it was to equalize everyone, providing additional justification for his execution by guillotine during the Reign of Terror. The bottles in the twenty-five cases from this barrel yield had been marked by a crescent, etched in the glass beside the vintage and the château. Thomas Jefferson, who had become obsessed with Bordeaux wines, had visited the region and Château Lafite in 1787. He ordered a case of wine from Pichard, but the winemaker replied that he had none left for sale, and for many years, it was assumed that Jefferson had never received any bottles from the 1787 Lafite vintage, let alone from Pichard's experimental barrel.

But among the papers that included Pichard's reference to *la chose secrète* was a copy of a bill to Thomas Jefferson for a single bottle of the 1787 vintage, dated several months after his initial, rejected application for an entire case. Wine historians could only assume that Jefferson had received it, but until the actual bottle came to light and its provenance was traced, nobody knew whether or not it still existed—if it ever had—and whether it had come from Pichard's experimental yield.

It had. A French family named Marquet had revealed the existence of the bottle, had it verified, and offered it up for auction. Thomas Jefferson's initials were etched just under the signifying crescent, indicating that he had, in fact, owned it. As far as anyone knew, this was the only bottle remaining from Pichard's experimental barrel.

And it might still be drinkable.

Sy Hampton had always been a history buff, and when history and wine converged, his gooseflesh became engaged. From the moment he heard old François's story, he swore to himself that, should Jefferson's fabled 1787 Pichard Lafite ever materialize, he would buy it and drink it. Wine had become his passion, but this bottle was his obsession.

He closed his eyes and, for the umpteenth time, imagined uncorking the wine that Thomas Jefferson could have drunk, but didn't. Just the thought of sampling a viable or even partially viable Château Lafite dating from the French Revolution was enough to make him tipsy.

The old woman next to Sy cleared her throat in an unmistakable bid for attention. Sy opened his eyes. She dipped her snowy head toward the open catalog in his lap. Like most bottles, which were intended to mature in damp, musty wine cellars, Jefferson's bore no label, only the etchings, but the present château, Lafite-Rothschild, had provided a beautifully calligraphed one for the occasion with an embossed gold crescent.

"You're not bidding on the Jefferson Lafite, are you?" she asked, eyeing him skeptically.

He arranged his face into a hangdog expression and nodded eagerly.

She pursed her plum red lips smugly, gave a little sniff, and returned her attention to her own catalog.

His dislike for her compounded instantly, and not just because the Escada suit reminded him of something that Marianne, the first and nastier of his ex-wives, would wear. Although Sy knew how far he would go to get the wine, he had no idea how far the dowager would. Clearly, she knew the history of the bottle, and from the way she was dressed, Sy guessed she could make it a very expensive day for him. So be it. He had lived with the promise of this bottle for so many years that he felt it was his already. It was inconceivable to him that he might leave Shoreham's today without it.

Sy glanced around the sleek, understated elegance of the Park Room. It was more crowded than usual, with over a hundred people gathered for the two-hour evening session, rather than the usual fifty or so, but there were more than 450 lots for sale, and several other notable ones besides the Jefferson Lafite. Sy scanned the long mahogany banquettes on either side of the room, each manned by three Shoreham's employees at telephones. That was the variable, he knew. The Lafite was listed roughly three-quarters of the way through as lot 345. He'd have plenty of time before then to size up the competition he could see. But who would be bidding anonymously by phone? And was the auctioneer commissioned to bid on behalf of some unnamed collector?

He spotted several familiar faces, including Peter Blomgard, his only remaining friend from his early days at Randall Ventures. He and Peter had a long history of slugging it out at Shoreham's over coveted parcels, with each maintaining that his lifetime tally was higher than the other's. But Sy knew that the Lafite was out of Peter's range. No, Peter was likely there for one of the two Domaine de la Romanée-Conti lots: the rare case of magnums of Grand Cru 1969 or the jeroboam of La Tâche 1962 Côte de Nuits. He guessed the Grand Cru would go for somewhere between twenty and forty grand, and the La Tâche anywhere from forty to fifty. Ordinarily, Sy would have delighted in making his friend sweat over either of those, but not today. Blomgard could have them.

A gentle tinkling of Debussy interrupted his thoughts, and the dowager retrieved a jewel-encrusted cell phone from the inside pocket of a large brown leather tote bag.

"Hello? It's about to start." She glanced sideways at Sy, who was purposely doing a poor job of pretending not to listen. "Oh yes, I think I'll be able to get it. I'll try not to go over three. I doubt I'll have to." She snapped the phone shut, replaced it in her tote bag, smoothed her snowy coif, and settled back in her chair as Antony Farrell took the podium.

With his ruddy cheeks and shock of golden hair, Antony Farrell, senior director of Shoreham's International Fine and Rare Wines Department, looked like an overgrown British schoolboy, which he more or less was. But Sy knew his looks were deceiving. Farrell was Cambridge-educated, whip-smart, and wildly ambitious. They had met at several wine events and had dined together once at Sy's home, where Sy had taken great pleasure in serving several prestige bottles from his cellar.

Farrell had been duly impressed both with the wine (which included a 1982 Pétrus) and Sy's state-of-the-art cellar. Sy had converted the entire basement level of his town house on East Sixty-fourth Street into a climate-controlled Mediterranean-style cellar and tasting room, complete with tile floor, marble table, wrought-iron grilles, stone archways, and a complex racking and filing system. It was the one part of the house he had refused to let Marianne design. He'd had to trade away the rest of it, including his study (the one room he had bothered to redecorate after they divorced), in order to get the basement. But it had been worth it, especially to see an expert like Farrell trying not to salivate at the sight of it.

Farrell spotted Sy almost immediately and gave a barely perceptible nod in his direction. Sy glanced sideways at the dowager, but she was staring fixedly at her catalog and seemed not to have noticed. It wouldn't be long before she realized whom she was up against. He consulted his Vacheron Constantin Great Explorers watch, which he considered his good-luck charm. He'd purchased the limited edition $70,000 watch the morning he and Warren closed their first billion-dollar deal. Five o'clock.

It was time.

Farrell pounded the hammer and the auction began.

"Lot number one! A lovely Château Margaux 1983. Do I have three? Three it is, and three-five? Three-five! Four from me—four-four against me, I'm out, it's in the room at four-four, do I have five? Five! Five-five? Yes? Last chance . . . selling at five-five . . . all done at five-five to . . . sorry, sir, can't see your paddle number . . . sold to paddle number 107! Do you want another? There's one more in the lot . . . come now, take it off my hands, won't you? Yes? Good. Throw a party!"

Despite Farrell's rapid-fire patter, the minutes turtled by. There were quite a number of parcels that, under normal circumstances, would have piqued Sy's interest, but he felt it prudent to remain invisible until the critical moment.

"Lot number 146! Six magnums of Château Mouton Rothschild 1945, do I hear thirty?"

Sy watched longingly as those passed to a young Asian couple in the front row for two hundred grand, and he was pleased for Peter Blomgard when he scooped the '62 La Tâche out from under them at fifty-two.

"Lot number 212!" called Farrell. "A case of 1961 Châteaux Margaux . . ."

The dowager excused herself, took a small purse from her capacious tote bag, and squeezed past Sy. Like Sy, she had yet to place a single bid. As he watched her salmon bouclé back recede, he took the opportunity to scan the room once more, and his eyes fell on the wooden banquettes. The telephone traffic had been fairly quiet so far, with most of the anonymous bidding filtering through the young blond operator on the end, whose name was Angela. Maybe they were all waiting for the Lafite. He was glad this auction wasn't online as well. The muted phones would bring him competition enough.

Sy glanced down suddenly at the old woman's tote bag. A terribly wonderful and devious thought had just occurred to him, and he found himself acting on it before his conscience could voice an objection. He couldn't do anything about the anonymous phone participants, but there might be something he could do about the bidding biddy . . .

Keeping his gaze on the door, he bent down and extracted her cell phone from the pocket just inside her tote bag. He quickly scrolled through the options screen until it displayed her phone number, which, even as his hands trembled, his easy head for figures absorbed. Then he scrolled to the alerts menu and made a slight alteration to her ringtone and volume level. Suppressing a chuckle at his choice, he replaced her phone in her tote bag. He pulled out his iPhone and added her number to his Favorites, temporarily replacing his office number. Although his heart seemed to be skipping every other beat, he was staring innocently and intently at Antony Farrell by the time the dowager returned.

"Lot number 239! Two jeroboams of 1961 Haut-Brion. Do I have five?"

The remaining lots sped by in a blur, and then, in a flash, the Lafite was up.

"Lot 345. A very special bottle, of course," Farrell purred. "One of the Jefferson Bordeaux, Château Lafite 1787. That's right, this wine dates back to the French Revolution, and legend has it that it could still be drinkable." Farrell paused for effect. "If it is, it would be a treasure beyond imagining."

Sy swallowed hard and gripped his white plastic paddle.

"Do I hear thirty thousand to start the bidding?"

Sy's hand shot up.

"Thirty-five. Do I hear thirty-five?"

The dowager's hand was up almost as fast. Almost immediately, two other people in the front of the room emerged as serious contenders, a stocky fellow in a rugby shirt who looked no more than twenty-five—it was harder and harder to tell who had money and who didn't—and an older, professorial-looking gentleman. Among them, the dowager, Sy, and several phone bidders, the price was driven up to $300,000 within minutes.

"Three, do I have three-five? Three-five to the lady. Three-ten? Three-ten, Sy. Three-fifteen, Angela on the phone."

And on it went, until the kid in the rugby shirt dropped out at $350,000, the professor dropped out at $380,000, and two of the three phone bidders hung up at $400,000. The mood in the room was palpably tense. It had become a three-way race, and the on-lookers looked dazed as the three hands—Sy's, Angela's, and the dowager's—chased one another into the air in quick succession.

"Do I have four-fifty?"

The dowager had brought the bidding to $445,000. Sy could have jumped in, but Angela was frowning over the receiver, and he felt certain her bidder was about to drop out. Angela looked at Farrell, shook her head, and set down the phone.

It was between Sy and the dowager now, as he had known from the start it would be.

His desire for the bottle had exploded with a new, unexplained intensity. Somewhere he had crossed the line between wanting the bottle and needing it with a desperation he didn't fully understand, and could not have articulated if asked. He suddenly felt that his whole future depended on his owning this wine, and that terrible things would happen if he lost it. Had he been able to think ration-ally, he would have admitted that this degree of blinding need was out of proportion with the bottle's actual worth, but in the mo-ment, all he knew was that he would stop at nothing to get it.

The sweat was running down the side of his neck onto his col-lar, but he didn't care. He wasn't using his right hand for any purpose other than to lift his paddle in the air, which he did again and again whenever the dowager brought hers down.

At $485,000, he decided he'd had enough. His iPhone was still in the palm of his left hand. He pulled up his Favorites, tapped the number, and waited.

The "Marseillaise" suddenly blared at top volume from the dowager's brown tote bag, and the whole room gave a collective gasp of distaste. Sy thrust his paddle into the air and upped his own bid by $5,000, then $5,000 more, while the dowager rummaged in her bag, trying to silence her phone. Sy gazed purposefully at Antony Farrell and raised his paddle three more times.

Farrell gave a slight nod in Sy's direction and pattered, "Five-ten . . . selling at five-ten . . ."

The dowager's white head shot up from her bag.

"Five hundred ten thousand dollars . . . going once, twice . . ."

She blinked her small blue eyes, unsure whether to bid further. Farrell let her indecision hang for a second longer, then brought the hammer down.

"All done at $510,000 to number three! Well done, Sy. You'll have to tell us how it tastes!"

The room broke into restrained applause. The dowager was dumbfounded. She stared at Sy and then down at the jewel-encrusted phone in her hand, the realization of his treachery taking hold.

"You son of a bitch," she seethed, her plummy lips writhing.

Sy shrugged as he rose from his seat. The room was coming back into focus, and his composure was returning to normal, even if his heart rate wasn't.

"All's fair in love and wine," he said with a wink.

He returned his empty champagne glass to the table at the back of the room, where the red-haired young man who had served him smiled and said, "Nicely done, Mr. Hampton."

Sy thought, not unkindly, that the amount of money he'd just dropped on the Jefferson Lafite was probably more than the waiter would see in his lifetime. Ah well, nothing he could do about that. Sy turned back to the room, and with a grateful nod to Farrell and a prayer of thanks heavenward, he dabbed his glistening brow and left to arrange for delivery of his prize.

PART ONE

THE SELECTION

ONE

"SO I SAID TO HIM, 'FOR THE LAST TIME, I'm not marrying you!' And he says, 'What have I been wasting my time with you for if you're not gonna marry me?' And I said, 'Well, screw you! If you think being with me is a waste of time, then you're not worth marrying!' "

Valentina D'Ambrosio chewed her red pinky nail in consternation as she adjusted her headset and finished, "But I don't know if I did the right thing, because I keep thinking about him."

Her confessional was greeted by silence.

"Trish? Trish! You still there?"

"Yeah, I'm thinking," answered the voice on the other end, throaty from a lifetime of cigarettes.

"I hate it when you think. It means you don't know how to tell me I'm wrong," Valentina said shrewdly.

"Not wrong exactly, but if you love him, maybe you gotta take him on his terms," said Trish.

"Everyone I ever knew who was married was miserable. Starting with my parents and ending with you."

Trish hacked her smoker's cough and said, "I'm okay. I made my bed. But you—I don't understand you! First you say he's not worth marrying, now you're saying you don't ever wanna get married. I think you don't know what you want!"

"My gut is telling me not to hitch myself to Jerry," said Valentina firmly. "But even if he's not Mr. Right, I still don't see why he can't be Mr. Right Now."

"Three years is too long for him to be Mr. Right Now if that isn't what he wants. You gotta shit or get off the pot, Val."

Valentina sighed. "Funny, that's exactly what Jerry said."

"What did your mother say?"

"I haven't told her yet. You know she's gonna flip. She thinks Elisa and I are old maids already at thirty-two."

"Well, you are. Between the two of you, she's running out of excuses to tell her friends. You know you're gonna send her to an early grave."

"Thanks a lot." Valentina glanced up and then whispered, "I gotta go. The dragon lady is coming. I'll call you later."

Without bothering to wait for Trish's response, she disconnected her headset and returned to her computer, where she began randomly clicking documents into folders, trying to look undisturbable.

"Valentina!"

She closed her eyes briefly before swiveling her chair around.

"Good morning, Miss Banks."

The tall, haughty black woman gave a magisterial nod of approval. At least Valentina had remembered this time. Miss Banks, whom Valentina guessed to be pushing fifty despite her flawless ebony complexion, was from British Guyana and very correct. Not only did she not want Valentina or anyone else calling her Henrietta, she refused to tolerate the customary "Ms." For Valentina, remembering to say "Miss" had been harder than remembering how to spell "leverage" correctly.

"Mr. Hampton just telephoned from the car. His breakfast at the Regency with Mr. Soros went long, but he's on his way in, so look sharp." Miss Banks glowered at the telltale headset that was still hooked around Valentina's thick auburn hair. "Even when neither of us is here, you do not have carte blanche to yammer on the phone with your friends. Do you understand?"

Valentina hastily removed her headset. At least I have friends, she thought.

"Now," continued Miss Banks crisply, "I need you to telephone the River Club and cancel his tennis this afternoon. His knee is acting up. Then telephone Serena Hart and see if you can arrange for her to make a home visit this evening."

Miss Banks always used "telephone" as a verb. She never said "call," although Valentina abbreviated it for herself as she jotted the notes on her pad. Serena Hart was Mr. Hampton's physical therapist, but Valentina didn't think for a minute that she spent her time tending to his knee.

"Wipe that smirk off your face, missy," scolded Miss Banks, clearly reading her thoughts. "One more thing. Telephone Salon Bouvier and make an appointment for me to get my hair cut with Marcel sometime this week. Doesn't matter which day, any time after five."

Valentina dutifully scribbled another note, trying not to let her disgust show on her face. Miss Banks could just as easily have made that call herself, but she never passed up an opportunity to remind Valentina who her boss really was.

Although Valentina had technically been hired as Mr. Hampton's secretary, she was actually Miss Banks's slave. Miss Banks was Mr. Hampton's Assistant with a capital A—the keeper of his keys, both personal and professional. The other partner, Mr. Sage, had Laura and Tracy, but they seemed to share the responsibilities equally. It was all jolly first names over on his side of the office, but Mr. Hampton was only ever Mr. Hampton. Valentina was pretty sure that was Miss Banks's doing, and that he wouldn't have minded being called Sy.

It's all wordplay, thought Valentina. Just so Miss Banks can feel superior and plump herself up, when she's really only a glorified secretary. The thought cheered Valentina momentarily, but depressed her again almost immediately because of what it made her: a secretary's secretary. She had hoped this new job at Hampton & Sage, LLC, would be a step up, but it seemed that being secretary to the CEO didn't mean much. Not when he already had an Assistant.

Valentina had always been proud to work in an office. She'd grown up in a big, Italian working-class family in Bensonhurst, and she and her twin sister, Elisabetta, were the first in the family to go to college. Valentina had gotten a business administration degree from Brooklyn College, while Elisa had studied English literature at Fordham. Although they were nearly identical physically, their personality differences had grown more striking as they pursued

their adult lives. Despite the endless commute into the city on the
D train, Valentina still lived a few blocks away from her parents, in
a first-floor rental in a small red brick house on Bay Twenty-fifth
between Benson and Bath. Elisa had moved closer to the city, to
Cobble Hill, where she paid more for a place half the size. While
Valentina was proud to be from Brooklyn, Elisa took great pains to
hide her broad accent. Valentina had never had the heart to tell her
sister that she gave herself away every time she said her own name,
the only words that she couldn't seem to mask. Sometimes
Valentina got annoyed at Elisa's pretensions, but Valentina knew
she had it over her sister in one important way: Elisa made far less
money as an editor at an academic publishing company than
Valentina could in business, even as a secretary's secretary.

Valentina's first and only job before joining Hampton & Sage
was at an insurance company, where she stayed until she and her
boss were downsized. Private equity, with its outsized personalities
and billion-dollar deals, promised more drama than insurance. But
the reality was that her new job encompassed the same mundane
tasks that she now realized were a constant at her level, regardless
of the industry: handling correspondence, filing documents, and
the like. It was no different. In fact, it was worse. At least at the insurance company she'd answered directly to the managing director.

Aside from Miss Banks, Valentina liked the people at Hampton
& Sage, and she knew that the second most important thing after
job advancement (which she was practical enough to realize was
unlikely here) was a friendly workplace. Laura and Tracy had been
welcoming and helpful, and after two months, Valentina had started
to get to know the assistants of the junior executives as well. The
only person who remained a mystery was Mr. Hampton himself.

He was always very polite to Valentina, though they'd never had
anything resembling a real conversation. She knew from delivering
the mail to his office that he was a big shot. His walls were plastered
with framed magazine covers with his photo, and there were several
ornate gold frames housing what even Valentina recognized were
valuable paintings. Underneath each painting was a small, lami-

nated card prepared by Miss Banks, which stated the name of the work, the date, the artist, and the declaration "From the private collection of Mr. Sy Hampton."

Valentina had never met anyone who collected art, but according to Laura, that wasn't even Mr. Hampton's real passion. What he really cared about was wine.

"Yeah, sometimes he'll take off a couple of months and work remotely while he lives on a ranch in Australia or in a château in France, to immerse himself in the local wines," Laura explained one day as she, Tracy, and Valentina ate deli sandwiches on a bench just inside Central Park.

"And he spent more on his fiftieth birthday party than Sumner Randall did on his sixty-fifth!"

"Who's that?" asked Valentina, munching, her eyes wide with curiosity.

"He's the head of Randall Ventures. That's the firm where Mr. Hampton started, and now they're rivals. If you're going to stick with us, you have to learn the names of the competition."

"Except that they're not always the competition," put in Tracy. "Sometimes the big guns like us and Randall team up to crush the little guy!" She waved a triumphant fist, then snorted and shook her head. "It's crazy."

"So how much did Mr. Hampton spend on his birthday party?" asked Valentina.

"According to the *Wall Street Journal,* it was four and a half million dollars. But, I mean, Randall spent four million getting Elton John and Mariah Carey, and all Mr. Hampton had was some chamber orchestra and two opera singers I've never heard of."

"Miss Banks assured us they're famous," said Tracy with a wink.

"They probably are," agreed Laura. "He is president of the Metropolitan Opera Guild, for Christ's sake."

"And the Racquet Club, don't forget," added Tracy in a fair imitation of Miss Banks.

"Then what did he spend four and a half million dollars on?" Valentina asked, confused.

Laura and Tracy looked at each other and burst out, "Grape juice!"

When their laughter died down, Laura added, "I overheard him talking to Warren about Sumner Randall's wines." She dropped her voice to baritone range. " 'Poor guy. The 2004 Louis Jadot Montrachet was the best he could manage.' Can you believe it?!"

All of this was equal parts fascinating and ridiculous to Valentina. She could understand squandering a fortune on art, because at least you could enjoy it for more than ten minutes. But wine? You finished the bottle, and that was it. It was gone. Or you could keep it in a dusty old cellar and never open it, and then who cares? Valentina didn't even particularly like wine. White wine was all right in the summer with a spritz of seltzer, but red wine gave her a headache, and it all tasted pretty much the same to her.

This obsession with wine made Mr. Hampton seem like some weird, exotic species that, thanks to Miss Banks, she'd never get close enough to really examine. Yet at the same time, there was something sort of sweet about him, even though to Valentina, it seemed like he was heading quickly toward the hill, even if he wasn't quite over it. He wasn't bad-looking, but he didn't exactly make the most of what he had. He dressed well, in designer everything, but he seemed to rumple easily. Certainly, he could afford a better dye job. His hair was an unconvincing ginger color and on top of that, he wore it a bit too long on the sides for a man in his fifties who wasn't Richie Sambora.

"Valentina!" Miss Banks's impatient bark interrupted her reverie. "Did you hear what I said about booking the NetJet to Bermuda next weekend? He'll fly from Teterboro, as usual. Do you have the number?"

"Um, yes, it's here . . . uh, somewhere."

"Really, girl, you need to be more organized."

At that moment, the subject of Valentina's musing and Miss Banks's fussing entered the office through the sliding glass doors that swooshed open at the swipe of an ID card. Miss Banks instinctively patted her glowing cheeks and turned to welcome

Mr. Hampton with a smile that radiated both enthusiasm and efficiency. Valentina, responding to Miss Banks's sudden movement, stood up and hovered nervously beside her.

"Good morning, Mr. Hampton," cooed Miss Banks. "Shall I take your coat? It's a bit chilly for September, don't you think?"

"I hadn't really noticed," he said, handing it over. "Will you set up the conference room for a meeting at ten? I'll need the research on the three Chinese banks and the latest spreadsheet on Asia Fund V."

"Of course. We've canceled your tennis and arranged for Miss Hart."

Valentina started to protest that she hadn't yet had a chance to make either phone call, but Miss Banks silenced her with a meaningful tilt of her head.

"What else do I need to know?" he asked.

"Francis Gilbert from *Opera News* called. The editorial staff has made their selections for the honorees at this year's awards."

Mr. Hampton nodded. "I'm sure he wants to discuss fund-raising for the event as well. Anything else?"

"That's it, at present."

Isn't that enough? wondered Valentina.

"Valentina, may I see you in my office for a moment?"

She was so startled that the headset, which she had only barely realized she'd been fiddling with, seemed to fly out of her hands of its own accord.

"Um, sure," she said, bending over to pick it up. As soon as her fingers grazed the carpet, she wished she'd let it lie. There was nowhere else Mr. Hampton's gaze could be falling except on her ass, which she could feel straining in his general direction against her tight red skirt.

"I'm happy to assist," Miss Banks volunteered, as Valentina straightened up, set the headset back on her desk, and tried, unsuccessfully, to avoid the other woman's glare.

"No, thank you," said Mr. Hampton lightly. "I need Valentina."

I need Valentina.

Valentina had no doubt that those three little words were as much a stab to the loyal heart of Miss Banks as they were a shock to herself. With a growing sense of unease, Valentina followed Mr. Hampton into his large corner office. She couldn't possibly imagine what service she could provide that Miss Banks couldn't supply more capably. Except the obvious, which could hardly be what he had in mind.

Mr. Hampton closed the door.

"Have a seat."

She hesitated, while he moved behind his desk to settle into the wide green leather chair, which gave a comfortable creak as it accepted his weight. He smiled at her as she sat opposite him, and she noticed for the first time that his eyes were a clear, twinkling blue.

"How are you settling in here?" he asked.

"Oh! Um, fine. Private equity is a lot more exciting than insurance," she declared, although she was still taking that on faith.

"You were with . . . which insurance company?"

"Avid. Do you know it?"

"Of course I know it. We own it." He brushed a long, stray lock of hair off his forehead. "Bought it about eight months ago. We downsized, and now we're refocusing on auto. We'll merge it with Royal Sun, which we bought about a year ago, then launch an IPO as soon as it makes sense."

Valentina seized on the one word that meant something to her.

"I was downsized. I think you downsized me."

Mr. Hampton looked slightly taken aback, then he recovered. "But we've made it up to you, right? Here you are!" He threw his hands wide, accidentally knocking a pile of papers to the floor.

Valentina, eager to make a good impression, scrambled to pick them up. "Yeah, but you didn't know that when I got axed." She set the papers back on his desk, though she didn't exert herself further to neaten them. "It was just luck."

He eyed her curiously and then smiled. "Thank you for not saying it was dumb luck."

"Um, what exactly did you need me for?" She gestured vaguely around the room.

He leaned forward with a conspiratorial smile. "Maybe 'need' was too strong a word, but I didn't want to give Miss Banks a loophole." Valentina stared at him, and he cleared his throat and sat back in his chair again. "I wanted to see how you were getting on. And to tell you . . . er . . . that you look lovely today."

Oh, dear, thought Valentina, following his gaze downward to the ballet neck of her white angora sweater, which was embroidered with pink and red hearts. Bending over to pick up her headset had definitely been a mistake.

"I went to a rare wine auction at Shoreham's yesterday, and do you know what I bought?" he said abruptly, as he stood and walked to the large picture window that looked out over Fifth Avenue.

Valentina frowned, wondering whether this was a trick question. "Um, a bottle of wine?"

"Yes!" he declared, so loudly she almost jumped. "And not just any bottle of wine. I purchased a Château Lafite 1787 that was once owned by Thomas Jefferson, the most artistic, creative, and brilliant of our founding fathers."

He paused expectantly.

"Wow. I didn't know wine that old still existed," she said finally.

"Oh, it's extremely rare. There are hardly any bottles left that date back to the French Revolution. And this bottle . . ." He leaned across his desk and spoke in an excited whisper. "This bottle is legendary, because there's a very good possibility it might still be drinkable!"

"Doesn't all wine get better as it gets older?" Valentina asked uncertainly.

She got the momentary impression that he wanted to pat her on the head, like a dog that had just caught a biscuit in its mouth.

"Yes, that's mainly true, although certain wines, Beaujolais Nouveau, for example, are meant to be drunk within six months. But even the best and biggest Bordeaux shouldn't age beyond, say, fifty years," he explained. "I don't know how much is still drinkable anymore from the legendary 1945 vintage. In any case, most wine is likely to be vinegar after 220 years."

"Then what's the big deal about the one you bought?"

He pulled from his jacket pocket a page torn from a catalog and smoothed it on the desk in front of her. It had a picture of a wine bottle. There was nothing particularly extraordinary-looking about it.

"The man who made this wine added something he hoped would make it last for centuries. We don't know what it was—he referred to it in his writings only as *la chose secrète*—the secret thing. Experts have reason to believe it may have been some kind of plant extract—citric acid, maybe, or even honey. He also left the skins, seeds, and stems in the wine longer than necessary to increase the antioxidants that preserve it. This man, Pichard, was determined to make a wine for the ages. And if he succeeded, and it's still viable, it will be like nothing you've ever tasted!"

"Why?"

"Because it's like a time capsule," he explained, pacing in front of the window as he talked. "You see, wines made before refrigeration are reputed to have been unsurpassable. On top of that, this one dates from before the phylloxera epidemic of the late nineteenth century that almost wiped out European vines altogether. Winemakers saved the vines by grafting the grape-bearing stalks onto American rootstock, which was resistant." He paused, gesturing toward his *Forbes* cover photo, as if he had forgotten all about Valentina and was lecturing to himself.

"To this day, European winemakers insist that the grafted stalks retained the characteristics of their own grapes, not the American stock, therefore making no difference to the wines. But who can say otherwise? Few people in modern times have ever had the opportunity to taste pre-phylloxera wines, but that's exactly what I'm going to do. The 1787 Lafite was rumored to be an exceptional vintage. This might very well be the most perfect bottle of wine in existence!"

He paused and rubbed his hands together as he spoke. "I had to fight to get it. There was an old woman next to me who wanted it almost as badly as I did. But I'll bet she was after the bottle only for its resale possibilities." He shook his head vigorously. "To keep a potentially drinkable wine on the market without ever uncorking it is heresy. Wine was made to be drunk, and I will not see this bottle's riches confined to the imagination!"

He turned to Valentina, his blue eyes glinting oddly, as if they were sweating. For a moment he looked quite unhinged.

"Valentina, I'd like to share this wine with you."

She stared at him, openmouthed. If this was what he needed her for, he definitely was unhinged.

"I—I don't understand," she managed.

Then the truth broke through her confusion. Aware that she probably sounded as disgusted as she was surprised, she blurted out, "Are you asking me on a date?"

This seemed to bring him up short, and he nodded, then shook his head, and then nodded again. If it weren't so bizarre, it would have been comical.

"Yes, I suppose I am," he said finally.

Valentina was stunned. She barely knew him well enough to have made up her mind about him one way or another. How had they gone from "Good morning, Valentina" to "Do you want to share Thomas Jefferson's rare, pre-whateveryoucallit bottle of wine with me"? And wasn't it against the law for a boss to date his secretary? Or at least against the rules? She desperately wished she could freeze him in time for a moment and run out to her desk to call Trish or Elisa for advice. It seemed incredibly rude to say no, but how could she possibly say yes?

"I've—I've got this boyfriend, you know, Jerry, and I don't think he'd like that very much," she spluttered.

Mr. Hampton drew a deep breath, seeming to collect himself, and nodded again. "Yes, I understand. But it doesn't have to be that kind of date."

She searched for some other excuse, but her mind was strangely blank.

He retreated to the window and waved his hand again, safely away from the papers on his desk. "Take the weekend and let me know on Monday."

She rose from her chair. "Was this wine, um, did it cost you a lot of money?" she asked hesitantly.

The corner of his lip turned up into a rueful smile. "If I share it with the right person, it will have been worth every penny."

Valentina couldn't fathom why he could possibly think she was the right person, but she nodded.

"Okay. I'll think about it."

"Thank you." He gestured toward the door. "Will you ask Miss Banks to come in?"

It was clear from Miss Banks's sudden and somewhat unsteady appearance at the adjacent filing cabinet that she had been kneeling by the door, listening.

"Your turn," said Valentina breezily.

As soon as the door closed after Miss Banks, Valentina ran to her desk, grabbed her headset, and punched in Trish's number.

"Candy's Nails, please hold," rasped the familiar, throaty voice. Valentina gnawed on the cuticle of her thumb and willed Trish to pick up again.

"Candy's Nails, may I help you?"

"It's me," whispered Valentina, keeping her eye firmly fixed on Mr. Hampton's door.

"What's wrong now? Is it Jerry?"

"No, it's not Jerry," said Valentina, and hurriedly explained Mr. Hampton's proposition.

"Fuck the wine, go for the money!" exclaimed Trish.

"What?!"

"Press a sexual harassment suit! Pick up some cold, hard cash and retire!"

"What are you talking about? This isn't harassment. It's an invitation! Jesus Christ, Trish, don't you even know the difference? I just want you to tell me if you think I should go with him to taste this wine. I mean, he says it doesn't have to be a 'date' date. He just wants me to go with him for some reason. God only knows why!"

"I know why, and so do you," said Trish snidely. "What other reason could he possibly have for wanting to impress you with this wine, if it isn't getting you into the sack?"

"I don't know. Maybe he thinks I'm interesting," said Valentina, her eyes still on the closed office door.

"Val, he doesn't know you. He doesn't know anything about you! Except he knows you've got great tits, hair that some of us would die for, and an ass that's as heart-shaped as your face."

"Maybe he senses something about me," protested Valentina.

"Okay, maybe, but do you sense anything about him? Val, honey," Trish croaked in what, for her, passed as sympathy. "I know you're still upset about Jerry. But just because Jerry's wrong doesn't mean this guy's right. If you really want to get to know him better that's one thing, but I swear this is the first time I've ever heard you use his name in a sentence. Don't get your head turned the wrong way just because he asked. *Capisce?*"

Valentina fingered the wire of her headset. Trish was right. She didn't want to jump out of the frying pan and land in another frying pan, even if it was a more expensive one. She wasn't particularly interested in Sy Hampton or in wine. What was the point of saying yes?

"Yeah. I guess you're right. He's probably already wishing he hadn't asked me."

"Maybe he should take the dragon lady," suggested Trish.

Valentina laughed in spite of herself. "Are you kidding? Then she'd be completely impossible!"

But as she hung up the phone, Valentina wondered whether there was any harm in trying something a little different for a change. Elisa was always on the lookout for new experiences, but, unlike her sister, Valentina often resisted them. Still, she sometimes found the missed opportunities haunted her, like the embroidered trench coat she'd tried on in Daffy's last April. It was in colors she never wore—all greens and browns—so she'd left it hanging on the rack, even though it fit like a glove.

She couldn't stop thinking about that coat for weeks.

TWO

WHAT THE HELL WAS THAT?

Sy wasn't thinking about the conversation he'd just had with Miss Banks, who had been uncharacteristically aloof. He was flashing back to his earlier encounter with Valentina. What on earth had he been thinking?

But that was just it—he hadn't been thinking.

Ever since his victory at Shoreham's, he'd felt as if a piece of his brain had disengaged and come loose, leaving him reckless and euphoric. First, he'd celebrated by splurging on his best champagne, Krug Clos du Mesnil Blanc de Blancs 1995, roughly $700 a bottle, and he was still on a high when he woke up this morning. He'd been so voluble at breakfast that he'd promised Soros $200,000 toward democratic fund-raising, to the surprise of the elder statesman financier. And when Sy saw Valentina standing by her desk, encased in a tight leather skirt and clingy sweater, with that beguiling expression of anxiety and defiance she sometimes wore, he was emboldened to invite her into his office for a private chat.

From her first day on the job, he had vaguely hoped to advance their acquaintance beyond their minimal exchanges about the weather and basic administrative tasks. Even the latter were infrequent, as Miss Banks was always quick to intercede. She was wonderful, Miss Banks, efficient, and always a step ahead of him. He'd become lazy about managing his affairs, because he had no need to be otherwise. No, he couldn't live without Miss Banks, but all the same, he'd lately been thinking he might increase her vacation days. Although he wasn't sure what good that would do, as she rarely used the ones she was already allotted.

Then, before he knew what he was doing, the first set of rash words escaped his lips, and he'd enjoyed a guilty rush of pleasure at Miss Banks's obvious displeasure.

"I need Valentina."

At last, he and Valentina were going to have a real conversation. He was itching to find out more about her. He knew she was from Brooklyn—her accent was unmistakable. Did she live, like he imagined, in one of those mansions in Bay Ridge, blocks from the shore, that had been segmented into apartments on the grand scale? Did she have a roommate, or perhaps live with her parents still? Did she sunbathe on the roof deck in a string bikini, or, better yet, naked? But the conversation had grown awkward as soon as she'd mentioned losing her former job at Avid Insurance, which, it turned out, was his fault. Then he'd clumsily knocked over his notes on Asia Fund V, which he'd been embarrassed to let her pick up, but not embarrassed enough to stop her. Eager to change the subject, he'd started chattering about himself. And the Lafite.

And the invitation had just popped out—like the cork from the Clos du Mesnil—which now made him wonder if perhaps, as with the champagne, he'd been twisting toward it all this time without realizing where he was heading. It was hard to say which of them had been more surprised.

But a strange thing had happened. As soon as the words were out of his mouth, he knew he meant them. For a split second the loose part of his brain tried to reattach itself and protest, but just as quickly, a fresh rush of exhilaration washed it away. As he silently willed her to accept his offer, he realized that now that he owned the wine he'd spent most of his adult life coveting, a new fixation was replacing the old. He needed a beautiful woman to perceive him as desirable, virile, and worldly.

Wine was sexy. He was not. It wasn't that he was unattractive, but he'd never thought of himself as the kind of guy women would sacrifice their friendships for. He'd been an adorable kid, with bright blue eyes that remained his best feature. More than one woman had told him he had sweet lips. At five feet ten, he had always been slender, but recently he'd been plumping up. Though he'd taken to working out in a specially outfitted room on the top floor of his house, he wished he'd stayed more active when he was younger. Within the first week of using his home gym, he'd injured his knee, necessitating regular visits from a physical therapist—which, he had to admit, had its advantages. But in general, his appearance had never been a priority.

For one thing, in his thirties and forties, his money and status were clearly his strongest attraction. Unfortunately, his recent market losses, though not as bad as others', had dulled his luster, while younger, richer men had catapulted beyond him. But all this was about to change. He had triumphed in battle to win the most famous, legendary, and, he had no doubt, most expensive bottle of wine in the world. He had emerged as its worthiest possessor, and it could prove to be his new passport to feminine youth and beauty. The Jefferson Lafite enhanced his pheromone cocktail of wealth and position with passion, color, texture, and a dash of youthful irresponsibility. It made him Dionysus. All he needed was Aphrodite.

Her name alone suggested her as the most likely candidate: Valentina D'Ambrosio. When he'd first seen it on the memo from Human Resources, it had struck him as improbably romantic— made up even. But that hadn't stopped him from immediately conjuring an image of a sultry raven-haired beauty walking into his office dressed in sinuous red silk, bearing a tray of coffee, which she would pour out for him before licking the spoon with succulent crimson lips. She'd smell like rosewater, and would let him bury his nose in every fragrant crevice of her body as they made love on his desk under his paintings in the shadow of Fifth Avenue.

Of course, nothing remotely like that had happened with the real Valentina, who bore little resemblance to his fantasy, except in one respect: she had consciously built a romantic identity around her name, though not one as provocative as his imaginings. She dressed almost exclusively in shades of pink, red, and white, favoring designs and decorations with hearts. But her hair was a luscious auburn, as thick and smooth as those silly hair care commercials where the model's tresses swirl in a perfect slow-motion billow. Valentina's hair really was like that, and it made him go soft in the knees. She wore it brushed back from a delicate widow's peak that rendered her face heart-shaped—a lucky boon from nature. Her eyes were extraordinary, too—cat eyes, green and almond-shaped.

Her earthiness was part of her appeal. It reminded him that she was a real person, and not a figment of his overactive, middle-aged imagination. He'd rather not think he'd fallen for a name; that would be pathetic. He considered it a plus that she did not hail from the circles in which he currently traveled. After all, he'd not been born to those circles himself, having grown up Jewish and decidedly middle-class in the Hudson Valley, and attended public high school in Poughkeepsie. It wasn't a leap to imagine Valentina in his high school, which had always had a fairly substantial Italian-American population. She'd have been the prettiest girl at the center of a bevy of less pretty girls who wanted nothing to do with the likes of him, and at the time, he'd have been equally dismissive of her. They wouldn't have crossed paths, as she'd hardly have been likely to be taking advanced placement calculus, and he wouldn't have been taking bookkeeping. But he'd have lusted after her just the same, and would have been hurt by her inevitable rejection of him, had he risked pursuing her.

As far as the real, current Valentina was concerned, the fact that she was even willing to consider his invitation gave him hope. Everything in life is negotiable, he reminded himself. That was his credo, gleaned from the most unlikely source: the handyman in the first building he lived in when he'd moved to New York, straight out of Dartmouth. It was funny how random people could say things that lodged in your brain. In this case, those five words had proved to be a formula for success. He wondered if Ronnie the handyman had parlayed that morsel of understated brilliance into something better for himself than air-conditioning repair.

If it came down to it, he would negotiate with Valentina. He would give up—what—in order to get her to taste the wine with him? Would he sign an agreement stating he would never nuzzle that voluminous hair, never taste the soft skin in the hollow of her neck? If that was the case, then what was the point?

What was the point anyway, he wondered. Valentina was lovely, and private thoughts of her had been known to set his heart and other parts racing. But he had no illusions about her, no expectations of stifled genius lurking behind her gently confused demeanor. She was, decidedly, not his type. He was generally attracted to accomplished women with a strong sense of purpose. And look where that had gotten him. Divorce court. First with Marianne, the corporate lawyer whose hard exterior had turned out not to conceal the soft center he'd expected to find. And then with Pippa, who'd grown tired of his absence at her gallery openings because of long hours in the office or solitary trips to foreign vineyards. It was Pippa who had finally hurled the mother of all accusations at him:

"You love wine more than you love me!"

And there wasn't much he could say to that, because it was true.

He paused under his favorite Fragonard. It was time to rotate his office paintings back to his home gallery and bring in some new ones, but he thought he'd keep this one. It depicted a coquettish young woman reclining, with an admiring swain at her feet. He got a kick out of watching male guests more accustomed to abstract geometrics derail mid-sentence when their eyes lit on the woman's décolletage. He knew the erotic hedonism of the painting was out of place in an office, but he liked to be reminded that his hard work and earning potential was only a means to the end of acquiring and experiencing sensual beauty. It occurred to him now that the woman looked a bit like Valentina.

He yearned for a life like the one in the painting, based solely on pleasure, leisure, and mutual admiration. More time with wine and women, less time waging corporate war. He found he no longer desired intellectual firepower or creative spark from a mate. He wanted a woman whose chief accomplishment was her femininity. At the end of the day, it was all so simple, really. A man and a woman. That was all it took to close the circle of life. Yin and yang. One and another. The rest was merely distraction from the elemental self. He was ready to stop being Sy Hampton, financier and aficionado, married to Mrs. Hampton, overachiever extraordinaire. All he wanted was to be a man to a beautiful woman, and to that end, Valentina

D'Ambrosio was everything he could ask for.

The phone rang, interrupting his reverie.

"You can pick up Eric at the house at six tonight. He'll be with Ruby, and he'll be very upset if you're late like last time. I know what you're going to say—that he doesn't seem upset when he's with you, but I'm his mother, and I live with him, and I know. He gets very *disappointed* when you don't show up on time."

Marianne stressed the word in such a way that he couldn't fail to comprehend her real meaning. It was she who continued to be disappointed in him. He was no better an ex than he had been a husband. It was tempting to point out to her that being the primary custodian of their only child was not an automatic measure of how well she knew him. As it happened, Sy knew that Eric spent more time with his nanny, Ruby, than with his mother. Talk about disappointed.

"Anything else?"

"No, that's it," Marianne replied briskly, and hung up.

What a bitch, he thought. It was a wonder that Eric was turning into such a fine young man. He knew better than to credit himself—how much good could he do Wednesday evenings and one weekend a month? It was sweet-natured Ruby from Jamaica who was raising their boy. And there was precious little he could do about it, except try to be on time.

But now to work, he thought, glancing at his Great Explorers watch, which he'd been loath to replace with his everyday Tourneau. It was time to choose a Chinese bank to invest in. It was worth keeping on his good-luck charm for that. Perhaps it was the watch that had led him to invite Valentina to drink the wine, which more and more felt like exactly the right thing to do. Best to keep it on for a while longer. As he sifted through his notes on Asia Fund V, Miss Banks buzzed.

"Mr. Fisher and Mr. Wegman are here. I've put them in the small conference room, and Mr. Sage is on his way. Also, Mr. Farrell of Shoreham's is holding on line one. Would you like me to take a message?"

"I'll take it. Thanks." He depressed the button and picked up the call. "Hello, Antony," said Sy genially.

"Well, well, well," chuckled Farrell. "You made old Buffy Bagnold very unhappy yesterday."

"I can't take all the blame," said Sy.

"We gave her every opportunity. But you're a devil, Sy. That wine means a lot to you, does it?"

"Wouldn't it to anyone? I'm surprised you didn't bid on it yourself."

"Oh, I make a nice salary here at Shoreham's, but not enough for that treasure. So, inquiring minds want to know. Are you going to uncork or sell?"

"Uncork. Wouldn't you?"

"Oh, I don't know. You might turn it around, you know."

Sy laughed. "We both know I paid a premium for that bottle. Nobody would be foolish enough to pay more than half a million dollars for it!"

"Perhaps Mrs. Bagnold would."

"As you rightly point out, she had her chance. But are you suggesting a private sale?"

"No, not at all," replied Farrell. "I'm just confirming that you plan to drink the wine."

"I am."

"Have you thought yet about where? And with whom? Uncorking a bottle like that constitutes an important event."

Sy looked at the Fragonard Valentina and her swain. "I'm thinking it will be private."

"I see. At your home?" Farrell asked.

"Well—" Sy paused. He hadn't given much thought to anything beyond buying the wine, and now convincing Valentina to say yes. "Honestly, I haven't gotten that far."

"Were you planning . . . let me be frank," said Farrell, trying to sound offhand, although a hint of tension had crept into his voice. "Were you planning to invite any of your fellow oenophiles to sample this rarest of vintages?"

So that was it. Farrell wanted to know if he was going to share. He should have guessed.

"Actually, no," replied Sy lightly. "I hadn't planned on that. No."

There was silence on the other end of the phone. "Well, of course, it is your wine to do with as you please, but so often when a special bottle is opened, the wine community is invited to experience it."

Sy had a sudden vision of taking old Mrs. Bagnold out to dinner instead of Valentina, and he shuddered and chuckled simultaneously.

"I am aware of that tradition, but in this case I have other plans." He decided to give the auctioneer a sop. "If I change my mind, you'll be the first to know."

"That's some comfort, I suppose," Farrell said dryly. "Well, congratulations, Sy. I hope the wine brings you every happiness."

Sy hung up the phone and returned to where his *Forbes* cover, by far the most flattering of them, hung on the wall. Something was nagging him. What was it that Farrell had said about Mrs. Bagnold? "*We* gave her every opportunity." Did he think Sy owed him something for bringing the hammer down when he did? Farrell had seen that she was distracted, and surely, he could have—possibly, indeed, should have—checked in with her one last time. But the timing of the hammer was always at the auctioneer's discretion, and it wasn't as if Sy had asked Farrell to bend any rules on his behalf. He had done what he'd done of his own accord. There were no promises, no guarantees, and it was terrifically presumptuous of Farrell to think otherwise.

His intercom buzzed.

"Reminding you that Mr. Fisher, Mr. Wegman, and Mr. Sage are waiting for you in the small conference room."

"Thank you, Miss Banks. I'm on my way."

Despite their considerable differences in color and age, there was something of Mrs. Bagnold's sangfroid in Miss Banks. As he clicked off, it dawned on him that what he was feeling was a pang of conscience for the trick he had played on the old woman. Despite his glib excuse to her at the time, he had not played fair. He pressed the intercom button again.

"Mr. Hampton?"

"Get an address for Mrs. Buffy Bagnold. Then call Sherry-Lehmann and have them send her a case of magnums of the 2000 Lafite-Rothschild Pauillac. Note should say: 'Please accept this gift with my sincerest apologies and regards, Sy Hampton.' Got that?"

"Yes, sir."

A $10,000 apology was the least he could do. A case of the 2000, though lacking the history and sentiment of his new treasure, was rated an incredible 100 points, and would be good to 2050. It would give old Buffy a better, longer-lasting drink—if she lived that long, and a decent legacy for her heirs if she didn't.

As he collected the Fund V folder from his desk, Farrell's parting shot echoed once more in his ears: "I hope the wine brings you every happiness."

There was something unsettling about Farrell's choice of words, as if he intended happiness to mean the opposite of what the dictionary said it did. In truth, there were many things in Sy's life that should have brought him happiness but hadn't. He opened his office door and pushed Farrell's loaded wish out of his mind. It was hardly relevant, in any case. He wanted the wine to bring him only one happiness. And he steeled himself to walk emotionlessly past Valentina on his way to discuss his next great investment.

THREE

"Hey," Valentina chirped into the phone when she saw Trish's number come up on her caller ID.

"Have you seen the *Post* today?"

"You know I never read the paper."

"There's an article about your boss and his bottle of wine. Val, do you have any idea how much he paid for it?"

"A lot."

"Are you sitting down?"

"Why?" asked Valentina guardedly.

"He paid more than half a million dollars for it!"

Valentina gasped. "You're making that up!"

"Look it up online if you don't believe me."

Valentina swiveled to her computer and punched in "Hampton," "Shoreham's," and "Jefferson" and the article came up.

There it was on her screen: $510,000. Dear God in heaven, when he said the wine cost a lot, she was thinking $500, not $500,000! Who on earth spent money like that on a drink?

Sy Hampton had spent $510,000 on *her*. On little Valentina D'Ambrosio from Bensonhurst. How could she possibly say no to him now?

But how could she possibly say yes?

"Oh, Trish," she moaned. "Half a million dollars?"

"Plus tax," added Trish.

"What?"

"Read on. It says there's something called a buyer's premium on top of that, and then he's gotta pay sales tax. Do you realize that's almost another hundred grand? Might not mean much to him, but that's enough for us common folk to buy a nice little Mercedes."

"Stop, Trish! You're just making it worse!"

"Here's what we're going to do," said Trish firmly.

"W-we?"

"First, you're gonna say yes."

"What?!"

"You're going to accept his invitation to drink the wine. I take back everything I said. You're gonna say yes to him, then we're gonna teach you everything you need to know about wine."

"Who's we? You don't know any more about it than I do!"

"Just shut up and listen, will you? My cousin Vito is big into wine. If your boss bought a half-a-million-dollar bottle of wine just to impress you—no offense, Val—I've gotta revise my opinion of him. With a price tag like that, he's gotta be after more than sex. Go straight for matrimony, and then if it doesn't work out, take him for all he's worth!"

Valentina's head was spinning. What Trish was saying made no sense at all. Well, it made a little sense—the part about him being serious about her if he spent that kind of money on the wine—but this insistence that she somehow scam him through whatever lawsuit she could manage was really low.

"You know I don't believe in marriage," was all she could think of to say.

Trish squawked on the other end of the phone, "For someone who wants to drop cash like that on you, honey, you could believe in it!"

"But I hardly know him!"

"Maybe you should get to know him. Maybe he's more than a stuffy rich guy."

"I don't know . . . just because the bottle costs as much as a house doesn't change anything. Wine makes me nervous. You can't just drink it—people expect you to say things about it. And he's . . . well, he's a big business hotshot. What on earth would I say to him over dinner?"

"Come on, Val. How can you pass up a chance like this?"

"I'm going to sleep on it," Valentina said finally. "Elisa always says, 'Don't make a big decision until you've slept on it.' And this is turning into a big decision. Although God knows why it should."

"It's money, Val," intoned Trish solemnly. "Money changes everything."

Valentina hung up the phone, put her head in her hands, and tried to think. It was as if the ground had been pulled out from under her feet and replaced with something liquid and slippery. On either side of her was a coast she could reach for safety. On one side was everything she knew, and on the other was this strange man with his invitation to taste what had to be the world's most expensive bottle of wine. Right now she was sliding and skidding, and she knew no matter where she landed, she'd be on the wrong side.

Was there really any harm in it? It didn't have to go any further if she didn't want it to. He said as much—it didn't have to be a "date" date. And Trish's plan to learn about wine beforehand, well, there was something sensible about that. Maybe the only reason she didn't like wine was that she hadn't tried to like it. Lots of things in life were acquired tastes. So were lots of people.

But it still didn't answer the question. Why her? She couldn't shake the feeling that she was being bought. At a ridiculously high price, but bought just the same. That didn't make her like Sy Hampton any better.

It didn't make her like herself any better, either.

FOUR

"YOU'RE LATE."

Sy's heart sank as he caught the look of disappointment in his son's eyes. Did Eric really care that much about fifteen minutes, or had his mother conditioned him so well that he could no longer separate her disenchantment from his own?

"Only twenty minutes, squirt," said Sy, ruffling his son's smooth, blond hair.

"Dad, please don't call me that. I'm ten years old."

Sy cleared his throat and looked at broad, floral Ruby, who was smiling benevolently at him like a displaced island queen.

"He's got everything he needs in his overnight bag, including his blazer and tie for school on Monday." She squatted down and held out her arms to Eric, who ran into them for a hug, which she returned with ferocity. "You be a good boy for your dad, okay?"

Eric didn't seem to mind Ruby squatting down to kid level; in fact, it seemed to please him. But Sy knew better than to try a move like that himself.

"I thought we could go see that new Rugrats movie," suggested Sy. They settled into the back of the Lexus, as Bill, his driver, began to negotiate the traffic down Fifth Avenue.

"I'm too old for that stuff, Dad," scoffed Eric, looking out the window.

Sy frowned. "I thought you liked cartoons."

Eric kept his eyes on Central Park as the trees, just starting to glow with autumn-hued leaves, flitted by. "I'm into anime, Dad. That's something else."

"Oh." Sy absently turned the gold college ring on his right hand. It was the only piece of jewelry he wore except for his watch, now that he was no longer married. "Maybe you could explain it to me? I'd love to know why you find it so interesting."

Eric shrugged, and Sy stared at his son's bony shoulders, so eloquently rejecting his attempts at intimacy as the boy hunched over his cell phone, furtively texting his friends. It was going to be a long weekend.

When they arrived at the town house on East Sixty-fourth between Park and Lex, Eric shot past Sy's housekeeper, hurtling up the wide, curving staircase.

"Hey, Claudine," Eric called out as he disappeared around the second-floor landing.

"He's in a rush, isn't he?" Claudine remarked, taking Sy's coat.

"To get away from me," Sy answered, mugging a fake sad smile that was more real than he cared to acknowledge.

Claudine laughed. "I'm sure you did the same thing to your father when you were ten."

Maybe, but not for the same reason, Sy thought as he picked up the mail from the small marble-topped table and riffled through the envelopes.

"Dinner will be at seven," announced Claudine. "Would you like me to lay the table in the dining room?"

"Kitchen's fine," said Sy. "I'll have a drink in my study first."

Just as he started upstairs himself, his iPhone buzzed in his pocket. He pulled it out and read the reminder from Miss Banks. Serena Hart was due at six thirty.

When he'd asked Miss Banks to cancel his afternoon tennis and arrange instead for Serena, he had completely forgotten that it was his weekend with Eric. By the time Marianne had called to remind him not to be late, he'd forgotten about Serena. Miss Banks, lacking the imagination to comprehend Serena's real purpose in his life, had not thought to point out the conflict. Of course, if Serena were actually coming to administer physical therapy, there would be no conflict, but it was a tacit part of their agreement that once his knee had been massaged, exercised, compressed with both hot and cold, and stimulated by ultrasound, the stimulation would extend to other parts of his body. If he'd remembered that Eric was coming, he wouldn't have canceled his tennis.

He was dialing Serena's number when the doorbell rang. He

looked at his watch. She was right on time.

"I'll get it," he called out, and opened the door.

"Hi, Sy, my handsome guy," Serena said perkily. She was petite, pretty, and dark-haired, with a sinewy athletic body, and generally game for anything. On several occasions, she had brought along an "assistant," a slim redhead named Clara. Those had been memorable sessions, indeed.

He gave her a quick peck on the cheek. "Give me a moment, will you?"

He left Serena in the front hall to admire the Tiffany drop chandelier that she had once declared her single favorite thing in the house, and walked back to the blue and white kitchen, where Claudine was sautéing some chicken breasts.

"Serena is here for my knee. Can you hold dinner for an hour? You can feed Eric earlier if he's hungry."

"Maybe you should send Eric to me now," suggested Claudine. "That way he can watch his shows with me, and he won't disturb you on his way down."

Good old Claudine, he thought. Not only did she possess the imagination that Miss Banks lacked, she had the discretion to go with it.

"Thank you. I'll run up and get him."

Sy let Serena into his study to unpack her ultrasound equipment and closed the door. Then he took the narrow stairs two at a time to Eric's aerie on the third floor.

"Claudine's got dinner going, and you can watch TV in the kitchen until it's ready."

Eric shrugged and kept his eyes fixed on SpongeBob. "I'm good up here."

Sy shifted his weight uncomfortably and tried again. "She wants to catch up with you. Why don't you go on down now?"

Eric eyed him suspiciously and then shrugged again. "Whatever."

Sy led him down the stairs, past the closed study door. For once, Sy didn't mind that Eric was more willing to open up to his housekeeper than to him.

Serena was waiting for him on the hunter green chesterfield in his study, a small, square room with Moroccan red walls that allowed Sy to imagine himself a country squire. Although she'd set up her equipment on the desk, she'd also poured herself a glass of white wine from the wet bar, and from the way she was draped on the sofa, it was clear she had no intention of flipping on the ultrasound machine anytime soon.

Sy closed the door behind him and stood for a moment, unsure what he wanted. Serena broke the silence.

"You're going to have to remove your trousers if you want me to examine your knee," she murmured in her dusky voice.

"Serena."

"Pants."

Sy unbuckled his belt and slipped his trousers off. Serena rose from the chesterfield, walked over to the door, and turned the lock. Sy sat on the sofa and extended his right leg. She rejoined him and placed her hand on his leg, delicately probing his kneecap.

"It's not swollen." She cocked her head to the side and raised an eyebrow at him. "Shall we see if anything else is?"

Without waiting for an answer, she straddled him and glided her hand inside his boxers. She took hold of him, and for a moment, he allowed himself to yield to her touch. Then, with every ounce of willpower he could muster, he took her hand firmly and pulled it away. She drew her lips from his and stared at him, astonished.

"What is it?"

"I have Eric this weekend. He's downstairs."

"You're a grown-up, you're allowed," she admonished, and began to caress him again.

He stood up, causing her to fall to the side of the sofa.

"My time with him is extremely limited. This isn't how I choose to spend it."

"Wait a second, you called me!"

"I forgot he was coming."

"Means that much to you, does he?" she scoffed.

He could tell from her expression that she wished she could take it back, but he wasn't about to let her off so easily. He pulled his trousers back up and removed his checkbook from the drawer of his desk. Her eyes narrowed as he handed the check to her.

"This is for the service you charge for. We'll dispense with the one that you don't."

"Keep it," she said, dropping the check as if it had burned her fingers. It fell to the floor, where it lay accusingly between them. She drained her wineglass and slammed it on the side table. "Spend it on your kid."

She packed up her equipment in loaded silence, and they descended the stairs together. From the front hall, they could hear the television blaring in the kitchen.

"You shouldn't let him watch so much TV," she said pointedly.

"Exactly," he replied.

He hadn't been entirely honest with Serena, he thought, as he watched her stride angrily down the front steps. Eric was only part of the reason he had sent her packing. Call it superstition, call it karma; he sensed that succumbing to Serena's advances—even though he'd summoned her—would somehow reduce the chances that Valentina would accept his invitation. A biweekly fuck from Serena was no longer what was required. What he needed, as he had stated so simply to Miss Banks that morning, was Valentina. And he began to think that, as he had done with the Lafite, he would do whatever it took to get her.

FIVE

MIDWAY THROUGH HER THIRD WORD SEARCH PUZZLE, Valentina chucked the flimsy booklet across the room and buried her face in the red velvet pillow on her bed. The sunlight was streaming in her window, which faced east. In another few minutes, it would be too bright and hot for her to stay in her room. It was almost eleven on Sunday morning, and she had nothing to do, except laundry she should have finished on Saturday. She'd have to do it at some point today, unless she wanted to wear one of her non-clingy, non-heart-themed sweaters to work tomorrow. Which, all things considered, might not be a bad idea.

She had slept on Mr. Hampton's invitation, not once but twice now, and had finally made up her mind to refuse it. But rather than feeling relieved, she was more troubled than ever. Trish had invited her out clubbing the night before, but she wasn't in the mood to debate the question further with her. There were times when she welcomed her friend's Mack truck approach to life, but it seemed to Valentina that there were finer points to be considered here, which were utterly lost on Trish.

She had called Elisa, and her sister's response was predictable: go and be grateful for the chance. It wasn't surprising. Elisa was all about bettering herself. She went to foreign art house movies, even though Valentina suspected she didn't really enjoy them. The one time Valentina had let her sister drag her to a chamber music recital, Elisa had been the one to doze off. Still, Valentina had to give her credit for trying. But she resented Elisa's implication that declining the invitation meant Valentina had no desire to expand her horizons. It wasn't true. She just couldn't see what one night out with Sy Hampton could possibly accomplish.

Valentina's buzzer rang, interrupting her sulk. She had no idea who could be calling on her, uninvited, at eleven o'clock on a Sunday morning. It was probably a delivery boy hoping someone would let him in to drop off unwanted menus. She burrowed deeper under her covers, but the buzzer kept on, as if someone was leaning on it. With a sigh, she dragged herself out of bed and went down the hall to the kitchen, where the intercom was.

"Hello?"

"Val?"

She should have known.

"Jeez, Jerry, I'm still in my pajamas. You could have called first!"

"It's not like I ain't seen you in your pajamas. And I knew if I called, you wouldn't pick up. I gotta talk to you!"

The only thing worse than letting Jerry in would be letting him stand outside leaning on her buzzer all day, and she knew he'd do it, because he'd done it once before two years ago, when she broke up with him for a week. She pressed the entry button and ran to the bathroom to splash water on her face. She finished just as Jerry knocked on her door.

"What do you want? I don't have all day," said Valentina, swinging the door open, more violently than she intended.

"Shit, Val, can't I come in?"

She let him walk past her, then stood in front of the door with her arms crossed, as if preserving it as an escape route for herself, just in case he wouldn't leave.

"I been thinking . . . can I sit down at least?"

Before she could say no, he plopped down on the folding kitchen chair with the wonky leg, which wavered under his weight. Valentina could see him taking in the tattered T-shirt and shorts she had slept in.

"Sure looks like you got all day."

"It's none of your business."

He leaned forward, and she turned away from the pleading look in his eyes.

"Val! You're acting like we was enemies or something. You know I love you—that's what this is all about!"

She and Jerry had had fun together, and it was true she'd kept thinking about him after she made her decision to dump him, but she suddenly realized that since Mr. Hampton's invitation, he hadn't crossed her mind once, except when she used him as an excuse to get out of it.

"Look, Jerry, I told you. I'm not interested in marriage. Not to you or anybody."

Jerry nodded earnestly. "I know. That's why I came over. I been thinking, if you don't wanna get married, that's fine. I mean, we can just go on the way we were. And if we—if you—I mean, if we ever wanna have kids, we can talk about it again. Only 'cuz it's easier for them to have a mom and dad who's married. C'mon, Val, whaddaya say?"

Valentina gave up her position by the door and plopped down on the couch, where she picked up a round, pink-fringed pillow and held it in front of her like a shield.

"You just want to have your cake and eat it, too," she muttered.

Jerry held out his hands helplessly. "Val, I'm trying to show you that I'm serious about you. Talk about eating your cake! First I ain't serious because I don't wanna get married, then I ain't serious because I'm willing to do whatever it takes to keep you in my life!"

Valentina looked down at the pillow in her lap and plucked at a tassel. "I've moved on, Jer," she said quietly.

"Moved on," he snorted. "You're full of shit!"

It suddenly seemed that someone was shining a spotlight on her cluttered living room. The outlines of her curbside furniture sharpened, and the air in the room was shimmering. She almost felt as if she were having an out of body experience. It wasn't quite like being high or drunk, because she knew she was in control. But as she formed the words, she experienced a dizziness that was unnerving and exciting at the same time.

"I'm going out with my boss."

Jerry stared at her, then he burst out laughing. "Your boss? He's like, twice your age!"

"But he's rich, Jerry, and he's cultured. And he . . . he bought me a bottle of wine!"

Jerry looked astonished for a moment, then he threw back his head and roared even harder.

"Christ, Val, if all it takes is a bottle of wine, I'll buy you a bottle of wine! I'll buy you a whole fucking case of the stuff! I didn't think you even liked wine!"

"I don't," she admitted, before she could stop herself.

"Then what the hell are you talking about?"

"I'm gonna learn! Trish's cousin Vito's gonna teach me. And as for any wine that you could buy me . . ." For no reason at all that she could grasp, she felt a rush of anger. She hurled the pink pillow across the room at him, where it clipped him on the ear before landing in a dish of cat food. He started in surprise.

"You got half a million bucks, Jerry? Because that's how much Mr. Hampton spent on me! That's how much I'm worth to him— and he doesn't even know me yet! But that's how much it's worth it to him to find out!"

"Mr. Hampton, huh?" Jerry shot back. "Sounds like you're off to a real great start."

"Get out, Jerry. It's over. Just forget about me!"

A pained look crossed Jerry's face, and for a moment, she felt sorry for him. It wasn't really fair to compare what Mr. Hampton— Sy—could do for her to what Jerry could.

"Val, I love you, and we're good together. If you don't see that . . ." His voice trailed off.

"Just go, okay?" She pointed to the door.

"Well, I got news for you." He swallowed. "It ain't gonna work. You're from different worlds. You won't have jack shit to say to each other. He's only after one thing, Val. I ain't even met the guy, and I can tell you he just wants to get in your pants. You go out with him, and you're nothing but a high-priced whore!"

"GET OUT!!!" She scooped up the dish of cat food and the pillow and chucked the whole mess at him. She didn't feel sorry for him anymore. She would show him. She was meant for better than Jerry DiCicco, and this proved it, once and for all.

He was gone so suddenly that she was sure he would come back one last time, like the dead thing in a horror movie that pops up just when you think it's safe to go back in the bathtub. But he didn't, and after a few minutes, she was left alone with her words still ringing in the empty air.

She hadn't exactly made the decision; the decision had made her. Which, as Elisa would say, was close enough for jazz.

SIX

BILL MANEUVERED SY'S LEXUS LS 460 L AWD slowly through the Monday morning traffic up Madison Avenue, and if Sy didn't know any better, he'd have said Eric had been staring mournfully out the car window all weekend. But that wasn't, in fact, the case. There had been the Rugrats movie, after all, for lack of anything better to do, and a brief discussion about anime that had ended abruptly when Eric's friend Dalton called. There had been several meals during which Sy tried desperately to engage his taciturn son in conversation. The boy had no problem chatting away happily with his friends on his cell phone or with Claudine in the kitchen. But it seemed that every time Sy asked a question, Eric shot him a look that clearly said "Don't waste your breath."

Sy had considered telling Eric about the Jefferson Lafite and his hopes for it. But he wasn't sure how his son would take his confession that he was interested in a woman other than his mother, although he knew that was completely irrational, since there had been an entire wife in between Marianne and his current single status.

In the end, Sy was forced to admit that he wasn't sure what his son wanted from him on these monthly weekend visits. Did he want to do more with Sy—or less? Or was Eric so poisoned against him by his mother that their relationship was destined to be strained, no matter how hard he tried?

The Lexus pulled up in front of St. Bernard's School on East Ninety-eighth Street, and Eric grabbed his backpack and leapt out of the car as if the seat were on fire. Sy opened the door and walked around the car to stand with his son.

"Next time, why don't you tell me in advance what you'd like to do and we'll plan it. Anything you want, anything at all," Sy said, with a magnanimity he didn't feel.

Eric nodded. "Sure, whatever."

As Sy reached to give his son a hug, his iPhone vibrated in his pocket.

"Hang on." He glanced at the brightly colored screen, and his heart gave a tiny skip when he saw the name. He held the phone to his ear and tried to keep his voice even.

"Hello?"

"Hi, it's Valentina. D'Ambrosio. Um, I guess you knew that."

"I did."

"I could have waited until I saw you at the office, but I thought maybe we should keep this, you know, outside."

"Yes, yes, I see," said Sy, his pulse quickening.

"Can I ask you something?"

"Sure."

"Why me?"

Sy gestured to Eric to wait a moment, then turned away from him and the car. What could he say? His reasons were so complicated that he only barely understood them himself. But he knew that her answer depended on his.

"Why not you?"

When she didn't speak, he plunged on. "I know we don't know each other well. At all, really. But I sense something special about you, and this is a special wine. Believe me when I say that there are no strings attached. I'd simply like to treat you to a gourmet dinner and a once-in-a-lifetime bottle of wine. If that's all it ever is, that's fine. I can at least promise you a lovely evening. Don't you deserve that?"

There was silence on the line, and Sy pressed his Gucci loafer into the curb until his toes hurt, while he waited for her answer.

"I'd be honored to drink your Thomas Jefferson wine with you," she said finally.

"Thank you!" Sy felt his face warm with a glow that was from more than just the September morning sun. "I'll be receiving the bottle from the auction house this week, and it will need to settle. Perhaps the week after next?"

"I need to check on some things, but probably," answered Valentina.

"Excellent. Valentina, I'm so pleased."

"I better go. I'm just at the Starbucks, and I don't want to be late to work."

"No later than I'll be," joked Sy.

"Yeah, but you're the boss."

"Right," Sy said uneasily. "Well, I look forward to seeing you."

"Okay. Um, bye."

Sy replaced the phone in his pocket. He wanted to jump, to scream, to high-five the air. Whatever night they chose, it couldn't come fast enough. It would be a night to remember, he would make sure of it.

He turned to where Eric had been standing against the car, but the black doors of St. Bernard's were closed, and Eric was gone.

PART TWO

THE RESERVATION

SEVEN

Not for the first time, and probably not for the last, Annette Lecocq cursed her chromosomes.

I should have been born a man, she screamed inwardly, as the specialty foods vendor on the other end of the phone continued his rambling lecture about the benefits of goose foie gras over duck.

"Excuse me," she tried for the fifth time, but the man continued to ignore her. If he hadn't had the best price for the precise kind of duck liver Etienne needed to sear for his gourmet variation on Québécois *poutine*, she'd have slammed down the phone then and there. Instead, she set the receiver gently on her desk and let the wood veneer absorb his condescending babble, while she pulled up the reservations screen on the computer in her office.

It was dreary, even for a Wednesday night. Only thirty covers. Parapluie had been open for six months, and the restaurant wasn't taking off the way she'd hoped. Despite a respectable one star in *New York* magazine, she hadn't been able to get the *Times* in, and *New York* had come only because her former employer and mentor, MaryLou Sampson, had put in a good word with the critic. If business didn't improve very soon, Annette would be forced to close. She tried to still the rising sense of panic that was starting to become as dependable a daily event as Etienne's little fits of temper.

Annette picked up the phone, but the specialty foods vendor was still yammering on. "Mmmmm," she said, and set it down again.

She needed some buzz. Etienne was an exceptionally talented chef but had no reputation in New York. She'd poached him from Frisson, one of her favorite restaurants in Montreal. He was about as temperamental as they come, but she understood that was an occupational hazard. Annette had confidence in the menu, which she and Etienne had designed together to reflect the French-Canadian heritage they shared. It was sophisticated but offbeat, with an emphasis on game, maple syrup, and fruit desserts. But in New York City, with an eatery of some kind every two feet, it was possible she'd overreached herself, as superb as Parapluie was.

From the receiver on her desk, her name cut through her thoughts.

"Ms. Lecocq? Are you there?"

She grabbed the phone and her chance. "I'll take ten pounds of the duck foie gras. Bill me."

She hung up before she could be lectured again, and pushed her chair away from the desk. She still needed to call her game vendor and put in an order for wild boar, venison, and rabbit fillet, but she decided to take a break and engage in one of her favorite exercises. She left her small basement office, passed through the prep kitchen where the three line cooks were cutting bread, chopping herbs, and tasting sauces, and hiked up the narrow stairs. In the serving kitchen, the lunch cook had finished clearing up and was busily taking note of which items in his cooler needed to be replenished.

Annette entered the restaurant, which was empty in the two brief hours between lunch and dinner service. This was her favorite time on the floor. Lunch was like a curtain raiser before the main event. During this intermission, a sense of accomplishment lingered in the air, but the atmosphere was charged with the promise of an even more exciting show. At this time of day, Annette liked to pretend she was not herself, owner and general manager of Parapluie, but a customer, experiencing its interior for the first time.

The walls were papered in slashes of alternating white and scarlet silk, with raised diagonal streaks of hammered gold fashioned to look like rain, which lent warmth to the bold, straight lines. The floors were polished bamboo, the furniture sleek, blond wood, and the walls dotted with small paintings, mostly colorful oils housed in frames that were themselves works of art. All were modern except for a large, limited-edition reproduction of Gustave Caillebotte's *Place de l'Europe on a Rainy Day*. The muted gray and blue tones of the painting, subtle by themselves, stood out against the brash décor. Centered on the back wall, the painting drew the eye like a fine actor who knows how to get the audience's attention by speaking softly.

Annette found comfort in knowing that even in earlier, more formal times, people had to deal with getting out and about in the rain, despite their extravagant clothing. Whenever she had to fight her way down a crowded city street in a downpour, she always thought of the serene, well-dressed couple with their umbrellas on the Place de l'Europe, who appeared to accept the rain rather than battle it. It also served to remind her that neither rain nor any other perceived misfortune was a blight sent from above just to torment her.

She had been staring at the original painting in the Art Institute of Chicago, the week after she and Roland had split up, when she'd made the decision to move to New York. Thinking back on it now, it was difficult to say which had come first: the idea of opening her own restaurant or of naming it Parapluie. Although she had later toyed with several other names, the French word for umbrella captured the sense of chic whimsy she sought. It had taken her more than two years to get her proverbial ducks in a row. Now she had to find a way to keep them afloat.

Annette wandered over to the small, rectangular bar in the front of the restaurant and sat on one of the cushioned stools. She pushed off the base with her foot and spun it around, letting the swirls of red, white, and gold blend together in a dizzying comet tail. There had been two stools like this in the big wood-beamed kitchen of the farm outside Montreal where she'd grown up, and one of her favorite things as a child was to spin around on them, while her grandmother made pastries with fruit from the fields.

As the stool slowed to a halt, Annette caught her reflection in the mirror behind the neat rows of liquor bottles: her short mop of ash blond hair that demanded little tending, a face that was more pert and pixieish than she had ever felt, and round gray eyes that, right now, looked back at her with a straightforward gaze that masked her fatigue.

She couldn't plead ignorance. She knew how hard the restaurant industry was, particularly for women, but she drew strength from MaryLou Sampson, who had overcome greater challenges than anything she'd ever face. MaryLou, descended from slaves, ran one of the most popular restaurants in Atlanta, Sampson's. "Upscale soul food" was how she described it, but that was only one element of its success. MaryLou's outsized personality and upright piano drew as many customers as her lip-smacking fare. She made it look easy, but Annette knew what a struggle it had been for a black woman in the 1970s American South to become a successful entrepreneur. It took a special kind of perseverance, what MaryLou called "damn-ass stubbornness," not to mention an important patron, Caroline Wilbur, the mayor's wife, in order for her to stake her claim. On top of that, MaryLou had a natural majesty that commanded respect. "They'd no more sass me than they would their mammy," she once confided to Annette.

Annette was tenacious in her own way, but she lacked MaryLou's self-confidence. That was part of the reason she had abandoned her ambitions of becoming an executive chef. She had also begun to tire of the long hours and low pay of kitchen work. It was MaryLou who suggested she move to the front of the house and urged her to apply for a Master of Management in Hospitality from Cornell. When Annette graduated, she returned to Sampson's as MaryLou's general manager. It was then that she'd met Roland LeCroy.

Roland was a bass player, with melt-away brown eyes and black, Byronic ringlets. Restaurant work was not generally conducive to romance, but MaryLou had been sympathetic, so for a time, Annette had been lulled into thinking there was hope. She'd managed to have boyfriends before, but they'd never withstood the grueling round of restaurant life. But as a musician, Roland kept odd hours as well, and with MaryLou's allowances, a real relationship seemed possible. Annette also found she wanted it to work, in a way she never had before. She adored Roland. He was sensitive, sexy, and funny. For the first time, Annette found herself contemplating marriage.

When Roland's jazz band decided to relocate to Chicago, Annette bade a tearful good-bye to MaryLou and moved with him. But she was in for a shock. She hadn't realized just how accommodating MaryLou had been. The owners of Zanahoria, the restaurant in Chicago that hired her as general manager, expected her on the job twelve to fifteen hours a day, with every other Monday off. The money was far better than what MaryLou had paid her, but she definitely had to work for it, and Roland didn't make enough gigging around to support them both. She was making a lot more than he was, and that was how the trouble started.

"I feel like a kept man," said Roland.

"But I want you to be able to play your music, and I love my restaurant work."

"You don't have any time for me."

"I do," Annette protested. "It just has to start at one a.m. when I get home from work. Besides, that's when you're back from your gigs."

"But I'm tired then, and so are you. It's not the same. I want you during the daytime. You can't work both day and night."

"But I have to. That's the job."

And around and around they went. She could feel him slipping away, which only made her want him more. She started cutting out of work earlier and earlier, and eventually she was put on warning, but she didn't care. Then one day she showed up and found her services were no longer required. On the drive back to the small apartment she and Roland shared on the South Side, she decided it was for the best. If she couldn't have love and a restaurant career, she'd take love and transfer her hard-won management skills to an industry with a more flexible schedule. To hell with her hospitality degree. It wasn't worth losing Roland over.

Except that she'd already lost him. By the time she arrived home, she was so absorbed in her vision of a poorer, but happier, life as Roland's groupie that she failed to pick up the clues that were littered across the sparsely furnished living room. A pair of unfamiliar leopard-print panties penetrated her consciousness just as she opened the bedroom door. In the end, she decided that, too, was for the best. She needed to see his betrayal to accept it.

So she'd lost everything the same day: Roland, her job, and her self-respect. She'd kicked around Chicago for a month, sleeping on her friend Dodie's couch, and it was then that she'd had her brainstorm at the Art Institute while looking at the Caillebotte. She would devote herself single-mindedly to her career and forget about love. But if she was going to make a sacrifice of that order, she needed to be a stakeholder in her life, not an employee, so she vowed to follow MaryLou's example and open her own restaurant. Considering what she had given up, failing was, quite simply, not an option. She had to make a success of Parapluie. If she didn't, she'd have nothing.

As Annette headed down the stairs to her office, she heard her phone ringing. She hurried back to the small, airless space that felt more like home than her studio apartment on East Seventy-ninth Street and picked up the phone.

"Parapluie, this is Annette."

"Darling, it's me."

She instinctively smoothed her hair, as if Antony Farrell had just walked into the room and not called her on the phone. They had met at the New York Wine Expo at the Javits Center last winter and had almost immediately fallen into bed. Of course, the relationship fizzled during the run-up to Parapluie's opening, but Annette had expected as much. She was sorry about it, but she never again wanted to find herself tempted to chuck her career for a man, and if Antony wasn't willing to play second fiddle to her restaurant (he wasn't), that was that. But they'd kept in touch, linked by the memory of their four fiery weeks together, their mutual and often competing ambitions, and the tangential intersection of their livelihoods. She wondered which reason had prompted him to call this time.

"You seem quite confident that I know who this is," she said.

She hated when people left messages or started conversations without identifying themselves, no matter how well she knew them. She considered pretending not to know who it was, but it wasn't worth squandering a move so early on in the game. Conversations with Antony were always a skirmish. It was part of his appeal.

"How's the restaurant?"

"Brilliant! Did you see the notice in *New York*?"

"I did. Has it done you much good?"

Annette hesitated. It was tempting to lie. On the other hand, she was a bad liar and he was hard to fool.

"I'm thinking about hiring a public relations consultant."

"Yes, of course, you could do that," said Antony in measured tones, "but what's your story? You need a hook for the media. And wonderful as you are, darling, and splendid as Parapluie is . . . well, let's be honest. French-Canadian restaurateuse challenges with haute cuisine hotspot? Not much there on which to hang your chapeau, I'm afraid."

"Restaurateur," she corrected him. Of all the barbs lurking in his description of her enterprise, the chauvinistic inaccuracy galled her the most.

"I hate to say it, but if you choose not to play the gender card, you have even less of a story. My point is, even if you hire a publicist, you still need to give him something to publicize, beyond the existence of yet another French restaurant in Manhattan."

She felt her neck grow hot. "Is that why you're calling? To tell me I don't have a prayer of making this work, because I don't have a story to tell?"

"No, no! *Au contraire.* I'm calling you with a story you *can* tell. And, if you're lucky, sell."

She tapped a pencil against her green desk blotter. "I'm listening."

"Well, what you need is buzz, right? On that we're agreed."

"Go on."

"And what better way to generate buzz than with an event!"

"Antony, please come to the point. I can't sit here and engage in guessing games with you all day."

"Did you read about the Jefferson Lafite that went for half a million dollars last week?"

"Of course."

"There's a story behind that bottle. The winemaker, Pichard, supposedly experimented with one barrel, intending to preserve it so it could be enjoyed well into the future. He marked all the bottles from that yield with a crescent. As far as anyone knows, this is the only remaining bottle in existence."

Annette frowned. "It didn't say anything about that in the paper."

He sniffed. "Who are you going to believe, the *New York Post* or the senior director of Shoreham's International Fine and Rare Wines Department?"

"I don't see where you're going with this."

"Don't you?" He gave an irritatingly sexy little chuckle. "There's an excellent chance that this bottle is still drinkable, and I've confirmed with the purchaser, one Sy Hampton, that he plans to drink it—not resell it. If we can convince him to drink it at Parapluie . . . well, I think your imagination can take it from there."

A bottle of wine dating from the French Revolution, opened and sampled in her restaurant? It was an outstanding idea, an excellent publicity stunt.

There was only one problem.

"And how are we going to get this Sy Hampton to open his bottle here? Why should he?"

"*Courage, ma chérie!* I will bring him to dinner first, and you will serve us Etienne's finest. Don't worry, I will pay for it. He will experience your beautiful setting and realize that, with its superb cuisine and juxtaposition of classical and contemporary elements, it is the perfect place to bring an historical wine into the modern world."

"And you're sure he'll be amenable to the publicity?"

Antony paused, and for a moment she wondered if the call had been dropped. "I don't know that he'll be amenable at all," he responded finally.

"But you think you can convince him?"

"I'm not sure, for your purposes, how necessary that is."

Annette drew herself up in her chair. "Are you suggesting we lure him here to uncork his wine for—whomever he's uncorking it for—and we pack the place with paparazzi hiding behind potted palms?"

"You don't have potted palms, darling. And rightly so. They're utterly wrong for your décor."

"I'm not going to ambush a potentially good and loyal customer! If somebody with half a million dollars to spend on a bottle of wine likes Parapluie, he'll come back again and again. And tell his equally rich friends. That's all the buzz I need, thank you very much!"

"Annette, this man is used to being in the limelight. He's a well-known figure in the financial world. This sort of thing happens to him all the time. I'm sure he's not complaining about the lovely spread in the *Post*."

"Which, let me guess, you planted?" she asked.

She could almost see his innocent shrug. "Well, not me, exactly. We do have a press office, you know."

"Antony, I appreciate your concern and your . . . creative solution. Honestly, I do. But unless I secure Mr. Hampton's agreement to the publicity, I cannot consider it."

"Cannot or will not?"

"Antony—"

"Fine. Let me bring him to Parapluie, and we'll take it from there. If he thinks your restaurant is rubbish, there's no need for further discussion, is there?"

"All right. Bring your friend to dinner," she said icily. "And don't forget to bring along your best wine. I'm sure it won't be as good as his worst, but it will have to do under the circumstances, won't it?"

Touché, she thought, and slammed down the phone.

She knew he was baiting her, testing her desperation. He must have known, before he called, that she was struggling. He'd only need to walk past on a Saturday night to see how empty the place was.

Still, his idea had merit. Years ago, the Four Seasons had held a series of wine events, where historic bottles of Château Margaux were displayed, and the more recent vintages imbibed. The wine and food press had all attended. Not that the Four Seasons needed any help, but it gave them something chic, offbeat, and, most pertinent, newsworthy to help them compete with the upstart establishments that were threatening to unseat them at the time. If the idea was good enough for the Four Seasons, it was good enough for her.

Except that this Sy Hampton might not be willing. She wished she hadn't been quite so unyielding with Antony on that score. It had been extremely satisfying to take the high road, but the truth was, if Antony could somehow manage to convince Hampton to bring his precious Lafite to her restaurant, it would be very difficult to resist using it to her advantage.

First things first, she told herself firmly. As Antony pointed out, Sy Hampton had to like the restaurant before he could even consider it.

She pushed open the door to the prep kitchen and saw Etienne in his tall, white toque and black striped tunic. He must have come in while she was on the phone, and he was already busy rolling pastry dough for the mixed berry torte. She looked at the gleaming chrome surfaces where Esme was rinsing the salad greens and Howie was pounding meat, and admitted the truth to herself.

If Sy Hampton liked her restaurant enough to want to drink his historic bottle of wine there, she would invite every wine writer and food critic in the tri-state area to witness it, whether he wanted her to or not. It was a matter of survival, pure and simple, and time was running out.

EIGHT

As he always did before every audition, Tripp Macgregor sent up a silent, heartfelt prayer. He had long since moved beyond any real fear of wiping out, but like most performers, he had his rituals, and old habits died hard. So he stood in the wings of the Gerald Schoenfeld Theatre, formerly the Plymouth, where he had seen some memorable shows in his youth, including all nine hours of the RSC's *Life and Adventures of Nicholas Nickleby* and Stephen Sondheim's *Passion*. Now, Tripp clenched his hands into fists at his sides, closed his eyes, and prayed.

God grant me agility and grace, and the ability to move fluidly through time and space.

He knew that time didn't really apply conceptually, but it made his little mantra scan, and although he was primarily a dancer, he had a fine appreciation of a well-turned lyric.

He opened his eyes and looked around at the hard young bodies with whom he was competing for a spot in this much-anticipated Broadway revival of *A Chorus Line*. They had youth on their side, no question, but he had experience. And at thirty-nine, he was still in excellent shape. Nevertheless, he found it disconcerting that most of these boys were too young to have seen the original production, which he had first experienced in junior high school.

However, they were getting cuter and cuter. And there were more of them than there used to be. It seemed that young people in increasing numbers were being encouraged to follow their dreams—the crowded lounge at Actors' Equity was proof of that. It also seemed that being a boy obsessed with Broadway shows, Judy Garland, Gene Kelly, and dance in general was no longer the mark of Cain it once was. Certainly, being gay was easier for this generation. Although Tripp was himself too young to have clocked the Stonewall riots, his earliest dating years were marred by AIDS and the initial ignorance and promiscuity that had turned a disease into a plague. Many of these boys dancing with him today faced challenges, but they knew a freedom that he had had to learn. They received it as their due, without understanding the sacrifices that had made it possible. None of this, of course, made them any less attractive. On the contrary, the confidence born of liberation made them even more appealing.

Enough. He had to concentrate on the audition, and on the first combination, from the opening number, "I Hope I Get It."

Truer words were never spoken, he thought.

He'd performed the combination many times before, but never on a Broadway stage. If he got this job, it would be his first Broadway show, and it had been a long time coming.

Fortunately, he'd done *A Chorus Line* twice in summer stock, playing Bobby and then Greg. The casting director had said he was under consideration for both roles. Tripp considered himself more like Greg, with his droll sense of humor and Upper East Side pedigree. The character of Bobby had a father who wanted him to be an athlete. Tripp was a natural athlete, great at tennis and basketball, and his own father couldn't have cared less.

"Next group!" called the assistant choreographer. "Andrew, Clark, Timothy, Michael, Jorge, and Tripp!"

As soon as he heard his name, an icy cold washed over him, bringing with it a heightened awareness of his surroundings. This was it. He chanted his mantra once more, this time with his eyes open. If ever an audition demanded a repeat incantation, a Broadway callback was it.

Before he knew it, he was standing on the stage. The lights were blinding, but he could still make out the creative team, filling scattered seats in two center rows of the house.

"Hold, please!" the assistant called.

There was some whispering and passing around of résumés, while the assistant walked among the six of them and spoke quietly.

"You'll do the opening combination first, and they may ask all or some of you to repeat it. Then we'll do the ballet combination.

Hang in the wings for a moment afterward, and then I'll let you know who needs to come back and sing. Have fun!"

Tripp saw Timothy and Clark share a look that said "Fun, who is he kidding?" But Tripp intended to take the assistant at his word. He was about to dance on a Broadway stage. Even if he got no further, he was thrilled to be where he was.

Okay, who was *he* kidding? He'd be devastated if he didn't get it. But he pushed that thought out of his mind and resolved to show these kids how it was done.

"Ready? Five-six-seven-eight!"

The music began, and his body flew through the opening combination. It felt effortless in that wonderful, free-fall way things did when he was feeling great and on top of his game, and, just his luck, there happened to be an audience. He and Michael were asked to repeat it, which Tripp took as a good sign. The subsequent ballet combination was a breeze, and he was exhilarated enough to have a relaxed, natural smile on his face. He could see, out of the corner of his eye, that Timothy's was plastered on his.

"Great job," said the assistant to the assembled glistening faces. "Please wait in the wings."

The six dancers hovered offstage left, too nervous to look at one another. The assistant reappeared after what seemed like an eternity.

"Michael, Jorge, and Tripp, please stay. The rest of you, thank you very much." He looked up from his clipboard and waited as the other three, trying not to betray their disappointment, headed off toward the stage door.

"We'll need you back here at four o'clock. Be prepared to sing one complete song of your choice. You'll also be reading from the script. We'll hear the introductions of each character on the line: Michael and Tripp, please look at Bobby and Greg. Jorge, please look at Greg and Don. The sides are in the green room on the table. See you at four." He crossed the stage back to the others who were still waiting their turn in the opposite wing. "Next group!"

The three who had emerged victorious gave a collective sigh of relief and congratulated one another. But as Tripp gathered up the stapled sheets of dialogue from the table in the green room, his excitement began to wane. He was due at work at four, and his boss wouldn't be happy about him coming in late. He also couldn't predict how late he would be. But he had no choice. He was an excellent waiter, and he knew he could easily find another job if it came to that.

With his father a prominent doctor, and his mother a successful real estate broker, Tripp had grown up dining in fancy restaurants. A natural actor, he could slide as easily into the role of server as customer. When he interviewed for his first job waiting tables in college, the owner of the restaurant had asked him what experience he had. Tripp had replied, honestly, "None. But I've eaten in many fine restaurants." The owner, recognizing the merit of that perspective, had hired him at once, and Tripp's charm and flexible body had proven valuable assets as well. He had learned to nimbly maneuver through narrow hallways from kitchen to dining floor while balancing a loaded tray on one shoulder. He could discuss tennis and golf with old farts, charities with socially prominent women, and the latest Broadway hits with just about anyone. The only obstacle to a stellar restaurant career had been his performing career. He was an even better dancer than he was a waiter, and although Broadway had eluded him until now, he worked five to six months a year, which, given the unemployment statistics that Actors' Equity coughed up annually, was better than average. Restaurant managers usually tried to keep a spot open for him, but it wasn't always feasible.

So he knew if he lost his job, he could get another. And with any luck, he'd be in *A Chorus Line* on Broadway and wouldn't have to, at least for a while.

He squinted into the bright sunlight on West Forty-fifth Street, rummaged in his jacket pocket for his cell phone, and dialed.

"Parapluie, this is Annette."

"Hi, it's Tripp. Listen, I know I'm scheduled to work tonight, but I just got called back for the Broadway revival of *A Chorus Line*.

They want me there at four. I know it's last minute, but I'll do whatever I can to make it up to you!"

Annette cleared her throat. "Will you be able to come in at all, or will you just be late?"

"That's the thing, I don't know. I'll have to stay until they're finished. I doubt it will be later than seven o'clock, but I can't make any guarantees. This is a really important opportunity. I can't miss it!"

"Then you'll have to find someone to replace you tonight," she replied briskly. "I can't be short a waitperson, and I don't have time to make calls myself."

"Of course," he said, praying silently that someone would be available to sub for him.

"And in return, if I ever host a special event, I want you on hand," she continued. "You know you're my best waiter."

"Absolutely," Tripp said emphatically. "You just let me know when, and I'll be there. Promise!"

It sounded like Annette had hung up on him, but he didn't care. He had phone numbers for three of her other waiters, and he hit pay dirt with Shoshana, his first call.

"Sure!" she cried enthusiastically. "I'm happy to have an extra shift. Especially dinner. She's only given me lunches so far."

Tripp hesitated for a moment, but Annette hadn't specifically declared Shoshana off-limits. He'd found a replacement. That's what he'd promised.

"You're the best, Shosh. I owe you one!"

"Tickets to opening night will be satisfactory," squeaked Shoshana merrily.

"You got 'em!"

He snapped his phone shut and took a deep, triumphant breath of New York City's freshest. This was his moment. He was sure of it. He had worked hard, up through the ranks of summer stock, regional theater, and national tours, and he was in his prime. His acting skills and, if he was honest, his ability to handle the responsibility and the schedule, had all caught up with his dancing talent.

He felt ready for Broadway in a way he never had before. He was going to get this job.

Never mind that he'd made two promises in order to ensure himself the chance. He'd deliver on them, if and when the time came. Right now, he had more important things to do. A song to practice, lines to review.

His dance bag slung over his shoulder, Tripp took off at a run, and with a move of sudden lithe grace, he executed a perfect pirouette right on Forty-fifth Street, startling several elderly passersby. Then he continued down the street on his journey toward the Great White Way.

NINE

"Now, tell me the truth. Was it you who called that old bat on her cell phone in Shoreham's?" asked Peter Blomgard, as he closed his menu and handed it back to the waiter.

"What makes you think that?" asked Sy innocently. "I'll have the ceviche to start and then the Dover sole. And we'll have a bottle of the Montrachet, Blain-Gagnard 2005."

"Very good."

The waiter collected Sy's menu and skirted the white marble pool next to which Sy and Peter were seated in the Four Seasons' famed Pool Room. Sy had been lunching there the day three extraordinarily fetching young women had decided to skinny-dip in it. After that, he was always a bit disappointed when the best-looking diners remained clothed and dry.

"The timing was a bit uncanny, and you had this complete shit-eating grin on your face when you walked out," continued Peter.

"Did I? Must have been a coincidence."

"Are you going to open it? I mean, this is the one, right? The one you're always talking about?"

"Of course I'm going to open it."

Peter smoothed his graying blond hair and flashed Sy an ingratiating smile. "Do I get a taste?"

Sy groaned. "Not you, too!"

"Why, who else?"

"Antony Farrell. He wants me to plan a tasting event."

"Well, I think that's a great idea!" said Peter, so enthusiastically he nearly knocked the Montrachet out of the waiter's hands.

The waiter, unruffled, set the bottle down and went through the opening ritual. He gave Sy the cork, and then tipped a tiny bit into his glass.

"Sorry, that's not in the cards," said Sy, swirling the wine. He leaned his nose halfway into the narrow glass and inhaled, then took a small sip and let it roll over all the parts of his tongue, chewing it before he swallowed. "Excellent, thank you."

The waiter poured out full glasses for them.

Peter took a sip and gave an appreciative nod. "So you're just going to drink the Lafite by yourself?"

"You think I'm such a loser I have to drink it alone?"

Peter sat back and folded his arms. "Ah." He winked knowingly. "Who is she?"

Sy shrugged. "Nobody you know."

That wasn't entirely true, as Peter had met Valentina once when he came by the office. Peter ran a hedge fund that sometimes invested in Sy's portfolio companies. But she wasn't anybody Peter knew in the social sense, and Sy intended to keep it that way.

"She must be very special," pressed Peter. "Is she 'the one'?"

Sy could hear the envy in Peter's voice. Peter liked both Marianne and Pippa, and couldn't understand why Sy had thrown away two perfectly satisfactory wives. He had never been married himself, which Sy always found odd, as Peter was, objectively speaking, far and away the better-looking of the two of them. He was tall, fit, and Nordic, with a long, straight nose, hooded gray eyes, and permanently tanned skin. He could also be arrogant and sexist, which Sy supposed was the source of the problem, but he'd always trusted that Peter was smart enough not to say to any actual woman the kinds of things he let slip to Sy. But maybe Sy gave him too much credit.

Whether Valentina was "the one" was not a subject Sy wished to discuss with Peter or anyone else, for that matter. Right now, all he wanted was the chance to get to know her better and let his obsession—he realized it was only that—evolve naturally into something deeper. If and when it ever got to that point, he would risk the snide comments and sidelong glances of Peter and his other friends. If he found he loved Valentina, public opinion would not be able to touch him.

"She's the one who's drinking the wine with me," he affirmed, taking another sip of the Montrachet.

"Lucky gal," whistled Peter as their appetizers were served. "I suppose you'll open it in the privacy of your home?"

"Haven't decided. There are reasons both for and against." Sy nibbled the tangy ceviche. "If I do drink it out, where should I go?"

"Lots of choices," said Peter, munching thoughtfully on his gravlax. "You could come here. The Terrace Room would be romantic. Oh, I know!" he exclaimed, waving his fork. "You could reserve the Wine Cellar at Patroon. That's certainly the right atmosphere. Aretsky would be all over you."

Sy shook his head vigorously. "That's exactly what I don't want."

"He'd let you alone if you made it clear that you wanted privacy."

"You don't think he'd try to use it for publicity?"

"Mmmmm . . . you're probably right. Better to find someplace off the beaten path. If word got out you were uncorking at Patroon, it'd be a mob scene."

"Are you still up for Bermuda this weekend?" asked Sy, eager to change the subject. "I booked the jet."

"You bet. Warren coming?"

"He and Lillian have an event at the Union Club. A concert by that Gilbert and Sullivan group that performs for charity."

"Too bad. Your partner's a hoot when that witchy-bitchy wife isn't around."

"Mmmm," said Sy. Peter had once made a similar comment to Warren, and that, in fact, was the real reason his partner wasn't joining them. Warren hadn't much use for Peter after that, although he wasn't above making similar comments about his own wife to Sy.

"Drunk anything good lately?" Peter asked. "Think my price range, not yours. Everyday stuff."

Sy thought back to recent non-rare wine purchases from the three wine merchants he dealt with regularly. There had been several excellent, inexpensive finds.

"A remarkable Pinot. 2005 Livera Chapelle-Chambertin Grand Cru Reserve. Berries, cherries, and notes of spice, but all in balance."

It's intense and structured. You can drink it now, but if you hang on to it, it will really come into its own."

Peter flipped open a small notebook and began to write. "Livera Chambertin '05. Great."

"I forget. Are you a Syrah fan?"

"Que Syrah, Syrah," Peter sang out in a lusty baritone, to the amusement of the people at the surrounding tables. "Whatever you drink, I drink!"

"Try the 2005 Lily's Garden Shiraz from Two Hands. Australian—considered one of their recent best. Deep, swaggering, plums and cloves. Very flavorful."

Peter scribbled some more. "Give me a champagne, too."

"Why? You got a date?"

"Why should I tell you, Mr. Forthcoming?"

"There's one that I like a lot. Citrus, green apple, but also an overtone of maple. Oudinot Brut, get the 1999, but don't hang on to it more than three years. Still, it's worth having a case of that in the house—if you can find it. It'll pair nicely with your Chinese takeout."

The conversation went on in this vein, and by one thirty they had finished. Peter picked up the $925 tab to thank Sy in advance for the weekend at his Bermuda condo.

When Sy returned to his office, Miss Banks was waiting with a stack of checks for him to sign.

"Mrs. Hampton telephoned," she said.

This was one of those times when Miss Banks's obstinate adherence to formality grew tiresome.

"Which one?" Sy asked, looking up from the checks.

"Miss Pippa."

"You can just call her Pippa, you know. Or Ms. Kirk."

Miss Banks bristled at the admonition. "Miss Kirk, then. She wanted to congratulate you on your wine."

He knew Pippa would hate the "Miss" as much as the Mrs. Hampton she'd never been, but he didn't want to further annoy Miss Banks, who had been especially prickly of late.

"Where's Valentina?" he asked.

Miss Banks's nose twitched in obvious displeasure, and he realized he'd done exactly that. "She's gone to lunch."

"Why don't you take yours now?" he suggested.

Miss Banks shook her head. "Somebody has to be here to see to your telephone."

"I think I can manage it. And I'm sure Valentina will be back before long."

"I'm not hungry. Thank you."

Miss Banks returned to her desk, and Sy was swift enough to realize that she had scored doubly off that maneuver—she got to be a martyr, and she could monitor any conversation between Sy and Valentina, once the latter returned.

Not much had changed outwardly between him and Valentina, but Miss Banks had clearly grown suspicious after their tête-à-tête in his office. He was certain Valentina would never confide the nature of their conversation to Miss Banks, but he knew enough about women, office politics, and Miss Banks to know she felt threatened. He was grateful for Miss Banks's devotion over the years, and he realized that she was, in her way, attached. But he had no reason to think this attachment was in any way romantic. It was merely possessive, though it did render her unusually proprietary about her underling. Sy resolved from now on to ascertain Valentina's whereabouts without resorting to asking Miss Banks, unless absolutely necessary.

The phone rang, and as if to prove to Miss Banks that he was fully capable of picking up the receiver himself, he snatched it up. He was surprised to find Antony Farrell on the other end of the line. He braced himself for more hints about presenting the Lafite.

"I was wondering if you'd like to join me for dinner some night this week or next. I have a wine that I'd love for you to try. It's a 1970 Château Giscours. Considered one of the best Giscours ever made. Stark loves it, and I thought you might sample it with me. He gifted me a few bottles last year, but I've yet to uncork."

Sy hesitated. It seemed like a generous, comradely invitation, but there was something slightly odd about it. Then again, Sy had invited Farrell to his place once. Perhaps Farrell felt it was time to return the favor? Still, Sy couldn't help but suspect an ulterior motive. But it would be ungallant to ask what the catch was. He needed to take the invitation at face value and either accept it or not, and the truth was, he was too curious about the Giscours to pass it up.

"That's very thoughtful of you. Let me check my calendar."

He pulled up his schedule on the computer, which Miss Banks kept updated and synched regularly to his iPhone.

"I'm free tomorrow, if that's not too soon. Otherwise, I'm off to Bermuda on Friday, and next week is pretty booked."

"Perfect," said Farrell. "Seven thirty all right?"

"Sure. Where shall we meet?"

"There's a superb new place I'm eager to try. I've heard it's quite modern and unique in décor, but has lovely classic French dishes. Parapluie, on East Fifty-second Street. Do you know it?"

"No, not at all. Sounds terrific. Looking forward to it."

Sy hung up the phone and entered the date into his calendar himself. Perhaps the invitation was nothing more than what it appeared to be: an offer from one oenophile to another to try an unusual wine. But it seemed so much more likely that Farrell was setting him up to return this favor with the Lafite, rather than repaying his last.

To be fair, he might have reacted more positively to Farrell's suggestion of a public tasting event if he hadn't already been moved to invite Valentina. It was the sort of thing he'd be likely to do under normal circumstances. But Sy was not about to change his plans for the wine, unless Valentina backed out. Even then, he wasn't sure he'd want to go public with this particular bottle. Regardless, he might as well enjoy a good meal and a scintillating discussion about wine, complete with a first-rate specimen. But that was as far as he was willing to go, and he would make sure that Farrell understood that.

TEN

VALENTINA INHALED A TURKEY AVOCADO WRAP from the deli, and then made a beeline for Barnes & Noble. Trish had passed along her cousin Vito's suggestion that she pick up a copy of *Wine for Dummies,* and this was the first chance she'd had. She didn't like to order online, because there was nobody at home to take her packages during the day, so she fought her way east over several long blocks to the closest bookstore, which was on Fifty-fourth and Third. If she thought that by two o'clock there would be fewer people clogging the sidewalks, she was wrong.

She pretended she was a fighter in the jungle wielding a machete that could cut through the tangle of pedestrians, without killing anyone, of course. She swung her arm in an imaginary slice, nearly knocking the Louis Vuitton satchel off the arm of the woman in front of her. Trish's method of clearing a sidewalk was more effective. They were once packed in a crush in Times Square, stuck behind a waddling grandma in the kind of 1950s housedress her mother still wore to clean. Trish had growled in her nicotine-lined rasp, "Get the FUCK out of my WAY!" Which worked. Better than Valentina's imaginary sword.

When she finally made it to the store, she found the book easily. The title didn't thrill her, but she had to admit that in this case, the shoe fit. She paid for the book and struck out back across town toward the office on Fifth Avenue and Fifty-fifth Street, but as she drew closer, she felt her feet dragging. She'd been avoiding Mr. Hampton—Sy—in the office. Valentina knew she had to get used to thinking of him as Sy if she was going on a date with him. But that was the problem. She could never call him Sy as long as Miss Banks was hovering about. But how could he be Mr. Hampton at work and Sy outside?

She expected that after they drank the wine, things would be different, whether or not he put the moves on her. But their relationship seemed to have shifted already. For one thing, they suddenly had one. From the moment he'd asked her out, the vibe had changed, at least for her. She found herself experimenting not just with how to be around him, but with who to be. There were times when she pretended to be like Miss Banks, all business. Other times, she tried being the way she was when she and Jerry had first become interested in each other. Like they had a secret that no one else knew, and wouldn't everyone else be shocked if they found out. But both ways felt wrong.

As she neared Fifth Avenue, she was seized with a sudden desire to visit Shoreham's. She wanted a glimpse of Sy's world and to see and maybe hold a valuable bottle of wine, before she was faced with the Lafite. She recalled from the *Post* article that Shoreham's was somewhere on Madison Avenue. She dialed information and got the address: 679 Madison, between Sixty-first and Sixty-second. It was out of her way, and she'd already been gone an hour plus, but this was all for Sy. She was trying to learn everything she could so he wouldn't feel he was wasting his wine on her. How could he complain? It was almost like running an errand for him.

She walked uptown on Fifth, tempted more than once to use Trish's crowd-clearer on the plaza around the Apple Store at Fifty-ninth Street. She doubled back east and continued north on Madison, and soon Shoreham's gold-lettered glass storefront came into view. As soon as she entered the auction house, the clamor of the street fell away. Huge, heavy Oriental rugs hung from the walls, absorbing the sound and creating an elegant hush. Valentina cleared her throat and approached the front desk, where a young man in a dark suit and pink tie was watching her, a polite and patient smile on his face.

"May I help you?" he asked.

"I was wondering if there's a wine auction today?"

"We only hold them a few times a year, and we just had one."

"Is there, um, any wine I can see?"

The young man regarded her curiously. "What do you mean . . . see?"

"Like, do you have any bottles on display or anything like that?"

He shook his head apologetically. "No, I'm sorry, miss, but we don't typically display wine that we're auctioning. Have you seen our catalog?"

"Um, just one page from it."

He pushed a thick magazine toward her. He continued as she examined it.

"Other items are available for viewing. For example, we have an auction of American silver coming up, and those lots are on view right now upstairs, if you'd care to see them."

"No thanks." She flipped past page after page of fancy-looking bottles with long, pretentious-sounding descriptions. "It's really just wine that I'm interested in. Can I have this?"

"We usually charge twenty-five dollars for our catalogs, but . . ." Valentina felt his gaze alight on her chest. "You may as well take it. Auction's over anyway."

She slipped the catalog into the Barnes & Noble bag along with her book. As she turned to go, she knocked into a tall man with ruddy cheeks, blue-gray eyes, and a mop of unruly blond hair who had crept up silently behind her.

"Pardon me, but did I hear you say you're interested in wine?" he asked, looking her up and down with a practiced and apprecia-tive eye.

"Not . . . not interested, really," she stammered. "I mean a little interested."

He cocked his head to one side and smiled at her. "You don't seem quite sure *how* you feel about wine."

"You could say that. I have to go, though. I'm late for work."

She started to move past him, but he stopped her. "Perhaps I could be of assistance," he said, and the combination of his silky British accent and the pressure of his hand on her arm made her melt just a little. "I'm Antony Farrell, head of the wine department here. Was there something in particular you wanted?"

She hesitated. If he was head of the wine department, he must know Sy. Instinctively, she knew she shouldn't say anything about tasting Sy's most recent purchase.

"Um, I just sort of wanted . . ."

What did she want?

"I wanted to see what a really expensive bottle of wine looks like," she concluded. "But he said there weren't any to see." She indicated the young man at the front desk, who seemed to be enjoying their exchange.

Farrell winked at her and stage-whispered, "It depends whom you ask. I have several bottles of rare wine in my office. Do you have a moment?"

"I don't, not really," she started. Oh, what the hell. She'd gone this far out of her way. "I mean, I could spare a few."

As she followed Farrell up the wide staircase, she caught a smirk on Pink Tie's face. Farrell opened a door marked "Park Room" and ushered her in.

"My office is just through here." He waved a hand around the room. "This is where we hold our auctions."

Valentina glanced around, oddly disappointed. It looked more or less like a hotel event room. She had been imagining something more elaborate, with ornate dark wood paneling and chandeliers dripping with crystals. She followed Farrell up two steps and across a small stage, past a podium and a large projection screen to a door in the far wall, which he opened.

His office wasn't large, but this, at least, had the elegance she was expecting. A grand mahogany desk took up the far wall, and there was a small round table, with a set of glasses in what appeared to be permanent readiness. A large refrigerated wine cabinet held around twenty-four bottles, and resting on top of a side table, an elaborate wrought-iron rack supported twelve more.

"These are real beauties," Farrell said, gesturing to the wrought-iron rack. "Haut Brion, Lafite, Margaux, and this one . . . the jewel in my crown." He picked up a bottle from the top row and cradled it in the crook of his arm like a baby. "1961 Château Pétrus Pomerol. Just having it in here brings me joy, even if it's not mine to drink."

Valentina glanced at the bottle. The name was lettered in bold red, and there was a sketch of a little friar at the top. It was fancy enough, but so were a lot of wine labels. It would still be hard to know this one held anything special based on the outside alone.

"You haven't told me your name." Farrell interrupted her thoughts.

"Valentina."

"Valentina," he echoed. "Lovely."

"How much does this one cost?" She indicated the Pétrus.

"As much as anyone is willing to pay for it. I would estimate that a lot of six bottles of 1961 Pétrus could fetch somewhere between $35,000 and $50,000. So on its own, this one is worth roughly $8,000."

A few days ago, hearing that a bottle of wine could cost that much would have made her howl in disbelief. But after what Sy had paid for his, this one seemed like a steal.

She looked up to see that Farrell was watching her, an amused look on his face.

"I thought you'd be impressed," he said wryly.

"Oh! Well, I mean, it's a lot of money." She gave a nervous chuckle. "But compared to what that guy paid for the bottle of Thomas Jefferson's wine last week . . ."

"Oh, you read about that, did you?"

"Yeah, in the *Post*."

He nodded, as if everything about her now made a little more sense.

"And you came by to see what such a bottle looked like?"

She gave a shy smile. "I guess."

He set the Pétrus on the round table. "There's a mystery inside here," he murmured, tracing the curved neck with his fingertips. "Rare wines are magical. Everything about them—the bottle, the bouquet, the color, the taste—evokes another time and place. For people who have devoted their lives to the pursuit of fine wine, buying a specimen like this is a chance to sample ambrosia."

"That's my name!" she blurted, before she could help herself.

"I thought you said it was Valentina," he said warily.

"It is. Valentina D'Ambrosio."

Farrell raised an eyebrow. "That has to be one of the most deliciously romantic names I have ever heard. Love's ambrosia! Quite a lot to live up to, but I imagine you do."

He took a step closer to her, and she squirmed at the turn the conversation was taking. It was a road she'd been down before, one way or another. She let the bag from Barnes & Noble drop to the floor. It broke the mood, just as she'd intended.

"Allow me," he said, and bent down to retrieve it.

He smiled mischievously and looked inside, pulling out the book. She expected a mocking comment, but he simply replaced it in the bag and handed it back to her.

"An excellent place to start. When you've finished reading it, give me a call." He handed her a card, which she took without looking. "Should you decide you'd like to sample some high-quality wines, perhaps you would accompany me to a tasting. Or, of course, you're welcome to come here. Sometimes I sample a bottle from a cache that's being auctioned. I'm always happy to share," he said with a seductive grin.

"Thanks. Well, I gotta go. But this was, uh, very interesting."

Valentina hurried out through the Park Room as quickly as she could. She knew that Farrell had followed her out of his office, and she sensed him standing on the little stage, but she didn't look back. She slipped his card into the bag with the book. She'd keep it, just in case, but she didn't need his help to taste an expensive, high-quality wine.

She was already going to sample the best.

ELEVEN

THE FINAL CALLBACKS WERE SIGNIFICANTLY more stressful than the dance audition earlier that day. Tripp knew the job was his to lose, which made it difficult to relax. As a result, his voice felt tight when he read the two monologues, he took two extra, stupid breaths in the song of his choice, Gershwin's "I've Got a Crush on You," and now, dancing the opening combo once again, he tried to clear his head and tap into the excitement he'd felt earlier. But it was hard to ignore the fact that his lifelong dream was now truly within his grasp. He glanced out the corner of his eye at Michael, who had been in his group earlier. He was hot. Well-muscled, with dark hair and a slightly exotic look, as if his parents might be of some foreign extraction, and easily ten years younger than Tripp. He was a good dancer, too.

Turn, turn, arabesque, pull to *passé, pas de* . . . shit.

The momentary distraction made Tripp stumble, and when he looked up, he saw the director making a note on his clipboard.

Shit, shit, shit! Tripp thought. He forced himself to concentrate on the remaining portion of the combination, even as he sensed his dream evaporating.

He tried not to assume the worst when the stage manager dismissed them all and sent them down to the green room to collect their belongings. Besides, he would know for certain soon enough. The moment the person in charge of hiring him made a decision, Tripp's brain would somehow receive the message telepathically. He had a strange, instinctive antenna for these things, and in close to twenty years in show business, he'd never once been wrong.

"That was great, wasn't it?" said Michael, clapping him on the back with a euphoria that Tripp, unfortunately, didn't feel.

"I was nervous," admitted Tripp. Some demon possessed him in the next moment to tell the whole truth. "And then I looked over at you, and that was it."

Michael's eyes widened. "Are you kidding? I was messing up all over the place. I don't think you have much to worry about from me. I saw you out there, and you are solid. Really solid."

Tripp shook his head. "Thanks, but solid isn't enough. And I only barely gave them that."

"Don't be so hard on yourself. You don't know yet that it won't come through."

Tripp had no energy left to keep up the façade of being hopeful. He slung his bag over his shoulder and pushed open the stage door. Michael grabbed his own bag and followed him out onto the street. Tripp couldn't decide if he was annoyed or flattered.

"You'll have plenty of other chances," Michael called after him.

Tripp paused and turned around. "How old do you think I am?"

Michael jogged to catch up. "I dunno. Thirty-two."

"Thirty-nine. I've been knocking around this business for a long time. I'm flattered that you think I look younger, but I can tell you, it doesn't feel that way, and it's showing up in my moves."

"Hey, man, I didn't mean to upset you." Michael put a hand on Tripp's arm. "And I wasn't blowing smoke, either. You've got fabulous style and you're just so . . . graceful. Smooth and elegant, especially in the ballet combination."

Tripp looked into Michael's eyes, which were a greenish hazel, and saw that he was being sincere.

"I appreciate that," said Tripp. "Really. But I have a second sense about these things."

"Oh." Michael seemed to have run out of palliatives. "Well, what about me, then?"

Tripp gave a wry smile. All actors ever cared about was themselves.

"Future cloudy, try again later."

Michael laughed. "Got it. Where are you heading now? I'm just off to grab a bite. Do you want to join me?"

"Thanks, but I have to get to work," Tripp lied. Cute as Michael was, Tripp was done smiling for today. He preferred to go back to his one-bedroom in Hell's Kitchen and nurse his disappointment in private.

"Can I call you sometime?" asked Michael.

Why was it that whenever Tripp was pining for a pretty boy to hit on him, it never happened, and now that all he wanted was to be alone with a glass of Dewar's, this hottie was coming on to him? He had to hope that Michael found indifference attractive enough to try again another time.

He dug into his pocket and handed Michael his card, then they shook hands and Tripp started down the street.

"I'll give you a buzz sometime!" Michael shouted.

Tripp waved over his shoulder, surprised at his own lack of interest. But on some level he blamed Michael for being what he no longer was and for distracting him enough to make him stumble at the critical moment.

And as much as he sensed that he would not get the job, his gut told him Michael would.

TWELVE

ANNETTE WATCHED SHOSHANA try to balance a tray with five bowls of Etienne's white asparagus soup and wished Tripp had called someone else. Although Shoshana claimed to have a lot of experience, and her references had all been highly enthusiastic, she'd proven slow to learn the routine at Parapluie. Annette also found her name annoying: Shoshana Raquelle. Shoshana Raquelle . . . what? "Raquelle" was so obviously a middle name doing duty as a last name that it sounded unfinished, like someone singing "Happy Birthday" and stopping on "to." Was there really a Mr. and Mrs. Raquelle out there somewhere? Doubtful. And, of course, Shoshana was an actress.

Annette didn't mind hiring actors on principle. On the contrary, they had excellent people skills, and if they could work out their schedules without hanging her up, they generally made first-rate employees. But she hated when they screamed ACTRESS, like Shoshana. She was always overly made-up, but more than that, it was her manner, which was aggressively friendly to a fault. She remembered when she interviewed Shoshana. The girl made an ENTRANCE, thrusting her hand into Annette's and pumping it zealously. Then with wide eyes, and projecting her voice at a level appropriate for the biggest Broadway house, she proceeded to compliment Annette on her décor, which would have pleased her if the delivery hadn't been so grating.

Annette had hired her only because she was having trouble filling her last waitstaff spot, and Shoshana was the best of the applicants. Although thinking back on it now, she decided she'd been steamrolled. On the other hand, she thought, as she watched the girl chat up a young, well-dressed couple on a date, the customers didn't seem as put off by her as she was. Maybe it was a cultural thing.

She left Shoshana to her best performance in a supporting role and returned to the kitchen to see how Etienne was getting on. Her conversation with Antony Farrell was still unsettling her. She knew she needed a hook to grab the media's attention, but there was something about somebody else saying it—particularly when that person was Farrell—that made her fear she was already too late. The clock was ticking, and now she was obsessing that even if she could put his plan into action immediately, she'd be just as well served to shut her doors for good.

At the same time, his proposed stunt refused to sit well with her conscience. The idea of tricking a customer was as distasteful to her as Shoshana's brazen chumminess. It was fundamentally dishonest to turn someone else's personal property into your public relations calling card without that person's consent. It was the worst kind of bait and switch. And yet, it was impossible not to be tempted by visions of fawning food critics, impressed that Parapluie—not the Four Seasons, not Bouley, not La Grenouille—had secured Sy Hampton's patronage for such an important event. In her mind's eye, she saw the critics tasting the food, nodding their heads, and rolling their eyes back in sybaritic enjoyment, murmuring, "Ah, yes. Delicious. I see why he came here."

She shook visions of the cover of *Food & Wine* from her head and returned to the kitchen, where Etienne was making dissatisfied clucking sounds over the asparagus soup. Annette took a spoon from the draining board and tried some.

"*Cette soupe n'est pas piqué des vers,*" said Annette. And it was, indeed, delicious.

"*Ouais, elle n'est pas mal,*" Etienne muttered. He set down his spoon and removed the rabbit from the oven.

Not bad? He was crazy. "*Et le lapin?*" she asked.

He sniffed it cautiously. "*Bofff!!! Ça va le lapin, mais sans plus.*"

She suspected that the rabbit, far from being barely passable, was mouthwateringly divine. Etienne was his own worst critic.

"*Ne sois pas si sévère envers toi-même. Personne n'est parfait,*" she said.

He looked up, straightened his toque, and replied sternly, "*On n'excuse pas un mauvais chef, encore moins sa mauvaise cuisine!"*

He was right. There would be no excuse for bad cooking—if it were bad. She should have known better than to ask her perfectionist, self-hating chef what he thought of his own creations. Then again, without a brilliant chef, no amount of publicity would propel Parapluie to a top rating.

She knew that in her current mood, she'd be a nuisance on the floor, and besides, it was too depressing to keep counting heads. She only wished her kitchen staff were "in the weeds" with orders piling up faster than they could prepare them.

She returned to the oasis of her office and her box of Grandmother Lecocq's dessert recipes. Just handling the stained, softening index cards brought Annette back to the big farm kitchen and the long walks through the orchards with her grandmother. They'd ravage the blueberry bogs, pick apples, and pluck strawberries, separating out enough from the sale crop for the compotes, preserves, tortes, and pies that were her grandmother's specialty. As skilled as Annette had become in kitchens from Montreal to Lyon to Atlanta, and with as many compliments as she'd received over the years, she knew deep down that the sublime perfection of her grandmother's desserts would always elude her.

She was contemplating asking Etienne to try the peach blueberry cobbler when the front podium buzzed.

"Yes?"

"It's Antony Farrell for you on line two."

"Thanks, I've got it."

Grateful for the one distraction that jibed with her current mood, she answered promptly.

"This is Annette," she said, determined to keep it all business.

"I need a reservation for two tomorrow night at seven thirty," demanded Farrell.

"You could have told Justine. I don't handle reservations when she's here."

"You might want to handle this one. I'm bringing Sy Hampton for dinner."

"You are?!" she cried in spite of herself.

He continued, feigning indifference to her excitement. "I'll bring my own wine. Do an old mate a favor and waive the corkage fee?"

"I'll consider it."

"And here's one other thing you must do. Make sure the restaurant is full."

She felt the heat rise to her face. "You know I'm having difficulty doing that! Isn't that why we're considering this crazy stunt?"

"Yes, of course, but you have to look like a chic and successful establishment for him to want to display his wine on your premises."

"What do you expect me to do? Pull people in off the streets and offer them a free gourmet meal?"

"Just make sure the place isn't too empty. And get Etienne to whip up something classy—something that would perfectly complement the oldest drinkable Bordeaux in existence."

"Just a minute," she said, and before he could respond, she pressed the hold button.

Really, he was too infuriating! And the fact that he had a point made it worse.

She pulled up the reservations screen on her computer. Thirty-eight for tomorrow. She buzzed through to the front desk. "Justine? What kind of walk-in business are we averaging on Thursdays?"

"I'd say you can count on thirty," Justine answered in the cheery voice for which Annette had hired her.

The restaurant seated eighty, so that wasn't too bad, all things considered. She clicked back to Antony.

"Tomorrow night will be fine. You needn't worry."

"Excellent! If we can impress him, I think you can look forward to an outstanding publicity event."

"Just tell me one thing."

"Yes?"

Annette twisted her grandmother's silver ring on her right hand and wondered how best to frame her question. She decided to come straight to the point.

"I know you well enough to know that this little stunt would never have crossed your mind unless there was something in it for you. So, what do I have to do in return?"

"Seat me next to Sy Hampton when he comes back with his Lafite."

"That's it?"

"That's it. I'll get you the attention you need, as long as you make sure I'm as close to him as possible when the time comes."

"I'll do my best, but what exactly will that accomplish?" asked Annette.

"I should have thought that was perfectly obvious," replied Farrell. There was a pause, and then he said, in a voice sober with determination, "I want to taste that wine."

THIRTEEN

"DID MY PACKAGE FROM SHOREHAM'S ARRIVE TODAY?"

Sy could barely keep the excitement out of his voice as he handed his coat to Claudine.

"Yes. I've put it on the dining room table."

He experienced a flash of horror at the thought of Claudine, capable though she was, transporting his treasure herself.

She must have caught the look on his face, because she quickly added, "I didn't think it was safe to leave it in the front hall where anybody could knock into it, so I asked the delivery man to carry it in."

"Thank you, Claudine. That was the right thing," he assured her. "Excuse me. If you don't mind . . ."

He rushed past her to the dining room, which was beautifully decorated in Wedgwood blue damask, with accents of peach that at first he had hated, but now rather enjoyed. Whatever else he thought about Marianne, she did have exquisite taste, and this room, like the others Pippa had chosen to leave intact, reflected it.

He stared at the box from Shoreham's. The wine was here! In his house! He was almost afraid to open it. Where would he keep the bottle? He supposed he could just leave it on the sideboard in the small rack. He would be drinking it soon enough, so there was no real need to store it in the cellar. Even so, it didn't seem quite right to treat it like an ordinary bottle of wine. What if some wine thief read about his acquisition in the *Post* and broke in? What if Antony Farrell himself staged a theft?

Now, that was an insane and paranoid notion, if ever there was one. And yet, Sy couldn't help but wonder how far the auctioneer's desire to taste the wine might take him. Sy had other rare and valuable bottles downstairs, in a special locked cabinet in the back of the cellar. Yes, even though the Lafite was only visiting, he'd best lock it up with the other notables.

But first he had to unpack it. He took a knife from the kitchen and sliced carefully down the tape, peeling away the cardboard box. Inside was a padded wooden crate with a little latch. He unlocked it and looked inside.

The bottle appeared to be in fine condition. Sy noticed a sheet of paper nestled next to it. This turned out to be a history, compiled by the Marquet heirs, of the extraordinary voyage the wine had taken to get to his dining room table. In the course of verifying the bottle, they had managed to reconstruct its journey.

According to Pichard's bill of sale to Thomas Jefferson, the bottle had traveled across the Atlantic and had remained in the President's private collection until, apparently in need of funds, the estate sold it at auction to a collector from Williamsburg named Jeremiah Dossett in 1856. In 1888, Dossett reneged on an agreement to sell it to one Franklin Ritter, who reportedly hired highwaymen to slit Dossett's throat on the coach from Williamsburg to Philadelphia and steal the wine. Acquitted of any involvement, Ritter got to keep the bottle, ultimately selling it in 1906 to a young French collector named Alexandre Marquet, who eventually built up an extensive cellar in his family's château near Lyon. When the Nazis arrived, Marquet and his son, Charles, blocked off the most valuable bottles behind a false wall to hide them from the Nazis, who took over their home and depleted the rest of the cellar. Alexandre Marquet died of pneumonia and Charles lost his life fighting in the French resistance. After the war, the house reverted to Charles's children, passing then to his grandchildren, who—renovating the property and converting it into a hotel—discovered the false wall and the cache of valuable bottles. The Marquet heirs were now half a million dollars richer through Sy's folly.

Sy ran his fingers over the label. It had an intricate line drawing of the château, with the date printed in red ink, and it was positioned over the old etchings. He had never before owned—let alone handled—a wine this old. Was he really going to drink it? It had been in existence for so long. Would he be the one to vanish it?

He gingerly lifted the bottle from the straw packing. The green glass was so dark it was almost black, and he could tell from the irregularities that it was handblown. He ran his fingers over the thick gray lead of the capsule, where a bunch of grapes was raised in relief above the words "Château Lafitte." The thick glass made it considerably heavier than a modern bottle, and it was slightly larger as well. He found himself trembling, and he quickly set the bottle back down on the foam packing. The glass may have been thick, but it was also extremely old. It was truly amazing that it still existed at all. Jefferson had probably intended to enjoy it himself someday. But even if he hadn't, he couldn't have known that collectors would continue to turn a profit on his souvenir of Bordeaux into the twenty-first century.

He repacked the bottle and again contemplated storing it downstairs. He realized he was too nervous to carry it down the steps, and he wasn't about to let Claudine handle it. The breakfront had a locked compartment on the right side that was big enough to house the entire package. That was the perfect solution. He would keep it in there until his date with Valentina.

He felt an enormous sense of relief once the bottle was safely stowed. It wasn't as if he had never held a valuable object before. He had statuary and paintings that were worth more than the wine. But they were all insured, he reminded himself. Perhaps he ought to insure the Lafite?

If he planned to resell or display the wine, he would certainly insure it. But it had come to the end of its natural life, one way or another. He would be drinking it, and soon. Its value, at this point, was fixed. Wine by definition had both a transient element—the drink itself—and a permanent element—the bottle. The empty might fetch back a couple of thousand dollars at Shoreham's, but it was hardly worth insuring it for that.

He paced the dining room, restless. He had just held history in his hands, and he wanted to share the experience with . . . someone. Not Valentina. He sensed she would only be confused by the extent of his emotion. Eric was too young, and besides, he'd only think his father weirder and more alien than ever.

But there was one person who might understand. And he owed her a phone call anyway.

He called out to Claudine that he wasn't very hungry and whatever she could throw together quickly would be fine. Then he escaped to his study, where he dialed the gallery and hoped she'd be there.

"Pippa Kirk Gallery, may I help you?"

"Is Ms. Kirk there, please? It's her . . . it's Sy Hampton."

As the receptionist went to retrieve Pippa, he thought longingly of his ex-wife's long, red hair and pale, translucent skin. He had loved her, he still did, but even in their marriage, she had always seemed perfectly complete without him. In response, Sy had constructed a protective layer around himself, as if to prove that he didn't need another person to complete him either, but in the end, it had only doubled the distance between them.

"Sy?"

"Pippa! Miss Banks told me you called. How's the gallery?"

"Fantastic! I've got a new exhibit. I think you'd like it."

"Sounds great. I'll try to make it down soon."

"So, I read about your wine in the paper. This is the one you always swore you'd own someday, isn't it?"

"This is the one!"

"Well, congratulations! That's quite an investment."

"I didn't buy it as an investment. I bought it to drink."

"I know, but you paid an awful lot for it. It's still an investment—of a different kind." She paused for a moment. "Just be careful."

"Careful? Of what?"

"I know you, Sy. You have this habit of endowing people—and things—with a significance they don't really have. You did it with me. This wine might not be as amazing as you think. I hope for your sake it is, but just . . . oh, I don't know what I'm saying."

"You think I'll be disappointed?"

"I think sometimes you expect too much. And you've spent so

much of your life dreaming about this one bottle. When you open it, you might find it's not all it's cracked up to be. Don't make it some kind of . . . trophy. It's just wine."

Just wine?! She still didn't understand.

"The only thing that could disappoint me is if it's turned. But if it hasn't, it's going to be ambrosial! If Pichard's experiment worked at all, it worked completely. Don't you see?"

He could hear her impatient intake of breath over the phone. "Yes, yes. I do see. I hope the wine makes you happy, Sy. Truly."

"It will. How could it not?"

"Listen, I have to get back to work."

"It's good to talk to you, Pip. You sound . . . good."

"Thanks, Sy. Take care of yourself, okay?"

He hung up the phone, and only after he sat down again on the supple green leather of his chesterfield did he remember why he'd chosen this moment to return her call. He had wanted to express his feelings at handling the Jefferson Lafite for the first time. The wine was a work of art, and he'd been moved.

But it was only an appreciation for someone else's genius, and no manifestation of any spark of his own. In Pippa's eyes, he had always been a fraud, somebody whose interest in art and music, though real and deep, concealed a soul devoid of originality. She appreciated his enthusiasm and respected his critical response, but at the end of the day, no matter how ardently he admired her inspiration, she saw only his failure to inspire. And now, it seemed she was no longer willing to countenance his enthusiasm. Why was she so sure he would be disappointed?

With a rush of sadness, he realized that there wasn't a single person in his life—not even Pippa—who understood.

FOURTEEN

VITO SCARPARELLI'S HOUSE WAS LOUD, but nothing in it was louder than Vito Scarparelli.

"*Triiiiiiissssssshhhhh!*" he squealed, clutching her in a bear hug so immense that she almost completely disappeared. All Valentina could see of her friend was the top of her bleach-blond frizz. "Lemme look at you!" He held Trish at arm's length and tsked over her outfit.

"I *looove* the boots, purple leather, so funky! But the leopard shawl collar, now that is *fabulous!*"

While Vito checked out Trish, Valentina checked out Vito. He was barrel-chested, with lots of curly dark hair, and wore black leather pants and a red silk shirt, open at the collar. But instead of the gold chains that a lot of guys she knew wore, Vito's neck was swathed in a long, multicolored scarf shot through with glitter thread.

"And you must be Valentina! Come give cousin Vito a hug!"

Before she could protest, he had squeezed the breath out of her as well.

"Lemme look at you!"

He took in her outfit with a critical eye. She was wearing a white angora sweater with red appliquéd hearts and gray wool pants.

"Love the hearts. You go with that, girl. Whatever works!"

Valentina shot Trish a look. She had reached the obvious conclusion about Vito and was amazed that Trish had neglected to mention it. Just then, a short, round dumpling of a woman, with glowing skin and thick, black hair, trundled into the front hall, several small children hanging from her legs.

"And this is Roseanne, Vito's *wife*," announced Trish, with an emphasis that clearly telegraphed to Valentina that she should keep any observations about Vito to herself. "And these are . . . oh, help me out, Vito," continued Trish quickly. "They're all getting so big!"

"This here is Annamaria." He scooped up the littlest one, who looked to be about two, and gave her a big smooch on her squishy cheek. "That's Patricia, Trish's goddaughter, she's four." Patricia gave Trish a little wave and then hid behind her mother's legs again. "My boy is Charlie, he's six and a half, and that's Isabella, who's eight."

Vito set Annamaria down and threw up his hands over his head in a grand cabaret gesture. "And that's the Scarparelli family! Now get outta here, Daddy's gotta do some wine tasting. Scat!"

"Let's go," said Roseanne, ushering them back out of the hall-way. She turned to Trish and Valentina. "Don't let him make you feel like morons, just because he's got a tongue that does what other people's don't!"

"Outta here, woman!" Vito shouted with a laugh, and Roseanne laughed back, as if this was a practiced routine they'd gotten lots of mileage out of.

Vito lowered his voice to conversational volume. "Come on into the dining room. Roseanne'll give the kids dinner in the kitchen. I got three wines for us to try."

He turned and, as much as it was possible for a man his size, flounced into the dining room. Trish started after him, but Valentina grabbed her elbow. As Vito disappeared around the cor-ner, she whispered, "How can he be married? He's—"

"Shut up!" Trish hissed.

"Trish! Are you crazy? He's—"

"Eccentric!"

"He's gay!"

Trish rounded on her and spoke through clenched teeth. "Vito loves Roseanne, and he loves those kids. He's a devoted father!"

"But he must have a—"

"I don't know, and I don't ask. He's doing you a favor, so just keep your big, fat mouth shut!"

Trish freed her arm from Valentina's grasp and stalked off after Vito.

Valentina was completely bewildered. How could Trish pretend

Vito was anything but a flaming queen? Leather pants? A scarf? Those squeals? And forget about complimenting them on their outfits, how about noticing them in the first place? As Jerry always said, "The only thing straight guys notice about clothes is how easily they come off." Vito was as queer as a three-dollar bill, and these people were in complete denial.

"Val! You coming or what?" Trish hollered from the next room.

Valentina followed the sound of her voice down the hall. As far as she was concerned, other people's sexual preferences were none of her business, and she knew that most devout Italian Catholics would rather die or lie than admit to being gay. But when it was this obvious? Then again, the kids looked just like him, so clearly he was willing to pony up when he had to.

The dining room was a modest square off the kitchen. Through swinging doors, Valentina could hear the controlled chaos of Roseanne dishing up dinner. Banging pots, loud, demanding, high-pitched voices—they sure sounded like a happy family. Vito had set out three bottles of wine and was chattering at top volume to Trish.

"Here she is! Queen of hearts," sang out Vito when Valentina appeared. "Pull a chair up to Vito's table of vineyard delights and I'll give you a quick lesson. We're gonna stick to reds, since that's what's on the menu."

Valentina sat next to Trish, who kept her eyes on Vito and refused to look at her.

"Now, there's three things you gotta notice about the wine you're drinking. We're gonna skip all the label reading, because you got a pro who's handling all that, right?" He winked at Valentina. "You just gotta learn how to drink it properly, and what to say about it."

He picked up the first bottle of wine and filled three glasses about a third of the way. Valentina reached for hers, but Vito stopped her. "Wait for cousin Vito! And don't put your whole fist around the stem like that, you look like a baby with a rattle. You wanna hold the glass like this." He proceeded to pick up the glass daintily by the stem, supporting the bowl gently with his index finger. "You don't want the heat from your hand to cook the wine, but you don't want the bowl to pop off like a dandelion head!"

Valentina and Trish picked up their glasses.

"Good," said Vito. "Now, whaddaya see?"

Wine in a glass, thought Valentina, although she was pretty sure that wasn't the right answer.

"What color is it?" prompted Vito.

"Red," said Valentina. At least she knew that one.

Vito tsked. "Just red? Is it garnet, ruby, crimson, burgundy, cherry, tomato? If it's tomato, the guy at the liquor store really screwed me!"

"Garnet?" suggested Trish.

"You think? I'd say something lighter, like ruby or even cranberry," Vito said. "Now tip the wine up the bowl of your glass, tilt it, like so . . ."

Valentina copied Vito. The wine left little drips down the side.

"You gonna call this a light, medium, or full-bodied wine?" asked Vito. "Look at how it slides down the glass and doesn't leave much of a trail. The more noticeable the trail—or the legs, we call it—the heavier the wine."

"Light?" Trish tried again.

"Valentina, what do you say? Is she right?"

Why not? Valentina nodded yes.

"Good. Second thing, the nose. Just stick yours right in the glass and give it a good snort. Go on, don't be shy!"

Trish and Valentina did as they were told, but Valentina had to pull her face out to keep from sneezing into the wine.

"Valentina, you answer this one first." Vito leaned forward, his brown eyes glinting eagerly. "What does it SMELL LIKE?"

He raised his voice so dramatically that Valentina jumped.

"Um, raspberry, and also, maybe, turpentine?" she said uncertainly. "Like when you spray Glade in the bathroom after um, you know, and you get that gross mix of raspberry, turpentine, and . . ."

Valentina looked helplessly at Trish, who was staring at her, horrified.

"Shit, Val," Trish muttered under her breath.

"Well, I wasn't gonna say it!" said Valentina defensively.

"That's not what I meant!" hissed Trish.

"Actually," said Vito thoughtfully, after inhaling the wine one more time, "there is a bit of a chemical smell mixing up with the raspberry." He looked at Valentina and shook his head slightly. "Not how I would've described it, but at least you gave us some detail. That's a start."

Valentina could feel Trish kicking her under the table.

"Now it's time to taste it, and here's what you're gonna do. Take a medium-size sip, but don't swallow it right away. Swirl it around your mouth, so it hits every side of your tongue. Some people sorta chew it. Each part of your tongue's got different taste buds. Sweet in front, salty and sour on the sides, and bitter in the back, so give 'em all a chance. Then when you're done swirling, let the wine run over your whole tongue and down your throat, and see what flavor stays behind in your mouth and for how long. We call that the finish. Now, *drink*!"

Valentina sipped the wine the way Vito told her to. She didn't like it. It was too acidic, and there was a slight chemical aftertaste.

"Now, Trish, what do you think of the wine?"

Casting a sideways glance at Valentina, Trish said, "Um, it is fruity. Raspberryish and maybe strawberry, too."

"Valentina?"

"Yeah. And also a little chemical in the, um, finish."

Vito looked at them both and tsked again. "What am I gonna do with you two?"

He walked over to a small bookshelf that held more than its share of Bibles and pulled out a worn paperback thesaurus.

"You girls gotta improve your vocabulary as well as your taste buds. You gotta know how to talk about what you're tasting! Words like 'good' and 'fruity' only get you so far." He winked. "Present company notwithstanding."

Valentina shot a triumphant glance at Trish, who was staring purposefully toward the kitchen door, but Valentina didn't care. She winked right back at Vito and gave a conspiratorial giggle.

"Is it tart? Sweet? Acidic? Tannic? Suggestive? Robust? Limp? *What?!*"

"Tart!"

"Acidic!"

"Good! Now I'll tell you. This is no great shakes. It's a table wine from Argentina, which means it's a mix of grapes, and it cost me all of $4.99. I wanted to start you off with a cheapie and then work our way up. You gotta know the extremes, although nothing I got is anywhere near what your friend is gonna give you. But I got better than this plonk. Roseanne can use the rest of it for marinara."

Vito moved the first bottle aside and picked up the next. "Okay, here's number two. This time, when you get an idea what the wine smells or tastes like, look it up and find me a ten-dollar word!"

They tasted the second wine, which was a Merlot from Napa and darker in color—Valentina proposed maroon, Trish suggested crimson. Valentina thought it was loud, but maybe it was just the noise from the kitchen or Vito himself, although he seemed pleased by the description. Trish said it was robust. The third wine, a Super Tuscan, was even better than the Merlot, and by the time they got to it, Valentina and Trish were passing the thesaurus between them and trying to outdo each other with adjectives.

When they were finished, Valentina was a bit light-headed, but Roseanne came in with steaming plates of pasta primavera. They ate and talked, and Vito brought out a leather-covered binder, which he showed to Valentina.

"This is my vintage label collection. Take a look at these beauties."

He lovingly turned each plastic-covered page. Valentina pointed to one.

"Lafite! That's the kind Mr. Hampton bought."

"This is a 2006 Lafite. Cost a pal of mine $495. He was good enough to share it with me—and give me the label." Vito turned a page. "This one I didn't get to taste, but I bought the label off him, just to have it for my collection."

Valentina was surprised to recognize the bold red lettering and the little waving friar at the top from the bottle Farrell had shown her in his office.

"I've seen that one before, too!" she blurted out before she could stop herself.

"Really?" Vito eyed her curiously. "Where?"

"Um, in a catalog that Mr. Hampton has in the office. Only the year was different. It was 1960-something."

"Yeah, well, 1960-something would be worth about ten times this. This was an '81. Cost my friend about $800."

"Who's the guy on the top?" Valentina asked.

"It's Saint Peter, holding the keys to the estate. That's where the name Pétrus comes from."

"Your friend must be pretty wealthy if he can afford wines like that," Valentina observed.

"I always say, if you ain't gonna be rich yourself, make sure you have rich friends!"

Roseanne gave Vito a friendly swat on the head, and he took that opportunity to enfold her in a meaty embrace. Valentina shook her head in a wine-buzzed fog and decided there were some things in life she'd just never understand.

As they were getting their jackets to leave, Vito pulled Valentina aside and handed her his thesaurus.

"Don't tell Trish I gave it to you, she'll be jealous. But you need it more than she does right now. You're like Eliza going to the ball! We'll pass you off as Hungarian, or my name ain't Vito Scarparelli!"

Valentina smiled and nodded, although she had no earthly idea what he was talking about.

"Thanks," she said, taking the book.

"You'll come back again before the big night, okay? We've got a little more work to do on you." He gave her nose a friendly tweak and sang out, *"I coulda daaaaaaaaanced all night . . . and still have begged for MORE!"*

He let the screen door shut behind him as he waltzed back into the house.

Valentina joined Trish, who was waiting for her on the sidewalk.

"That Vito's a kick," Valentina said, somewhat drunkenly.

Trish took off at a clip toward Twentieth Avenue. Valentina hurried down the block after her.

"Trish? Trish! Wait up!"

Trish stopped and turned to her, a defiant expression on her face. "I know what you think about Vito."

"That's not what I meant! I really like him. He didn't make me feel stupid. He's funny and he's . . . well, he seems like a great guy."

Trish pulled a pack of cigarettes from her jacket pocket and lit up.

"Are you mad at me? I swear, I didn't mean anything," pressed Valentina.

Trish turned her head and blew smoke rings back toward Vito's house. "I'm a little jealous, you know," she admitted after a moment.

"Aw, come on!"

"No, I'm serious." Trish fixed her watery blue eyes on Valentina. "Nothing like this ever happens to me. I could never even get a guy to pick up the tab for me at the Red Lobster, let alone take me to fancy French places and give me designer wine. And I like wine more than you."

"Maybe you should go instead of me," Valentina suggested, falling into step beside Trish. "I'm not even sure I can go through with it."

"Yeah, Lou would love that," Trish said sullenly, taking another long drag on her cigarette.

Trish's husband, Lou, was a macho shithead, and a good caution to Valentina not to rush into marriage with Jerry or anyone else. Lou gave even Valentina's mother pause. Valentina supposed, looking sideways at her friend as they trotted along Twentieth Avenue in the warm September night, that the invitation from Sy must look pretty glamorous to Trish. Things hadn't exactly worked out the way she had hoped. Like many shitheads, Lou made a good first impression and only revealed his true colors later, after Trish was stuck. Valentina knew there wasn't much she could do to help her best friend, who believed in divorce about as much as she was willing to acknowledge homosexuality even when she was related to it.

Actually, that was one thing Valentina could do for Trish—resist the urge to press her any further about Vito. And the least she could do to repay Vito for his time and wine was to leave his cousin's illusions about him undisturbed. But Valentina couldn't help feeling she and Vito had an understanding of sorts, and as she walked silently alongside Trish toward her apartment, his happy parting song continued to echo in her head.

FIFTEEN

TRIPP WAS DREAMING that he was in the pit conducting *A Chorus Line* while all the waiters from Parapluie were dancing onstage. He had just cued Cassie to begin "The Music and the Mirror," only it was Shoshana, and she was galumphing around the stage in rain boots. Just as he was trying to decide whether to start the number over again, he woke suddenly to the "Liberty Bell March" blaring from his cell phone. He grabbed it off his nightstand.

"Hello," he mumbled.

"Ooh, sorry, did I wake you up?"

He glanced at his clock. It was eleven o'clock and that third scotch he'd had before bed was making it hard to recognize the phone number that appeared in the small screen.

"Who is this?"

"Michael Kleinfeld. We met at the audition yesterday."

Tripp sat up and tried to clear the fuzz from his brain. No wonder he hadn't recognized the number.

"Right, right. Sorry, I, uh, stayed up kind of late last night."

"I can call back another time."

"No, this is fine." Tripp massaged his forehead and forced his eyes to focus.

"I haven't heard anything yet," said Michael quickly.

"Me neither."

"You've been asleep."

"Right." Tripp squinted again at the screen on his cell phone. No message icon. "But I haven't."

"That isn't why I called, though. I was hoping maybe we could grab a cup of coffee today."

Through the cotton batting in his head, Tripp heard himself say, "Sure, great."

"What time is good?" asked Michael.

"Maybe around two? I have to be at work at four."

Tripp named a coffee shop not far from Parapluie, and as he hung up the phone, he tried to savor the experience of being pursued by a handsome, younger man. Jordan, his partner of eight years, had been ten years older, and age had never meant much to either of them, until Jordan was diagnosed with lung cancer. The hideous irony of it was that Jordan was a health nut who had never smoked a day in his life, but the cancer hit hard and fast, and he was gone in a shocking nine weeks. That had been four years ago, and Tripp still thought about Jordan every day. He had also developed an irrational fear of turning forty-five, the age Jordan was when he died. So there was something appealing about dating someone younger, for reasons other than the obvious.

Tripp spent what was left of the morning puttering around his apartment, trying not to obsess about the callbacks, although he did allow his thoughts to drift to Michael in his black spandex dance gear. At two o'clock, he pushed open the door to Java Life. It took him a moment to recognize Michael, but there he was, in a booth near the back. Michael spotted Tripp and waved.

"Hey!"

"Good to see you again," said Tripp, sliding in across from him.

Without the distraction of the audition, he was able to fully appreciate just how attractive Michael was. High cheekbones, short, medium brown hair combed away from a high, squarish forehead. His hazel eyes were overhung with thick eyebrows and sliced through with a slightly curved nose. Tripp was dying to ask how old he was, but he'd wait to see if it came up in conversation. If he made too much of it, and Michael was the eight to ten years younger that he guessed, it would only make Tripp seem old and paranoid. Both of which might have been true, but didn't need to be underlined.

They ordered their coffee and sat awkwardly for a brief moment, until they both said, at the same time, "Still haven't heard."

That broke the ice, and as they laughed it off, Tripp asked, "How long have you been in New York?"

"Four years. Before that, I was on the road with various tours.

And I did time on a cruise ship. How about you?"

"I grew up here. Never lived anywhere else, except for college. But I've been here working since right after."

They discussed various jobs, trading names of people they'd worked with, and Tripp remarked, as he often did, that there were only ten people in theater. It was, in its way, a very small world.

Eventually, the conversation turned to the personal front, and Tripp found himself talking about Jordan, in spite of his resolve not to.

"Wow, that's heavy," said Michael. "My dad died of lung cancer. Of course, he was a smoker, but it still sucks. How old was Jordan?"

"Forty-five."

"I'm thirty-six," Michael volunteered. "I'd hate to think I have less than ten years left."

"I thought you were younger," commented Tripp, oddly disappointed.

"And I thought you were, remember?" Michael raised his coffee cup. "Here's to us!"

"Who's like us?" said Tripp, picking up his cue.

"Damn few!" They finished together, completing the secret musical theater handshake of shared Sondheim lyrics.

"I'm finally ready for my close-up, you know?" Michael continued as their laughter receded. "Broadway has passed me by too many times, and I feel like this is it. In a way, I don't think I was prepared for it before now. My shrink says I never felt I deserved it."

"That's exactly how I feel," said Tripp.

For a moment the air between them hardened, then Tripp added, as dismissively as he could, "Yeah, but at the end of the day, it's just a job. A line on your résumé, and in three years it's like it never happened."

"You're an old hand at rationalization, aren't you?" Michael observed.

Tripp raised an eyebrow. "You know a better way to survive in this business?"

A grin split Michael's handsome features. "Yeah. By befriending the competition!"

Tripp couldn't help but smile. He found Michael's bluntness refreshing.

"So, can I see you again?" asked Michael. "We could go dancing."

"That would be great," Tripp said, nodding. "Can I call you? I've got to check my work schedule."

"You bet."

They stood up, hugged, and double cheek-kissed. "This was fun," said Tripp. "I'm really glad you called."

They walked out to the street together, where they waved each other off in opposite directions. Tripp headed uptown toward Parapluie with a newly springy step. Even if he didn't get the job, it might all turn out to be worth it, just to have met Michael. He knew better than to speculate about how he would feel if Michael got cast and he didn't. For now, he was content to enjoy the rush of adrenaline a new attraction brought with it and to relish the novelty of being pursued.

SIXTEEN

ANNETTE KNEW SHE WAS GETTING on Etienne's nerves. As the day crawled toward seven thirty, she kept darting into the kitchen to ask questions about the lentil terrine, taste the filet of venison with juniper berries and root vegetables, and fuss over the chocolate hazelnut mousse. When Tripp Macgregor arrived, she practically hugged him.

"Good, you're here!" she exclaimed, intercepting him as he emerged from the basement bathroom in his tidy uniform of black pleated pants, gold brocade vest, and bow tie. "We have special guests this evening. I want you to take them. They'll be in the nook."

The nook was a raised platform in the back left corner just to the side of the Caillebotte painting, with a large round booth that seated six. Even though there would be only the two of them, Antony Farrell and Sy Hampton, Annette was perfectly happy to give them her best table. It was an investment in the future, as was everything that happened tonight.

She had agreed to waive the customary corkage fee of twenty dollars a bottle for customers who brought their own wine, and although Antony had offered to pay for the meal, which she intended to make him do, she had planned a few extras. Etienne had prepared a *petite salade de foie gras et cèpes* for them to start with, and she would serve an aperitif, pear champagne sorbet as a palate cleanser, and a complimentary glass of Inniskillin Icewine with dessert—as long as they didn't order anything chocolate, which threw off the taste. Beyond that, she had to hope that Etienne was in a slightly less self-destructive mood than usual. Perfectionism was one thing, but as she knew from her own bitter experience, there came a point when it brought diminishing returns.

"Now." Annette returned to Tripp, who was patiently awaiting instructions. "They are coming in at seven thirty, the name is Farrell. It will only be two people, but they are important, which is why I'm giving them the nook." Tripp nodded, and she continued. "You'll have other tables, of course, but fewer than usual. I've brought Jonathan in as an extra hand tonight, to pick up the slack and to second you. Please use Manuel as your busboy. He's very reliable. I cannot *impress* upon you how potentially important this evening is to Parapluie's future."

"Got it," Tripp said solemnly.

"There's one more thing. Mr. Farrell will be bringing his own wine. One or two bottles, maybe more. As much as I am trying to impress him, he is also trying to impress his guest, so when you present the wine, please do it with as much precision, attention, showmanship, and expertise as you can muster. The way the wine is handled tonight is even more important than the meal. Do you understand?"

She looked into Tripp's handsome face, the tiny crinkles just starting to form around his round blue eyes, the smooth, fair, freckled skin, his coppery brown hair.

"First-class treatment, all the way," he said, holding steady under her gaze. He paused, and she felt sure he was going to ask what the fuss was all about, but instead he asked, "How did Shoshana do last night?"

Annette pursed her lips. "She's not you."

She left Tripp to his tables and joined Justine at the podium. The early reservations were arriving. To occupy her mind, Annette began to run numbers in her head, calculating what she could cut back on to hire a publicist. To the best of her knowledge, it would cost a minimum of three to five thousand a month, which she could ill afford, even if she stopped offering specials. The irony was that by the time she could budget for a publicist, she'd probably no longer need one. For the millionth time, she wondered how things might have been different had she been a man. There was a network, a skein of connections, a patchwork of whispered recommendations from which she would always be excluded, purely by virtue of her gender.

When she was about seven, she looked up the word "chef" in the dictionary and was puzzled to see it defined as "a cook, esp. a male head cook." This made no sense to her, since her mother and grandmother did all the cooking, as did her friends' mothers. She could only conclude, given the evidence of her personal experience, that the dictionary was wrong. She never trusted dictionaries after that. Until she'd started in professional kitchens and found that the dictionary knew exactly what it was talking about.

She stood with Justine and welcomed her customers as they arrived, seating them herself. She couldn't predict what time Farrell and Hampton would actually show up, and she wanted to look industrious when they did. She didn't want them to think they were getting special treatment, although the meal enhancements were, admittedly, a tip-off. She wanted to appear equally committed to all her guests, as, in fact, she was.

She was leading an older couple, tourists from Portugal, to their table, when she heard Antony's suave accents sail unmistakably over the gentle conversational hum. She hurriedly seated the Portuguese, gestured to Justine to present their wine list and menus, and dashed back to the podium, slowing down just in time to greet the two men with an air of what she hoped came across as poised largesse.

"Lovely to see you again, Mr. Farrell," said Annette, pointedly adhering to formality. "I'm delighted to have you back."

Antony's eyes flickered for a moment, but he said smoothly. "This is Sy Hampton. May I present Annette Lecocq, the proprietor of Parapluie."

"A pleasure to meet you," she said, shaking his hand. There wasn't much to distinguish him outwardly from any other middle-aged financier about town, although she did notice that his gaze was gentler and less aggressively probing than that of many men of his reputed acumen. He had nice features, though a smarter haircut wouldn't hurt.

"I didn't realize you two knew each other," Hampton said.

She glanced at Antony, who seemed to be trying to send her a telepathic message.

"The worlds of fine wine and haute cuisine frequently intersect,

Mr. Hampton," she replied breezily. "Come this way, gentlemen."

She led them through the restaurant and was pleased to see Hampton nodding appreciatively at the art on the walls.

"Here we are," she said, gesturing to the nook.

As the men slid into their seats, Tripp materialized silently at her elbow, the heavy leather-bound menus resting on his hip.

"This is Tripp. He will be your server this evening. I couldn't leave you in better hands. Please let me know if there's anything I can do personally to make your evening more enjoyable."

This was said without an iota of sexual suggestion, a tactic she had perfected long ago. With a pleasantly professional smile to Farrell and Hampton, she gave Tripp's arm an encouraging squeeze and forced herself to return to the front of the house.

She walked back through the restaurant, feeling a little like a queen on her way to an execution, nodding absently to the other diners as she passed. She chanced a backward look over her shoulders and saw Hampton smile in response to something Tripp was saying.

Thank heaven for Tripp, she thought. He'll take care of them.

SEVENTEEN

"GOOD EVENING, GENTLEMEN," said the young man called Tripp. "It is my pleasure to serve you tonight." He smiled at them both, then turned his attention to Farrell. "I understand you've brought a special wine this evening?"

"Yes, I have, thank you," answered Farrell. "It should aerate a half hour at least. We'll drink it with our entrée."

"Of course." Tripp inclined his head with a smile.

Farrell removed the promised 1970 Château Giscours from a leather wine carrier and handed it across the table to Sy, who examined the understated white label, with its coronet, and the oval embossing on the glass above.

"I'm looking forward to it," said Sy, returning the bottle to Farrell. "And whatever else you have in your bag."

Farrell winked mischievously and set the bottle on the table.

"I'll be right back with a carafe," Tripp said.

"Do you know wine?" Sy asked the waiter.

"In any other company, I might be inclined to say yes. In Mr. Farrell's company, and, I imagine, yours, I can only say I hope I might learn something this evening. In the meanwhile, Ms. Lecocq would like to offer you an aperitif. What can I bring you gentlemen?"

"Dry Sack, please," said Farrell.

"I'll have the same," said Sy.

Tripp gestured to another young man who was hovering nearby with two plates, each with a small, decorative salad, which he set in front of them.

"Please enjoy these while I prepare your wine. When I return with your sherry, I'll tell you about our specials this evening."

"Thank you." Farrell took a small amount of salad on his fork and sampled it. "Mmmmm, delicious."

The second waiter nodded deferentially and left them.

Sy was glad for a moment free from overly attentive staff. He was curious about something.

"I thought you said you'd heard of this place and were wanting to try it," he commented. "Seems like you've been here before."

"Yes, of course I have."

"But you said—"

"I said I knew of a superb place I wanted *you* to try. You must have misunderstood me." Farrell took another bite of salad. "You should taste this—it's divine!"

As Sy nibbled the excellent *foie gras et cèpes,* he tried to reconstruct their phone conversation. He distinctly remembered Farrell saying *he* wanted to try the place, something about the mix of modern décor and classic cuisine. He watched Farrell enjoying his foie gras and wondered, yet again, what he was up to.

"How long has this place been here?" he asked.

Farrell shrugged. "A few months, I think. I met Annette Lecocq at a party and thought I'd try it out."

Sy nodded politely. "It's just that I remember you saying—"

At that moment, Tripp arrived with a crystal carafe, which he set on the table.

"Gentlemen," he declared, somewhat grandly. They watched as he took the Giscours with a firm grasp and held it up for both of them to see. Then he deftly cut the capsule and pulled the cork. He decanted the wine into the carafe with great care and set the empty bottle back on the table.

"Let me tell you about our specials. We have game hens with a mustard maple glaze, accompanied by a black truffle risotto and roasted Brussels sprouts with shallots."

"Sounds rich," remarked Sy.

"It is, a bit," agreed Tripp. "I prefer the venison in juniper berry sauce with duchesse potatoes and grilled asparagus. The savory of the game balances the sauce, so it's not too sweet. We also have a turbot with celery remoulade, and an outstanding herbed rack of lamb. For appetizers, we are featuring *escargots de Bourgogne en croûte,* and cream of lobster soup."

He disappeared again and Sy asked Farrell, "What did you have last time?"

"Coq au vin from the regular menu. Simple, but delicious. Then a hazelnut mousse for dessert."

This misunderstanding was odd, thought Sy. Either he wasn't Machiavellian enough to imagine an ulterior motive for Farrell's duplicity, or it was simply an honest mistake. But he knew what he'd heard.

"Do you know that painting?" asked Farrell, pointing to the large canvas on the back wall above their heads. It depicted a couple in Victorian clothes walking down a cobblestone street in the rain.

Sy shook his head. "It seems familiar somehow, but I can't place it."

"It's called *Place de l'Europe,* by Gustave Caillebotte. Not particularly famous, but I've always rather liked it. I believe it hangs in the Art Institute of Chicago." Farrell returned to the menu. "What will you have?"

"I'm leaning toward the venison. You?"

Farrell nodded in agreement. "I was thinking the same. I believe game dishes are a specialty of the house."

Tripp reappeared to take their orders, bringing with him another complimentary hors d'oeuvre of baby artichokes fried in oil and herbs.

"We seem to be getting the royal treatment," Sy observed.

"I had the complementary foie gras salad last time, too," said Farrell nonchalantly. "But I believe the artichokes are a boon."

Their artichokes were followed by a palate cleanser of pear champagne sorbet, after which Tripp returned with wineglasses.

"It's been thirty minutes and your entrées are almost ready. Would you like me to decant your wine now?"

"Please," Farrell nodded.

Tripp poured a small amount of wine into a glass for Farrell, who held it up to the light, swirled it, and smelled it. Then he took a mouthful, closed his eyes, and gave it a long, deep taste. When he opened them again, he looked immensely proud of himself.

"That—is sublime," he pronounced. "Rich blackberry and cassis, with a tantalizing hint of tobacco." He signaled to Tripp, who filled both glasses. Farrell raised his.

"To Bacchus!"

The wine was a deep ruby, almost purple, and when Sy stuck his nose into the glass, a burst of black and red berries assailed him, fringed with the promised tobacco. He took a sip and let the wine cascade over his tongue and down his throat.

Farrell was right—it was sublime. Rich and intensely full-bodied.

"It's bodacious, orotund. Don't you think?" Farrell said. "With just a whiff of, dare I say it, manure."

"Manure?" Sy laughed.

"Just an overtone, but yes," said Farrell, quite seriously. He cocked his head at Sy and said, "You don't get that?"

Sy didn't want to appear to have a palate unworthy of the Giscours, let alone his precious Lafite, so he took in the bouquet again.

"It's earthy, I'll give you that," he said in compromise, "but I can't honestly say I get anything beyond that, no."

Farrell shrugged, and they lit into the tender, succulent venison. It was indeed an excellent complement to the wine, and once Sy was able to put Farrell's manure comment out of his head, he enjoyed his meal tremendously.

"Ms. Lecocq would like to offer you some Canadian ice wine. Might I suggest a plate of assorted cheeses as an accompaniment?" asked Tripp when they'd finished.

Sy glanced up from his dessert menu and met Farrell's eye. They both nodded.

Tripp collected their menus and returned to the kitchen. Farrell drained the last of his Giscours, set his glass down, and looked squarely at Sy.

"I suppose you're wondering why I've called you here," he quipped.

At last, the truth.

"I take it it wasn't just to taste the Giscours?"

"It wasn't." Farrell leaned forward with a conspiratorial smile. "Although you have to admit, that alone would have been worth it." Farrell reached into his wine carrier and produced a second bottle, which he set on the table.

Sy read the label. It was a Haut-Brion, 1961. Potentially a wow.

"Here's the thing," continued Farrell. "It's had a bit of rough treatment, and I fear it may be slightly oxidized. As you know, this was one of the great vintages."

"Yes," Sy nodded. "This and the '45. So they say. I've yet to come across one of those."

"But you've tasted a '61 before?"

Sy shook his head, and Farrell brightened.

"Good! Then let's try it out. Perhaps we'll agree on its level, perhaps not. In any case, I thought it would be more interesting to open it in the company of a fellow oenophile."

Sy was intrigued. Superb as the Giscours had been, a 1961 Haut-Brion appealed more to his sense of adventure. He was also relieved to learn, finally, that this had been Farrell's secret agenda, and not the Lafite. While they waited for Tripp to return with the cheeses, Sy finished off his own Giscours and focused once more on his surroundings.

The restaurant appeared to be busy, but it didn't have that bustling feeling of some New York eateries, where the goal was to turn over as many tables as possible. Then again, maybe that wasn't so much by design, but was rather a function of the fact that Parapluie hadn't yet caught on. Still, it was intimate without being cramped, with plenty of room between tables for waiters and customers. In fact, Sy realized, Annette Lecocq could have put in more seating and clearly had chosen not to. He liked the raised slashes of gold down the walls, which were obviously meant to suggest rain. If rain were that shiny and attractive, perhaps nobody would mind it.

The food was first-class, and they certainly knew how to handle wine, at least this waiter did. Perhaps he should reenact this entire evening, with Valentina and the Lafite replacing Farrell and his Haut-Brion. Sy liked the fact that despite the restaurant's quality, it was still apparently flying under the radar.

"You look miles away," said Farrell, interrupting his thoughts.

"No, I was right here, actually," chuckled Sy, enjoying his private joke.

Tripp returned with a plate of Canadian blue, Taleggio, and a vodka currant cheese and decanted the Haut-Brion.

"Shall I leave it for you?"

Farrell shook his head. "Best not to give it too much air. We don't want to risk losing it."

Tripp poured the wine, which was browner than the expected garnet. Farrell frowned and inhaled the bouquet, while Sy looked on. He wasn't surprised by Farrell's reaction after tasting it.

"Well, that *is* disappointing," he said. "Pungent, yes, but flaccid. Too reticent."

"May I?"

Tripp obliged by pouring a bit into a fresh glass for Sy.

It was, sadly, a shadow of its former, lustrous self. From what Sy knew of this vintage, it should have been exuberant and memorable—truly a wine deserving of a special meal, more so even than the Giscours. It should have been robust, with overtones of red and black fruit, cedar and chocolate. Those flavors had receded, over-weighting the cigar box aroma and spoiling the finish.

"You just never know, do you?" Farrell said, shaking his head. "You'd think two grand would guarantee you something drinkable. But I suppose it's my comeuppance. I've presided over enough auctions where people have dropped a bundle on expired wines. It's a crapshoot, isn't it?"

"There are some people who like that aged, old wine taste," Sy reminded him, and, for the hell of it, took another sip. "It might rally given a bit more time in the glass. Perhaps we're rushing it."

"You may be right. Let's enjoy our cheeses and revisit it, then, shall we?"

Wine was subjective, that much was true, Sy reflected. Most

things in life were. As somebody once said, one man's trash is another man's treasure. It didn't go quite that far with wine—vinegar was vinegar, after all—but to a certain degree, it was subject to opinion. There was also the bottle's history to take into account, plus the life of the winemaker, and the journey from vine to table, whether it took ten years or one hundred. There was more to wine than wine. And in the case of the Jefferson Lafite, there was the added significance of the wine's future, as well as its past. There was what the wine might bring him.

Sy took another sip of the tawny liquid. Already the Haut-Brion was improving. The smoky flavor was more in balance, with the fruit emerging to the foreground.

A feeling of well-being, validated by his instinct about the Haut-Brion, suffused him. Parapluie would be the perfect spot for an intimate tasting of both personal and historical significance. It was here that he would bring Valentina. Forget Patroon, or even the Terrace Room at the Four Seasons. Parapluie was the perfect choice, right down to the red décor, which would certainly please Valentina.

It was here that his practically lifelong investment in fine wine would both culminate and usher in a new era of romantic happiness. As he looked across the table at the fair head of his distinguished companion, he realized that he had another reason for which to be grateful to the auctioneer. In addition to sounding the hammer before old Mrs. Bagnold could get her gnarled, manicured fingers on his Lafite, Farrell had led him to the best spot for drinking it. It seemed Sy had utterly misjudged him.

EIGHTEEN

SCARLET, RUBY, BURGUNDY, CHERRY . . .

No, not burgundy, thought Valentina. That means something else. A place, somewhere in France.

Audacious, gallant, persistent, capacious . . .

Why couldn't she just say bold, brave, stubborn, and big?

"Improving your vocabulary?"

Valentina jumped and set Vito's thesaurus on the desk face down. Miss Banks picked it up and leafed through its well-worn pages.

"You could stand to learn a few words with more than four letters," she remarked snidely.

Before Valentina could think of a response, Sy's door opened and he gestured toward them.

"Could I see you a moment?"

Miss Banks started toward his office, but Valentina knew immediately from his startled expression that he meant her. Sy gave a nervous laugh.

"Sorry, I meant Valentina."

Miss Banks stiffened as Valentina walked past her without giving her a second look. It was a delicious moment. Far better than any retort she could have come up with herself.

"Have a seat."

Sy closed the door. He sat down on the small sofa and gestured for her to sit beside him. She did, but was still surprised when he reached for her hand. She instinctively pulled away, then, realizing her rudeness, extended it again. But his hand had retreated to his lap, and he was smiling awkwardly at her.

"We haven't really spoken about our . . . about drinking the wine. Not since you agreed to join me."

"I haven't changed my mind," said Valentina.

He smiled and seemed to relax. "I'm glad to hear it."

"I've been trying to learn about wine. My friend Trish, she's got this cousin Vito, he's into wine, too, and we went over there and tried some. One of them tasted like turpentine, but the others were okay and he showed us how to do it. So I know a little bit more about it now, because I didn't really before, although I still don't know anywhere near as much as you."

Valentina felt her face flush, but Sy's blue eyes glittered with happiness.

"That's—that's great of you! The reason I wanted to talk to you is that the shipment has arrived from Shoreham's, so let's set a date."

Valentina thought of the thesaurus on her desk and panicked. She had barely memorized the more obscure shades of red, let alone adjectives that could be used to describe flavor.

"Are you free Saturday night?" he asked.

She needed more time, but maybe it would be better to get it over with.

"I think so."

Sy seemed to deflate with relief, as if he'd been holding his breath. "I've found a perfect little restaurant. The food and service are outstanding, and best of all, nobody knows about it yet, so it will be private."

She nodded. Private was good. There would be fewer people to overhear any stupid comments she might make about the wine.

"It's called Parapluie," Sy said.

"Para-what?"

"It means umbrella in French," he explained.

"What does an umbrella have to do with food unless some waiter is dropping soup on your head?" she asked before she could stop herself.

Sy laughed. "Got me! But it's a nice place. You'll like it."

Saturday was so soon! She had to get back to Vito's again right away. There was still so much to learn, and she didn't want to be a disappointment to Sy. Or to herself. She wanted to be a worthy date for the real thing, even if she wasn't the real thing herself.

Sy rose from the sofa, scribbled something on a Post-it, and handed it to her. "Here's the name of the restaurant and the woman who runs it. You'll have to look up the number. Seven thirty on the twenty-fifth, and say that I will give her a call to discuss some special arrangements for the wine."

She glanced down at the unfamiliar-looking names and wondered how to pronounce them. Her first test, she thought, as she left his office to make the call. At the same time, she realized, with a twinge of resentment, that things hadn't changed as much as she thought. She was still his secretary.

NINETEEN

"WHAT'S TAKING HIM SO LONG?" Annette asked Farrell over the phone, trying unsuccessfully to keep the edge out of her voice.

Farrell gave an exasperated sigh. "It's only been three days!"

"Four. You were here on Thursday night, and now it's Monday."

"I know perfectly well how long it's been, as you've called every day to remind me. Now I really must insist that you stop pestering me. I'm not going to call him! Good Lord, I've created a monster."

Annette was silent for a moment.

"He's not coming back," she said glumly.

"He hasn't reserved yet," Farrell pointed out.

"It's the same thing," she snapped.

"Annette, he loved the meal. And the ambience. Everything he said that night leads me to believe that he will choose Parapluie, but he may or may not arrive at that conclusion—or even intend to drink his wine—immediately. And as I've told you before, I cannot be the one to suggest it. You blew my cover when you blabbed that I'd been there before. If you hadn't done that, I might have been able to propose the idea. But my hands are tied, because of your indiscretion!"

"I don't know why you lied in the first place," she said peevishly. "It was entirely unnecessary."

"I want to taste that wine," Farrell intoned in a low, steady voice. "He knows I want to taste it. We're not mates—I don't generally call him up and invite him out to dinner. If, on top of that, he knew I was bringing him to a restaurant owned by an ex-lover, he might think I was up to something."

"I don't see why," said Annette.

"Don't you? I wanted him to think the idea of opening the wine at Parapluie was his idea. I had planned to gauge the conversation and see if I might subtly lead him there, but once he knew you and I had a connection, I couldn't possibly."

"Well, you might have let me in on your strategy in advance," she growled irritably. "I don't believe he's going to come back."

The second line rang. Annette glanced at the clock on her wall. It was only ten. Justine wasn't in yet, and she was in no mood to speak to anyone, even to take a reservation.

Well, that's just foolish, she thought. You can't afford to let one slip away.

"Just a moment," she said, placing Antony on hold.

"Parapluie, this is Annette. May I help you?" said Annette.

There was silence, and then a raucous New York voice said, "Um, is this Para-plooey?"

Annette massaged her forehead wearily. One of those. "Yes, it is. What can I do for you?"

"Can I make a reservation for Saturday night?"

Annette pulled up the reservations screen on her computer. "Is that this Saturday, the twenty-fifth?"

"Yeah."

"For how many?"

"Two."

"What time?"

"Seven thirty."

"Name?"

"Sy Hampton. That's H-a-m-p—"

Annette sat up straight as if someone had just poured a bucket of cold water over her and wrenched her from a sound sleep.

"Sy Hampton? Yes, of course, absolutely. May I . . . may I take a number for confirmation?"

"You can call me."

"Thank you, but may I get Mr. Hampton's direct line?"

"That's it. I'm his secretary. I mean, I'm his assistant's secretary. But I answer his phone most of the time. Oh, yeah, he told me to tell you—is this Miz LeCock?"

Annette cringed. "Lecocq," she repeated, stressing the long *o* sound, though she knew it was futile. "Yes, it is."

"He said he'll call you, because he needs to make a special arrangement."

Annette's heart quickened. "A special arrangement? How intriguing," she said, trying to sound casual. "Do you know what it's regarding?"

"He's bringing his own wine. It's a very old bottle that was owned by Thomas Jefferson. It's a Lafite," the secretary said with obvious pride.

Annette stood up and danced the tiniest jig. If she could have, she would have screamed with joy.

"Wonderful!" She hoped she sounded simply pleased, rather than ecstatic. "Please let him know I'm delighted he'll be returning to Parapluie, and he may call me at any time to discuss the arrangements for his wine. Tell me your name?"

"Valentina."

Annette made a note on her pad next to the phone number. "Thank you so much, Valentina. Tell Mr. Hampton we'll see him on Saturday the twenty-fifth at seven thirty."

She hung up the phone, clenched her fists, and let out a squeal. Then she remembered Antony. She doubted he was still holding, but the light was flashing, so she pressed the button.

"Antony? Are you there?"

There was a muffled clatter as he took the phone off speaker. "It's not very considerate keeping me on hold—"

"It was Sy Hampton! Not him, his secretary. But he made the reservation! He's coming this Saturday! I'm sorry I was such a beast. *Je t'embrasse mille fois!*"

"Well, well, well." Farrell was unable to disguise his satisfaction. "What time?"

"Seven thirty."

"Perfect. And how many people will be joining him?"

"Just one."

"Just one," Farrell repeated thoughtfully. "That's what he thinks." Farrell cleared his throat. "Well, my dear, we have a lot to discuss. We have plans to make."

Annette was struck anew with a pang of conscience at the strident purpose in Farrell's voice.

"I'm still not sure this is right. It's dishonest. Isn't there another way? We could let him dine in private with his date and hope the experience is so good he'll tell everyone he knows. He must have friends in the press. Maybe he would make some calls on my behalf after the fact!"

"Annette," said Farrell coolly, "how much longer can you afford to stay open at your current rate?"

She bit her lip. She had another month, maybe two, if she was lucky, but she refused to admit to Farrell just how desperate she was.

"I understand your hesitation, but believe me, opportunities like this do not fall in one's lap readily," he continued without waiting for her response. "The thing is done, reserved. It will be quite a show, and every show needs an audience."

"But—"

"*Chère* Annette. You worry about Etienne and the menu, and get that classy waiter back. Just leave everything else to me."

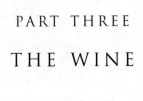

PART THREE

THE WINE

TWENTY

TRIPP COULDN'T REMEMBER A BETTER WEEKEND. He'd met Michael for dinner at a cozy little place on Forty-third and Ninth, where his friend Margaret tended bar. She always gave Tripp a little bite off his bar tab, so he was able to order a really nice bottle of Barbera to complement their pasta and veal. Michael had been impressed both by Tripp's knowledge of wine and the amount he was willing to spend (Tripp hadn't bothered to disclose his discount). They had continued the name game and discovered they'd both had similarly disastrous but mercifully brief relationships with a certain narcissistic choreographer.

After dinner, they'd gone to Xanadu, then to Homo Erectus (Tripp didn't particularly care for the ambience, though he gave the place points for its name), finishing up at Michael's place for a sweaty night between his purple and black Egyptian cotton sheets. The whole experience had been delectable from start to finish, and he was surprised that dating a man close to his own age with a similar professional trajectory was so comfortable. In his twenties, Tripp would have found such a person to be a mirror of himself, and therefore a threat. He'd have seen the other person's accomplishments as his failings. Now, pushing forty and having lived through Jordan's illness and death, he was more inclined to relish the common experience, rather than fear the competition.

As he stretched out in his own bed Monday morning, he found himself reliving the highlights of Saturday's hedonism. It almost made him forget about *A Chorus Line*. Almost—but not quite.

They still hadn't heard anything. Which could mean something, or nothing. Tripp had been offered jobs on the spot, a day later on his voice mail, and as much as a month later, though in those cases it was usually because someone had dropped out. One of the things he'd found hardest to get used to about show business, even after all these years, was the fact that there was no road map, no career plan, no timeline. There was no "first you take this job, which leads to this position, which then lands you on Broadway." What rules existed were broken more often than they were obeyed, and little about career advancement could be gleaned from other people's experiences, let alone one's own.

As Tripp showered, he determined to do what he always did when he was waiting to hear about a job. He'd immediately set something else in motion. He didn't yet know for sure that he hadn't landed *Chorus Line,* but it was safer emotionally to proceed as if that were the case. Then if he did get good news, it would be a wonderful surprise. If he didn't, well, as his friend Margaret liked to say, "You get twenty-four hours to be depressed when you don't get a job. Forty-eight if it's Broadway."

He dried himself off, dressed, and went online to scout out casting notices. There was a production of *La Cage aux Folles* at a regional theater in Philadelphia where he'd worked once before, and a New Jersey *Music Man* with the narcissistic choreographer. He figured he'd take a pass on that one—he liked the show, but it wasn't worth it—but he decided to head over to the Equity building to sign up for the *La Cage* call. He contemplated contacting the agent he was freelancing with to see if she could get him an appointment, but he still hoped to call her with the news that he'd gotten *A Chorus Line.* For all the protective armor he was amassing, he still wasn't quite ready to declare it dead in the water. Calling her with anything less than that career-bolstering news would feel like an admission of defeat.

He walked east toward the Equity building on West Forty-sixth Street and turned his thoughts from last weekend to this Saturday night. He and Michael were planning a repeat performance, only there were two new clubs they wanted to try. Tripp was seriously considering inviting Michael back to his place afterward. He hadn't had a man over since Jordan's death. It might be time to make that leap. Perhaps Michael would be the one.

Tripp breathed in the cool morning air and smiled. He found he liked the idea of inviting Michael to spend the night. He paused on the corner of Forty-eighth and Eighth, stepped out of the stream of foot traffic, and closed his eyes. He imagined Michael sitting in the big wicker chair in his living room, which he had kept from his grandparents' long-sold summer house and re-covered in a sweet yellow chintz. Jordan had loved that chair, but when he'd gotten sick, he'd stopped sitting in it. He didn't want to take the chance of getting it dirty from spilled medicine or, as he euphemistically put it, "intestinal malfunctions." But when Jordan had stopped sitting in it, Tripp had stopped, too, until after Jordan's death. It hadn't seemed fair that he should enjoy the chair when Jordan couldn't.

Tripp opened his eyes and walked on toward the Equity building, picturing Michael in his bedroom, his kitchen, his bathroom. It worked. He could see it. He was willing to see it. Like his first Broadway show, the time had come. But unlike with his career, Tripp could schedule the milestone of inviting a new lover to spend the night in his and Jordan's bed.

He pulled his cell phone from his pocket and flipped it open to call Michael, but was surprised to hear a female voice coming out of the tiny speaker. Confused, he put the phone to his ear.

"Hello?"

"Tripp? Is that you?"

"Yes, who is this?"

"It's Annette Lecocq. That's funny, the phone didn't ring."

"I was just making a call," he hinted, hoping she'd excuse herself and hang up. She didn't.

"I wanted to thank you again for the excellent service you gave last Thursday to Mr. Farrell and Mr. Hampton."

"Just doing my job," he said agreeably, although the compliment pleased him.

"In fact, Mr. Hampton was so impressed that he's chosen Parapluie as the place to uncork a bottle of wine he purchased at auction for $510,000."

"For $510, did you say?" shouted Tripp as a truck rumbled by.

"Five hundred and ten thousand dollars," she repeated loudly.

Tripp stopped abruptly, causing a delivery boy behind him to bump into him and start cursing him out in Spanish.

"That's crazy! What kind of bottle is worth that kind of money?"

"I don't claim to understand it myself," said Annette. "But this is a Lafite that dates from the French Revolution and was once owned by Thomas Jefferson. On top of that, there's good reason to believe it's still drinkable."

"Amazing," was all Tripp could think of to say.

Amazing didn't even begin to sum it up, he thought. Absurd was a better place to start.

"Mr. Hampton is coming back on Saturday night, and I want you to serve him again. I believe you're a large part of the reason he's chosen Parapluie."

Tripp swallowed. "This Saturday? The twenty-fifth?"

"Yes."

"I'm not scheduled to be in on Saturday," he said slowly, as his vision of Michael sipping a mint julep in Jordan's yellow chintz wicker chair evaporated.

Annette's voice modulated from ingratiating to steely. "You promised you'd fill in for an important event if I ever needed you. In return for letting you off for that audition, remember? Well, I need you. There's no one else on the waitstaff I'd even remotely consider letting handle a half-million-dollar bottle of wine."

What could he say? He had promised. Although a fat lot of good that audition had done him. He'd rather have had the date with Michael.

But he might never have met Michael in the first place if he hadn't gone back for that late-afternoon callback. He had no good excuse to refuse Annette. A date was hardly enough. Besides, he had to agree with her—there wasn't another waitperson on staff who was up to it. He wasn't entirely sure he was.

"What makes you think this guy is going to let me anywhere near his wine? Won't he want to decant it himself? I wouldn't trust anyone with a bottle that valuable!"

"I still want you there. It needs to be a perfect evening in every way. We need to put our best foot forward, and it's likely you'll have to handle the bottle in some way. A lot is riding on this. Can I count on you?"

There was only one possible response, unless he wanted to start looking for a new job immediately.

"I'll be there," promised Tripp.

He sighed and flipped his phone shut. There was no need to make that call to Michael so quickly. Saturday was the only night Michael had off from his own restaurant job, so it looked like Tripp would have to shelve his fantasy of a bedroom romp in three acts, at least for the immediate future.

He continued on toward Forty-sixth and Broadway, but his enthusiasm for the *La Cage* call had dwindled. Rather than welcoming the opportunity to go after another job, he found himself resenting the fact that he'd been unable to successfully jump off the treadmill.

Someone had once told him that a performer's real job was to audition. But these days, he felt like his real job was waiting tables, and theater was nothing more than an expensive hobby. It was tempting to think he was indentured to Annette Lecocq, but the truth was, he was indentured to his own ego.

He tried to look on the bright side. It would be something to see a bottle of wine dating from the French Revolution. If only he could taste it as well. But he knew that would never happen. As far as the likes of Annette Lecocq and Sy Hampton were concerned, he was a waiter and that's all he would ever be. And in his current mood, he couldn't help feeling they were right.

TWENTY-ONE

EVERYTHING WAS PROCEEDING according to plan, reflected Sy. The wine was bought, paid for, and safely locked in his dining room; Valentina had committed to an actual date mere days away; a reservation had been made at an excellent but discreet restaurant.

And yet . . .

At the end of the day, he was going on a date. If he had imagined that showing up with the world's most expensive bottle of wine would keep him from feeling like a pimply teenager with unruly hair and big feet, he was mistaken. The details were settled, but there was still the girl part to contend with. He'd never been much good at sitting across the table from a woman and making casual conversation, when all he really wanted to do was get her in bed.

And what then? Suppose he successfully navigated the minefield of small talk. Was he such a Casanova in the bedroom? Both Marianne and Pippa had grown bored with him. It was, he was forced to admit, another reason for his failed marriages, particularly to Pippa, whose imagination didn't stop at her canvases. Serena Hart had seen him as a challenge, and he took some comfort in knowing he'd improved under her tutelage. But he feared he was as uninspired and uninspiring a lover as he was at everything emotional or artistic. The only talent he had was for managing money. While he knew there were many people who would happily trade a little sexual spark for financial acumen and the security it brought, he had to face the fact that all the billion-dollar deals and half-million-dollar bottles of wine in the world wouldn't make him any more comfortable naked.

Sy looked around his Moroccan red study, at the books on his shelves, most of which he'd never had time to read, the artwork on the walls, much of it supplied and left behind by Pippa, and asked himself the question he'd been avoiding since Antony Farrell had first put the thought in his head.

What if the wine didn't bring him the happiness he sought?

He picked up his vodka tonic and paced the Oriental rug, purchased at auction at, where else? Shoreham's. He was seized with the crazy thought that he'd purchased his entire life at auction. He'd tried to buy happiness, but he'd only bought possessions, which he knew, realistically, were the only things one could buy. Even if owning this wine and a piece of history miraculously made him irresistible to Valentina, how long would the glow last before he became himself again, Sy Hampton from Poughkeepsie, self-made multimillionaire and perennial bore?

He paused in his perambulations to pick up a photo of Eric in a silver frame. Eric was about five, astride a pony at a petting zoo in Queens. He sure as hell wasn't fooling his son. Eric wasn't impressed by possessions and wealth, but Sy didn't know what else to give him. Love, obviously, but Eric seemed to shrug that off as well.

When I was a child, I thought as a child. But when I became a man, I put away childish things.

Except that he hadn't put away childish things or childish thoughts, despite the counsel of First Corinthians. He still yearned for the flashiest toys, thinking they would make people admire him. His own child recognized that quality in his father, and it disgusted him. Eric wanted a father who was a man, someone to look up to. Not a playmate.

Sy decided to turn in early. He left his study, but instead of padding across the hall to his bedroom, his feet led him downstairs, where he could hear Claudine rattling around in the kitchen, putting away pots and pans. He entered the dining room, and with the spillage from the Tiffany chandelier in the hall casting a kaleidoscopic glow on the blue and peach walls, he unlocked the breakfront and removed the Lafite from its resting place.

What if he drank it, alone, right then and there?

Before he knew what he was doing, Sy had the bottle upright on the dining room table, his best corkscrew in hand.

Well, why the hell not?

Even with the help of her wine-loving pal, whatever his name was, Valentina wasn't going to appreciate the wine. He knew that.

He had known it from the start. In the end, he had bought the wine for himself, and he should drink it himself. Who deserved to commune with the grapes of history more than he did?

But it was so unceremonious to drink it alone. If a wine cork pops in a dining room and there's no guest to hear it, does it count? Without a witness, would it register in the world, or would he wake the next morning, with a histamine headache no doubt, and wonder if the whole thing was nothing but a half-million-dollar dream?

He'd invite someone over, that's what he'd do. He looked at his watch. It was only nine thirty. He could call Peter Blomgard, or hell, he could even call Antony Farrell. What was he doing wasting the wine on Valentina? Was it worth sacrificing something this valuable in a misguided attempt to make himself more attractive? He had a vision of calling old Mrs. Bagnold and inviting her over to share the wine. Even that would make more sense than drinking it alone or using it to try to impress a girl who, he suspected, probably didn't return his interest.

Or would it? Maybe, at the end of the day, the only way this wine was ever going to satisfy him was for it to be his alone. His prize, his treat, his toy. It was a bottle of wine, nothing more. Not a status symbol, not an aphrodisiac, not a mark of how far he'd come or an indication of where he was going, but a beverage to be hoarded and savored in solitude as a fitting reward for a lifetime of devotion to the cult of fine wine.

He flipped open his corkscrew and unfolded the knife. Grasping the bottle firmly around the neck, he made a cut in the capsule. A shiver went down his spine, and he set both bottle and corkscrew back on the table. For no reason that he could think of, his grandmother's voice rang inside his head, as loud and as present as if she were standing beside him.

"You could buy a house with that! You could sell it and donate the money to the poor! But what are you going to do . . . drink it?! That's pouring money away, let me tell you!"

Suddenly, Sy began to laugh. It was madness! They must all be jeering at him, not just his dead grandmother editorializing inside his head. What was he thinking, paying that kind of money for a bottle of fermented grape juice that, legend or no legend, would probably be more useful taking the smell out of old sneakers?

He sat down heavily on one of Marianne's shield-back chairs. He was ridiculous. His wine was ridiculous. Even his fellow oenophiles were probably laughing at him. It was all a joke. In the annals of impotent, self-aggrandizing gestures, paying half a million dollars for a bottle of wine and inviting your secretary out to dinner to drink it had to rank pretty close to the top.

That settled it. If he drank the wine, nobody could mock him anymore. Valentina would probably be relieved.

He would be relieved.

He grabbed the corkscrew and sliced off the leaden capsule below the lip of the bottle, revealing a thick layer of greenish mold across the opening. He knew the cork underneath would be fragile, but with any luck it would have good color. The mold told him that the bottle had been stored in properly humid conditions. It also provided the cork with added protection. Sy gently excised the mold, tipping it onto the table. The top of the cork was dark brown and didn't seem to have any red seeped into it. Another good sign. He took a cloth napkin from a drawer in the breakfront and wiped off the bottle neck. Now he needed a glass. He retrieved a crystal Riedel Vinum Bordeaux from the sideboard. Then he picked up the corkscrew and tipped the point gingerly into the cork.

"Mr. Hampton?"

For a split second, he almost lost his grip on the bottle. He set the wine and the corkscrew down and saw that his hands were shaking furiously.

"Jesus Christ, Claudine! You almost made me drop it!"

His whole body was trembling now and, to his surprise, he felt his eyes fill with tears.

"My goodness! I'm sorry! I just wanted to tell you I was leaving," said Claudine.

They stared at each other across the dining room, and Claudine's gaze moved to the bottle. Sy blinked back the moisture in his eyes, and as his body began to relax, a feeling of guilt stole over him. He couldn't have been more embarrassed if his mother had caught him with *Playboy* under the covers.

"Isn't that the Lafite?" said Claudine.

"It is. I . . . er . . . decided to drink it myself."

"Oh." She frowned. "Seems a pity to waste it. Seems like you should have a party for it or something."

It's not a waste, his brain screamed. Why is it a waste for just me to drink it? I paid for it, who are you to say it's wasted on me? Am I that insignificant?

"Yes. Well, thanks, Claudine. I'll think about it."

"Good night, Mr. Hampton."

He heard her slide the bolts and let herself out the front door, leaving him alone in his glorious, empty, Marianne-decorated and Pippa-accessorized town house.

He looked at the denuded cork on his Lafite and felt as if he'd just been pulled back from a precipice by the hand of God.

What on earth had come over him?

Sy's hands were still quivering as he wrapped a wine capsule preserver around the cork. He carefully replaced his prized possession in the breakfront, where he secured it safely once more under lock and key. Then he headed back upstairs to his study to pour himself a good, stiff drink.

TWENTY-TWO

"Thank you, Shoshana," Annette said to the relentlessly energetic waitress who was setting down steaming crocks of cassoulet before her and Antony. Shoshana lingered over their table, fussing over their water levels (fine), the cleanliness of the silverware (God forbid), and her arrangement of the peonies in the vase (likely to have their stems broken by overhandling). Didn't the silly girl know that the best way to impress the boss was to be discreet and efficient? But, of course, that wasn't Shoshana's style. That was why Annette had determined to keep her far away from Parapluie on Saturday night. Twittering, hovering staff was out of the question.

"That's all for now, thank you," Annette dismissed her firmly, and the girl gave a last deferential bow before retreating to the kitchen.

"What an odd little creature," remarked Antony.

"Unfortunately, actors make the best waiters," said Annette, scooping up a savory spoonful of duck and smoked sausage.

"Why unfortunately?" asked Antony. "They have charisma and flexible schedules, don't they?"

"Yes, but they're always so 'on.' Like that one." She indicated the closing kitchen door with her fork. "I always expect her to sing the specials."

Antony shrugged. "Could be your publicity hook, singing waiters," he said, munching. "Cassoulet is divine."

"Thank you."

"I quite liked the young man who waited on us the other night. He had some style. I suppose he's an actor, too?"

"Dancer. But he comes from a wealthy Upper East Side family. Breeding trumps career. In his case, at least."

"And you've secured him for Saturday?"

"Oh yes, I've seen to that. *She* won't be anywhere near." Annette indicated Shoshana, who had reappeared and was listing the desserts at top volume for a table of attentive Japanese businessmen.

"Lunch business isn't too bad," observed Antony, following her gaze.

"No thanks to Shoshana," sniped Annette.

Antony gave an attractive, and therefore annoying, smile. "I wouldn't be so sure about that. You, as a woman, don't respond to that sort of thing. A man, on the other hand, would find all that attention rather flattering."

"Yes, well, let's get back to the matter at hand, shall we?" said Annette.

"Right. " Antony took a deep gulp of his Painted Rock Merlot and pushed a small notepad toward her.

"Here's who we want. Rand at the *Times*—he covers both food and wine. Churchill from *Wine Spectator*, DiFranco from *Wine and Dine*, Myerson from *Food & Wine*, and of course, St. Alban from *Bon Appétit*. Let's also try for someone from *Forbes* and *Robb Report*, good targets for the high net worth set. Definitely someone from restaurantgirl.com—Danyelle herself if we can get her—and other key bloggers. My feeling is that we need to crowd the place with actual customers, so it looks like a thriving enterprise."

Annette bristled. "Saturday looks quite good already."

"Define good."

She bit her lip, determined not to be put on the defensive. "About what I had last Thursday."

Antony shook his head. "Not good enough. You'll have to get more people in."

"If I knew how to do that—"

"Can you extend some kind of half-price offer to friends of the staff? Theaters do that all the time, it's called papering the house."

"Yes, thank you for that little tidbit," she said tightly. "I'm aware of the term and the concept. It goes against the grain, but I will do it if you think it's that important."

"I do. I'll call the wine writers, and you e-mail the bloggers." He wagged a finger at her. "Don't discount them, they are quite important."

"I'm not a Luddite, Antony."

"In fact, you should consider having *her* in for their benefit," he said, indicating Shoshana, who was hovering expectantly nearby.

"Absolutely not!"

"Take my word for it. She helps you look hip. Now, what shall we say to them all." He cautiously lapped the silver end of his Tiffany pen with his tongue. Annette stirred the remains of her cassoulet disconsolately.

"We'll say that the bottle of Château Lafite 1787 recently purchased at Shoreham's for a record $510,000 is being uncorked at Parapluie on Saturday the twenty-fifth at seven thirty. Now, here's the sticking point, or points." He looked seriously at Annette. "We cannot, in good conscience, promise them any chance of tasting the wine, as that is not ours to promise."

"Obviously."

"The best we can do is indicate to them that the event is taking place. If we're lucky, perhaps Hampton can be persuaded to say a few words about the wine after he tastes it."

Annette squirmed in her chair and looked anxiously at the Caillebotte painting on the back wall.

"This is what disturbs me, Antony. We can't promise that either without discussing it with him first."

"It's simple," he said, brushing off her concern. "When the time comes, just tell him that you extended offers to members of the press to review your restaurant—"

"And they all just happened to reserve for the same night?"

"When a critic knocks at your kitchen door, you don't say, 'Not tonight, I have a stomach ache,'" he said, raising an arched blond eyebrow.

Annette watched Shoshana balance their empty cassoulet crocks on a tray and navigate the aisle back to the kitchen, where Etienne, in the throes of self-doubt, would probably jump on her for a blow-by-blow of how they liked it. She knew ego and insecurity often went hand in hand, but in all her years in the restaurant industry, she had never met a chef who was quite so obvious about it. It made her wonder how genuine Etienne's insecurity really was; she suspected that if she ever told him one of his dishes tasted like garbage, he'd scream at her that she was out of her mind and then quit.

She turned her thoughts back to the matter at hand, which she wanted to avoid but couldn't any longer.

She knew what they were doing was underhanded. She wanted to debate the point with Antony one more time, and yet when she tried to define wherein the dishonesty lay, she could find no tangible evidence of wrongdoing.

It would be one thing if she had promised Hampton discretion, but she had not. He likely assumed it, but that was his mistake. She was free to invite whomever she wanted to her restaurant, whenever she liked. And although she knew the right thing to do would be to alert Hampton to the publicity, the businesswoman in her warned against it. She knew that if told, Hampton would withdraw his reservation and drink his wine elsewhere.

It was the media's job to find out about important events. The information, the tip-off, wasn't traceable. It need not have come from her, and Hampton need never discover the source of the leak. She had gone this far, and time was running out. Was she really going to throw a gift horse away on principle? Principles got you nowhere in this or any other business, and there was too much riding on the success of Parapluie. Too much pride, too many years of training and planning, and too much capital. But it went deeper than that. Her identity was at stake. If she were forced to close, she would be nothing but another failed female entrepreneur, washed up at thirty-six. It would mean desertion by the one lover she thought she could count on.

She glanced down at Antony's notepad. "You've left someone off your list," she said.

Antony turned it toward him and scanned his notes. "Who?"

Annette gave a smug smile. "The *New York Post*. The ones who made such a to-do over the purchase of the bottle in the first place."

"The *Post*," he scoffed. "They're only concerned with money and scandal. I doubt they'll care very much about the actual quality of the wine or the historical relevance of the event."

"Add them," Annette insisted. "They covered the bottle once, and this is their chance to follow it up for their readers."

"Fine," said Antony, scribbling the addition to the list. "Although I wouldn't expect much from them."

You're just annoyed that you forgot them, Annette thought.

She sipped her coffee and watched Shoshana press her hands together in a polite dip to the Japanese businessmen, one of whom slipped her a wad of bills, which she pocketed with a megawatt smile.

Annette was doing this for herself, but also for Etienne, Tripp, Jonathan, Manuel, silly Shoshana, and the rest of her staff. For MaryLou Sampson, her beloved mentor, and women restaurateurs everywhere. She supposed she was also doing it for Antony Farrell, although she stood to gain much more from the evening in practical terms than he did. He must realize that the possibility of Hampton offering him a taste of the Lafite was still a long shot.

As she considered all this, the nagging thought that had been lurking just beneath her conscious objections burst forth, and she was forced to confront it.

MaryLou Sampson would never pull a stunt like this. Even if her restaurant were struggling, she'd find some other way.

Annette squinted and rubbed her eyes. There it was, the root of her discomfort in its starkest form. MaryLou would not approve.

Well, MaryLou had a patron. Annette did not. Atlanta was not New York. It was not as newsworthy to be a successful Canadian woman in a northern U.S. city as it was to be a black woman, descended from slaves, establishing a destination restaurant in the South. Who was to say that MaryLou, in Annette's position, wouldn't do the same?

One did what one had to do, it was that simple. Sy Hampton was a big boy and could take care of himself. As a businessman, he would have to appreciate her predicament. She couldn't afford to worry about him any longer.

TWENTY-THREE

"VAL, IT AIN'T ROCKET SCIENCE! It ain't science at all, come to that. All that matters is what you think of the wine, and nobody knows that but you!" said Vito, his arm around Valentina's heaving shoulders.

"But I s-s-s-said the wine was indigent!" she sobbed.

Next to her, Elisa gave a little chirp. Valentina shot her sister a dirty look through her tears, but a second gulp confirmed that Elisa really did have the hiccups.

Elisa covered her mouth daintily and added, "It's a good word, Val. Honest! It just doesn't mean poor like you meant poor. You wanted to say that you thought the wine wasn't good qua-ha-lity."

"Which is true," said Vito, nodding. "It only cost me six bucks."

"But the thesaurus said 'poor,' and then it said 'indigent' right next to it. How the hell was I supposed to know it meant something else?" Valentina was trying very hard not to get Vito's purple silk shirt wet, but somehow she couldn't stop the tears coming.

"Indigent means you don't have any mo-ho-ney," said Elisa, hiccupping again. "It isn't a word you use about wine."

"Jesus Christ, drink some water, will you?" snapped Trish, pushing a glass across the table.

"Hold my ears," gasped Elisa.

Valentina sat up and squeezed her sister's earlobes between her fingertips. Elisa took several short sips of water.

"What the hell are you doing?" crowed Trish. If Valentina was occasionally put off by Elisa's upwardly mobile aspirations, Trish was openly offended by them.

"It's the only thing that works to cure hiccups. Better than leaning over the glass and drinking upside down," said Elisa when she had finished. She handed the glass to Valentina, who drank gratefully. "Jill, my roommate at Fordham, taught me. It opens the Eustachian tubes."

Valentina saw Trish's brow furrow and knew that she was taking exception both to the mention of Fordham and the scientific term.

Somehow, Trish wasn't bothered by the fact that Valentina had gone to college, but then again, she didn't mention it at every opportunity.

"This is the worst idea ever. I don't know why I said yes," Valentina said gloomily.

"You know, maybe I led you down the wrong path," Vito said, patting her hair thoughtfully. "Maybe you should just stick to words you know. They don't have to be fancy. Not at the stage you're at. You just stick to good, bad, poor, sour, bitter, sweet . . ."

"Fruity?" she sniffled.

"Yeah, fruity. Lotsa wines are fruity. And old Bordeaux wines, like the one you're gonna drink, they got a lot of fruit aromas. Blackberries, currants. You know what?" He lifted Valentina's heart-shaped face and stared into it, his black eyes sparkling beneath his neatly weeded eyebrows. "All you really gotta say is thank you. He don't expect you to be smart about the wine. That's his job—he's the expert."

"But he'll respect me more if I have an opinion."

"When have you ever not had opinions?" asked Elisa.

"Yeah," said Trish, nodding in rare agreement. "You know if something tastes good or if it tastes like turpentine. So just call it like you taste it."

Valentina wiped her eyes and looked at Vito. "But what if it does taste like turpentine?"

"Well, it might taste like vinegar," said Vito. "It's part of the mystery of wine that old. Think of it as an adventure. *La grande avventura!*" He threw his hands wide, nearly clocking Roseanne, who had come up behind him and was murmuring sympathetically. "It might be the best thing you ever tasted in your goddamn life! It might be ambrosia, like your name."

"Or it might taste like piss," put in Roseanne helpfully. "You should taste some of the crap that Vito brings home from wine sales. I don't know much about wine, but I know when it tastes like something better found in a litter box."

Valentina couldn't help but laugh. They were right. She was overreacting. Sy was fully aware that she knew nothing about wine.

That seemed to be part of the point of the evening—he wanted to impress her with his knowledge and expertise. He wanted to teach her. It didn't matter if her opinion was different from anybody else's. And, she reminded herself, there wasn't anybody else, there was only Sy. It wasn't as if there would be a hundred people watching her, waiting for her to say something smart.

"Gimme that thesaurus back," said Vito.

Valentina handed Vito the book, and he tossed it over his shoulder without looking, knocking a ceramic jug off a bookcase. It broke into three large pieces on the floor, but neither he nor Roseanne seemed to care.

"Just be yourself, Val. Use words that mean something to you. Now, let's have some of this next one, and you tell me—in Valentina-speak—what you think of it."

He pushed aside the six-dollar bottle and pushed forward a bottle of Beaujolais. She blew her nose, then set the tissue aside and took a sip of the wine.

"First of all, do you like it?" asked Vito.

She didn't know what to say. It was okay.

"Um, it's okay."

"Fair enough. If you had to say what it tasted like, what would you say? Quick, the first thing that comes into your head!"

"Tangy," she said. "And it's got a little fizz in it, like soda, which I don't think I like so much in red wine, only white."

"There!" Trish declared triumphantly. "You just had an opinion, not even just about this wine, but all wines. You don't like red wine with fizz!"

"Valentina, Valentina," Vito sang, and took her hands in his. "You are figuring out what you like and what you don't, and that's what wine is all about."

"That's what life is all about," advised Roseanne sagely. "You figure out what you like, and you take it, no matter what anybody else thinks."

She was standing behind Vito, and she put her hands on his shoulders and gave them a loving squeeze.

"I can't figure out if I like him," Valentina blurted out.

Roseanne cackled. "That's all right, he's already taken!"

"No, not Vito! I love Vito." She flashed him a grateful smile. "I mean Sy. The guy I'm going on the date with. I just don't know. He's kind of intimidating."

"He beats the hell out of Jerry DiCicco," remarked Elisa.

Valentina turned to Elisa. "Yeah, I'm through with Jerry. He's not for me, either. At least, I figured that out in time."

"Jerry DiCicco? You were dating Jerry DiCicco?" Vito set down his wineglass, surprised.

"Yeah, for three years. He wanted to get married, but I never want to get married."

"Never say never," counseled Roseanne.

"I went to high school with Jerry DiCicco," said Vito, shaking his head. "I always thought he might turn out, you know . . ." Vito waggled his hand limply.

The room went silent, and Roseanne chose that moment to shuffle across the room and pick up the ceramic pieces. Valentina glanced at Trish. There were about a hundred things she wanted to say, like what made him think that, did he know this from personal experience, and the obvious "takes one to know one," but all she said was, "Are you kidding me? Jerry's an animal! That was part of the problem."

That broke the tension, and everybody laughed with nervous relief. Roseanne excused herself and brought the broken pottery into the kitchen, where a child had started to wail.

"Back to the wine," Vito said, and Valentina was thankful. She was on surer ground with wine than with the question of Vito's sexual orientation. And that was saying something.

"So, this is a Beaujolais. It's a young wine, tangy and crisp. You gotta drink it within a few years of the vintage."

"What's vintage exactly?" asked Elisa.

Elisa knew damn well what vintage was, Valentina thought, irritated. She was just trying to make her feel less stupid.

"It's the year the grapes were harvested. It don't matter so much with American wines, but wines from the Old Country, you know

France, Italy, Spain . . . The weather's kinda screwy over there. Sometimes it's hot, sometimes it's rainy. And that can make a big difference in the wine. But California is California, the weather don't change."

"So it pays to buy American?" joked Elisa.

Vito nodded thoughtfully. "Well, yes and no. There's lots of great wine out there from all over the world, so you don't wanna limit yourself."

"I was making a joke there, Vito," said Elisa in a prickly voice, as Trish gave a satisfied little snort. Apparently, the charm of looking stupider than Valentina had worn off.

"And New York wines are a different story altogether," Vito went on, ignoring her. "The East Coast gets a whole host of problems that California doesn't have to deal with. Humidity, rain, cold weather, less sun. But the result is some damn good wines. You should try some from the Finger Lakes, or there's some really good labels in the Hudson Valley. Most folks don't realize that there's more to American wine than California. You'd be surprised how many hotshot experts don't know shit about New York wines."

Vito's littlest girl came running into the room and slid onto his lap. He gave her a loud kiss on the cheek, and she settled into a comfortable snuggle, ogling the grown-ups around the table with saucer eyes. Vito ruffled his daughter's hair and turned to Valentina.

"So when's the big night?"

"Saturday," said Valentina, her stomach giving a little lurch.

"You'll be fine. I've taught you all the basic stuff. You know how to hold the glass, you know you're actually supposed to stick your snout right down into it and smell the wine, right?"

Valentina nodded.

"You've tasted enough wine tonight and last week to know that there's some you like and some you don't. You're only gonna use words that you know, and you're gonna enjoy yourself. You don't gotta impress nobody. And you said yourself, you aren't even sure if you like the goon. So what's to worry about?"

Valentina nodded again.

"And you learned that if the goon fires you, you're gonna be indigent!" Vito threw his head back and laughed heartily. Trish and Elisa joined him, and in a minute, Valentina found herself laughing, too, in spite of herself.

"Come on, let's get some pizza," said Trish as they left, with the whole Scarparelli clan waving them off from the front door. "It's early, and I got a headache from all that wine."

"You know, professional tasters spit out their wine. That's how they can do it all day and not get drunk," said Elisa.

"That's dumb," sneered Trish. "What's the point of that?"

"I'm still trying to figure out the point of any of this," said Valentina as they paused in front of Gino's Pizza. She pushed the door open for Trish, but Elisa held back.

"Aren't you coming?" Valentina asked.

Elisa looked at her watch. "I don't know . . . I've got my book club tomorrow, and I'm behind a few chapters."

"Yeah?" asked Valentina. "What are you reading?"

"*Middlesex* by Jeffrey Eugenides. It won the Pulitzer Prize, you know."

"I only ever have great sex, not middling," said Trish.

Elisa rolled her eyes. "It isn't about sex. I mean, it sort of is, because the narrator is a hermaphrodite—"

"Seriously?" Trish gaped. "I thought they were mythical creatures!"

Valentina could see that Elisa was having difficulty deciding whether Trish was baiting her on purpose, which Valentina was pretty sure she was. Inevitably, whenever she was with both her sister and her best friend, she wound up trapped in the middle. But Trish had done her a real favor introducing her to Vito, so she resolved that the best course of action was simply to shut down the conversation and send Elisa on her way as quickly as possible. But Elisa surprised her with a decisive nod of her head.

"You know, I think I will have a slice," she said, and pushed past Trish into Gino's.

"Why'd you have to invite along Miss Know-It-All anyway," Trish grumbled as they followed Elisa inside.

"I was telling her about Vito and she said she'd always wanted to learn about wine from an expert," whispered Valentina.

Actually, it was Valentina's spot-on impersonation of Vito that had made Elisa beg to be included.

They slid into a booth in the back, where they ordered Cokes and a large mushroom pie from an exhausted-looking waitress. As soon as the pizza came, they devoured it.

"You've never told me what Vito does when he's not tasting wine," Valentina said, hoping to lighten the mood.

Trish shrugged. "Nobody really knows. But whatever it is, he makes enough money for his family."

"Most Italians I know don't know much about French wines. He must get out a lot," remarked Elisa.

"How should I know? I'm not his mother!" Trish snapped.

Trish took her cigarettes out of her pocketbook, pulled one from the pack, and rolled it absently between her fingers, her substitute for lighting up ever since Mayor Bloomberg's ban on smoking in restaurants.

"That work for you?" asked Elisa pointedly.

"No. But it's better than nothing. Why?"

"'Cause you could always just go outside and take a ciggie break."

Valentina saw Trish's eyes narrow dangerously.

"Yeah, I could. Back in a few."

Trish scooped up her cigarettes and stalked off toward the door. Valentina glared at her sister.

"That was really rude."

"I don't know why you still hang out with her. She doesn't do much for your social profile."

"She's been my best friend since ninth grade."

"You're not in high school anymore, Val," said Elisa, sipping her Coke.

"Why are you in such a bitchy mood? Why did you even come?"

"Because you invited me, remember?"

Valentina turned her head toward the glass front of the pizzeria, where Trish was pacing back and forth on the sidewalk, smoking furiously.

"You could be a little nicer to Trish. She is doing me a big favor, you know."

"I wish somebody would invite me out to taste a half- million-dollar bottle of wine," Elisa said after a moment.

"Yeah, well, I'm sure there are strings attached, even if he says there aren't. I kinda feel like I have to sleep with him if he wants."

"Val, if all he wanted was to get you in bed, he could've done it a lot cheaper, no offense."

"Then what does he want from me?" asked Valentina, feeling panic rise again.

Elisa popped a stray mushroom in her mouth thoughtfully. "Maybe he doesn't know." She signaled to the waitress, who looked relieved at the prospect of being done with them so she could go home. "But one way or another, it'll all be over by Sunday. And you don't have to see him again if you don't want to."

"I work for him, remember?" Valentina dropped fifteen bucks on the table and pulled her leather jacket on. "This is for Trish and me."

Elisa stretched her arms over her head and ran her fingers through her auburn hair, which, with its highlights and chic cut, made her look far more sophisticated than Valentina. "I feel a little sorry for the guy."

"Sorry for him? How come?"

Elisa scooped up the check and Valentina's money. "Sweetie, don't take this the wrong way, but if this guy's got no wife, no girl-friend, no friends, and you're the only person he can think of to share this famous bottle of wine with . . . don't you think it's just the teeniest bit pathetic?"

Elisa took the check and the money to the cash register, leaving Valentina steaming.

How dare Elisa say Sy was pathetic because of her?

Then again, it was nothing she hadn't thought herself a hundred times. It was just worse to hear Elisa say it. Until this moment, Valentina had hoped that nobody else had noticed. And if Elisa noticed, wouldn't everybody else?

And if everybody noticed, and if everybody agreed, wouldn't that mean it was true?

TWENTY-FOUR

"Hey, man, is that your dad?"

The shrill prepubescent voice carried over the clamor of rough-housing schoolboys with such clarity that it caught Sy's attention. He looked up from his iPhone, on which he had been e-mailing Warren Sage, and realized it was coming from the boy walking with Eric. Sy looked down at the tiny screen again, keeping his ears trained on them, curious to hear how his son would respond.

"Yeah, that's him," Sy heard Eric say, although he had to strain to hear the quieter voice. It was a noncommittal answer, although his tone suggested that the other boy already knew something about Sy, and probably nothing very flattering.

"What's up with the hair? Man, that is some freaky-looking do!"

Sy's head shot up, and this time his eyes met Eric's. Eric must have known that Sy had overheard them, because he quickly bade good-bye to his loudmouthed friend and hurried over to the car. Sy was at least amused to note that the other kid's body and voice were on different timetables. He was about five feet four, but he still sounded like a first grader. Sy gave a friendly wave and the kid turned away, embarrassed. Sy climbed into the Lexus next to his son.

"Who was that?" he asked.

"Jack Wobeson. He's kind of a jerk," offered Eric.

Sy was wise enough to recognize this as a filial olive branch. "So, what do you want to do this afternoon? Do you have a lot of home-work?"

"Just math and social studies."

They rode downtown in silence. As they made a sharp turn, Sy slid into Eric, and he got a moment's pleasure from the unexpected physical contact with his son. But as he sat up again, he caught a glimpse of himself in the rearview mirror.

Jack Wobeson might be a jerk, but he was right. His hair looked awful. Sy had been going for years to Franco, who worked in a small salon near his office. Franco always did whatever Sy asked, but maybe he didn't want to risk losing a long-standing, high-profile customer by pushing back. Or maybe Franco thought this looked good. Sy rarely gave his hair much thought, but seeing himself through the eyes of Eric and his obnoxious friend, he realized that Franco wasn't doing him any favors.

"Where does your mother take you for haircuts?" Sy asked.

"Kozy Kidcuts. But I don't need a haircut. I just went a few weeks ago," Eric said quickly.

"Not for you, for me." He leaned forward and addressed his driver. "Bill, do you know a good barber?"

Bill glanced over his shoulder. "I go to a shop near my house. You probably want something fancier."

"Dad, your hair's fine. I told you, Jack Wobeson is a jerk," said Eric, shifting uncomfortably.

"I think I need a new look, don't you?" He leaned closer to Eric. "I've got a hot date on Saturday."

From the look of horror on Eric's face, Sy realized he'd completely miscalculated. Eric didn't think it was cool that his dad had a date. He thought it was gross.

"I'm kidding—it's not that kind of date," Sy backtracked. "It's really with a bottle of wine."

Eric looked at him like he'd grown a second head, also having a bad hair day. "Dad, I don't think a bottle of wine is going to care what you look like. Can we just go back to your place?"

My place, thought Sy sadly. Not "home," not even "home away from home," or "our place." He decided to try a different tack.

"The wine is very rare. It's from the French Revolution, and it was once owned by Thomas Jefferson. You know who he was, right?"

"Dad," groaned Eric.

"I could show it to you, if you like. It's a collector's item."

"You don't have to," said Eric. "It's just a bottle."

Bill pulled up in front of the house, and Eric followed his father inside.

"Hey, kiddo," said Claudine, greeting them at the door. "I just baked some cookies."

"Cool!" Eric dropped his backpack in the front hall and followed Claudine to the back of the house.

"I'm making pork chops and those cottage fries you like," she said over her shoulder, as Eric trotted behind her like a puppy that hadn't been fed in a week.

Sy didn't know why he bothered leaving his office early on Wednesdays. The only thing Eric seemed to enjoy about these visits was chatting with Claudine in the kitchen and eating her treats. He could just as easily have Bill pick up Eric and deliver him right to her. This court-ordered father-son time was clearly a chore for the boy, a sentence to be served for a crime he didn't commit.

Sy took refuge in his study, but before he made himself comfortable on the chesterfield, he went into the small bathroom and turned on the light. How was it he'd never noticed that the color Franco used oxidized to a reddish blond? And the length. It grew over his ears, the ends were frizzy, and the whole mess, brushed back from his hairline, overemphasized his high forehead.

Now that he'd made the decision, he couldn't get his hair cut fast enough, although nothing could make up for the months, probably years, he'd been walking around looking like a "before" photo. Without a word to Eric or Claudine, he slipped out of the house and walked over to Madison Avenue. He had no idea whether there was a salon nearby, though it seemed to him that there should be. Ten blocks uptown he came to a fancy-looking place called Salon Rivoli. After waiting twenty minutes, Sy was handed over to a stylist, whose name tag announced him as Jeffrey.

"Hmmmm, this is overdue, isn't it?" Jeffrey said, pulling strands of Sy's hair up through his fingers. "What kind of look do you want?"

"Anything but this," said Sy.

Jeffrey laughed. "Let's just concentrate on reversing the damage, shall we? We'll start with color. Your natural color is a medium brown, right?"

Sy nodded.

"We can bring it back to that, but honestly"—Jeffrey parted Sy's hair as if he were looking for bugs in tall grass—"I'm more inclined to let you go gray. It would be more flattering than the brown at this point in your life—if you don't mind my saying so. And I'd like to bring up the sides, here . . ." He pressed Sy's hair down above his ears. "The dyes are just not as flattering on men, and with gray hair as fine as yours, you'd get a nice salt-and-pepper look. Very distinguished."

This wasn't at all what Sy wanted to hear. He was going on a date—a date that he hoped would reinvigorate him and make him feel youthful.

"Can you try to match my old color, please? I don't much care about the cut as long as it looks neat, but the color . . ." His voice trailed off.

Jeffrey held up his hand. "Leave it to me."

An hour and a half later, Sy barely recognized himself. His hair was a warm chestnut brown and much shorter. He hadn't realized it, but the long hair made him jowly.

"I still think," counseled Jeffrey, "that graceful gray would actually make you look younger, although this is still a major improvement."

"Maybe next time." Sy thanked Jeffrey and slipped him a sizable tip.

While he didn't feel entirely like a new man, at least he no longer sported a "freaky do." He supposed he had Jack Wobeson to thank for that. Sy started back down Madison Avenue. It was getting dark, and the amber glow of the streetlights suffused the September twilight with an unseasonable holiday magic. Sy passed a small Italian clothing boutique, where a suit in the window caught his eye. It was charcoal gray with a delicate pinstripe. On a whim, he went inside.

"This is perfect on you," said the clerk when Sy came out of the fitting room. "It doesn't even need to be tailored. Might I suggest this pink tie?" The clerk leaned forward. "Ladies like pink on a man.

It's a well-kept secret. Many customers don't believe me, but the ones who do . . ." He winked and made a suggestive gesture.

Thinking that Valentina might appreciate the pink tie particularly, Sy took it and threw a new white shirt into the bargain. When he arrived home, Eric was sitting on a stool in the kitchen, watching more SpongeBob.

"Look at you! Very handsome," said Claudine, nodding appreciatively.

"Eric? What do you think?"

His son turned from the television and his eyes widened. "Dad! That looks so much better!"

"No more freaky do, huh?"

"Dad," Eric said, the color rising in his cheeks. "I told you . . ."

"I know, Jack Wobeson is a jerk," Sy finished. "But I did need a haircut." He looked at his watch. "Listen, we've still got some time before I take you home. Are you sure you don't want to see that bottle I was telling you about?"

He wasn't sure what made him ask again, but to his surprise, Eric flicked off the television with the remote and hopped off the stool.

"Is it all full of cobwebs?" he asked, following Sy into the dining room.

"No, it's been cleaned up. It even has a new label."

Sy gestured for Eric to sit at the table, then unlocked the breakfront. Unlike the last time Sy handled the bottle, his hands were steady and confident. He set his treasure down in front of his son.

"Can I touch it?" Eric asked.

"Gently. Here, let me show you something." Sy ran his finger over the label, felt what he was looking for, and gingerly peeled back the top right corner.

"Look." He pointed to the engraved letters he had revealed. "Château Lafitte, 1787. Wineries don't put labels on bottles until they ship them to stores. In the old days, they etched the information right into the glass. The spelling has changed, too—now it's Lafite, with only one *t*. And see just below? Th. J., for Thomas

Jefferson. After he bought it, they marked it as his."

"Why don't they use labels?"

"Well, wine needs to be cool and damp to stay viable, and that's not a good climate for paper. It just gets moldy and rotten, so wines that are made for the long haul used to get etchings. Nowadays they get dog tags, like soldiers. This label was printed up especially for the auction where I bought it."

"Who'd you buy it from?" asked Eric.

"A man named Charles Marquet owned it earlier this century. He had to build a fake wall in his wine cellar to hide this and other valuable bottles from the Nazis. His grandchildren found the hidden chamber, and that's who I bought the wine from."

"Wow, that's pretty cool!" Eric sounded genuinely impressed. "And you're gonna drink it on Saturday?"

"I am."

"And that's why you got your hair cut?"

"It's a special occasion."

"Is it going to taste really amazing?"

The look on Eric's face was one Sy hadn't seen in a long time. He really did think it was cool, and he, Sy, was the source of the cool. The moment felt so fragile that Sy didn't dare do anything to break it. He longed to stroke his son's rounded cheek, which he knew would not stay cushiony and sweet for much longer, but it wasn't worth the risk of him pulling away.

Instead, he picked up the bottle from the table, clasped his other hand on Eric's shoulder, and answered, "I sure hope so."

TWENTY-FIVE

"*À MOINS QUE JE NE ME TROMPE, j'ai la drôle d'impression que tu veux prendre ma place derrière les chaudrons?*"

"*Mais non, Etienne, quelle idée!*" Annette said patiently. Etienne was very much mistaken! Of course she had no desire to replace him in the kitchen. She simply wanted to prepare the peach blueberry cobbler and the mixed berry torte herself for Saturday night. They were her grandmother's recipes after all, and it was her prerogative.

"*Par contre, je veux simplement t'aider avec les petits desserts aux fruits. Car comme tu le sais, ce sont des recettes que je tiens de ma grand-mère.*"

"*Je le savais, tu n'aimes plus ma cuisine,*" Etienne said, shaking his head.

She was hardly maligning his cooking. But she supposed she should have anticipated his reluctance. It wasn't the first time he had objected to her helping out in the kitchen, and it probably wouldn't be the last.

"*Etienne, essayes de comprendre. Je ne remets pas tes compétences en doute—loin de là. Ce sont plutôt des raisons personnelles qui me poussent à vouloir les faire.*"

She did not owe him any explanations. He simply had to accept that she was the boss and she had personal reasons for wanting to prepare her grandmother's desserts. Her superstitions were none of his business. Etienne squinted and raised his head to the ceiling. Amazingly, his tall *toque blanche* didn't fall off. She sometimes wondered if he taped it to his shiny bald pate. He gave her a steely look, but she didn't flinch.

"*Bon. C'est d'accord—mais juste pour cette fois.*"

"*Un gros merci, chef!*"

She returned to her office, distinctly put out. Etienne had managed to turn the tables on her and make her feel as if he were doing her a favor—just this once—when it was she who employed him! It didn't help that this exchange came on the heels of a frustrating conversation with Antony Farrell, who was pushing her to comp the bloggers, which she could ill afford to do.

She returned to her office to review the specials for Saturday night, although she'd been over them so many times she could recite every ingredient from memory. She would repeat the venison with juniper berry sauce, since it had gone so well with Antony's Bordeaux. She would do foie gras in a puff pastry rather than salad, but she'd repeat the escargots and the fried baby artichokes. She wanted to change the soup to a watercress and zander broth with braised endive, even though restaurant critics rarely ordered soup, and she thought she'd flatter Etienne by asking him to substitute his fillet of rabbit in bitter chocolate sauce with quince, or maybe pressed duck, in place of her grandmother's game hens.

She leaned back in her chair, pushed her notepad away, and put her head in her hands. Saturday night was going to make or break her. If she could have set it up any other way, she would have. Banking everything on one meal was a terrible idea. And it appeared they were all coming.

She had worked practically her whole life to get to this point. She'd been barked at, cursed at, lambasted, scalded, and, worse, ignored, on food lines on both sides of the Atlantic. She had distinguished herself at Cornell and successfully transitioned to front of house. As she had promised herself on that day in front of the Caillebotte in Chicago, she had traded romantic for culinary happiness, and if Parapluie failed—well, she couldn't imagine what she'd do.

Her intercom buzzed, and Justine's cheery voice rang through.

"It's Sy Hampton on line two for you."

Annette's heartbeat quickened, as she picked up the phone. "This is Annette Lecocq."

"Sy Hampton here. How are you?"

"Fine, thank you. We're looking forward to seeing you on Saturday."

"That's why I'm calling."

For a horrible instant, Annette thought he was going to cancel, but, of course, his secretary had said to expect a call.

"What can I do for you?" she asked, pressing her cheekbones up into a smile with her fingers, which she knew would keep her voice bright and reduce the chances of her sounding nervous and brittle.

"I'm bringing with me an extremely rare and valuable bottle of wine."

Annette felt herself relax. It was as she'd hoped.

"Yes, your secretary mentioned that. Is there anything special we can do to accommodate you?"

"It will need to be decanted, but I don't think it should aerate long. A wine this old might not last too long in the fresh air. I wonder if the young man who waited on us the other night will be there?"

"Yes, he will. As a matter of fact, I made sure of it, as soon as your secretary made the reservation."

"Excellent," said Hampton. "Will you be serving the venison again as well? It went so well with the Giscours, and while it would be misleading to say the wines are similar, they are both vintage Bordeaux."

"I will, yes, along with a rabbit fillet," she said, deciding on the spot to jettison the duck.

"You seem to have thought of everything."

"We try to keep our special customers happy, Mr. Hampton," she said, feeling more relieved by the minute.

"I'd like to get that nice booth in the back again, the one underneath the painting."

"That won't be a problem at all, Mr. Hampton. We call that table the nook, and we frequently reserve it for special customers."

"Frequently" was something of a stretch, but it was certainly her intention to use the nook for that purpose, assuming she could draw more "special customers."

"Much appreciated. Well, then, we'll see you Saturday night."

"Yes, see you Saturday," said Annette, and hung up the phone.

She left her office and went back upstairs, where lunch was still being served to a few late diners. She stopped at a table or two and graciously accepted compliments on the food. After pouring herself a glass of 2003 L'Orpailleur Rosé at the bar, she sat in the empty nook and observed the room. There was Shoshana, entertaining an elderly woman and her companion with some amusing imitation—there was Jonathan, serving coffee to a party of business associates with appropriate sedateness.

She sipped her wine, a Gold Medal winner at the All Canada Wine Championship, and looked up at the imperturbable couple strolling down the shiny cobblestones in the Caillebotte painting. Sy Hampton's call was the last piece falling into place. There was no turning back now. Everything was on track for a spectacular Saturday night at Parapluie.

Her moment had arrived, and she was as ready as she'd ever be.

TWENTY-SIX

TRIPP HAD NEVER BOUGHT INTO THE IDEA of waking up on the wrong side of the bed, but his eyes were open for barely a minute on Saturday morning before he knew something in the universe was out of sync. He lay back on his pillow and tried to trace the source of his ill humor. He'd dreamed about *A Chorus Line* again. He was in the pit conducting, but this time, it was Michael onstage singing "I Can Do That."

And there it was. Tripp had not gotten the job. Somewhere out there in the world, the decision had been made. Tripp knew it as surely as he knew it was ten o'clock on Saturday morning and he was lying in his bed. He had been harboring a secret hope that this time, his fears were just a natural defense mechanism preparing him for the worst. He had allowed himself to test the mental waters of not being cast, but he had not entirely believed it, until now. Similarly, while he had feared that Michael would get cast and he wouldn't, he was now as certain of it as if Michael were standing beside him breaking the news. This was Tripp's gift, and his curse. It was like those old ads for the yellow pages: "If it's out there, it's in here." His sixth sense, or whatever it was, had received both messages loud and clear.

He closed his eyes, desperate to return to the comparatively blissful state of not knowing, where he was free to play mind games with himself and create the future any number of ways. But he couldn't, and he knew that, too.

His disappointment over *A Chorus Line* was deeper than he expected, and it would only worsen when he spoke to Michael. He'd wait until he confirmed what he knew to be true, and then he would scream, pound his couch pillows, and wallow in the humiliating misery of rejection for the prescribed forty-eight hours. In the meantime, he went to the gym. Counting reps was the best way he knew to drown out unwanted mental chatter, and he spent almost two hours bench-pressing, cycling, and rowing until his body ached.

Making matters worse was the fact that he hadn't seen Michael all week, and because Annette Lecocq was calling in her chips, there was no chance of a rendezvous until Tuesday at the earliest, when they both had off from work. But now Tripp was uncertain about continuing to see Michael. For all his earlier bravado, he wasn't sure he'd be able to swallow his pride and straddle the gulf that had suddenly opened up between Broadway dancer and East Side waiter.

By three o'clock Michael still hadn't called, and the tide of Tripp's unease was rising. There was no reason he shouldn't pick up the phone and call Michael. Maybe Michael was feeling awkward about getting the job. But Michael had no way of knowing Tripp hadn't gotten it. So why hadn't he called to say, "Hey, I heard from the casting director. Did you?"

Unless Tripp's intuition was totally off this time. He was willing to acknowledge the possibility, but at the same time he was growing increasingly suspicious of Michael's radio silence. By the time Tripp arrived at Parapluie, he was feeling prickly and unmoored.

He found the restaurant hectic with preparations. Annette was micromanaging everything from the silverware placement to the temperature of the sauces. In the right mood, Tripp would have found the singularity of the occasion exhilarating, but in his current frame of mind, it only reinforced the fact that this was the closest he was going to get to an opening night anytime soon.

"Tripp!"

He emerged from the downstairs bathroom to see Annette waiting for him at the top of the stairs.

"I need you to make sure that one of the large crystal carafes is thoroughly washed and preset on the table in the nook. They're coming at seven thirty, but before then I'll need you to seat some other important guests."

The feverish look in Annette's eyes told him there was more to the evening than he knew.

"What other guests?" he asked hesitantly. He could feel anxiety wafting off her body like a toxic cloud.

"There's food and wine press coming."

Tripp swallowed. "Tonight?"

"They're coming to see the uncorking."

"You didn't tell me Hampton arranged a press event!"

Annette glanced furtively into the serving kitchen, then took Tripp by the elbow and steered him back down the stairs to her office, where she shut the door.

"I had to take advantage of the publicity. It's unlikely that he'll recognize any of them. None of us knows what they look like, and under normal circumstances, we wouldn't even know they were coming."

Tripp blinked, incredulous. "Are you telling me he doesn't know?"

"If he asks, we invited the press to review the restaurant sometime this month, and they all coincidentally reserved for tonight."

"What if Hampton walks out when he realizes he's got an audience?"

"He wouldn't. It would be too embarrassing for him. Besides, we're not asking him to do anything. We would never presume to request that he share his wine. Only his reaction once he and his companion have tried it."

"But—"

Annette held up her hand to stop him. "The most important thing is that our distinguished guests will be feasting on a fabulous meal. Etienne has been preparing all day and I made the desserts myself."

Tripp felt his mouth go dry. *He* felt set up, and it wasn't even his wine! He did not want to perform tonight. It was bad enough having to serve Sy Hampton's famously expensive bottle of wine without a roomful of reporters watching his every move.

"I'm giving you Mr. Rand from the *Times* and Mr. St. Alban from *Bon Appétit,* both parties of two. Jonathan and Roberto will have the *New York Post, Forbes,* and whoever else is left to split between them. I've got Shoshana in for the bloggers."

"I thought you hated Shoshana," said Tripp, still trying to process what Annette was telling him.

"She's young and hip, and the bloggers will like her. So will Antony Farrell," she added somewhat snidely.

"Farrell is coming, too?"

"Yes, and he'll be seated near Hampton. The table on the right, just down of the nook."

"Tell me, do you have any regular customers tonight or are they all plants?" Tripp asked, unable to hide his disgust.

"This won't affect you, but we're comping the bloggers," she said, ignoring his remark.

"What about Hampton?" Tripp asked, still trying to process the magnitude of the evening, which had just exploded exponentially.

"Waive the corkage fee," said Annette. "But for everything else, he pays."

TWENTY-SEVEN

VALENTINA SPENT MOST OF SATURDAY with a knot in her stomach. As she sat in the salon, having her hair set, she considered the benefits of not eating. After all, she would be having a multiple-course meal of fattening French food, so it was probably best that the only thing she'd been able to choke down all day was half an apple.

She kept reminding herself that it was just dinner, and it was just grape juice. Still, she couldn't shake the sense that as much as she had mentally and physically prepared herself, there was some unforeseen curve ahead.

"You look gorgeous," said Dawn, the stylist. She patted Valentina's hair and spun the chair around. Valentina barely recognized herself in the mirror. The updo made her look elegant, like a movie star.

"I guess I clean up okay." She giggled nervously.

"I'll say. You're gorgeous! So? Whaddaya gonna wear?"

"Red leather pants and a pink and white cashmere sweater. I want to look nice but not too, you know, suggestive."

Dawn winked. "You playing hard to get?"

"No, it's not that. I'm going out with my boss. It's, like, a work thing."

Dawn raised an eyebrow. "It's a work thing and you're getting your hair done?"

"It's hard to explain."

"Okay, whatever. Anyway, you're finished."

Valentina paid the cashier, slipped Dawn a few extra bucks, and walked the four short blocks back to her apartment. As she walked, she practiced a few phrases, and for the first time in her life experimented with suppressing her accent.

"I can't thank you enough for inviting me this evening."

"You're right! This is the most astonishing wine I've ever tasted!"

"What a lovely restaurant. The food is excellent."

She found it wasn't so easy to alter her Brooklynese inflections, which gave her a new appreciation for Elisa's efforts. No, she would stick to what Vito advised and just be herself. Sy could have invited anyone else, but he hadn't. He was expecting her, though she still found it hard to understand why.

When she turned the corner, she saw somebody sitting on her front steps. As she drew closer, her heart sank.

"What the hell are you doing here?"

"Val," said Jerry, popping to his feet like a jack-in-the-box. "I gotta talk to you."

"Why? Something you wanna tell me about Vito Scarparelli?" she asked, turning her key in the lock.

Jerry looked genuinely confused. "Who?"

Valentina gave a bored sigh. "From high school. Vito Scarparelli. He's kinda, you know." She imitated Vito's gesture, waggling her hand from side to side.

"Oh, yeah, I remember him. He was always giving me the eye. A total faggot. What do I gotta tell you about him?"

Valentina whirled on him. "It just so happens that Vito is a very knowledgeable wine expert."

"So what?"

"And . . ." She paused for maximum effect. "He's married and he's got four kids. Which is more than you can say, Jerry!"

She pushed the door in. Jerry tried to follow her, but she was ready for him, and she turned quickly, blocking his entry with her body.

"Well, bully for Vito," Jerry said. "Folks can swing both ways, you know."

"Any particular reason you're sitting on my steps?"

"As a matter of fact, yeah. I wanted to tell you that I'm dating somebody."

Valentina felt a slight pang of regret, but only a slight one. "That's nice, Jerry. I'm happy for you. Now, do you mind?"

"Wait!"

"What?"

"I mean, I just wanted to tell you, because if you see me out with her, I didn't want it to be, you know, like a shock."

"Okay. So you told me. Now I know."

She was tempted to ask who it was, but she didn't really care.

"You got your hair done," Jerry commented.

"Very observant. I've got a date tonight. There, I told you, so if you see me out with him, it won't be, like, a shock."

Jerry blinked, and Valentina suddenly understood that he wasn't really dating anybody else. It was just another trick to get her to feel sorry for him. Whereas it was obvious from the fact that her hair was piled on top of her head and sprayed within an inch of its life that she was telling the truth.

Jerry shuffled his feet. "So, uh, who is it?"

"My boss."

Jerry snorted. "You told me that one last time. Mr. Whatshisname and his fancy vino. You weren't serious . . . were you?" Jerry asked, looking suddenly concerned. "You were bullshitting me, right?"

Valentina shook her head. "No, Jerry. I was telling you the truth. So if you don't mind, I have to get ready."

"That old guy? What the hell for?"

She thought for a moment. "Because, Jerry, I don't want to be indigent!"

She left him staring at her, bewildered, and shut the front door firmly behind her. But as she continued down the hall to her apartment, she realized she was trembling all over. Despite the show of bravado she'd just put on for Jerry's benefit, her confidence was fading again, fast.

In her bathroom, Valentina applied her makeup and tried to put Jerry out of her mind. Satisfied with her face, she pulled her red leather pants and matching sweater from the closet. But even before she put them on, she knew they were all wrong. She slipped into them anyway, but they were off her body and crumpled on the floor within moments. She needed something more sophisticated.

Something to go with the hair.

She had a suit, which she'd bought for her job interview at Hampton & Sage. It was a nice navy blue pencil skirt with a tailored jacket, but with her hair up, she felt like Miss Banks, and she knew if Sy had wanted to go on a date with Miss Banks, he'd have asked her. She tried on and discarded a full-skirted party dress in a tropical print, a leopard sheath, and silk pants with a beaded top. The beaded top was close, but the hair was wrong with it, too severe. Barefoot, in the silk pants with the top unzipped in back, she rooted through what was left of her closet. She had nothing else that was remotely appropriate. There was only one thing to do.

Cringing at the thought of throwing forty bucks down the drain, she undid her hair and let it fall loose around her shoulders. Yes, that was better, but there was so much gel and spray in it, she'd have to wash it, and there was hardly time left to do that and dry it properly.

She cursed herself for not planning better and for not accepting the car Sy wanted to send for her. She had stupidly insisted on getting to the restaurant on her own steam. But it was five o'clock already. Suddenly everything seemed impossible, every little step toward her date an insurmountable hurdle.

What on earth had she been thinking?

She sat on the edge of her bed and began to cry. She should call Jerry and say she didn't mean anything she'd said to him. She should admit that he was the best she could do, that this date with Sy was a joke. She would tell him it was a ploy to make him jealous. What else could she do? She'd ruined her hair, and now her makeup was running down her cheeks.

And then it hit her. She realized what she should have done all along. Why hadn't she thought of it sooner? She glanced at her watch. It was late, but still, it was worth a shot. Mopping up her tears, she brushed out her hair with a newfound resolve and set to work.

TWENTY-EIGHT

SY REGARDED HIS REFLECTION in the full-length mirror in his dressing room, and for the first time since he bought the Lafite, he felt at peace with himself. The charcoal suit made him look even trimmer than it had in the boutique, and the pink tie brightened his face in a way the long hair never had. It also carried a hint of adventurousness, which he certainly felt, and the color would be a nice complement to the shades of red that Valentina would undoubtedly be wearing.

He descended the curving staircase to the front hall, where Claudine and Bill were waiting for him, like proud parents seeing their son off to the senior prom.

"My, you look very handsome, Mr. Hampton," cooed Claudine appreciatively.

"Thank you, Claudine." He allowed himself a smile and almost immediately felt himself on the verge of erupting into giddy laughter.

"Bill, is the car out front?" he asked, clearing his throat for cover.

"Yes, sir."

"Good. I'll be out in a moment with the wine."

From the dining room, he heard the front door close as Bill went out to start the car. For the last time, Sy unlocked the breakfront, where the star of the evening was waiting to make her entrance with little fanfare.

Feeling slightly foolish, and glad nobody was watching, Sy took the bottle from the compartment, hugged it to his chest, and kissed the crescent on the label. Then he slipped it into the shoulder carrier he'd had made especially for transporting fine wine. It was made of hand-stitched brown leather. Although it was strong enough to hold several bottles, Sy supported the wine underneath, just as he used to do when he carried Eric in a baby sling.

Bill had the car door open for him, and Sy slid carefully into the backseat with his prize. He set the carrier beside him and fastened the seat belt around them both. He was glad he'd decided not to drive out and pick up Valentina, though he'd have felt better if she had accepted his offer of a car service. He wanted a few more moments alone with his Lafite. As he opened the flap of the carrier and caressed the neck of the bottle, it occurred to him that what he'd said to Eric was true.

His date really was with the wine.

TWENTY-NINE

"GOOD EVENING, MR. RAND," said Annette in her most gracious hostess voice. "It is a great pleasure to have you with us tonight. This is Tripp. He'll be your waiter this evening. We have some additional items that are not on the menu, and I am also delighted to offer you some specially chosen appetizers to supplement your own choices. If there is anything else you require, please let Tripp know. He and I will make every effort to serve you well this evening." She nodded her head, eyes shut, in a gesture of what she hoped read as humility, but which, in actuality, was intended to calm her beating heart.

The silver-haired *New York Times* critic took the menu from Tripp and looked around the room.

"Where's Hampton?"

Annette felt a twinge of annoyance. The wine was supposed to be the lure, but only the lure. At least for the food writers. She signaled to Tripp to bring the complimentary foie gras and to present the wine list, as she hurried over to greet the next arrival, Tony DiFranco of *Wine and Dine*. She ran through the same routine with him, only to be met with the same inquiry: where was Sy Hampton?

"He'll be here presently," she replied as politely as she could. The hulking, curly-haired man with DiFranco gave her an ostentatious wink.

"We wanna see the famous bottle! We've heard a lot about this wine, Tony and me."

Annette smiled indulgently. Tony DiFranco was an understatedly effeminate fellow, but his companion was flamboyantly dressed in a gold silk shirt with some sort of fringed scarf tied around his neck.

Chacun a son goût, she thought. To each his own.

"Well, perhaps we can arrange for you to speak with him when he arrives," she said, signaling Jonathan to bring their appetizers.

This is what it would feel like to cater my own wedding, she thought, moving on. Justine had seated three tables of—kids was the only way to describe them. But as soon as Shoshana took over with her nonstop chatter, Annette realized Antony had been right. The bloggers were responding with ready smiles and energetic inquiries.

"And this is Chris Fabian of the *Post*," Justine was saying. Annette extended a hand in queenly welcome first to him, then to his companion, whom she was somewhat taken aback to see had brought along a rather conspicuous Nikon.

"You don't object, do you?" asked Fabian, following Annette's gaze to the camera.

"No, of course not," she assured him. "I'm sure you can be discreet," she added with a meaningful glance.

The photographer nodded, and Annette, quickly evaluating sightlines, suggested sotto voce that Justine reassign them to the banquette across from the nook. She was beginning to wish for the potted palm that Antony had joked about, when the front door opened and Antony himself arrived. She hurried over to him.

"Well, well, who's here?" He rubbed his hands together eagerly as they surveyed the dining room together.

"Everyone who said they were coming, I think, except the guy from *Robb Report*."

Antony squinted and peered in the direction of the Caillebotte. "Hampton not here yet?"

Annette glanced at her watch. "Should be any minute."

At that moment, a party of three distinguished-looking men arrived.

"Stark for three," said one of them to Annette. She glanced at the reservations screen, and there they were. She took three menus and handed them to Justine.

"Justine will assist you. Enjoy your meal."

The man called Stark winked at Annette. "It's the wine we've come for," he said. "Good to see you, Antony."

Before she could respond, he turned to follow Justine toward the back of the house. Annette fixed a cold eye on Antony.

"That wasn't Richard Stark, was it?"

"I believe it was."

"You invited the most influential wine expert in the world?"

"I didn't exactly invite him," Antony demurred.

"But you told him?"

"It may have slipped out in conversation."

"And who was that with him?" asked Annette, feeling slightly faint.

"If I had to guess, I'd say it was Joseph Adler and Dennis Waggoner."

"You know damn well who they are," Annette hissed. "Hampton may not recognize the food press, but he'll certainly know them! Why did you invite them? Antony—what did you promise?"

Antony gave her hand a squeeze. "I don't know what you're worrying about," he said. "The evening is going to be a crashing success."

"What did you promise them, Antony? Antony!"

But he was already walking away from her toward the restrooms. Annette wanted to scream at his retreating back, to demand that he answer, but she knew she couldn't do any such thing. He clearly had something up his sleeve. But what was it? And why hadn't he told her?

THIRTY

THE LEXUS PULLED UP IN FRONT OF PARAPLUIE. Bill opened the door, and Sy got out of the car, cradling his wine.

"Let's say ten o'clock," said Sy.

"Just call if you need me sooner. Or later." Bill winked.

Sy watched Bill return to the driver's seat and pull the car away. Then he pushed open the door to Parapluie.

"*Bon soir,* Mr. Hampton!"

Annette Lecocq was standing by the podium with a broad, bright smile on her face. It was clear she'd been waiting for him. He extended his free hand and took hers.

"We are honored to have you back," she said.

Her eyes flicked past him, over his shoulders, and he said quickly, "My companion is meeting me here. Miss D'Ambrosio."

"Ah. I don't believe she has arrived yet," said Annette. "Let me show you to your table."

Sy followed Annette toward the Caillebotte painting in the back. The restaurant was quite a bit busier than it had been last time. Perhaps word was spreading. He hugged the wine carrier closer to his side and climbed the three small steps to the nook.

"Here we are," Annette said.

Sy sat down and carefully withdrew the bottle from the carrier, setting it on the table next to a handsome crystal carafe and a delicate glass decanting rod.

He thought he heard a gasp from somewhere behind him, and several diners turned in their seats. A few began to whisper among themselves. Perhaps they recognized him from the *Post* article. Or maybe they were simply reacting to the fact that he'd been seated in what was clearly the most desirable table in the place.

"Nice crowd," he commented to Annette, adjusting the bottle's position on the table.

She smiled modestly and beckoned to Tripp, who set down two

puff pastries on the table and shook Sy's hand.

"Good evening, Mr. Hampton. Nice to see you again."

"You, too," Sy responded. "My date should be here any—"

"Excuse me, I'm meeting Mistah Hampton?"

Loud, Brooklyn-accented tones cut through the hushed restaurant and Annette seemed to jump. Sy followed her gaze toward the door.

"I think that's my—good Lord."

Sure enough, Valentina had just come into the restaurant.

And Antony Farrell was kissing her hand.

"Valentina D'Ambrosio, ambrosia of love! What a delightful surprise!" Antony was saying to the young woman whom Annette realized must be Sy Hampton's secretary. She'd know that voice anywhere.

"Sorry, but I don't—" Valentina started.

"Antony Farrell, Shoreham's Wine Department. We met the day you stopped by to learn a little something about wine," he said, winking at Valentina.

Valentina's face broke into a smile of relief. "Omigod, of course. How could I forget?"

"Your reasons for improving your wine education are suddenly clear. If you're here to meet Mr. Hampton, you must be here to taste his Lafite."

"That's the one."

Mon Dieu, thought Annette, who had rushed to the front of the house and was observing this exchange, unsure how to break in. Please tell me he isn't squandering that invaluable wine on this floozy!

Annette recovered herself and pried Valentina's hand from Antony's.

"I believe we spoke on the phone. I'm Annette Lecocq."

"Oh, Miz LeCock. Sure."

Annette cringed. It sounded even worse in person.

Valentina peered into the dimly lit restaurant. "Can you, uh . . ."

"Certainly, come this way," said Annette. She shot Antony a murderous glance and led Valentina to the nook, where her date and his wine were waiting.

Valentina looked stunning. She had confounded his expectations by wearing black, a silky wraparound dress that accentuated her hourglass figure. Her only nod to her name was a large heart-shaped pin of red rhinestones. There was something different about her hair, too, but he couldn't put his finger on what. Whatever it was, it was very flattering.

He stood up and extended a hand. She relaxed visibly.

"You are a sight for sore eyes," he said, aware that he sounded more like an old fuddy-duddy than ever.

"You look pretty nice yourself," she said, sliding into the nook next to him.

"Friend of yours?"

"Huh?"

Sy pointed to a barrel-chested man with curly hair and a rather loud shirt who was waving furiously across the room.

Valentina gave a little gasp. As she waved back, the man winked and turned to say something to his companion.

"Who's that?"

Valentina flashed Sy a sheepish smile. "Uh, nobody. He must think I'm someone else."

"How do you know Antony Farrell?"

Valentina looked over her shoulder toward the entrance to the restaurant, and Sy followed her gaze. Annette and Farrell were striding purposefully across the floor to their table.

"Oh! I, um, stopped by Shoreham's one day to learn more about wine."

Sy was about to inquire further when, to his surprise, Annette seated Farrell at the two-top just below the nook.

Farrell smiled benignly at them, and Sy felt a sudden chill over-take him, as the significance of Farrell's presence broke through his delight at finally being alone with Valentina.

Annette Lecocq had tipped him off. Obviously, their acquain-tance went well beyond the casual, despite Antony's protestations. Sy had never doubted what he had heard on the phone that day. Had this been the plan all along? Was this why Farrell had brought Sy to Parapluie? What was he hoping to do? Steal a sip when Sy went to the bathroom?

"Are you okay?" Valentina was asking.

"What? Oh, yes, I'm fine, thanks," he said. "Would you like me to order for you? There are some dishes that will be perfect com-plements to the wine."

"And this is it?" she said, pointing to the bottle.

"It is, indeed."

He held up the bottle so she could get a better look.

It was as if all the sound had been sucked out of the room. The sudden silence was so shocking that Sy set the bottle down. Farrell was looking at him with an unguardedly hungry expression on his cultured features.

But it wasn't just Farrell.

Sy felt the collective energy of many eyes on him. He peered more closely at the diners in the restaurant, and he realized they were all staring at him, in varying degrees of wonder and expecta-tion.

In an instant, the truth hit Sy full force.

Annette Lecocq and Antony Farrell had set him up.

A movement caught his eye, and his gaze traveled to a ginger-haired man with a goatee sitting across the room. On the table in front of him was a camera. A professional model, with a zoom lens. It was all making sense now. Farrell had delivered a publicity stunt to Annette Lecocq in return for a chance to taste wine that was not hers to promise. There was no privacy to be had here. He should take Valentina and leave. Now.

But wait, wasn't that . . . oh, Lord, it was. Richard Stark, Joseph Adler, and that must be Dennis Waggoner. This was getting worse by the minute. The room was full of wine eminences. Farrell wasn't the only one who would pressure him for a taste. If he refused, he would look utterly churlish. And what if Farrell had told them all they were there at Sy's invitation?

This was not how it was supposed to be, not at all.

"Sy?"

The touch of Valentina's hand on his brought him back.

"Have you tried your . . ." His voice trailed off as he found himself temporarily unable to think of the word "appetizer."

Sy was damned if he was going to let any of them have even the tiniest sip of his precious Lafite. He'd drain the whole goddamn bottle right in front of their eyes.

"Have you decided?" Tripp asked, hovering unobtrusively at the foot of the short staircase that led to the nook. At least the waiter was giving them some breathing room.

Sy looked down at the menu and named the first items his eyes lit on.

"We'll have the watercress soup and the venison."

"Very good," said Tripp, taking the menus from them. "When would you like to decant your wine?"

"Not just yet," said Sy, letting his eyes wander over the other diners, most of whom had returned to whispered conversations. If they'd come for a show, he'd make them wait.

"Can I bring you an aperitif in the meantime?"

Sy shook his head, but Valentina said, "Just some seltzer—I mean sparkling water, please?"

"Of course."

"Are you sure you're okay?" asked Valentina after Tripp left them.

"Fine. I'm just glad to finally be here with you. I notice you're not wearing pink and red."

Valentina absentmindedly touched her neck, as if to remind herself what she had on. "Oh, well, you know. Black is more sophisticated, and this is a special night."

"You should wear it more often. It suits you."

"You think?"

"I do. You look especially lovely tonight."

As Tripp served them more complimentary hors d'oeuvres, and then their soup, Sy struggled to make conversation with Valentina, but he found himself stumbling along like the old Fiat with the wonky clutch he'd driven in high school. Although he knew the assembled connoisseurs were there for the wine, he felt as if he were on a reality show. "First Date: Old Fart and Secretary Edition." He was keenly aware of the impression he and Valentina must be making. He knew if he didn't say something soon about the wine, they might choose to comment instead on his choice of company.

He wanted to explain to her why the other guests kept staring at them, that they were going to have an audience when the moment came to uncork the wine, that they were no longer anonymous. But she seemed more nervous tonight than he had expected her to be, and it was possible that in this case forewarned was not forearmed.

It suddenly occurred to him that Annette Lecocq was not the only possible source of the leak. Valentina had gone to Shoreham's. She had obviously spent enough time with Farrell for him to recognize her and kiss her hand. Could she have been the one to betray him? Is that what was making her so uncomfortable?

He didn't want to believe it. Surely, she had some sense of discretion. Or maybe she didn't. Why wouldn't she have gone bragging to everyone she knew about where she was going and why? Farrell must have probed the reasons for her interest in wine. Why wouldn't she have boasted the truth?

There were no safe subjects left. Anything he could think of to say to Valentina was suddenly and unexpectedly radioactive. There was only one thing left to do, and there was little point in putting it off any longer.

He looked around for Tripp, but the usually solicitous waiter was nowhere to be seen. He spied Annette, lurking near the kitchen door, and waved her over. The entire room followed her movement as she hurried over to his table. Sy was grateful that he hadn't had an aperitif. He needed every ounce of authority and composure he possessed as he announced in a steady, commanding voice, loud enough for all to hear:

"Please tell Tripp I'm ready to decant my wine."

THIRTY-ONE

ALL THE IMPORTANT GUESTS were seated, their appetizers served and their orders taken. Tripp glanced at his watch. Eight fifteen, and he still hadn't heard from Michael. The dour stares of the food press were stressing him out. He knew they were scrutinizing every word he spoke and every move he made, and as much as he relished being doted on by an audience, there was a big difference between dancing at a distance and waiting tables up close and personal.

He felt at odds with his surroundings, with himself, with Michael. There wasn't much he could do about the pressures of the restaurant, but at least he could put himself out of his misery where Michael was concerned. That might help him steady himself. One loose end raveled. And now that the thought had occurred to him, he couldn't stand it any longer.

He removed himself to the bottom of the stairs, was relieved to see he still had one bar on his cell phone, and dialed Michael's number.

"Heeeeeey! This is Michael's cell phone! Who's this?"

Tripp started. It was a male voice he didn't recognize. It certainly wasn't Michael's. He could hear loud music and whooping in the background.

"Tripp Macgregor. I'm Michael's—I'm a friend of Michael's. Is he there?"

"Yeah, yeah! We're just celebrating. Michael's gonna be a big Broadway star! He's doing *A Chorus Line!* Whoo-hoo!"

Tripp closed his eyes. "I know. What part is he playing?"

"Hey, Mikey! What part is it again?"

There was a rustle in the background, and then the man came back to the phone. "He's playing Greg. You wanna talk to him?"

"Who is this, anyway?" Tripp asked again.

"Jake. Michael's boyfriend. Who's this?"

Just then, Tripp looked up to see Annette heading down the

stairs, loaded for bear. He snapped his phone shut and shoved it into his pocket.

"Where the hell have you been? Sy Hampton wants to decant his wine. NOW!"

Annette returned to the nook with Tripp. Sy swallowed hard. This was it.

Tripp addressed Sy in an oddly flat voice. "Would you like me to uncork the wine or would you prefer to do the honors yourself?"

"I'd like to do it."

"Of course," said Tripp, handing Sy his corkscrew.

But Sy set the corkscrew on the table and took hold of the bottle instead. As he stood up, it seemed that the entire restaurant drew a collective breath.

"Look at this!"

He was facing Valentina, but he made sure his voice was loud enough for all to hear. Seizing the loose edge of the label that he had peeled back for Eric, Sy ripped it, roughly and dramatically, tearing it completely from the bottle. Behind him, magnified in the stillness, were tiny clicks of a camera at work. Valentina was looking uncertainly from Sy to Tripp.

"The etchings," declared Sy. "There they are. Do you see? Château Lafitte 1787. Th. J. for Thomas Jefferson. And the crescent. Pichard's secret code—his message to the future, his time capsule. This wine should be a treasure for the ages. And it's for you and me. And nobody else."

He spoke the last words with such force that there could be no doubt about his meaning. Now Sy picked up the corkscrew. The wine was like an old friend, and for a brief moment, he felt guilty about violating it. But all friends served a purpose, and this one was no exception.

With every eye in the room on him, Sy cut away his replacement capsule. Ever so gently, he pointed the corkscrew into the old cork, slowly coaxing it up. At first, the cork didn't want to leave its housing, but finally the top half came free and slid out soundlessly. Sy set it on the table. Tipping the bottle slightly, he edged the corkscrew back in to detach the remaining bit of cork. He got part of it out, but the rest dropped back into the bottle. Sy lifted the bottle to his nose and breathed. The luscious aroma of earth, chocolate, fruit, and smoke was dizzying. Sheer, unadulterated desire overtook him, and his entire body grew weak.

"Tripp, would you?" asked Sy, indicating the crystal rod and decanter.

"Of course," the waiter answered.

Sy handed him the bottle.

Grasp firmly and pour, Tripp told himself.

With the bottle in one hand, and the rod in the other, he began to transfer the deep reddish purple liquid into the decanter. As the blood red wine trickled down the length of crystal, he heard the voice again in his head:

"Jake. Michael's boyfriend. Who's this?"

Tripp closed his eyes for the briefest of seconds, as if he might blot out one sense by blocking another. He opened his eyes again and looked up, just as he felt his left hand, the one holding the rod, start to quiver.

A blinding flash came out of nowhere.

Startled, Tripp instinctively took a step backward as if retreating from an advancing foe. But he had forgotten that he was standing on the small flight of steps that led up to the nook. The floor seemed to give way, and he tried to steady himself, but the rod left his hands as if it had been snatched away by an unseen force, taking the carafe with it. He reached for the table, but as one foot caught round the other, it seemed to move away from him. Tripp felt the bottle leave his grasp as he slid and tumbled down the stairs, landing on his back with a resounding thud.

Annette watched in mute horror as the half-filled carafe flew toward the wall. It hit the hammered gold ridges with musical discord, raining down shards of shattered crystal. The decanted wine splattered her ivory silk dress like blood. She tried to catch Tripp, but the photographer's flashbulb went off again and again, like a strobe light. Between flashes, she saw the bottle itself take to the air as Tripp careened backward, away from her rescuing arms.

It seemed to Sy that the bottle took forever to fall. In fact, it seemed to pour itself out first, turning itself neck over end, protesting all the way. When it finally hit, it split into several large wedges of thick glass. The jagged neck rolled toward Tripp, who lay stunned and motionless on a bed of broken crystal. There was a moment of shocked silence before the world jump-started itself into real time again, and a tsunami of bodies rose up as one. Sy thought at first they were rushing to Tripp's aid, but as the flying forms converged on the ground, they kicked the broken glass aside and, abandoning any pretense of dignity or decorum, pushed and shoved one another like squealing pigs at a trough. As if from a great distance, Sy heard himself erupt in an impotent scream, while history pooled in garnet rivulets on the bamboo floor, and the freeloaders greedily lapped up what was never theirs.

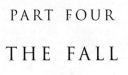

PART FOUR

THE FALL

THIRTY-TWO

ELISABETTA D'AMBROSIO AWOKE in a strange bed, with a pounding headache. As she rubbed her stinging eyes, she took in the shock of blond hair on the pillow next to her. She only barely recognized the face, which in sleep resembled a sweetly dreaming six-year-old, but slowly, she began to piece together the events of the night before.

It was the guy from Shoreham's . . . what was his name? Not Anthony. Antony. That strange British mutation of the name. And suddenly, it came flooding back, starting with Valentina's panicked phone call at five o'clock. Elisa lay back on the navy satin pillowcase and replayed the last fourteen hours in her head.

"You've gotta help me!" Valentina had wailed into the phone.

"We haven't pulled the switch since high school. I can't pretend to be you anymore, we're too different now!"

"Sure you can," insisted Valentina. "Use small words, wear the red heart pin I gave you—anything. I need you, Elisa. Just this once, and I promise we won't ever do it again."

"You can do it, Val, you've been studying so hard!"

"I *caaaaan't*," Valentina had sobbed hysterically. "I never should have said yes. This is all a big mistake. *Pleeeeeeease,* Elisa. I'll do any-thing!"

The truth was, from the moment Valentina first told her about the invitation, Elisa had felt an uncharacteristic surge of envy to-ward her sister. After everything Elisa had done to broaden her horizons, how could her disinterested twin be given a once-in-a-lifetime chance to taste wine dating from the French Revolution? When she'd joined Valentina for Vito's wine tasting, her suspicions were confirmed: pearls before swine. And the strangest part was that Valentina didn't seem to want to go. A certain sisterly "I told you so" coupled with her sense of entitlement had led Elisa to over-come her reluctance to answer Valentina's SOS.

So she had agreed, even though it meant blowing out her naturally wavy hair straight, the way Valentina wore it. Valentina also didn't have her coppery highlights, but there was only so far she was willing to go. Let him think she'd had her hair done specially. It also meant letting herself slip back into the accent she tried so hard to lose, with, she knew, only partial success. Every once in a while a "cawl" or a "poo-ul" would fly out of her mouth and she was powerless to stop it. A tiny part of her had enjoyed exaggerating her twin's Brooklynese at the restaurant, even though she was the only one present to appreciate the joke.

But almost immediately, she knew she'd gotten in too deep. First there was Antony—she'd have to ask Valentina what that little visit to Shoreham's was all about—but at least he'd told her what she needed to know before Sy grilled her. But what the hell was Vito doing there?! She had been completely unprepared for that! If Valentina knew, she hadn't mentioned it, unless Vito had been planning to surprise her all along. Then there were all the food and wine reporters. Elisa was pretty sure that Valentina wasn't expecting that little wrinkle. It was clear to Elisa that Sy had been completely blindsided, and Antony had confirmed as much later—yes, it was all coming back now—in the cab on the way to his place. It was a scheme he'd cooked up with the owner. She wanted publicity, and he wanted to taste the wine.

In the end, they'd both gotten what they'd wanted, although, Elisa mused, not exactly the way they'd planned. She was sure the broken bottle had eclipsed the food in the minds of the press, and she expected that Antony would have preferred to taste the wine from a glass, not off the floor.

For in the mad minutes that followed the crash, that was exactly what happened. Before she knew it, the floor was swarming with bodies. There they were, all those wine freaks in their fancy suits and ties on their hands and knees, desperate to lick the goddamn wine off the floor. Some quick-thinking person had slid the chunks of heavy glass out of the way, and after a moment, Elisa had thought, What the hell? I came to taste the wine, I may as well taste it! So she had fought her way through feet and elbows jabbing at her from every direction to join the writhing mass. The little bit Elisa managed to lap up was rich and plummy. It hadn't taken much to realize that had the bottle not broken, it would have been an extraordinary drink, a fact that Antony confirmed after his own frantic slurping.

She felt a flash of guilt about abandoning Sy. He'd screamed bloody murder—she'd never heard a man howl like that before—then he'd sat down, his face totally white, and blankly watched the chaos on the floor below him. That was the funny thing, she realized now.

Unless she was mistaken, the only person there who hadn't tasted the wine was Sy Hampton.

By the time she'd sat up, dazed, Sy was gone. The journalists had stumbled back to their tables, their ecstatic moans replaced by sheepish justifications, and she was sure she'd seen a man with a camera running out. Then Antony had invited her to join him for dinner—somewhere else. So she'd left on his arm—why not? And as they left, she saw the owner, that uppity woman, huddled around the fallen waiter with the rest of her waitstaff, while the busboys mopped up the mess.

They'd gotten a cab and gone to some other French restaurant whose name she couldn't recall, where Antony had ordered two very fancy bottles of wine. She'd drunk her share much too quickly, although she did recall saying yes when he invited her back to his place.

And here she was.

She had no desire to stay. The sex, what she could remember of it, had been okay, but they'd both been too drunk for it to be much more than sloppy groping. He was cute, but not *that* cute. And after the charm of his accent wore off, she'd begun to suspect that he was a bit of a jerk. Careful not to wake him, she slipped her dress and shoes back on, grabbed her coat and purse, and quietly let herself out.

She shivered in the early morning air and realized she had absolutely no idea where she was, though she knew she was still in Manhattan. She looked up at the street sign. She was on Lexington Avenue and Eightieth Street. Her head began to clear in the cool air, and she walked downtown toward the subway. What she really needed was a cup of coffee.

A deli loomed into view, and Elisa pushed the door open and went inside. It took a moment for the image and the words to register. When they did, she felt her stomach drop with a sickening lurch. Slowly, she turned around and went back outside, where the morning papers were lined up on a squat wire rack.

There, on the front page of the Sunday *Post*, was the headline "Butt-a-boom!" and a photo of her ass, draped in her clingy black wrap dress, high in the air as she licked the wine off the restaurant floor.

THIRTY-THREE

VALENTINA SLAMMED DOWN THE PHONE AGAIN. Where the hell was Elisa? Her cell was obviously off, because Valentina's calls kept going straight to voice mail. She tried to decide if she should be worried, but a horrible thought suddenly occurred to her.

Was it possible she'd gone home with Sy? Had Elisa slept with her boss, pretending to be her?

Well, that would be a neat sort of payback, wouldn't it, Valentina thought. She knew that Elisa hadn't been happy about the plan. The few times they'd pulled the switch on boyfriends in high school, it had caused more problems than it solved. Valentina wasn't surprised that Elisa had resisted the idea, but she didn't know what she'd have done if her sister hadn't come around in the end.

Her buzzer rang, loudly and repeatedly.

She hurried over to the intercom. "Who is it?"

"It's me. Let me in!"

Valentina immediately buzzed, then opened her front door and stuck her head out the door, holding her bathrobe closed around the neck. In a few seconds, Elisa appeared in the hall, and Valentina could see that she was still dressed up from the night before.

Elisa walked through the open door, past Valentina, threw off her coat, and sat down heavily on the rickety folding chair in the kitchenette.

"Omigod," breathed Valentina, taking in her sister's disheveled appearance. "Please don't tell me I slept with Sy."

Elisa massaged her forehead. "No. You slept with Antony Farrell."

"Who the hell is that?" Valentina asked, vaguely horrified.

"The guy from Shoreham's. Apparently, you went by there one day and had a little private chat with him about fancy wines?"

The British guy who looked like Prince William. Of course.

"How did that—"

Elisa held up her hand. "But wait, there's more. I think you wanna sit down."

As Valentina pulled the other kitchen chair up to the table, she saw that Elisa had a newspaper tucked under her arm. She suddenly knew that the evening had not gone well.

Elisa threw the paper onto the table. Valentina stared at the headline and the image.

"Holy shit, Elisa. That's your ass on the front page!"

"Nuh-uh," said Elisa, shaking her head. "That's *your* ass, honey. As far as everyone there last night knew, I was you."

"Oh. My. God," gasped Valentina. "But why were you—"

"Read."

Elisa flipped open the paper to page three, where the headline screamed in bold capitals: "TRIPP TRIPS, SPILLING HISTORIC BORDEAUX!" Then, underneath it, the subhead, which read "Winos Hit the Deck to Lap It Up."

There were photos, too. A grainy one of Sy pulling out the cork, and a clearer one of a waiter falling backward with a carafe in midair. The caption read, "Waiter Tripp Macgregor drops Jefferson Lafite." There was also a photo of Sy standing up, fist in the air, apparently screaming, and another close-up of Elisa's rear, with a pull quote to the side:

"Valentina D'Ambrosio, secretary to Sy Hampton and his date for the evening, threw caution to the winds and dived onto the floor with the assembled food and wine aficionados at Parapluie last night, when the aptly named Tripp Macgregor went flying down a flight of steps, sending half a million dollars' worth of vintage Bordeaux crashing to the ground."

Valentina folded the paper shut and shoved it away.

"You get the gist," said Elisa, pulling a cigarette from her bag and lighting it.

"Poor Sy." She stared at Elisa, tears forming in the corners of her eyes. "Do you have any idea how much he paid for that wine?"

"We all know. Half a million bucks. That's fucking crazy, Val."

"You think he deserved this?" Valentina asked, her voice rising.

"Calm down, I didn't say that. It's just, I mean—even if the bottle hadn't broken, would it really have been worth that much money?"

"You tell me. You tasted it."

Elisa's lip curled into a wistful smile. "It was pretty amazing. Although it had hints of bamboo, which it wasn't supposed to." Valentina stared at her, uncomprehending. "The floor was bamboo," Elisa added. "It was a joke."

"This isn't funny!" Valentina slammed her fist down on the paper. "He must be devastated! I should call him or—I don't know what to do!"

"Well, first let me tell you what you *did* do. Just calm down and let me fill you in."

Valentina only half listened. She couldn't stop thinking about Sy. If only she had been there, the real her, it all might have happened differently.

"Did you know he was going to be there?"

"What? Who?" Valentina focused again on Elisa, who was glaring at her impatiently.

"You're not listening, are you? Did Vito tell you he was going to be there?"

"Vito?!" Valentina exclaimed. "What are you talking about?"

"He was there, Val. He waved at me!"

"What the hell was Vito doing there?" It was all too unbelievable.

Elisa, frustrated, threw up her hands. "That's what I'm asking you! And, for the record, he was definitely on a date with one of the reporters. Male."

On second thought, it was entirely believable.

"Did he taste the wine?" Valentina asked.

"Yeah." Elisa nodded. "You know, I think the only person who didn't was Sy. Poor guy. I didn't spend much time with him, but he seemed decent."

"What happened to him, after . . . you know, after."

Elisa shrugged. "I dunno. He erupted like a volcano, and then he looked like he was in shock. When I got up from the floor, he was gone. That's when Antony grabbed my arm and said, 'Let's get some dinner.' So I went with him, and one thing led to another."

"You didn't tell him who you really were, did you?"

Elisa considered this. "I don't think so," she said finally. "But I was so drunk, maybe I did. No, wait a minute, I seem to remember him calling out something about ambrosia of love or some bullshit, so he must have still thought I was you."

"Great. Do I have to, like, call him or something?"

"Are you kidding? He set you up—you and Sy. He's an asshole. And besides, I think that hoity-toity restaurant owner has a thing for him. She looked fit to be tied when we left."

"Miz LeCock?"

"Yeah, her. What a name."

"If the shoe fits . . ."

The phone rang and they both jumped.

"Don't answer it!" Elisa put out a cautioning hand. "It might be the press."

The answering machine clicked on and registered a hang-up. After that, the phone rang about every two minutes. The fifth time, it was Trish, who left a message asking if Valentina had seen the *Post* and what the hell happened? But Valentina didn't want to talk to anyone. She didn't even want to talk to Elisa anymore.

All she wanted was to dial back the clock so she could do it over again and go to Parapluie with Sy like she had promised. She should never have sent Elisa in her place. It was all her fault.

Because she knew that while her being there might not have kept that poor waiter from tripping and dropping the wine, she would never in a million years have thrown herself on the floor to drink it like Elisa had. She never cared about the wine. But she did care about Sy, she realized now. And there was no way she would ever have skulked off with that sleazeball, Antony Farrell. She'd have stayed and taken care of Sy. But as far as he knew, she had abandoned him, just like everyone else.

She could only imagine what he must think of her now.

THIRTY-FOUR

IT WAS HIS WORST NIGHTMARE come true. Actually, it was worse than anything he could ever have imagined.

For his whole life, Tripp had always secretly feared that names were a window into destiny. Out of this fear, his mantra was born: "God grant me agility and grace, and the ability to move fluidly through time and space." Obviously, he hadn't been specific enough. He should have prayed, "God grant me agility and grace, and don't let me wipe out on my ass or my face." Then again, he'd been so thrown by his conversation with Michael's "boyfriend" that he hadn't remembered his mantra at all before he served the wine. He wasn't sure it would have occurred to him in any case. He had never used it for anything other than performing, although if his mind had been clear at the time, he just might have thought to do it for this.

But he hadn't, the inevitable had occurred, and he couldn't remember ever being in so much pain, both physical and psychic. He'd been cut up pretty badly by the crystal. There were scores of scratches of varying depths all over him. The force with which he'd hit the floor had turned the crystal shards into tiny bayonets. They'd driven right through his shirtsleeves, although the brocade vest had offered a little more protection to his chest. His back and legs ached so much from his roll down the steps, he could barely move. All he could do was lie in bed, staring at the ceiling, reliving the disastrous moment over and over again. It was a torture to do it, but it felt even worse not to.

He blamed his parents, of course. If only they had named him William Macgregor III. But no, they figured he'd just be called Trip anyway, for being the triple William, so they'd saved the bus fare and made it his given name, adding the extra p to make it seem more legitimate. Not that the extra p had bought him much. Whenever he gave his name, other kids heard "Trip" and the teasing would begin. He'd experimented with introducing himself as

"Tripp with a double *p*," but that had led to ribbing of a different order. Of course, this was all in childhood. Adults rarely commented. Still, he couldn't begrudge the *Post* for making a meal out of it. It was a gift. The headline that wrote itself. Even in his despair, Tripp was forced to admit that if he'd been in the editor's position, he'd probably have done the same thing.

The funny thing was, he'd never seriously considered changing his name. By the time he hit high school, there were plenty of kids with names that were far weirder, like Brick and Boat. And if you took the meaning out of it, Tripp was a jaunty, lively, happy-go-lucky sort of name. It sounded like he had hours of leisure time to relax on his yacht and sip mint juleps, his favorite drink. Despite the ever-lurking danger of living down to his name, he'd resigned himself to a love-hate relationship with it.

And now he'd ruined . . . well, just about everything he could think of. He'd ruined his good name (or rather, his good name had ruined him), he'd ruined the restaurant's chances, he'd taken out both his dancing career and his food service career in one slip—who would ever hire the most notoriously disaster-prone person in history? And of course, he'd completely destroyed Sy Hampton's life.

Lying on the floor of Parapluie, stunned and bleeding, Tripp had been aware of the bustle of movement all around him. But from his vantage point, the only thing he could see and hear clearly was Sy Hampton standing in the nook, screaming his head off. Tripp couldn't begin to imagine what Hampton must have been feeling in that moment. He couldn't get much beyond what he was feeling himself—guilt and mortification so debilitating, he feared he'd never leave his apartment again.

He had failed spectacularly and publicly at the most delicate task he had ever been entrusted with. Nobody would ever expect anything from him again. If he'd injured himself in performance, torn a ligament or something, he'd have been welcomed back to the world once he was healed. But he had caused damage. He was dangerous to himself and others, not to mention defenseless inanimate objects.

He was clumsy.

He didn't want to talk to anyone. His friend Margaret, she of the forty-eight hours' depression dispensation for Broadway gigs lost, had left a message helpfully suggesting that this could be expanded to a full week, possibly two, to incorporate the addition of total career ruination. His parents had called several times, but they were the last people he wanted to talk to.

Michael had not been heard from, but that was hardly a surprise.

In hindsight, there were signs he should have recognized, like Michael's protestations that he was too tired to meet after work. If he even had been working. How had they managed that one Saturday night? Maybe Jake had been away. Maybe they had an open relationship, and Jake knew all about Tripp.

Or maybe it was just Michael's show business survival mechanism. He was simply befriending the competition. Screwing the competition was more like it. And now that Tripp hadn't gotten the job and Michael had, he was no longer competition, and therefore no longer necessary.

As Tripp lay in his bed, he tried to reconstruct the moment before he had dropped the bottle. What had been going through his mind? He had a vague idea, but it was too terrible to give voice to, even within the confines of his own head. Yet, now that he had opened it a crack, he couldn't shut the door to his thoughts.

Just at the moment the photographer's flash went off, Tripp had been filled with fury. Anger so deep and all-consuming that his whole body had begun to shake. He was furious that he hadn't gotten cast in *A Chorus Line.* He was furious that Michael had lied to him. He was furious that Annette had set him and Sy Hampton up by packing the place with reporters. And he was deeply furious and resentful that he was forced to be a latter-day servant, when by virtue of his upbringing, he should have been the one being served.

Finally, the question that he'd been avoiding over the last forty-eight hours burst through in all its awful significance.

Could he have dropped the bottle—even subconsciously—on purpose?

THIRTY-FIVE

THE *NEW YORK TIMES*, THE *NEW YORK POST*, the magazine websites, and, of course, the blogs had all had a field day with the debacle.

But the worst, the absolute worst—for which Annette was totally unprepared—was YouTube.

One of the bloggers had recorded the critical moment and posted the brief clip for eternal replay. Not that Annette needed to see it on her computer screen to recall the moment in all its horror. Every scream, every flying shard of glass, every spatter of wine would be ingrained in her memory forever. She had her own video running on an infinite loop in her mind's eye. But now everyone else did, too, and Parapluie would forever and inescapably be known as That Restaurant Where the Waiter Dropped the Wine.

She put her head in her hands and pulled at her short blond hair until her scalp hurt. She was exhausted—she'd hardly slept since Saturday—and disaster or not, she still had a business to run. Or, more accurately, to save. The event had certainly put Parapluie on the map, but in the worst possible way. She forced herself to look again at the newspapers on her desk. She picked up the *Post*. Their headline was utterly predictable, going for the cheap joke off Tripp's name. If she weren't so incensed, she'd feel sorry for him. The *Times*—well, she had to give them some credit for putting her in the headline, with "Unexpected Showers at Parapluie." Unfortunately, that was about the extent of Gene Rand's mention of the restaurant. He'd dismissed it with one sentence: "The food was excellent, although it was eclipsed by the central event of the serving, and the dropping, of the most expensive bottle of wine in the world."

And that was the basic tenor of all the articles. Some hadn't bothered to mention the food at all. There was no opportunity— no reason—for any of them to give the restaurant a proper review. Not when there was such a juicy story to report, complete with visuals.

She'd given the media a hook, all right. And hung herself on it.

She paced around her overflowing office. Thank goodness the restaurant was closed on Mondays. Somehow she had gotten through Sunday without falling apart. She supposed there were greater disasters in the annals of food service. MaryLou Sampson had once told her of a place in Atlanta that had a grease fire on its first night and burned to the ground. But it hadn't done so in front of every important food and wine writer in the city. The smoldering wreck hadn't been preserved for posterity on YouTube.

Goddamn Antony Farrell! She realized now that he had everything to gain and nothing to lose from this little scheme. There had been risks involved for her, which she hadn't fully understood. But Farrell had, the shifty bastard. The evening had cost him nothing. She had agreed in advance to comp the bloggers, who were not working on expense accounts, but once the bottle broke, she had been forced to throw all kinds of extras at the journalists to get them to focus on the food. She had acted in desperation, and it hadn't even worked. She couldn't bear to think about how much money she'd lost.

The most galling thing of all was that Farrell had somehow managed to keep his name out of the papers. It was appalling that his greed, which had caused such a mess, had not been punished, but rewarded. He'd fled with that floozy of Hampton's and gone—she could only imagine where—but she was sure the final destination had been his bedroom. Tripp was cut up and injured, not to mention fired, her business was ruined, Sy Hampton . . . well, she had no idea what this had done to him. And Farrell? He'd gotten laid for his trouble.

A tiny voice reminded her that she'd always known ambushing Hampton was a bad idea. She'd tried so hard to justify it as survival of the fittest, but now that the worst had happened, there was no getting around it. It was a disaster, but she had brought it on herself. The one possibility that had never occurred to her was that Tripp might lose his composure, but she realized now that she had ambushed him as well. The pressure of decanting that wine in a room full of reporters—well, she probably should have given him more advance notice. But he was a performer. He was supposed to be able to deliver, regardless of nerves.

In a burst of teary frustration, she kicked her filing cabinet. She'd worn her sneakers just for the purpose. It felt so good, she kicked it again and again.

Various banalities came to mind. There's no such thing as bad publicity. When life gives you lemons, make lemonade. Everything happens for a reason.

Fine, she thought as she sat down to massage her right foot. She would put every ounce of culinary wisdom she had to use, and figure out how to juice lemonade out of this horrible publicity that had happened for some reason of which she was not yet aware.

And once she'd done that, she'd find a way to get even with Antony Farrell.

THIRTY-SIX

THE MONDAY MORNING SUNRISE over New York Harbor was magnificent, even more beautiful than the one on Sunday, which he'd watched over the East River from Carl Schurz Park. The colors reminded him of Pippa's paintings, and one in particular. It was called Birth of the Goddess, and it occurred to him now that the sunrise must have been her inspiration. The striations, the complementary warmth and coolness of the colors, they were all there, both in her painting and in the actual experience. As the sky lightened, Sy watched the Staten Island Ferry pull into Whitehall Terminal, and he hoisted himself up from the bench where he was sitting and shuffled inside.

He had not been home since the fall of the wine. The first hours afterward were a blur. At some point, he had found himself on the number 4 train, heading north toward the Bronx. He dimly remembered the subway clerk explaining to him that the MTA had stopped using tokens in 2003, and she sold him a MetroCard instead. Once on the subway, he'd let his eyes glaze over the map. He couldn't recall the last time he'd ridden the subway. What was the V train? And what had happened to the 9? He was glad at least that it still ran every hour of the day and night, even in this economy. He got off at the last Manhattan stop, 125th Street, and began walking back downtown. But he wasn't heading for his house. He wasn't heading anywhere, he just needed to walk. And as he walked, he noticed things, the kinds of things he never bothered to notice. Peeling paint on the base of a streetlamp, flies swarming around piles of overstuffed garbage bags, a brownstone with a Venetian stone balcony, a bright blue door. He forced himself to focus on what was around him, because he couldn't bear to acknowledge what was going on inside.

So he walked and walked, south and east, until he reached the Roosevelt Island Tram Plaza at Fifty-ninth and Second. He hiked up the stairs, swiped his MetroCard, and squeezed onto the crowded gondola seconds before the doors shut. The tram, loud and packed with revelers, began to glide through the air. Sy found himself sandwiched between two bulky college-age Manhattanites who seemed unable to get over the twinkling skyline view to the south. He barely noticed it himself, and when he did glance up, the lights had an odd halo that made his forehead throb. He'd called Bill on his cell and, in a voice that didn't sound like what he remembered his own sounding like, told his driver he would be walking.

And he had kept walking when he disembarked from the tram, eschewing the twenty-five-cent red bus that rounded the island. He trudged north, past the sterile blankness of the stores and apartment complexes, all the way to the lighthouse, and although he longed to rest, he would not allow himself that tiny comfort. Instead, he doubled back downtown toward the tram station.

Back in Manhattan after another, even louder, more raucous, and more uncomfortable tram ride, he set out north again up Second Avenue until he reached Eighty-sixth Street, where he veered east toward Carl Schurz Park. When his fatigue could no longer be ignored, he allowed himself to sit on a bench, and after a few fitful hours of upright sleep, the glorious late September sunrise awoke him, and he resumed his wanderings.

He made the long horizontal hike west, disappearing into the thickets of Central Park, where he trailed the Park Drive until he emerged at the top of Seventh Avenue. He continued downtown past Carnegie Hall, through the madness of Times Square into Chelsea, where he bought a cup of coffee and a cruller from a cart on the corner of Twenty-third Street and Seventh Avenue. He plunged farther downtown into the maze of Greenwich Village, where the breakdown of order from the grid of uptown Manhattan into the chaos of overlapping streets pleased him. He paused for a moment on the perennially unhelpful corner of West Fourth and West Tenth Streets. The improbability of that juncture felt just as incongruous as the crossroads at which he found himself personally, and he suddenly found himself laughing uncontrollably. People walking by picked up their pace, those with children hugged them close and crossed the street to avoid him. Sy knew he was making a spectacle of himself, and he could not have cared less. The release of violent sounds from his body was overwhelmingly satisfying, and when inevitably his laughter gave way to a torrent of deep, soul-sucking sobs, those were just as welcome.

Gradually, he pulled himself together and continued his trek through the winding streets of Soho, Tribeca, and the Financial District. He'd always loved the vertiginous feeling he got looking up from the narrow streets to the tops of the tall buildings, the oldest in the city, which seemed like they could topple at any moment from the weight of the money exchanged within their hallowed halls. At night, the Financial District emptied out, and then he felt truly simpatico, a ghost wandering among the spectral shadows of commerce.

He'd allowed himself to sleep lying down on a bench in Battery Park, and at dawn he stumbled through the glass-fronted Whitehall Terminal, drawn in by the giant purple letters advertising the ferry. He used the bathroom and sat for a while on one of the stone benches listening to a folk guitarist. As the morning advanced, the terminal filled with tourists, and he found himself following a mass of them onto the nine o'clock ferry. He was surprised to discover it was free. The last time he'd taken it, it had cost twenty-five cents for a round-trip—a cheap and convenient way to spend time alone with a girl when you had roommates. He stood at the stern, watching the gulls wheel over the boat's wake, and found comfort in the idea of leaving Manhattan behind. It was Monday. Claudine would come in and find the house empty, his bed not slept in. Would she worry? Perhaps. Warren Sage, his partner, would come to the office and find his door shut. Would he notice? Perhaps. Marianne would call him on Wednesday to warn him not to be late picking up Eric, but he wouldn't answer. Would she care? Definitely not.

And Valentina?

She had been revealed in all her coarse, uncouth, indiscreet splendor. Sy could understand Stark, Adler, and Antony Farrell, that fucking bastard, diving to the floor to taste the Lafite. But Valentina—that had shocked him.

Now he knew the truth about her. He had never had grand expectations, but how could he have been so far off? She had thrown herself on the floor only because everyone else had. At least they cared about the wine. She was shallow, mindless, a lemming shamelessly writhing on the ground with her ass in the air for no reason that meant anything to her. She had betrayed him, but worse, she had betrayed herself. It was as if, in that moment, someone had switched on a spotlight, and he saw her for what she was.

He had seen himself, too. And he had fled.

I am the wandering Jew, he thought now, as he walked upstairs to the outside deck and paced past the orange benches, his hand brushing the cold, damp railing. Cursed to walk aimlessly forever for the sins I have committed: the sins of lust and excess, ego and hubris.

I am no longer myself.

THIRTY-SEVEN

As THE CLOCK TICKED SLOWLY on toward nine, Valentina still hadn't made up her mind whether or not she was going to work. She felt paralyzed—unable to commit either way. She couldn't bring herself to finish getting dressed and walk to the subway, nor could she manage to pick up the phone and call to say she wouldn't be coming in. By eleven o'clock, she was still pacing her bedroom in her bra and underwear, thoroughly undecided about what to do, when the phone rang.

This time, when she heard Trish's throaty rasp on the answering machine, she snatched up the receiver.

"Where the hell have you been?" screeched Trish. "You know your ass is all over the Internet?"

"What?!" Valentina froze. "You mean the paper!"

"No, honey, the Internet. Some bozo filmed it, and it's on YouTube! The whole thing! That waiter falling, the bottle breaking, and all the people on the floor trying to drink the wine. With a nice close-up of your butt, wiggling back and forth. Good thing you go to the gym, that's all I gotta say. My ass wouldn't look half as good."

Valentina sat down heavily on her bed. "It isn't funny," she sighed. "And it isn't my ass."

"What are you talking about?"

"It's Elisa's ass. I made her go instead of me."

"You—what?!" Trish choked. "You've gotta be kidding me! That wasn't you?"

"Nope."

"It was Elisa?!"

"Don't you remember when we used to do this in high school? At the last minute, I just couldn't go through with it. Nothing I put on looked right with my hair. Dawn gave me a really fancy do, but it felt like I was trying to be someone else. And then I realized that I couldn't just be myself, not at some fancy restaurant with that crazy bottle of wine, and not really sure why I was going in the first place. Everything about it was just *wrong*."

"After all that time Vito spent with you?" said Trish in disbelief. "How are you gonna explain why you didn't go?"

"He was there," Valentina said wearily.

"What do you mean, he was there?" Trish paused, confused. "Who was where?"

"Vito was at the restaurant on Saturday night. Elisa saw him. I'm sorry, Trish, I'm not pretending about Vito anymore—he was on a date with another guy. One of the wine reporters."

Trish was quiet for a moment.

"Trish?" Valentina asked. "Are you mad at me?"

"No. Yes. I don't know."

"I'm sorry about Vito. But I'm not gonna lie about it. He was with another—"

"I heard you. Are you gonna tell Sy it wasn't you?"

"I don't know which is worse! For him to think that I sent my sister because I didn't want to go on a date with him, or to think that I left him standing there screaming while I licked the stupid wine off the floor."

"You should never have said yes if you weren't gonna go through with it."

"But I didn't know until that night," protested Valentina. "I really was gonna do it, I swear! Otherwise I wouldn't have spent all that time drinking wine with you and Vito. I don't even like wine. I hate the fucking stuff, if you wanna know the truth. I hate it!"

She sobbed into the receiver for a full minute, and she could hear Trish choke as she pulled too deeply on her cigarette.

"I don't know if I can go to work today," sniffed Valentina as her sobs subsided. "I mean, he'll be there, and what am I gonna say?"

"Well, it's eleven o'clock already. Are you gonna quit?"

Strangely, the thought hadn't crossed Valentina's mind, but of course that was exactly what she should do. She should call up Human Resources and tell them she was finished. That way she'd never have to see Sy Hampton again.

Could she really do that? Talk about chickening out. Then again, what would she have done if the evening had gone off as planned?

In her hysteria on the phone trying to convince Elisa to go, she hadn't bothered to think it through. What if Sy and Elisa had actually drunk the wine together? Sy would have had memories of an experience they had shared, and Valentina would have had nothing more to go on than whatever details Elisa remembered to tell her. For Sy, their relationship would have advanced a step, but not for her. At some point, she'd have had to come clean. She didn't know what to do. But she knew she needed more time before she faced Sy.

"No, I'm not quitting," she said finally. "Not yet, anyway. I'll call in sick today. Maybe tomorrow, too. Give it a couple of days. Then I'll go in and tell him it wasn't me at the restaurant. What do you think?"

Trish was quiet again, but this time, Valentina didn't wait for her to respond.

"I'll talk to you later," she said. And before Trish could advise her further, she clicked the receiver and immediately dialed Miss Banks's extension.

"Hello, Sy Hampton's office. This is Miss Banks speaking."

"It's Valentina."

"Oooooh, Miss Thing," drawled Miss Banks, in a decidedly un–Miss Banks–like fashion. "I didn't think we'd be hearing from you today!"

Valentina took a deep breath, determined not to take to the bait. "Will you please tell Mr. Hampton I'm sick and I'm not coming in today?"

"I can't. He's not here."

"He's not?"

"No. And I don't believe he's called. Then again, his secretary isn't here to take the message."

"Well, if he does happen to call, will you tell him?"

"I suppose," said Miss Banks.

Valentina hung up the phone, troubled. For all that she had been wrestling with whether to show her face in the office, it had never occurred to her that Sy himself wouldn't come in. But now she realized that he probably didn't want to face her. Or Miss Banks—or anyone, for that matter.

What had Sy done after he'd left he restaurant? Where had he gone? Where was he now? Valentina chewed on her red pinky nail as she paced her kitchen. She hoped he was okay, but the more she thought about it, the more she realized he couldn't possibly be.

THIRTY-EIGHT

HAL'S DISCOUNT WINES & LIQUOR on Stuyvesant Place didn't open until noon, so Sy climbed onto the S74 bus toward Tottenville. He decided, latter-day wandering Jew that he was, that the bus's journey could stand for his own, so he moved to the back and sat down. It was almost empty. He didn't really know where he was going, and he didn't care. He was through making plans. He now had a personal appreciation of what happened to the best laid of them.

He tried to interest himself in his surroundings and maintain his concentration on all things external, but it was becoming increasingly difficult to keep his roiling thoughts at bay. He could sense them massing behind a dam in his brain, and he began counting red cars on the road. Anything to keep the flood from breaking through. Two Hasidic boys sat down next to him and began to talk, though it sounded more like they were chanting prayer. Eventually, Sy grew restless and jumped off the bus at Richmond Road and St. Patrick's Place. He crossed the busy thoroughfare, feeling somewhat daredevilish as cars honked their disapproval at his obliviousness, and started up the hill. A sign pointed the way to the Visitor's Center of Historic Richmond Town, but upon closer inspection, it appeared that the picturesque enclave was closed on Mondays. He sat down heavily on the stone steps and stared at a small blue frame house across the way.

He would experiment. He would let one small thought creep through.

If only he had drunk the wine alone that night in his dining room.

The pain was so intense and physical that he wanted to scream again. He jammed his fist into his mouth and writhed on the steps, kicking and thrashing, his Gucci loafers scuffing against the stone. He bit his knuckles so hard that they began to bleed. Unable to stand it a moment longer, he hurled himself to his feet and ran down the steps.

What had kept him from drinking the wine that night? The lack of ceremony, the fear that it wasn't enough of an occasion, the absence of witnesses? He had traded in a private moment of ecstasy for a sideshow, a bastardized christening, a bacchanal. Tears stung his cheeks, as his feet pounded down the center of a wide, quiet street lined with large houses. He doubled back and ran down the hill to Richmond Road, where another bus, headed back to St. George and the ferry, was pulling up. He raced to the doors and wiped his brow, hoping the driver would think he was crying from his efforts to catch the bus.

He swiped his MetroCard, but it was empty. He reached into his pocket and found he was out of change.

"Excuse me," he said, his voice still sounding foreign to him. "Does anybody have change?"

This bus was more crowded, and the other passengers glanced away from him with varying expressions of distaste. It was only then that he realized what he must look like, his new charcoal suit wrinkled, his pink tie stained, his face unshaven.

He cleared his throat. "Does anyone?"

The bus driver was shaking his head and pointing toward the door when a light-skinned black teenager in a baggy satin jacket called out, "Yeah, man. Over here."

Sy walked down the aisle to him. As Sy reached out to trade his bills for the coins, the kid purred, "Cool watch."

Sy looked down at his failed good-luck charm, his Vacheron Constantin Great Explorers watch, and suddenly he felt sickened by the wastefulness of owning such a toy. It was a symbol of the uselessness of his life, the great, checkbook-crashing pointlessness of his wealth. He didn't deserve any of it. What was the son of a hardware store owner and a teacher doing with a $70,000 watch?

He slipped the watch off his wrist and threw it in the kid's lap.

"Take it," he said, and returned to the front of the bus to pay his fare.

"Shit, man—that shit's real!" he heard the kid exclaim behind him.

Of course it is, Sy thought wryly. And it was insured. If Sy ever needed that money, he could always report it lost or stolen.

He should have insured the wine.

Squeezing his forehead as tightly as he could stand against this unguarded and unwelcome thought, he reminded himself that even if the evening had gone off as planned, on this day, Monday the twenty-seventh, the wine would still be gone. It was the experience he had lost, and that could not have been insured in any case.

When the bus eventually pulled up again across from Hal's Discount Wines & Liquor, Sy got off. Even if the bottle had not broken, dinner wouldn't have taken much longer than his impromptu tour of Staten Island. Moments passed, life went on. Perhaps he could convince himself that he *had* drunk the wine. He stood on Bay Street as the bus rumbled past him, and closed his eyes. He tried to imagine what the wine had tasted like. He was enough of an expert that he could almost reconstruct it.

A glorious burst of red fruit, soft tannins, complex layers of cedar, spice, chocolate, and tobacco that lingered and changed and deepened from nose to finish. For he knew, without a doubt, that the wine was viable. He knew from the brief bouquet he'd inhaled that it had been, as advertised, ambrosial. He knew, too, from the delirious, ecstatic smiles of the thieves on the floor.

So would he be feeling any better today if the wine had been a dud?

It was a useless question, just like the others. An expired wine would have denied him the experience just the same. One thing was clear to him now: he was never meant to drink the Lafite. He didn't deserve it. Pippa had understood, and she had warned him. But even she couldn't have known that the bottle had been damned from the start. Antony Farrell had cursed it with his loaded wish, not just for the one happiness Sy longed for, but worse, every happiness. In possession of the most exciting wine in the world, he had been blinded by hubris and had denied other palates at least as deserving as his. He had stolen it—with Farrell's help—from Buffy Bagnold (whether she was any more worthy was immaterial), and he had not rewarded his partner in crime. He had not dealt fairly. He had manipulated Fate, and now he was paying the price.

He opened his eyes and crossed the street, barely bothering to look, and entered Hal's Discount Wines & Liquor, where a beefy black man was behind the counter.

"What's the cheapest red wine you have?"

The black guy, whose name tag said Ara, cocked his head at Sy. Sy knew what he was thinking—that he was a wino, down on his luck. A bum looking for the fastest way to get drunk. Let him think that. That wasn't it at all.

"I got a table wine from Chile that's on sale for $3.99."

Sy nodded. "Is that the cheapest? I want the absolute cheapest. I don't care what it tastes like."

"That's my rock bottom." Ara gave a knowing snort. "And believe me, it's no Lafite."

A bolt of horror shot through Sy's heart. Ara knew who he was. But before he could say anything, Ara went on.

"Did you read about that guy who broke the wine? That was one epic fail!"

Sy nodded weakly and turned his watering eyes to the floor. It was only a matter of minutes before Ara recognized him. If he'd seen the story, he'd seen the photos.

He handed over five dollars, took his change, and left in what he felt sure was the nick of time. Safely on the sidewalk, he chanced a look back to see if the light bulb had gone on yet, but Ara had turned away and was straightening some bottles on the counter.

Sy walked slowly back to the St. George Ferry Terminal. The fatigue was beginning to hinder his ability to move. This time, he sank onto a green bench inside the ferry and zoned out to snatches of meaningless cell phone conversations and the thrum of the engine underneath. Back in Manhattan, he hailed the first cab he saw.

As soon as Claudine heard his key in the lock, she yanked the door open. Sy, half asleep, propped himself against the door frame.

"Mr. Hampton! My God! Where have you been? I've been worried sick about you! I read about the—"

He held up his hand and shook his head wearily, though even in his fog, he was touched by her concern.

"And your bed wasn't slept in. You look awful! You need a hot bath."

"I am not taking any phone calls, and I am not receiving any visitors," he said hoarsely. "I do not want to be bothered under any circumstances."

"But, Mr. Hampton—"

"Under any circumstances," he said again, as firmly as he could manage.

"Have you eaten anything? Come back to the kitchen and have some soup."

Sy shook his head again and went upstairs to his study, locking the door behind him. He used the small bathroom, which felt luxurious after two days on the street.

Then he took a corkscrew from the wet bar and tried to peel the foil from the top of his cheap table wine, but it wouldn't come off. He started to laugh, a thin, maniacal, defeated cackle. Of course. It was so cheap, it didn't even have a capsule or a cork. It had a screw top, like a bottle of soda. He flung the corkscrew aside and twisted open the bottle.

He poured the wine into a glass and began the ritual. He held it up to the light to determine the color—a thin cranberryish red— tilted it to see if the wine even had legs, and the streams of liquid disappeared almost as soon as they formed. He stuck his nose in the glass. It was not promising.

Then he took a gulp of the wine. Acidic, slightly sour, a bit chemical in the finish. But this was his world now. He would never again spend substantial amounts of money on a bottle of wine. He was starting at the bottom of his new universe. It was important to reestablish the boundaries. Although even as he sipped the cheap wine, he knew he could never survive on this kind of crap. He would work his way back up—but with a limit. No more thousand-dollar bottles of Bordeaux or Burgundy, he would drink wine the way most people did. He was done being a snob. He would turn his attention to the wines that he had snubbed on principle: Italian wines, Spanish wines, better quality South American wines, and North American wines, from Sonoma, Paso Robles, Long Island, the Finger Lakes.

He had learned his lesson. He would never again put all his dreams in one bottle. He'd never again let his heart be broken like that.

The wine from Hal's got a bit more drinkable as he went on. By the third glass, his mind and his mouth were so numb that he was ready to play the game he had devised.

Sy closed his eyes and pretended that this was his priceless Lafite. First, he imagined that it had spoiled, and this was what it tasted like: weak, expired, bitter. Then he repeated the tasting ritual from the beginning and pretended it was the ambrosial nectar of the vine he had staked his life on. He could almost convince himself that it was. It wasn't difficult, not at all. Wine was completely subjective. It was whatever he decided. A bottle of $3.99 plonk could—if he chose to let it—bring him the same pleasure as a bottle of $510,000 Château Lafite 1787. And the new Sy Hampton would be finding his pleasures in very different places from now on.

The Moroccan red walls began to swim before his eyes. He staggered over to the desk and unplugged the phone. Then he threw himself backward onto the chesterfield, drained the bottle, and fell into a deep sleep.

THIRTY-NINE

TRIPP WAS HAVING THE *CHORUS LINE* dream again. Only this time, as he stood in the pit waving his baton, the dancers were lined up across the stage doing the bottle dance from *Fiddler on the Roof*. As the dancers squatted down and jumped up Cossack-style, the bottles fell from their hats, one by one, like a wave down the line. But they didn't break. Instead, they rolled into the pit, where they flew toward Tripp, pelting him like angry rocks. Then Thomas Jefferson broke through the line, singing "The Music and the Mirror." Tripp knew it was Jefferson, because the man wore a powdered wig and Revolutionary waistcoat, but he had Sy Hampton's face. Although the correct words were somehow issuing from the man's mouth as he pirouetted about the stage singing, his face was frozen in an elongated, horrified scream, like the Munch painting. As Tripp pondered this impossibility in his sleep, he realized that the words were actually coming from his own mouth. It was he who was singing, as he conducted Jefferson/Hampton/Cassie, yearning from the deepest reservoirs of his soul to be allowed to dance again.

The house phone woke him up with a start. Tripp barely knew what day it was, let alone what time. He pulled himself out of bed, wincing as his back readjusted itself, and forced himself to answer the intercom on the off chance—though he knew it was pretty far off—that it was Michael.

"It's Shoshana. I brought you something."

He liked Shoshana well enough, certainly more than Annette did, but he wasn't sure he could stomach her relentless cheeriness in his current state of mind. On the other hand, she had been at the restaurant that night. She knew he'd been set up. She'd seen the accident. In fact, she might even be able to confirm that it was an accident, since more and more he'd been tormenting himself with the idea that his subconscious had sabotaged him.

"Come up," Tripp said, pressing the intercom button. He knew he looked like shit, but he didn't care. Shoshana had seen him thoroughly humiliated. That was the one positive thing about his situation. Things couldn't get much worse.

"You look awful," said Shoshana as he opened the door to let her in. "I've been worried about you. I brought you chicken soup with ginger. It's good for everything that ails you."

"Thanks. I'm really touched."

"I'm a Jewish mother waiting to happen." She smiled, gently patting his cheek.

He took the soup into the kitchen, and when he returned, she was sitting in Jordan's wicker chair. Before he could say anything, she spoke.

"This is a beautiful chair. It feels like a throne," she said expansively. "What? You're staring at me."

"It's just that . . . well, my partner, Jordan. I always thought of it as his chair. He died four years ago. Nobody but me has sat in it since then, so it just sort of took me by surprise, that's all."

Shoshana jumped to her feet. "I'm so sorry!"

"No, no, sit," he assured her. She hesitated. "I mean it. Sit. The chair looks good on you."

She sat down again, tentatively. "I love the pattern. It's very 1950s beach house."

"That's exactly what it is. My grandparents had a house in Long Beach. It was one of those wonderful old 1920s houses, with a brick deck that ran around the side to the backyard. There was a little one-car garage with a honeysuckle vine that snaked up the stucco wall. This chair was in the sun parlor."

"It sounds nice," she said, running her hand over the broad wicker arm.

"I have very clear memories of it," said Tripp, sitting across from her on the couch. "Sometimes when I can't sleep, I imagine walking through that house, room by room. On the ground floor, there was a bedroom in back, which had a scary African mask on the wall over the bed, and I was afraid to go in there. My grandparents had a black maid named Savannah, who baked the most fantastic gingerbread. I once burned my chin trying to inhale a whole pan of it. God! I've never told anyone this stuff. Not even Jordan."

"What happened to the house?" asked Shoshana.

"My grandmother and my parents sold it after my grandfather died. I was about ten. But I still miss it."

"At least you have the chair," she said sympathetically.

"At least."

They sat for a moment in silence.

"I don't know what to do," he said finally.

"What do you mean?"

"It's all over. Nobody will ever hire me again to wait tables, let alone dance."

"What are you talking about?" Shoshana said dismissively. "Just because you had an accident? Accidents happen. Everyone knows that."

Here it was. Faster than he'd imagined they'd get to it, but it was his chance to ask. And he found he couldn't.

"Everyone in the entire city is talking about me," he said instead.

"For five minutes. Give it a week, nobody will remember. This, too, shall pass."

He shook his head. "The general public may forget. But I guarantee you, the next time I go to an audition, they'll look at me and go, 'Tripp Macgregor . . . why do I know you?' And even if they don't figure it out on the spot, it will come to them later. It'll be like this dark cloud that follows me around for the rest of my life."

Shoshana shrugged. "Then give it up. Switch careers. Do something where it won't matter. Move somewhere else."

"I can't do that!" he cried.

She gave a Cheshire cat smile and stretched her arms over her head. "Of course you can't. I'm just trying to show you how silly it would be for you to let this drag you down. *You'll* never forget it, but other people will. And someday"—she leaned forward earnestly—"someday, it will be a story you tell on yourself. You'll be on Letterman, he'll make the obvious joke about your name, and you'll give a self-effacing laugh and say, 'You know, Dave, I actually *did* trip once! Let me tell you about it.'"

"I ruined a man's life," said Tripp somberly. "That will never be funny."

He got up from the couch and went into the kitchen to make some tea, wondering if such a future were possible. Not the Letterman part, that was obviously a pipe dream, but being able to joke about it.

"Ruined his life?" Shoshana asked. She'd come into the kitchen behind him, and her voice jolted him back to the present. "Don't you think that's a bit of an exaggeration?"

He lit the burner under the kettle and turned to her. "Shoshana, he spent half a million bucks on that wine. How would you feel? You're an actress, put yourself in his shoes."

He expected her to shut her eyes and begin a Method exercise, but she waved him off. "It was a stupid thing for him to do in the first place," she said.

Tripp wasn't fooled. The only reason she wasn't exercising her imagination was that she'd already done it. And she knew Tripp was right.

"You know," he said, "I suppose I ruined things for Annette, too, but I can't honestly say I feel too bad about that."

"I don't think you should," said Shoshana. "Did Hampton know she was inviting reporters? Did he ask her to get publicity for his wine?"

"She used him to lure them there. She told me as much."

"Then she had it coming to her," declared Shoshana. "Maybe you should sell that story to the press."

Tripp handed Shoshana a cup of tea, made one for himself, and sat down at the kitchen counter. "What good would that do?"

"It would let everyone know she's a scheming bitch."

Tripp shook his head. "She's never understood what it means to us to be performers. But we know what it is to pour your soul into something. I'm not saying what she did was right, but I can understand why she did it. This is going to suck enough for her as it is. I don't want to bring her down."

"You're too noble," said Shoshana. "It would make you look better."

Too noble. When she heard the truth, she'd change her mind about that, thought Tripp.

He took a long sip, then set down his teacup and looked at her. "Can I tell you a secret?"

"Sure."

"You have to promise you won't tell anyone."

"I swear," she said solemnly, resting a palm across her heart.

He took a deep breath. "I dropped it on purpose."

The color drained from Shoshana's face, and her cup quivered in midair. She set it down slowly.

"You didn't. You couldn't have."

"I might have. I can't swear that I didn't."

"I don't . . ." She shook her head. "What are you talking about? I saw you fall. You went flying backward down those steps."

Tripp got up and began to pace his galley kitchen. "Just before I came out to serve the wine, I called this guy I've been seeing, Michael." Tripp closed his eyes as a pain sliced through his chest and threatened to derail his voice. "In the same phone call, I found out that he got *Chorus Line* and I didn't, and that he already has a boyfriend. Annette interrupted my conversation, and then I went right out to serve the wine."

He glanced at Shoshana, whose face was the color of the countertop, a flat white against her long brown hair.

He continued hurriedly. "I was angry. I was boiling inside, and suddenly there I was, having to tamp it all down, having to act, to pretend everything was fine, when I was dying inside. And I was furious about being a waiter and having to serve. And"—he paused, steeling himself—"just before the photographer's flash went off, my hand . . . my hand started to shake, and I remember thinking in that moment . . ."

He put his hands over his eyes. Here was the part that he hadn't even allowed himself to fully remember, and now he was going to say it out loud, to confess. He kept speaking, with his face hidden.

"You know when you're driving and you have the urge to steer into oncoming traffic? Or you're sitting in the theater, and it's a really quiet moment, and you have to put your hand over your mouth to keep from screaming? I had one of those moments. The last thing I remember before that flash went off was the urge to throw the bottle against the wall."

In his mind's eye, Tripp saw the words drift across the small space to Shoshana, making her recoil slightly as they reached her ears.

"But you didn't," she whispered. "I saw what happened. You didn't throw it. You were startled. You slipped."

"But did I let it go on purpose?" he asked, daring to look at her again. He gripped the kitchen counter. "Could I have hung on to it? Or did my subconscious take over in that moment?" Tripp's throat had gone dry, but he said the words anyway. "You don't understand. I wanted to break the bottle."

"No, I know you," said Shoshana firmly. "Maybe on some level you thought you did, but you didn't want that. Not really."

"There's a part of me that wants to call the *Post* and tell them everything I just told you. Because I can't honestly say one way or another. And if I dropped it on purpose, I'm not a klutz."

Shoshana closed her eyes for a moment, and then she opened them and took a deep breath.

"Tripp, that is the most fucked-up thing I have ever heard in my life."

He prayed silently for her to keep talking, hoping there would be absolution in whatever she said next.

"You wouldn't be a klutz," she went on, "you'd be an asshole. One is forgivable, the other is not. You fell. That's what happened. Why you fell is immaterial. It wouldn't help matters any, and you'd only make people hate you." She took a sip of her tea.

It wasn't quite absolution, but she had a point.

"Bury that thought, Tripp!" She shook a warning finger at him. "Pretend you never had it, and I'll pretend I never heard it."

"But I feel powerless. I feel like I have to defend myself."

"A false confession isn't defending yourself!" Shoshana exclaimed. "If you want to take back the power, forge ahead with your life! Get another restaurant job. Go to an audition. Get back on the horse that threw you!"

"It will only throw me again. Nobody in their right mind would hire me."

Shoshana drained her cup and stood. "Don't be too sure of that. A little notoriety never hurt anyone." She pointed to the deli bag on the counter. "Eat the soup. It will make you feel better, honest."

He followed her to the front door. "It was really sweet of you to come by. Nobody else has bothered."

"Nobody else who cares about you was there. And talk about putting yourself in someone else's shoes." She let out a long, low whistle. "That could have been me, although we both know she'd never have let me anywhere near that bottle. I'm surprised she even let me in the restaurant that night. I'm a terrible waitress."

"And Sy Hampton?" he asked.

"Look, if you really want to put closure on this for yourself, don't go blabbing bullshit to the *Post*. Tell Sy Hampton how sorry you are for what happened. Apologize. For the *accident*," she added pointedly.

She gave him a peck on the cheek and disappeared into the elevator, which dinged and closed behind her.

Tripp returned to his kitchen, rinsed out his teacup, and poured himself a mug of Shoshana's soup. He sat in Jordan's chair and sipped the healing liquid, letting his mind's eye travel through the Long Beach house, from the sun parlor, through the dining room and scary downstairs bedroom, up the stairs to his grandparents' room, with its demure twin beds and chenille bedspreads, out to the small, tar-floored balcony that overlooked the garden with its vapor of honeysuckle. But eventually his thoughts returned to the present, to his apartment, and to Shoshana's advice.

"Tell Sy Hampton how sorry you are."

It was a new thought—one he hadn't come to on his own, although it seemed so obvious now. And in spite of his well-stocked arsenal of mental games, he knew that once the idea had lodged in his head, it wouldn't leave until he acted on it.

FORTY

IT HAD TO BE A JOKE, Annette thought. She couldn't believe what she was seeing.

The restaurant was full.

She'd arrived late on Tuesday. During lunch, in fact. And it was so busy, the waiters were furiously trying to juggle their tables. She was even more surprised when she pulled up the dinner reservations on her computer.

Ninety covers. Her biggest night yet. And it wasn't even one o'clock.

Was it possible that there really wasn't such a thing as bad publicity? Had their crazy stunt worked in the end? Or—she held her breath for a moment as she contemplated this bizarre twist—had the accident actually made it even better?

If that proved to be the case, she might have to give Tripp his job back. She might even have to thank Antony Farrell.

She quickly stashed her things in her office and returned to the floor, beaming with good-natured interest at the lunchtime customers and ready to lend a hand to her harried waitstaff. As she looked more closely at the tables crammed with diners, she saw that they weren't the usual businesspeople wandering in because of the restaurant's proximity to their offices. To all appearances, Parapluie was on its way to becoming a destination restaurant.

"I'm sorry, but you'll have to ask Ms. Lecocq. I wasn't here," Sarah, the lunch hostess, was saying to a table of middle-aged ladies. "Annette!" Sarah waved her over. "These ladies would like to know where the wine bottle fell."

"Ah, yes," Annette said, with a broad smile. "It was just over there. That table up the steps, under the painting."

"Thank you!" cried one of the ladies. "Come on, Gertrude. I want a picture!"

With that, they rose en masse and hurried over to the nook,

where a family of four was eating.

"Sorry, do you mind? We just want a quick picture," said Gertrude to the family.

"Look!" The first woman pointed to the floor. "You can still see the stain!"

Gertrude held up her camera as the other two ladies huddled together on the steps of the nook with wide smiles.

"Here, I'll take one of all of you, then you take one of us," offered the father. "We didn't realize we were sitting at *the* table!"

The cameras were passed around and the guests posed, making faces and pointing at the floor, while Annette looked on in disbelief. She returned to Sarah, who was explaining to another table what the photo circus was all about.

"Sarah, could I have a word?" whispered Annette.

The hostess excused herself and came over.

"I'm just curious. That table of ladies. What have they ordered?"

Sarah flagged down Jonathan, who was waiting on them.

"The prix fixe," he confirmed, consulting their bill.

"Are they enjoying the food?"

He shrugged. "Seem to be."

"Excellent. *Continuez,*" said Annette, fluttering her fingers in dismissal. Jonathan returned to his work, but Annette put a restraining hand on Sarah's arm. "Still, let's try to discourage that sort of thing," she said, indicating the party at the nook.

"But that's why they came," Sarah pointed out. "They want to see where the wine fell."

"I understand, but this is a restaurant, not the scene of a drive-by shooting. I'd like to maintain some kind of decorum."

Annette left Sarah and moved off to chat up her new clientele. Are you enjoying your meal? Yes? *Parfait!* If there's anything else I can do for you, please let me know. Yes, we're open for dinner. Of course, we can do a private party. The wine list? Just one moment.

Despite her fears, the lemonade was juicing itself. And it seemed that all Annette had to do was hold the pitcher underneath and let it fill up.

FORTY-ONE

VALENTINA DIDN'T THINK TWICE THIS TIME. She called Miss Banks's line before nine o'clock, knowing she'd get voice mail, and left a message saying she was still sick.

She waited until ten o'clock, which seemed a reasonable hour, and then left her apartment and took off down the street toward Vito's house.

She found Vito at home, as she suspected she would, but he was alone.

"Come on in! Roseanne's out with the kids. The little ones. Big ones are at school," Vito explained.

Valentina followed him into the dining room, reflexively sitting where she had for both wine tastings.

"Coffee?" he asked.

"Sure."

He disappeared into the kitchen and reappeared a few moments later with two steaming mugs. "It's like I knew I'd have company!"

Valentina took a sip of her coffee, which seemed to be flavored with something.

"It's hazelnut," Vito offered, noticing the look on her face. "You're tasting subtle flavors. That's good!"

"Vito, about the other night . . ."

"Yeah," he said, looking suddenly uncomfortable. "I'd, uh, rather you didn't tell anyone that you saw me there."

"That's the thing. I didn't see you there."

He gave her a wink. "Good girl. I knew you'd understand."

"No, I mean it. I didn't see you there, because *I* wasn't there."

"What are you talking about? I saw you!"

Valentina took a deep breath. "It was Elisa."

Vito's head gave an incredulous twitch. "What?!"

"Vito, I chickened out at the last minute. I couldn't do it! I meant to, I really did, and I'm so grateful for all the time you took with me and everything, but I just felt like a complete phony. It was all a big mistake, and I should never have said yes in the first place. And the thing is, now I realize that I actually *do* care about Sy, because I feel terrible about what happened, and I let him down, because if I was there, I would've stood by him and not thrown myself on the floor like Elisa did. And I let you down, too!"

She buried her head in her arms and sobbed as if her heart would break. When her tears finally subsided, she waited for Vito to say something. When he didn't, she lifted her head and saw that he was gone.

That's it, she thought. I've ruined everything.

She was about to leave when Vito returned with a bottle of brandy. Without saying a word, he poured a generous capful into each coffee mug.

"You're disappointed in me," said Valentina weakly.

"A little bit," said Vito, nodding. "But maybe in a way I'm kinda relieved."

"Yeah?" she sniffed.

"When I saw that poor guy standing there screaming, and you—I mean, I thought it was you—on the floor with everyone else, at first I thought, 'Hey, I turned her into a real wine expert!' and then I thought, 'Shit, that poor slob is dying up there and she's just ignoring him!' So I guess I feel better knowing it wasn't you."

"I'm really sorry. After all the time you took with me," she apologized again.

Vito leaned across the table and patted her hands between his. His palms were incredibly soft. "All I was doing was helping you get through that dinner. And if you decided in the end you couldn't do it, that's no skin off my nose. Does he know it wasn't you?"

Valentina shook her head. "I have a secret now, too, Vito. Just like you."

"Look, what I said before about seeing me there." He blinked at Valentina. "There's things I do in my private life that gotta stay private. You get me?"

Valentina smiled ruefully. "I got you the moment I met you.

Only how come you never told me you were going to be there?"

"Tony called me at the last minute, when his date canceled. Seems there were a lot of last-minute switcheroos on Saturday night."

Vito stood up and walked over to the bookshelf, where a kid's papier-mâché vase had replaced the pottery that had broken when he tossed the thesaurus.

"You shouldn't keep that kind of secret, Val. I gotta keep my secrets because, well, I gotta. It's the deal I made with myself." He paused, then went on. "Years ago, I met this rich, hunky guy named Danny in a bar. He started taking me to wine tastings and expos, and I realized I had a palate that was, you know, discriminating. There's kind of a group of us, we've done a little traveling together, you know, and there are certain bars . . . Well, that's how I met Tony. And he and I . . . okay, I don't gotta spell this out for you. I think you get the picture." He turned to her, his expression solemn. "But your situation is different. You gotta fess up." She shook her head vigorously, but he continued. "You know you do. You gotta tell Sy it wasn't you."

"But why? What does it matter now?"

"Because it wasn't fair poker. He was doing something exceptional for you. And you let him down. But then Elisa let him down worse."

"I know," said Valentina. The honesty of his words made her wince.

"That's why you gotta tell him. You can't leave him thinking the wine was more important to you than he was."

"But what do I say—'I never really wanted to go with you in the first place, so I chickened out'? Won't that only make him feel worse?"

"Given the way it all played out, it'll probably make him feel better."

Valentina shook her head. "It'll just mean that everything about the evening was a disaster. Even the me part."

"Then make it up to him."

"How can I do that?"

"Start by telling him the truth. Maybe there isn't anything else you can do, but you owe him that at least."

Vito was right, but it just didn't seem like enough. And what would Sy say to her when she told him? Horrible things, probably. Or worse—nothing at all.

"Did you get to taste the wine?" she asked.

"I did."

"Was it amazing?"

Vito sat down again next to her. "Well, it was on the floor. But under the right circumstances, it would've been killer."

They sipped their brandy-spiked coffee in silence. Valentina was grateful for the liqueur, which was taking the edge off her despair.

"I gotta admit, I feel a little guilty, too," said Vito after a moment. "I mean, I didn't pay for that wine, and I wasn't his guest. And I'm telling you, Val, the man was destroyed. I've never heard a grown man scream like that."

Valentina shut her eyes. It hurt to imagine it.

Vito went on, "It was like when that bottle broke, he broke, too. That's a broken man right now."

"You think Sy's okay, though, right?" she said, rolling the mug between her hands anxiously. "You don't really mean he's broken, do you?"

"I do, Val," said Vito gravely. "If he was my friend, I'd be good and worried."

The key turned in the front door, and Valentina heard Roseanne's voice ordering the kids to go to the bathroom and wash their hands.

"You're gonna have to help him get back to himself, and the only way you can do that is by telling him the truth." Vito stood up and linked his fingers through the handles of the coffee mugs. "But you knew that. That's why you came over. You just needed to hear somebody else say it."

He patted her hair with his free hand and carried the mugs back into the kitchen, where Valentina could hear him greet Roseanne with a noisy, wet kiss.

FORTY-TWO

SY HAD NO IDEA HOW LONG he'd been asleep. The cheap wine had left him with a nasty headache, and he stumbled from his study down the hall to his dressing room, where he downed two ibuprofen and ran the shower as hot as he could stand it. Then he rummaged around in the back of his closet and pulled out an old pair of jeans and a flannel shirt. Clothes he hadn't worn in years. The jeans might have been tight a few days ago, but now he was able to snap them with minimal effort.

"Well, you're looking much better," said Claudine, who was ready with a steaming cup of coffee when he appeared in the kitchen doorway. "You need some food. What sounds good?"

Sy hadn't thought he was hungry, but as soon as he took his first sip of coffee, he realized he was ravenous.

"Bacon, eggs, and toast would be great."

"Nothing wrong with breakfast at three o'clock," Claudine smiled.

"Three o'clock," he muttered. "Monday?"

She gave him a motherly look. "Tuesday. You've been asleep for more than twenty-four hours. You must have needed it."

"Has the phone rung a lot?"

"Oh, yes. I've been letting it go to voice mail," she said as she scrambled his eggs.

He moved over to the kitchen phone and dialed his access code.

Unsurprisingly, the mailbox was full. Most of the calls were hang-ups. The press, he figured, a suspicion that was borne out by the decrease in calls over the past day. He was old news already, and they were onto the next, which was fine with him. Pippa had called to say how sorry she was and that she hoped he was okay, and Warren was worried because he hadn't come into work or called. He'd be taking care of that today.

Then he heard a message that made his heart skip a beat.

It was Eric. Sy swallowed hard when he heard the little voice. Eric always sounded about four years younger on the phone than he did in person.

"Mom told me what happened to your wine. It was in the paper, I guess. I hope you're not feeling too bad about it. I know it was a special bottle and all that, and you were looking forward to it. So, I, um, just wanted to say I was sorry about it breaking. Okay. Bye. Oh, this is Eric."

Claudine set the plate down on the table behind him. "Come and eat. You can listen to those later."

Sy deleted the entire mailbox and hung up the phone. He ate in silence at the granite-topped table, while Claudine vacuumed the living room. He remembered when Eric was born, Marianne had a rough delivery, and her doctor advised her to set herself a single, manageable task per day until she felt like herself again. Sy imagined he had suffered a similar shock to his system, and it struck him now as useful advice. He gave himself permission to demand nothing more from himself today than the single phone call he intended to make.

He poured himself a second cup of coffee and brought it up to his study, where he plugged the phone back in and dialed.

"Warren Sage's office."

He cleared his throat. "Tracy, it's Sy Hampton."

"Mr. Hampton! Are you—I mean, we heard about . . . I'm so sorry about your . . . your . . ."

"Thank you. Is Warren in?"

"Sure, I'll get him," said Tracy, sounding distinctly relieved not to have to quantify his loss.

His partner came on the line almost immediately.

"Sy! Where have you been? Are you okay?"

He knew the polite thing would be to apologize for not calling sooner, but he had no energy left for sparing other people's feelings.

"I want out," Sy said bluntly.

There was silence on the other end of the phone, and then

Warren Sage spoke in that deliberate tone one uses when handling a volatile personality. Sy had heard Warren use it on other people, but never on him.

"Are you sure you're in the right frame of mind to make that kind of decision? There's no need to commit to anything right now. Why don't you sleep on it?"

"I've slept on it, and I'm certain. I'm done. Done with the lifestyle, the trappings, the work, all of it. We'll need to divide up the assets, and since I'm leaving the business altogether, you can retain my clients, although we'll need to adjust for that in the buyout."

"Sy, you can't just end your entire career in one conversation!"

"I'm only informing you in one conversation. We'll take all the right steps to disband properly."

"That's not what I mean. We have a successful partnership. I still think we could achieve tremendous returns," said Warren, parroting their brochure almost verbatim.

"This has nothing to do with you. It's about me and what I want—or, more to the point—don't want anymore. I'm not setting up a competing firm, so based on our commitments to the limited partners, my exit shouldn't trigger key man provisions. Our positions are equal, so the LPs should be okay with you running the show."

"Sy, think about this some more. There's no need to rush into anything. We can carry on without you here for a while. Take whatever time you need."

"The decision is made. The switch is flipped. Done."

Sy could practically hear Warren's brain riffling through his compendium of arguments, but there wasn't anything at the ready to combat "no, for the sake of no."

"Shall I call Joan Greenfield and Ben Stratton? Or will you?" asked Warren finally.

Sy thought about leaving it to his partner to contact the lawyer and the accountant, but he wanted to expedite things.

"I'll take care of it. You still have work to do, and I don't.

My resignation is effective as of this moment."

Warren cleared his throat. "Sy, as a friend, may I tell you something?"

"If you like."

"Valentina hasn't been in since . . . since the weekend."

"I don't see why you should be telling me that as a friend. She is my secretary."

"It's just that . . ." Warren seemed to be struggling. "I didn't know if she was with you. I assumed that she might be, but then I thought, maybe since things hadn't turned out . . . In any case, she hasn't been here."

"That doesn't really concern me," said Sy coldly. "Although I'll have to ask you to spare Tracy or Laura to help Miss Banks pack my things. I won't be coming back in at all."

"I understand," said Warren. "But we'll speak again soon?"

"Of course," said Sy, knowing they wouldn't. "Will you do one more thing for me?"

"Of course."

"Call Human Resources and tell them Miss D'Ambrosio's services will no longer be required. Unless you want to keep her on."

"No, I don't think so."

"You can do what you want about Miss Banks. Thank you, Warren. And I'm sorry," said Sy with finality. He hung up the phone and unplugged it again.

It was amazing. In ten minutes, he'd terminated an almost thirty-year investment career. He felt no triumph, no liberation, only certainty that the time for retirement had come. If he had hoped that uncorking the Lafite would forestall middle age, it had instead had the opposite effect. He had been made old overnight. The blankness he felt at having cut the cord of his professional life seemed perfectly in sync with the absence of all other feeling. He was drifting. And although it struck him that, in fact, he'd been drifting for some time, now he was drifting by design. The sensation was not altogether unpleasant.

He returned downstairs, where Claudine was washing up after his delayed breakfast.

"I'll take dinner tonight, Claudine. Whatever's easiest."

"I've got roast chicken and garlic rosemary potatoes, if you want to select your wine."

"I'll go down to the cellar right now. Please tell Bill I won't need him for a few days. He should take a vacation."

"Don't you want him to pick up Eric from school tomorrow?"

"No. I'll get him myself. Thanks." He started down the steps to the basement level, then paused. "Claudine, thank you for everything."

"Of course," she said cheerily. "It's no bother."

And it's what I pay you for, thought Sy as he continued downstairs. He appreciated her not pointing that out, and with an odd sense of detachment, he reflected that the person who knew him best was his housekeeper.

Well, that would change. A lot was going to change.

For one thing, he would no longer keep a wine cellar. He opened the door to the little subterranean room, and the cool air felt refreshing. If there was one thing he had learned, it was that you can't take it with you. Not even to a restaurant.

There was only one worthwhile way to dismantle a wine cellar, he thought as he scanned the large leather-bound wine log. One bottle at a time. He selected a bottle of Rioja, the only one he owned, a Bodegas Faustino, "I" Gran Reserva, 1982. It seemed as good a place as any to start.

FORTY-THREE

TRIPP KNEW SHOSHANA WAS RIGHT, both about getting on with his life and making some sort of apology to Sy Hampton. An apology, he reminded himself, not a confession. She was right about that as well. There wasn't anything concrete to confess, only an impulse, a thought, and as far as Hampton was concerned, Tripp would certainly rather be thought of as a klutz. He resolved to put any question of intent from his mind forevermore. His doubt would remain one of his soul's secrets. It was a fruitless inquiry in any case, since it was ultimately unanswerable. Even if it were not, the truth would do nothing to change the outcome.

As he sat in Jordan's chair and stared at the same wall he'd been looking at for three days, he wrestled with his options. He could try to get a restaurant job, try to get an acting job, or apologize to Sy Hampton. He could, of course, do nothing, but wallowing in misery was starting to lose its appeal. There was something about having survived his encounter with Shoshana, and feeling marginally better for it, that gave him hope for interaction with others.

Confronting Sy Hampton was, in its way, the hardest of the three options, but Tripp knew it was also the most likely to bring relief. Even if Hampton refused to accept his apology, it wouldn't keep him from getting on in the world. He'd continue to feel like shit, he'd feel worse, in fact, but it wasn't quite the same as having either of his two career doors slammed in his face. Then he really would be nowhere.

Before his courage could fail him, Tripp dressed and looked up Hampton on the Internet. He located only his company, Hampton & Sage, so he left his apartment and walked across town to the address on Fifth Avenue. He hadn't been outside since Saturday night, and he sensed that in those few days the world had passed him by. New discoveries had been made, technology advanced, there had been births and deaths, comings and goings, while he hibernated in a cocoon of self-loathing.

When he arrived, he rode the elevator alone to the seventh floor and took a deep breath before pushing open the gold-lettered door to Hampton & Sage, LLC. He wasn't exactly sure what he was going to say. He was counting on his acute need for forgiveness to motivate the right words in the moment.

He approached an attractive middle-aged black woman with gold and black glasses who looked like she'd been crying.

"Excuse me," he said, as deferentially as he could, "I'm here to see Mr. Hampton."

She pulled her glasses down onto her nose and peered over them before raising them again.

"He doesn't have any appointments today."

"I don't have one. But I'd like to see him, if he's in."

"He's not. And he's not expected back." Her voice broke. "Excuse me," she hiccupped, and fled past him into the hallway, weeping.

At that moment a tall, balding gentleman with a long, aquiline nose and prominent ears emerged from an office with a stack of papers, which he handed to a young blond woman seated at a desk nearby.

"Tracy, these can be filed," he said.

"Thanks. I think this gentleman is here to see Mr. Hampton." Tracy indicated Tripp.

The man, who Tripp thought looked like an aging British colonel, shook his head and said, "I'm sorry, but he's not in. Can I help you?"

Tripp decided he couldn't let this be a dead end.

"My name is Tripp Macgregor. I was serving Mr. Hampton his wine the other night when the accident happened, and I'd like to speak to him. To er"—Tripp coughed self-consciously —"apologize."

Tracy and the man exchanged a glance, and the man said, "I see. Come with me."

Tripp followed him into a long, spacious office with a spectacular view downtown, aware all the while of the young blond woman's eyes boring through his back.

The man shut the door and gestured to a chair opposite his desk. "I'm Warren Sage, Sy's partner."

"It was a terrible accident," said Tripp as he sat. "You see, there were food and wine reporters there, and nobody told either of us. The owner went ahead and invited them. She didn't ask Mr. Hampton's permission, and she didn't tell me until right before I served the wine. It was nerve-wracking, to say the least, and all of a sudden flashbulbs started going off, and I was standing on some steps, and it was so startling and blinding that I lost my balance."

That's my story, and I'm sticking to it, thought Tripp.

Sage shook his head indignantly. "The owner should have made it clear to Sy. And to you. That wasn't right, springing the press on you like that."

"No, it wasn't," agreed Tripp, relieved to have a sympathetic ear.

Sage paced over to the window and looked at the view. "Sy is a bit of a romantic. His head is always in the clouds. I think he had invested this wine with an importance it didn't have. I know the history of it, but that's not what I'm talking about. You saw the woman he was with."

Tripp nodded. "She was very pretty."

Sage gave a knowing smile. "If a bit coarse. Valentina D'Ambrosio. The name says it all, don't you think? I'm sure you could tell he was infatuated with her, even though she wasn't . . . well, not really his type. She was also, until today, his secretary. Do you see where I'm going with this?"

"I'm, um . . . not exactly."

"You're a man," said Sage with a vague gesture. "You know what it's like to want to impress a woman."

Actually, I don't, thought Tripp, but he let it pass and nodded as enthusiastically as he could.

"I think this really struck at Sy's pride. At his sense of self," continued Sage. "Look, I'm about ten years older than Sy, and I've been through this. Yes, the owner of your restaurant set him up, but he

set himself up for a disappointment. Because I don't think this secretary, Valentina, really cared that much for him. And even if she
did, I think eventually he'd have realized that she was . . ." Sage
winced. "This sounds awful, but I'm going to say it anyway. That
she wasn't good enough for him."

Tripp shifted uncomfortably in his chair and tried not to imagine what Sage must think of him.

"Sy is one of those people you can read like a book. Oh, not in
business circumstances, he's got as good a poker face as anyone
when it comes to facts. But his feelings are always very transparent.
You see, anyone else would be apoplectic about losing his financial
investment, but for Sy, that bottle breaking was about something
else. Something deeply personal."

Great, now I really feel like shit, thought Tripp.

Sage took a notepad from his desk and scribbled. Then he tore
off the page and handed it to Tripp.

"The reason I'm telling you all this is that I think it's admirable
of you to want to apologize, even though from what you're telling
me it wasn't entirely your fault. Seems like the owner owes him
more of an apology than you do. In any case, here's Sy's home address. He may see you, he may not."

Tripp pocketed the paper. "Thank you. This is very"—he
searched for the right word—"decent of you. I appreciate it."

"No, you're doing the decent thing. But I thought, under the
circumstances, I should give you a heads-up on where he is.
Emotionally. You know."

Before he could talk himself out of it, Tripp left the office, past
Tracy, who was whispering excitedly into her phone. He was no
longer certain that an apology would do either of them any good,
but after what Hampton's partner had told him, he was more determined than ever to try.

Fifteen minutes later, he crossed Park Avenue and continued
east on Sixty-fourth Street. As he drew near a gracious red brick
town house with a swirling white stoop, he saw the front door open
and then close. A woman ran down the stairs, paused on the side-

walk, and then sat down on the bottom step. From her hunched position, Tripp could tell she was upset. He stopped in front of her and matched the address on the paper to the number over the door.

"Excuse me, are you all right?" he asked.

She looked up, her eyes red and watery, and he recognized her immediately.

"You were at the restaurant with him," Tripp said.

She blinked at him. "No. I mean, yes. Oh, what the hell, whatever." She put her head down and started crying again.

He rummaged in his pockets. "I'm sorry, I don't have a tissue or anything."

"It doesn't matter." She shrugged and squinted at him. "Who are you, anyway? Are you a reporter?"

She began to scramble to her feet but he stopped her, his hand on her shoulder. "You don't remember me? I'm Tripp. The waiter who . . . you know, tripped."

She sighed heavily. "This is like having amnesia."

"Did you hit your head or something?" he asked, concerned.

She wiped her eyes on her sleeve. "I know you think I should know you, but I don't. You think you met me at the restaurant, but you didn't."

Clearly, the girl had a screw loose, or she'd drunk so much she didn't know which end was up.

"Well, I did. I remember it, even if you don't," he said.

"You met my sister. It wasn't me. Only he doesn't know, and now he thinks I'm a horrible, unfeeling bitch!"

She burst into tears again. Tripp sat down next to her and put his arm around her heaving shoulders.

"It wasn't you?" he asked, trying to make sense of what she was saying.

She shook her head.

"It was your, what, your evil twin sister?"

She gave a squawk that was half a laugh and half a cry. "Elisa. I'm Valentina. We're identical twins. And I came by to tell him, only he won't see me. He won't see anyone!"

"Maybe he'll see me," Tripp said, jumping to his feet as quickly as his still aching back would allow.

Valentina's head shot up. "I'm serious. There's a lady answering the door, and she says he won't see anybody. This is all my fault!"

"Your fault?" asked Tripp, coming back down to her. "How on earth is it your fault? You weren't even there! I was the one who dropped his precious wine."

She peered closer at him. "Yeah, I recognize you now from the newspaper. It's got my ass all over it, only it ain't my ass!"

This was such a bizarre statement that Tripp burst into laughter before he could help himself. "I'm sorry, that's just so . . . unintentionally funny."

They sat for a moment, Tripp laughing and Valentina sniffling, until finally he said, "I came by to apologize."

"Yeah, so did I."

They watched the cars and taxis chase each other down the tree-lined street, until finally Tripp said, "Can I buy you a cup of coffee? Maybe it'll do us some good to talk. Maybe we can make each other feel better, even if he's not ready to hear from either of us just yet."

Valentina wiped her eyes. "Yeah, okay."

He held out his hand and pulled her to her feet. Then, tucking her arm through his, Tripp led her to Lexington Avenue, where he hoped they'd find a coffee shop nearby, and some comfort in conversation.

FORTY-FOUR

SY DIDN'T REMEMBER MUCH from his subway jaunt to 125th Street in the moments immediately following the accident, having been blinded by the chaos of his soul imploding. Now, taking in his fellow passengers on the 6 train as he headed uptown to pick up Eric, he found that he both did and did not belong. Surprisingly, he felt little kinship with the suited men rushing off to meetings or escaping early from their offices. He felt no impulse to identify himself in some way as a compatriot, because he wasn't one, not anymore. At the same time, he sensed no connection with the young parents or babysitters with their kids, or the blue-collar workers commuting wearily to or from their low-paying jobs. And yet, Sy was aware that the subway, and the apathy of those who rode it, provided unconditional acceptance and anonymity, which suited his new self just fine.

He exited the subway at the still slightly seedy corner of Ninety-sixth Street and Lexington Avenue and walked west. It was funny how this neighborhood, like so many in the city, changed from block to block, as the arm of gentrification spread the wealth farther uptown and east. There was a new apartment building on Ninety-sixth and Madison with a fancy paper store on the ground floor. Years ago, there had been a shoe store and a dry cleaner, both of which he might, quite literally, have been caught dead setting foot in.

The world was shifting, advance and retreat, and he was aware of a newfound indifference as he eyed the city in preparation for a third divorce.

It's just not working out anymore, he said to the storefronts on Madison Avenue as he strolled past them. Sy wasn't sure where he was going or what he planned to do, but he knew that he was not going to stay. He no longer loved New York, because he'd learned that New York was all too eager to reject him with loud, public mockery. It had always been a one-sided relationship. He'd just never noticed.

The doors under the carved stone archway of St. Bernard's opened and gave forth a wave of boys in matching blazers. After a few moments, Eric emerged with his buddy Jack Wobeson, and Sy saw him shade his eyes in the afternoon sun, looking for the Lexus. He said something to the other boy, muttering that his dad was late, no doubt, and Sy stepped forward and waved. At first Eric looked past him, then he squinted again and trotted over to where Sy was standing.

"Where's the car?" asked Eric.

"I took the subway," said Sy.

Eric was clearly surprised by this, which pleased Sy. He was anticipating a perverse enjoyment in proving himself to be something other than what Eric was expecting.

Eric hesitated. "I wasn't sure if you were coming today."

"Why wouldn't I?" asked Sy.

Eric shrugged. "I dunno. I thought maybe you were . . . I dunno."

Sy gave his son an enigmatic half-smile. "I am. But I came anyway."

They turned the corner onto Fifth Avenue's Museum Mile and strolled downtown, past the elegant dove gray Jewish Museum and the expansive grandeur of the red and white brick Cooper-Hewitt. Sy felt no compunction to break the silence. He was happy in his cocoon of privacy, letting Eric be in his. Father and son, together, but not.

"Um, what are we doing?" Eric asked finally.

"Up to you."

Eric pointed toward the familiar corkscrew building looming ahead of them. "Can we go to the Guggenheim? There's a special exhibit on anime, featuring Hayao Miyazaki. He's made a bunch of great movies—I think he's really amazing. He did *Princess Mononoke, Spirited Away, Howl's Moving Castle*. . . He's really an artist."

Sy glanced sideways at his son. "I think that's the longest sentence I've heard from you in five years, aside from your phone message the other day."

Eric was so taken aback that he stopped walking. Sy quickly added, "It's okay. I was just pointing it out, that's all."

They continued toward the museum and Eric muttered quietly, "I didn't think you were all that interested."

"Of course I'm interested. I'm your father," said Sy. He knew he wasn't being entirely fair, but it was time to shake things up a little. He went on, "I'm sure your mom probably spends a lot of time telling you what a boring jerk I am, and I suppose in some ways she's right. But I do love you, and I want us to get along."

"We get along!" said Eric quickly, his eyes bright. "It's just . . ."

"What?" Sy stopped and turned to him.

Eric looked down at his shiny black school shoes. "I don't know. Like sometimes you just sort of try too hard. And then you give up too easy." He stole a glance at Sy. "I know that sounds sort of mean, and like it's two different things . . ."

"No, that's okay," said Sy. "I understand."

"And Mom doesn't say you're a jerk," added Eric. "She felt really bad about your bottle breaking. She said she knew how much it probably meant to you, although she said it was insane that you spent that kind of money on it."

"Did she tell you how much it cost?"

"Yeah. But I know you're rich. You can afford it. Right?"

"Well, since you mention it, I'm going to have to tighten my belt a little from now on," said Sy. "I'm retiring."

"But you're not *that* old!"

Sy chuckled in spite of himself. "No, but I'm that tired."

"I've never seen you wear jeans before," Eric commented. "Not even on weekends."

Sy shrugged. "I'm changing a lot of things about myself," he said.

"What are you going to do?" asked Eric.

"I'm going to the Guggenheim with you, because I want to see your anime guy. That's about as far ahead as I'm willing to plan."

Sy put his arm around Eric's bony shoulder and led him into the museum. They took the elevator to the top floor and began a slow promenade down the corkscrew ramp.

"Tell me what you like about this. " Sy stopped and pointed to a painting of a woman being menaced by a winged, dragonlike creature with a man's face.

Eric unconsciously straightened his school tie. "Well, it's got elements of anime. See how the woman's eyes are large? And she's scared of the dragon, so there are extra lines around her mouth to show her fear. See how detailed the dragon is? It's not a cartoon, because it's paint." He pointed to the plaque by the side of the frame. "Oil paint, I guess it says. I don't know this artist. But look over here." Eric took Sy's arm and pulled him over to a tiny frame. "This is a still from *Howl's Moving Castle*. That's Sophie, the heroine. She looks like the lady in the dragon painting, don't you think?"

Sy nodded, marveling more at the urgency with which his son had taken his arm than at his comparisons. "So you like the way their faces are exaggerated," he observed.

"Yeah. You always know what's happening. No, that's not it exactly—it's that you always know how they feel about what's going on. I think people aren't really like that."

"Do you think it would be helpful if they were?"

"Yeah, kind of," said Eric.

"I don't agree."

"You don't?"

They continued down the ramp, stopping to admire more work by Miyazaki and drawings by Yuriy Norshteyn, the Russian animator who influenced him.

"I can understand it from the point of view of the observer, but I think people often have good reason to hide their feelings," Sy continued.

"But then the observer might say or do something they shouldn't, and if they knew what was really going on in their friend's mind, they'd act differently."

"So you're all for emotional transparency?" asked Sy.

"I think it's important to know where you stand with people, if that's what you mean."

"You hungry?" Sy asked as they left the museum. "We could go somewhere and get a snack."

"Can I get a hot dog from the cart?" Eric asked. "Mom never lets me."

"Then you definitely can."

Sy bought them both hot dogs and they sat on a bench on the cobblestone walk parallel to the park, where they had a good view of the unique building.

"I told you what I like about anime. Why do you like wine so much?" asked Eric, as he licked the neon mustard off his fingers.

"Right at this moment, I don't like wine very much at all. I'm mad at it."

Eric laughed. "Dad!"

"I'm serious," said Sy. "I feel like I was betrayed by a friend."

"But Dad," said Eric earnestly, "that was just one bottle. It's like cutting off all your friends because one of them was mean to you. Besides, it wasn't the bottle's fault. It was the waiter's fault."

Sy shook his head. "It wasn't even. I mean, it was, but there was a man from the auction house who was there. I blame him. And I have to say I blame myself a little, too. It's complicated."

"Still, that waiter must feel pretty bad," said Eric, crumpling the foil from his hot dog into a ball.

"I haven't given him much thought," said Sy. He brought their used wrappers to a garbage can a few feet away and tossed them in.

In fact, he hadn't given Tripp any thought at all. Sy imagined he felt terrible, not to mention humiliated. But he must have known there would be press there, and photographers. He was supposed to exhibit grace under pressure, and he hadn't. In that sense, at least, he was at fault.

Sy returned to the bench, where Eric was watching him warily.

"What?" said Sy.

"You still haven't told me why you care so much about wine. What's so great about it?"

Sy sat down next to his son and tried to rearticulate feelings he'd taken for granted in happier times.

"The taste, for one thing. The fact that wines can have so many different, complex flavors. Those take a while to recognize—your taste buds have to mature and you have to be attuned to all kinds of subtleties. Then there's the way wine pairs with food. A wine can taste bitter or acidic on its own, but partnered with the right meal, it turns into a superstar. Then, of course, there's the history of the bottle."

He stopped. This was the facet of wine that he didn't want to discuss, but Eric seemed to sense that, and he said, "That's okay. You told me that part last time."

"Wine is also an investment," Sy went on. "A cultural and hedonistic investment. Do you know that word? Hedonistic?"

"Like enjoying something with the senses?" Eric asked.

"Nice to see they're teaching you all the important stuff at St. Bernard's," Sy said wryly. "But yes. A wine cellar is an investment financially, but also an investment in pleasure. If you have a full cellar, you'll always have the right bottle of wine on hand. It is, in its way, the ultimate luxury. You don't always pay . . . a huge amount . . . per bottle, but if you collect enough wine, you'll have a substantial asset on your hands. People sell collections, inherit them."

He thought back to the Rioja from his cellar that he had laid waste to the night before. Perhaps he should save his collection after all and bequeath it to Eric.

"How do you make wine anyway? Is it just ordinary grapes like you buy at the store?"

Sy regarded his son. Somebody, somewhere had a twisted sense of humor. How was it possible that just as he was aiming to divorce himself from wine, Eric was showing an interest?

"If you're really curious, we could visit a winery," he said steadily. "There are plenty within driving distance, on Long Island and even in the Hudson Valley on the other side of the river from where I grew up. I'm not so familiar with the ones upstate. Maybe we can explore them together. I understand that New York wines are pretty different from what I'm used to drinking. I'm pretty sure my buddy Peter Blomgard knows a guy who has a winery somewhere up there."

Eric took a breath like he was about to ask a question, then seemed to change his mind and not know what to do with the air he'd taken in. He held it for a minute, then exhaled slowly.

"What?" Sy asked.

"Nothing."

"You sure? You looked like you were tanking up for a biggie."

Eric started to laugh, then stopped himself. He swallowed hard.

"Were you really mad when the bottle broke?"

Sy squeezed his eyes shut for a moment.

"Yes," he said finally. "But not mad like you mean it. Mad crazy." He opened his eyes and stared at the button on the sleeve of Eric's blazer. "I went a little nuts."

Eric didn't say anything, and Sy continued. "Do you remember how you felt when your computer crashed, before I got you the backup drive, and you lost all your data?"

Eric winced. "Yeah."

"What was the worst part about it?"

Eric looked up at the sky and then back at Sy. "The photos. I had them all organized chronologically. It was like a slideshow of my life, and then it was gone." Sy could see Eric blinking back tears at the memory. "It was like I lost a whole part of my life."

Sy nodded. "It's not exactly the same, but probably the closest you can imagine. And, like you did, I'm starting all over again. Compiling new data and images and burying what I lost." Sy stood up and stretched his legs. "What time is it?" He hadn't bothered to put on his everyday Tourneau since he'd given away the Great Explorers watch. He liked feeling adrift in time, even if he was no longer adrift in space.

"Four thirty," said Eric, consulting his watch.

"What do you want to do now?" asked Sy. "Walk through the park? Catch a movie?"

"Can we just go back to your place?"

"Sure, if that's what you want."

Eric nodded enthusiastically. "I bet Claudine's making me something good for dinner."

FORTY-FIVE

TRIPP SCANNED THE EQUITY LOUNGE for familiar faces, but didn't see anyone he knew. It had taken all his courage to come to the *La Cage aux Folles* chorus call that he'd signed up for the week before, and he still wasn't feeling entirely himself. But since his attempt to apologize to Sy Hampton had failed, he had to do something to get on with his life. Securing a new restaurant job was far less important to him than proving that he could still dance gracefully. Besides, if he landed a theater job, he wouldn't need to worry about a day job for a while.

He was also playing a little game with himself. He wanted to see if anyone recognized either his face or his name, and whether that would affect his chances. So far, he hadn't noticed anyone smirking or pointing, but the real test would come inside the audition room.

He glanced down at the white index card he'd filled out with his contact information, which he held together with his photo and résumé. He was going to need a new headshot soon. This one was almost ten years old, and he had changed. Jordan's death had given him a gravitas that he'd lacked at thirty. The edge was off his optimism as well. Maybe he'd quit altogether, change careers. The union offered career transition seminars precisely for people like him.

Don't rush into anything, he reminded himself. This is not the time to make a big life decision. One step at a time.

Tripp's group of ten was called into the large studio to dance. The monitor collected their materials and handed them to the creative team who were seated behind a long table. Tripp watched as they scanned the pictures, résumés, and contact cards, passing them among themselves. He saw the artistic director glance at his résumé. She looked up, caught his eye, and gave Tripp a little wave, which he returned.

Doesn't count, he thought. She remembers me from *On the Town*.

The choreographer demonstrated a combination that wasn't particularly challenging—nothing compared to what he'd had to do for *A Chorus Line*—and the ten of them danced it through twice.

"Just a moment," the choreographer said.

He consulted with the table and collected a small stack of cards. Then he called three names, Tripp's among them, and dismissed the others. The three who were kept watched one another sing their sixteen-bar excerpts. Tripp sang his standard "I've Got a Crush on You" and got no response from the stone faces at the table.

The director finally spoke. "Thank you. Callbacks are next Thursday. We'll let you know."

The monitor ushered Tripp and the other two back into the lounge and brought in the next group of ten.

He'd done it! He'd danced well enough to be asked to sing, and he'd sung as well as he usually did. But most important, nobody had made any reference to his misadventure. He'd never been so relieved to get no reaction at all from a table of auditors. Perhaps there was hope after all.

"Tripp?! Hey, aren't you Tripp Macgregor?" called a voice from across the room.

He cringed as several heads turned to look his way. But just as quickly, the heads, unimpressed, returned to whatever they'd been doing before, and a shortish, baby-faced man headed toward him.

"Hey, I'm Jake. Michael's boyfriend. I gave him your message, did he ever call you back?"

Tripp was suddenly having difficulty breathing. This . . . pip-squeak was Michael's boyfriend? Then again, maybe that explained why Michael felt the need to dally elsewhere.

"No, but that's okay," he managed to answer. "He doesn't have to."

"Well, just so you know, I did tell him."

"Thanks."

"So, how do you know Michael?"

"We, uh, met at the *Chorus Line* callbacks."

Jake nodded. "I recognized your name when they called you inside. At least you got to sing," he added enviously.

Jake had been in his group and Tripp didn't even remember seeing him there. He found he felt a little sorry for the guy.

"Well, good luck," Tripp said.

"Thanks, but I already know I'm out of it. Maybe you have a shot, though," said Jake, trying to sound upbeat.

"I meant with Michael," said Tripp.

Tripp left Jake pondering his parting words and exited the building as quickly as he could. He'd passed the test he'd set for himself. Even if he didn't get called back, he'd gotten on the horse and stayed put for a good long jump. He'd been recognized, but only because of who he was, not because of what he'd done.

It wasn't until he crossed Times Square that he realized he'd forgotten to recite his mantra before the audition. On the other hand, the worst had already happened to him. There was no need to chant it ever again.

FORTY-SIX

VALENTINA COULDN'T STOP THINKING about poor Tripp Macgregor. It didn't seem fair that Sy wouldn't see him, or her, or anybody, for that matter. She knew he felt angry and betrayed, but at some point he would have to face the world again, just as she and Tripp were doing.

And then this morning, the phone call had come. Her services were no longer required at Hampton & Sage. Effective immediately.

Now she and Tripp were both out of a job, all because of that smarmy wine dealer from Shoreham's with the cheeks that looked like they'd been slapped. She'd love to slap them now—good and hard. There was no doubt in her mind that he was really to blame. Especially now that she knew Tripp hadn't been warned until the last minute that there were reporters coming. If Antony Farrell hadn't convinced the owner to invite the press, Tripp wouldn't have been startled by the flashbulbs and fallen. He was as much a victim as Sy.

Sy must really hate her to have fired her, she thought as she walked down her block toward the shops on Twentieth Avenue. It was worse than she'd imagined. He never wanted to look at her again, even in the safety of his office, where all he really had to do was give her orders—and even those could be indirect, through Miss Banks. Fine. Let him find another secretary, and she'd find another job. She'd forget all about him.

Except that she couldn't. Not without first telling him the truth. But how could she even get him to listen to her now that he'd fired her and instructed his housekeeper or whoever she was to bar the door?

She stopped at a deli and bought a packaged pound cake slice. There was a playground a few blocks away, and she sat down on a bench to eat it, watching the kids run around while their babysitters ignored them and gossiped among themselves.

Maybe she could be a babysitter. The money wasn't as good, but the hours were flexible and it would be more relaxing. She could find a job nearby and not have to commute an hour and a half each way into the city.

A toddler running toward her fell splat on his face and erupted in earsplitting screams. His negligent sitter hauled her bulk up from the bench and ambled over.

Then again, maybe not.

She chucked the cake wrapper into a garbage can and returned home, thinking about Tripp. Even if he hadn't dropped the wine, he would still be a waiter who'd just lost a Broadway show and a boyfriend, working in a restaurant nobody had heard of. She'd still be a secretary who had no idea what to say to a boss who thought he'd been on a date with her, but hadn't. And Sy—well, Sy would have gotten to drink his precious wine. But how would he have felt the next morning? Wouldn't it be like waking up the day after winning an Academy Award? Valentina had always imagined that to be the worst day of a movie star's life. What did a Best Actress do with herself the next day? Go to the gym? Valentina thought she would just take her statuette and walk straight into the Pacific Ocean, because really, after that, what was left?

As she drew up in front of her building, she spotted a familiar form sitting on the steps. Unbelievable. He was like a bad penny.

Jerry jumped up as soon as he saw her. "Val!"

"What do you want, Jerry?" she said, already weary of the conversation they hadn't yet had. "To rub it in?"

He blushed. "Well, it don't sound like your date with Mr. Big Balls worked out so good. But hey, at least you got your, um, face in the papers."

"Nice, Jer. Thanks for stopping by. Come again when you can't stay as long."

She rummaged in her bag for her keys.

"No, really," he said, taking her arm. He scanned her face hungrily. "You gotta know it was never gonna work out. You gave it a go, you lived in the fast lane for a night, and now maybe you can give me another chance. What do you say?"

"Oh, Jerry." She pulled her arm away. "You and Sy have nothing to do with each other. I know I told you that's why I didn't want to go out anymore, but the truth is . . ."

She thought of Tripp and how brave he was to attempt to face Sy, and she took a deep breath.

"I don't love you, Jerry. I should have told you a long time ago, but it was just easier to go along with it. Even after I dumped you, I kept thinking about you, and at first I thought maybe I'd come back. And if you wanna know the real truth, when Sy first asked me out with him, I told him I couldn't because you were my boyfriend."

She sat down on the top step and gazed out into the street. She was aware of Jerry still hovering above her.

"But I realized that I'd only have gone back to you for the same reason I stayed too long in the first place. Because you'd have me. And that's not a good enough reason."

She could sense Jerry shifting his weight back and forth, and he finally sank down next to her in defeat.

"I've been a bitch, and I know it," she continued, keeping her eyes trained on a group of boys tossing a ball on the sidewalk across the street. "I used you, and I was shitty to you, and I'm sorry. You're not a bad person, Jerry, and maybe we can still be friends."

"So it's not that you don't wanna get married."

She shook her head.

"And it's not that you're in love with this Sy guy."

"No."

"You just don't love me."

It sounded so stark. No wonder she hadn't been able to say it before. But she knew this would finally free her from Jerry. There was no arguing with the truth.

"I'm sorry."

They sat for a while in silence, and finally Jerry said, "Well. I guess we know where we stand." He made a grunting sound, which almost sounded like crying, but she didn't want to take the chance and look.

"I brought you something. It ain't much. It ain't what he gave you, but I wanted you to see that I'm no slouch."

He stood up and handed her a bag from the liquor store.

She pulled out the bottle. The label, lettered in red and black, read "Château Bourgneuf Pomerol," with a red seal above the name. It didn't look cheap.

"Jerry."

He shrugged and started down the steps. "Just gimme a thought when you drink it." He looked back at her with a wan smile. "And don't drop it."

Before she could think of anything to say, he was gone. She contemplated running after him. It seemed wrong for her to accept his gift when she'd just stomped on his heart. She hadn't even noticed him holding it. He could easily have taken it away with him and she'd have been none the wiser. But he'd given it to her all the same. The only thing to do was to accept it as a peace offering, and take comfort in knowing that she wasn't likely to find Jerry squatting on her steps again anytime soon.

Valentina turned the key in the lock and trudged down the hall to her apartment. She set the bottle on her kitchen counter and tossed the crumpled bag under the sink. She went into the bathroom and switched on the light over the mirror to examine her teary face.

And it was there, in the bathroom, where all brilliant ideas are born, that Valentina had hers.

She ran out to the kitchen and examined the wine again.

"Thanks, Jer," she whispered under her breath.

Then she grabbed her jacket, purse, and the bottle and flew out of her apartment, down the steps. She ran as fast as she could down Twentieth Avenue, past the architectural jumble of apartment buildings and two-family houses until she reached Eighty-second Street, panting from the exertion. Vito opened his door wearing black jeans and a tight black T-shirt stretched over his barrel chest.

"Valentina!"

"Vito," she said, sucking wild gulps of air. "I need your help again."

"Are you okay?" he asked, moving aside to let her in.

"I have a plan." She turned to him and prodded his chest with her long, red fingernail. "But don't you worry. This time, there is no way in hell I'm chickening out."

PART FIVE

THE HARVEST

FORTY-SEVEN

"HELLO, THIS IS ANNETTE LECOCQ. May I speak with Jim Wedekind?"

"Speaking."

Annette took a deep breath and launched into her elevator speech.

"I'm the owner of Parapluie, a new haute cuisine restaurant in Manhattan with an unusual mix of modern décor and classic French and French-Canadian dishes, mostly from traditional family recipes, and I don't believe anyone from *Fine Dining* has visited us yet. We'd love to—"

"Do you have a website?"

"Yes. It's—"

"I'll Google you."

"We're featuring a tasting menu all next week. Our chef de cuisine is Etienne Marceau from Frisson in Montreal, and—"

"Yes, thanks. I'll check out your site," the editor said, and hung up.

Annette crossed *Fine Dining* off her list. There wasn't much chance Wedekind would come. But at least he hadn't said what the editor of *Cuisine* had said:

"If I'm not important enough to invite to the uncorking of the Lafite, I'm surprised you're so interested in me now."

I can't win for trying, Annette thought wearily, as she picked up the phone again and dialed the editor of eatmedrinkme.com.

"Yeah, sure! Restaurants like yours never think of us, and we're trying to upscale a bit. You know how it is," giggled the young woman in charge, who sounded like she was only barely out of high school.

Annette did know how it was. Eatmedrinkme.com was not exactly her target audience. But it was just about all that was left to her, and at least she'd gotten a positive response. Annette put them in the "yes" column underneath the neighborhood weekly free paper. She knew she was scraping the bottom of the barrel, but the publications that were most important to her had come and gone and were not likely to return.

Nor, it seemed, were her new customers.

For more than a week, business was better than she could have hoped. And then it tapered off. She was astonished at how quickly the numbers returned to their pre-disaster lows.

She knew why, and it served her right. They hadn't come for the food, they'd come to gawk. Even if they'd enjoyed their meals, they weren't telling their friends. They weren't returning to repeat the experience. Her fifteen minutes of fame were over, and there was no hope of it lasting, because it had attracted the gapers, the tourists, the schadenfreude crowd. Not the foodies.

She pushed her chair back from her desk and ran her hand through her hair, which, she realized idly, she hadn't washed in a week. There had to be other ways to get customers in. She desperately wished that she hadn't let Antony convince her to invite all the A-listers the same night. There was simply nobody left to ask.

What she wouldn't give for a return to the frenzy of those first few days after the accident: excited guests having their photos snapped under the painting, or the more discreet ones examining the floor during long, purposeful walks to the restroom and back. The stressed-out waitstaff, the mounting receipts, Etienne swearing in the kitchen, and the line cooks in the weeds. Annette had recouped her losses from the night of the accident, but her daily take was dropping again. Soon she'd be right back where she started. On the verge of closing.

"I'm leaving for the night," she said to a surprised Justine, who was busy explaining to two young men that the table where the wine fell was occupied at present, but the stain on the floor was visible from just about anywhere.

Her folly would be forever memorialized in the bamboo floor. Why had she ignored the decorator's recommendation to do thick veneer? Never mind, she thought bitterly, she should just put a fence around it like an excavated ruin and charge extra for viewing.

Annette walked up Lexington Avenue in a supremely surly mood. She needed some perspective, and she needed time to think. As she headed uptown, she counted restaurants. Within ten blocks there were fifteen, only one of which appeared to be French. But Annette knew that most of the French restaurants were clustered on Madison or hidden down the side streets. Besides, Lexington wasn't even restaurant central. Third Avenue—Second even more so—was home to clumps of them. And this was only the East Side. There was downtown, the West Side, the Theater District. What was she thinking? What on earth had possessed her to choose New York? And when would she decide enough was enough? When she ran through her capital?

She turned down Seventy-first Street toward Third Avenue and passed a tiny little restaurant with twinkling lights, set down a small flight of steps. She paused and looked at the menu. It was called Auvergne, and the bill of fare looked similar to hers, minus the Canadian influence. On impulse, she went inside.

"*Bon soir,*" said the hostess, a plumpish, ruddy-faced woman of about sixty.

"*Bon soir. Je suis seule,*" said Annette. She had long since stopped being bothered by dining alone.

The woman smiled. "*Un moment.*"

She consulted with a waiter, an older gentleman, who then gestured to Annette.

"*Suivez-moi, Madame, s'il vous plaît.*"

She followed him down the long, rectangular space, where he seated her at a banquette in the rear. The restaurant was doing healthy business for a Thursday night. Much better than the stragglers she'd just left at her own. Annette took her menu from the waiter and thanked him.

"*Ce restaurant existe depuis longtemps?*" she asked.

"*Vingt-trois ans, madame,*" said the waiter, with a slight bow. "*Voudriez-vous voir la carte des vins?*"

"*Oui, merci.*"

She took the wine list and scanned it. Auvergne had been here for twenty-three years. This was what she was up against. Perhaps she'd been foolish to try to be both cutting-edge and traditional. It set her up in too many categories. Perhaps she should be one thing and stick to it. Perhaps she should fire Etienne and return to the kitchen herself.

She ordered coq au vin, which she considered a good touchstone for a French restaurant, partnering it with a half bottle of Pinot Noir from an Oregon vineyard she'd never heard of. It was quite nice, but a further glance over the wine list confirmed that hers was superior. She started with *moules marinières* and finished with a raspberry soufflé.

It was all delicious. It was also, she was discouraged to see, close to twenty dollars cheaper than what she'd have charged for the same meal. Even though she was trying to reach a loftier crowd, aiming to be a destination rather than a neighborhood restaurant, the fact still gave her pause.

She paid the check and thanked her doppelgänger.

"Tout était delicieux."

The woman gave a demure smile. *"Merci beaucoup."*

"Vous êtes la propriétaire, madame?"

The woman held up her hand in a defensive gesture. *"Pas moi. Mon mari, Monsieur Poulet. Moi, je m'occupe des clients en salle."* She gave Annette a conspiratorial wink.

Of course. The owner was a man, and his wife was the mannequin in the window. She should have known.

But as Annette continued on her way uptown, warmed by the wine and the fine meal, a plan was taking shape in her head. It wasn't the sort of plan she'd originally intended to percolate. This one didn't involve revenge on Antony Farrell, although she did hope he'd cut his forked tongue on the broken glass. No, tempting though it was to try to engineer some kind of retribution and jeopardize his reputation, she knew that he wasn't worth wasting any more energy on. She wasn't going to stoop any further to his level. If there was such a thing as karma, it would find him, but she wouldn't be the instrument of his destruction. Her priority was to save herself and her baby. She knew exactly what she needed to do.

FORTY-EIGHT

"Now, you're clear about how this is gonna work?" Valentina asked Elisa as they emerged from the subway and elbowed their way through the crush around Rockefeller Center.

"For the hundredth time, yes!" said Elisa impatiently.

"If we can pull this off, everything might be okay," said Valentina fervently. Sensing that Elisa was about to protest, she forged ahead. "I don't want to hear all the reasons why it won't. I swear to you, if it goes wrong, I'll take all the blame. Honest. But it won't. Not if we do what Vito told us."

"I can't believe I agreed to this," said Elisa, her voice dripping with regret, as they turned onto Madison Avenue.

They were getting plenty of stares as they made their way uptown. They were dressed identically, and provocatively. Tight black miniskirts, red leather jackets, transparent white blouses over pink lace spandex camisoles, stretched to the limit by their pushiest push-up bras. They had hot-rolled their hair so that it draped seductively away from their widow's peaks, and were wearing more makeup than either of them was accustomed to. They did their best to ignore the stares and catcalls, and finally they arrived around the corner from their destination. Elisa shifted her weight impatiently.

"Come on, let's do this."

"You gotta give me enough time, but not too much," urged Valentina one last time, patting the large red satchel at her side.

"I know, I know!"

"Okay. Here goes!

Valentina pushed open the glass doors to Shoreham's.

It was a different young man behind the front desk this time. Valentina approached, smiling disarmingly and trying to ignore her heart, which was beating so hard she was sure he was about to ask what all the racket was.

"I have an appointment with Antony Farrell. Miss D'Ambrosio."

The young man ogled her greedily and nodded. "He's expecting you. Just up the stairs, second floor. Go into the Park Room on the right, and his office is through the dais in the back."

"Thanks," said Valentina. She went up the stairs, did what she needed to do, and came back down.

"I think the door is locked."

The young man frowned. "Really?"

Valentina gave an innocent shrug.

He left his post behind the desk and led Valentina up the stairs, pulling a key ring from his pocket. She knew that as soon as he was out of sight, Elisa would come in. He fit a key into the handle of the Park Room door.

"That's odd," he said. "I wonder why he locked it."

He didn't, thought Valentina, smiling to herself.

The young man turned the key and pushed the door open. He took two steps into the room and pointed to the platform and the door to the side that Valentina knew led to Farrell's office.

She lingered in the doorway, blocking the entrance for a moment, and was relieved to hear footsteps behind her and the door to the ladies' room open and close.

Sending a silent thank-you to Vito, whose familiarity with the layout of Shoreham's was crucial to the plan, Valentina followed the young man into the room.

"Oh, yeah, now I see. Okay, thanks," she said.

He left her, closing the door to the Park Room behind him.

Valentina double-checked that the tiny button under the inside handle was back in the unlocked position. Then she crossed the room, stepped onto the stage, and knocked on the door to the side. Farrell opened it.

"Well, hello again, Miss Ambrosia," he purred.

"Hi," she said, with a shyness that was not coy. After all, he had memories of a night in bed that she did not.

"Come in." He gestured beyond into the handsomely decorated office. "I'm all ready for you.

She entered the small room, glanced briefly at her watch, and looked around.

There were two open bottles of wine and two glasses on the small round table. She also noted, with some disgust, that there was a large, inviting leather couch against the wall that she hadn't registered the first time, although she supposed it must have been there. The small wine rack on the side table still held its twelve bottles.

"You know," he said, closing the door behind her, "I was surprised to hear from you. Your silent disappearance from my apartment sent a very definite message. But perhaps I misread it."

He turned the small lock on the office door.

"So, what exactly brings you here?" he asked, facing her, his back to the door.

She sat down on the couch and crossed her legs alluringly. "I got all excited about tasting the wine that night, but then it tasted like floor."

Farrell threw his head back and laughed. Valentina wondered if he knew how unattractive it made him look.

"So you thought you'd take me up on my offer to savor something rare and valuable?"

She rose from the couch and walked over to the wine rack.

"Uh, uh, uh! Not those," Farrell said. "Those are a bit too rare and a bit too valuable, even for you, my dear. The ones I've opened will do for the purpose."

"Mmmmm." Valentina nodded, her gaze brushing over the labels on the racked bottles. The Pétrus had migrated to the middle of the second row.

Okay, Elisa, she thought. Now would be a good time for you to knock.

But no knock came. Farrell returned to the table, where he poured from one of the bottles, and handed her the glass.

"This is a 2005 Haut-Bailly, appellation Pessac-Léognan."

She instinctively dipped her nose into it, the way Vito had taught her, and was pleased to notice that she did it without thinking.

"Berries. And kind of earthy or woody," she said, with more confidence than she'd ever felt before when tasting wine. Maybe it was because she could not have cared less about impressing Antony Farrell.

"Well, well." Farrell raised an eyebrow. "You surprise me. Now taste."

Valentina took a sip of the wine. Even she could tell it was in a different class from Vito's best.

"It's elegant, isn't it?" asked Farrell.

She nodded. "Tell me about where it's from."

As much as she was, to her surprise, enjoying herself, she knew her little visit wasn't going to stay about wine for much longer, especially with a couch in the room.

What was taking Elisa so long?

Farrell set his glass down and took hers from her hand, placing it next to his on the small round table so that their rims touched.

"Later, perhaps. You were a very naughty girl to run off like that and leave me to nurse my hangover all alone," he murmured as he kissed her hair.

What an arrogant son of a bitch, thought Valentina. Elisa, where are you?!

She pulled away. "Let's try the other wine."

Farrell grabbed her arm and kissed her forcibly on the lips. The linger of the wine on his lips was more acidic than in the glass, and although she wanted to pull away, she knew she had to play along.

"Come over here," he said breathily as he pulled away. "Put your bag down." He indicated the red satchel on her arm.

Oh, no. No way, she thought, hugging the bag closer.

"Here, let me take that for you," he said.

Valentina froze. Oh, God, Elisa, what the hell is taking so long? she thought desperately.

As Farrell reached for her bag, there was a loud knock at the door. He jumped back.

"Yes?" he called out, annoyed.

"Valentina? Valentina? Are you in there?"

Farrell looked at her, instantly suspicious. Sending up a prayer of thanks, she gave a relaxed, bored sigh.

"It's just my sister. I told her to meet me here. She wants to try the wine, too, and she actually knows something about it. You'll like her," said Valentina as suggestively as she could. "She once tasted a Lafite." Valentina couldn't resist that last jab, knowing that he wouldn't figure it out until much later.

He glared at her and crossed the room to unlock the door.

Valentina seized her chance. She quickly pulled Jerry's Château Bourgneuf Pomerol from her red satchel and grabbed the Pétrus from the wine rack. As Farrell unlocked the door, she swapped it with Jerry's Bourgneuf, which was no longer immediately recognizable as such, now that Vito had pasted the 1981 Pétrus label from his collection on it. The extra time Farrell took standing there staring at Elisa in quiet shock was just enough for her to safely stow the real Pétrus in her bag.

By the time he whirled around, his face ashen, Valentina was standing as she had been, her bag at her side.

It was clear he knew he'd been had, but was struggling to work out precisely how. "Valentina, who the bloody hell is this?" he asked unsteadily.

"I'm Valentina," said Elisa, looking over Farrell's shoulder at Valentina, who nodded ever so slightly to indicate that the task was accomplished, and they should make their point and get the hell out of there.

"That's my sister, Elisa," said Valentina. "*I'm* Valentina."

"Oh, *thaaaat's* right. *You're* being Valentina today," said Elisa with a bewitching smile. She turned innocently to Antony. "But which one of us was Valentina at the restaurant?"

"And which of us was Valentina in bed?" added Valentina, crossing the room.

Farrell closed his eyes for a moment and shook his head as if he were trying to wrench himself awake from a bad dream. When he opened them, Valentina was standing next to Elisa, and she knew that the effect of the two of them, identical to begin with and now dressed in matching outfits, must be making his head spin.

"Well, I'd say it was me," said Elisa, turning to Valentina, "except he was such a forgettable fuck, I can't remember."

Valentina's eyes flashed. "You got one thing right, sis. He is a fuck."

"What do you want?" asked Farrell hoarsely.

"Stay away from Sy Hampton," said Valentina in a hard voice. "You've done him enough harm, and I think if he ever sees you again, he'll rip your fucking head off."

"And stay away from us. Both of us," said Elisa in her broadest Brooklynese. "We won't rip your head off, we'll get our family friend Vito to do it for us. And I think you know what I mean when I say *family*."

"You bloody bitches," hissed Farrell. "Get the hell out of here!"

They didn't need to be told twice. Valentina turned and stalked out after Elisa. She could feel Farrell's hot, angry eyes on her ass and gave it an extra teasing wiggle, which prompted Farrell to slam his door. They bolted through the Park Room and down the steps.

"Excuse me, please don't run—" the young man began. When he saw the two of them together, he gasped. "Hey! What the—"

But they didn't stop to enjoy his confusion. Farrell's had been satisfying enough. When they reached the street, they began to laugh hysterically, slapping their palms in the air and hooting with glee.

It was, beyond a doubt, the most rewarding switch they'd ever pulled.

FORTY-NINE

As hard as Tripp tried, he couldn't get a read on the *La Cage aux Folles* audition. He'd been called back for one of the cross-dressing cagelles, and it had gone well enough. But then a strange thing happened. He completely forgot about it. When it finally occurred to him to wonder whether he'd gotten the job, he opened his mind to receive his usual message from the universe.

And there was nothing.

Not even the certainty that no decision had yet been made—nothing. It was as if that channel, that sixth sense he'd always had about auditions, had been switched off. He'd never known how or why it happened in the first place, so there was no way to tap into whatever psychic energy stream he had always instinctively and unconsciously found to receive that information.

Had the show been cast? Had he been cast?

He'd have to wait to find out through normal channels, just like everyone else.

Even stranger, he found he truly didn't care one way or the other. If he didn't get the job, he thought he might use the time to reconnect with old friends. People he hadn't seen much since Jordan died.

As he strolled through the Chelsea greenmarket, he decided not to be so quick to look for either a theater job or a waiting job. He had enough money in the bank to float for a while. Most important, he had proven to himself that he could do it again. He wasn't scared of failing anymore. And for all his fear that people would be pointing and staring at him on the street, nobody gave him a second look. Of course, it probably helped that he'd holed up in his house for the first several days nursing his wounds, but the incident had proven to be a fleeting New York minute, relegated now to urban legend.

Shoshana was right. Already he could, if not quite appreciate it himself, at least acknowledge that there did exist an awful humor in it. In the irony of the broken bottle being the most expensive one on record. In the utter loss of propriety of the assembled wine experts—including the head of the wine department of Shoreham's, for God's sake—abandoning themselves in a moment of savage animal desire. They had shown their real selves, those slurpers of the spilled wine. It was like a sci-fi cartoon where the face of the sweet-looking princess flashes away for a moment, revealing the fanged, sharp-eared alien who has taken up residence inside her.

No such ignominy had befallen Tripp. He hadn't revealed his true self, he had merely fulfilled the destiny of his name, and, as far as he was concerned, there was now nowhere to go but up.

When he looked at it that way, it was pretty damn liberating.

Besides, it was all so silly—drinking expensive wine was as inane as playing a drag queen in a musical. How could he—or anyone else—think these things were important, when people hurt, bled, loved, and lost?

He decided that if the producers of the theater in Philadelphia did call to offer him *La Cage aux Folles,* he would not accept. Thanks, but no thanks. For once, he felt like the audition had been the job, and it was enough. He had better things to do with his life. He wasn't entirely sure what they were, but that didn't worry him. He was game to try anything that appealed. He sat down on the steps of a brownstone and contemplated his colorful purchases, a shiny, waxy red pepper, purple-headed broccoli, long green and white leeks.

Tripp had never realized just how terrified of failure he was. He was paralyzed by the fear of it. And as he stared at the florets on the head of the broccoli, he realized that he had always insulated himself against failing at too high a level, where too many important people would see and bar him from the temple of theater forevermore. He had, mistakenly, thought that he'd been psychologically ready for a big Broadway show, but he realized now that he hadn't been at all. There was still a layer of self-preservation in operation—the mechanism that made him turn his head to admire Michael's smile just as he was about to execute a difficult turn—

that soured things just enough before someone else's opinion did the job instead.

He could see this now, because he had failed spectacularly and publicly—and survived. Who cared? Big fucking deal. He knew that if he had the *Chorus Line* audition to do over again, he'd ace it.

And he also knew, paradoxically, that even if he was given that chance, he wouldn't take it. As he pulled his denim jacket tight against the chill of early October, he realized that he no longer had any interest in performing. None at all.

FIFTY

VITO SMACKED HIS LIPS and handed the 1961 Pétrus back to Valentina. "I'd love to uncork this beauty right here and now."

Valentina hugged the bottle to her chest. "Well, you can't. That's not why I took it. So what do you think? Will it get his attention?"

"You'd better believe it. This baby would go for anywhere from $6,000 to $9,000."

"Farrell said $8,000." She glanced nervously at Elisa. "What if he gets in trouble?"

"That snake?" snorted Elisa, who was sitting next to Valentina at Vito's dining room table. "I wouldn't worry about him."

"But it isn't his wine. It belongs to the auction house."

"Don't tell me you're sitting here feeling sorry for him!" crowed Elisa.

"You know," said Vito, looking across the table at them, "when Elisa straightens her hair out and you wear the same clothes, it's almost impossible to tell you apart. It's freaky."

"Yeah, yeah, we know," said Elisa, with a dismissive wave of her hand. "Okay, I've gotta run." She pushed her chair back and stood up. "Thanks for helping us out, Vito." She turned to Valentina. "Sorry it took me so long to get into Farrell's office. When I was hiding in the bathroom, I realized I actually had to go."

"That's okay. Thanks for everything."

"Sure. But you know, Val, you should give yourself more credit. You could have gone that night. You'd have been fine. You'd have behaved better than I did, that's for sure. And I gotta tell you, from the way Sy Hampton was looking at me, I don't think he gives a shit whether you know anything about wine or not."

Valentina hugged her sister and watched her go. Then she turned back to Vito.

"I bet Farrell's steaming mad right about now about Jerry's Bordeaux. I mean, how's he gonna sell that?"

A sly smile crossed Vito's face. "You wanna have some more fun?"

Vito winked at her and pulled out his cell phone.

"Hey, Tony, it's Vito here. Listen, I've got a little unofficial information that you might wanna follow up. It involves a bottle of 1961 Pétrus. I happen to know that our friend Antony Farrell seems to have misplaced it . . . I'm afraid I can't reveal that. But let's just say it's a nice little scoop for you in return for bringing me along . . . I'm just saying you might want to see what Shoreham's has to say. Yeah . . . you got it. Ciao."

Valentina gasped, her eyes wide. "I can't believe you just did that."

"What? You don't think the creep deserves to be outed in *Wine and Dine?*"

"He does, but—"

"Listen, a guy like that—he thinks it's all about him. Attractive as all hell, but fucking dangerous, that kind." He glanced toward the kitchen, where Roseanne was making a ricotta cheesecake. "Take it from me," he whispered.

"Will they fire him?" Valentina asked.

Vito shrugged. "I would. But even if they don't, Tony's blog is huge. It'll be enough so people might start taking their business back to Christie's or Sotheby's if they think Shoreham's is unreliable. So yeah, if it were up to me, I'd sack him."

"Jeez, Vito. Remind me never to piss you off!"

Vito laughed heartily, then let his gaze rest wistfully once again on the Pétrus.

"So when are you gonna give it to him?"

"Tomorrow, I guess. I've had enough excitement for one day."

"And what are you gonna say?"

Valentina bit her lip. "I was just gonna leave it with a note."

"Chicken shit," scolded Vito. "Don't you wanna see the look on his face when you hand him a bottle of eight-thousand-dollar vino?"

"But that's nothing to him!"

"Yeah, but coming from you, it may as well be eighty thousand."

"It's not like I paid for it. Christ, Vito, I stole it!"

Vito flung the loose end of his scarf over his shoulder. "Nothing like a little petty larceny to show you care." He saw the horrified look in Valentina's eyes and quickly added, "The point is, no matter how you slice it, it did cost you something. You're making it up to him in the only way you can, and he's gotta at least stop and hear you out."

Valentina walked over to the low bookshelf and ran her fingers over the spines of a set of old hardcover kids' books. "I used to think he was just this ritzy, stuffy snob, but I'm really worried about him."

"Take the Pétrus and go see him," said Vito. "Believe me, it will mean something to him."

Valentina turned around to face Vito. "I don't understand wine—or him. But what I really don't understand is why I care so much if he's okay or not. It doesn't make any sense."

"It will," Vito said, nodding sagely. "Do what I tell you, and it will."

FIFTY-ONE

Sy pulled the Lexus into the curved driveway of a low frame house nestled underneath the long white ridge of the Shawangunk Mountains.

"We're here," he called to Eric, who was in the backseat slurping the last of a Coke from the Stewart's where they'd stopped for gas.

Eric jumped out of the car and pointed to the jagged heights. "Wow! You think anyone ever climbs them?"

"Probably," said Sy. "Come on, leave that in the car."

Eric threw the empty cup onto the floor of the backseat and slammed the door, and they started up the driveway together.

The front door opened, and a tall, slender man with iron gray hair emerged.

"Mr. Hampton?" he asked.

Sy extended his hand. "Please. Sy."

The man smiled and came forward. "Rick Tague, nice to meet you. Welcome to Stony Kills Vineyard."

"Thanks for making time for us. This is my son, Eric."

Eric dutifully held out his hand. "Have you ever climbed up there?" he asked, indicating the mountains once he got his hand back.

"Yeah. It's pretty awesome."

"Can we go?" Eric asked excitedly.

Sy patted his shoulder. "Mr. Tague was kind enough to offer us a private tour of his winery, and that's the order of the day."

"Please, call me Rick. You, too," he added, winking at Eric. "Now, are you guys hungry? It's a bit of a drive from the city."

"We're fine, thanks," said Sy, looking around. "I always forget how beautiful it is up here."

"I wouldn't live anywhere else." Rick smiled. "Come on, and I'll show you around."

Rows of vineyards stretched endlessly before them. Sy could see four men in the distance, moving slowly among the vines.

"We're harvesting now, so you can see how heavy the grapes are," said Rick, cradling a bunch in his hand.

"Can I taste one?" asked Eric.

"I think I can spare a grape or two." Rick plucked a few plump dark globes. "This is a Cabernet Franc grape. They're popular in the Hudson Valley. Less fussy and more easily grown in this unpredictable climate than the Sauvignon grape."

"I'm not all that familiar with Cab Franc, to tell you the truth," said Sy.

"There are a few varietals we cultivate that you may not know about. Interesting thing about Cab Franc—especially to a fan of Bordeaux, like I know you are—is that recent DNA testing on the grapes proved that Cab Franc is actually the father of Cabernet Sauvignon. Most people aren't aware of that."

"You're right. I wasn't," said Sy.

"Who's the mother?" Eric piped up.

Rick laughed. "Sauvignon Blanc. A white grape." Rick turned back to Sy. "Cab Francs are spicier, more herbal, lots of berry flavors. I'll have you try one when we get inside. You'll see what you're missing."

"Mmmm . . ." Eric licked the grape juice from his lips. "Those are even better than the grapes Mom buys from Eli's."

"What you eat are table grapes."

"Can you make wine from those? Like could I take a bunch from my lunch and squeeze them and make wine and sell it to the other kids?"

Rick ruffled his hair playfully. "A little entrepreneur! Yes, you could, but it wouldn't taste that great. Although before Napa Valley reshaped the wine industry, that's pretty much what we got here in the States."

They moved from the vineyard into the winery, where Rick showed them the stemmer-crusher, the massive steel fermentation tanks, and the heavy wooden barrels wreathed with metal reinforcements and labeled in chalk with varietal names that were, to

Sy's surprise, unfamiliar: Baco Noir, Seyval Blanc, Vignoles.

"How much do you know about the history of winemaking in the Hudson Valley?" Rick asked, noting Sy's interest in the names.

"I'm embarrassed to say, nothing at all. And I grew up in Poughkeepsie!"

"Without knowing exactly how old you are, I'd guess you were living here during the fallow years," said Rick. "Things have really changed. Here, have a seat."

Rick pulled up chairs for Sy and Eric and leaned against a metal rail.

"The Hudson Valley has both the oldest commercial winery and the oldest vineyard in the country. Brotherhood Winery has been operational under one name or another since 1830, and Benmarl has vines dating back to the eighteenth century. The *terroir* is difficult, though, and it's taken a long time to figure out that what works best here are French-American hybrids like the ones you're looking at."

Rick gestured to the barrels behind him and continued.

"Even during the fallow years, the region was always known for its fruit wines—apple, pear, peach—and we've also got a few more or less native varietals like Niagara and Cayuga. Everett Crosby unlocked the region when he started High Tor in the 1950s, which soon became the best-known winery on the East Coast. After Crosby came Mark Miller, who founded Benmarl on the site formerly owned by Andrew Caywood, an important mid-nineteenth-century grape hybridist and pioneer. Miller really kicked Hudson Valley winemaking up a notch—his wines even made it onto the list at the Four Seasons, which was a first. Now we're getting more and more small artisanal wineries. Basically, we're about where Napa and Sonoma were in the mid-seventies, before the Paris Judgment and the influence of Robert Mondavi. On the verge of an explosion."

"This is all rather eye-opening," admitted Sy. "Every time I visit a winery, I'm always struck anew by the details of winemaking. But it's been a while since I've stumbled across an entire region I knew nothing about."

"If you don't mind my being candid," began Rick, "I think that oenophiles who have large discretionary budgets don't often bother with the likes of us. Come on, there's more."

Sy and Eric followed Rick to several racks of green bottles. Rick held one up.

"Here's a bottle of champagne in progress," said Rick. "Only a few wineries in the valley make it. Brotherhood does, and so does Whitecliff. Ours is a *blanc de blanc,* which means it uses Chardonnay grapes, which not many vineyards grow here. You have to add yeast into the second fermentation to get all those great carbon dioxide bubbles. Here, look."

He held it up to the light, and Sy and Eric could see sandy particles swimming around in the clear liquid.

"It's chemical reaction central in there right now. We have to keep rotating the bottles until the yeast has finished its work. Then we tilt them down to get the yeast up to the neck and flash-freeze the sediment into a solid chunk. Twist off the top, take the yeast out, slam in the cork and you're ready for New Year's."

They moved on to the tasting room, where several bottles were waiting.

"Now that you know how it's made, would you like to taste some wine?" Rick asked Eric. He turned to Sy. "That's okay, right?"

Sy nodded. "Absolutely."

Rick poured a glass of golden liquid and handed it to Eric.

"See what you think of this."

Eric took a tentative sip. "It's sweet. Kind of tropical."

"That's a Vignoles. It's a semisweet wine." He poured a different wine and handed it to Sy. "I want you to try a Seyval Blanc."

Sy examined the wine and then tasted it. "Crisp and citrusy. A little like a Sauvignon Blanc. Very refreshing."

Rick poured out two different reds and handed one to Eric, who took a big sip. "Yum! This tastes like Kool-Aid!"

"Easy, sport. It's got a kick to it! Here, you should spit it out after you taste it. We don't want to get you drunk and your dad arrested!" He turned to Sy. "It's a Concord," he explained. "For you, a Baco Noir."

Sy took a sip. "Not unlike a Pinot Noir, but a bit of lavender and mint mixed in there. Very interesting!"

"You've just tasted the Hudson Valley's two signature grapes: Seyval Blanc and Baco Noir."

"Not at all what I expected," admitted Sy.

He tried two more wines, a Vidal Blanc and a Cab Franc, both of which stood up as well as the others.

"I have to say, it's really an honor to have you here, tasting my wine," said Rick.

"Truly, the pleasure is all mine," Sy replied sincerely. "Can you mix a case for me of the Baco Noir, the Cab Franc, and the Seyval Blanc?"

"Absolutely," said Rick. He turned to Eric. "Do you want to pick out a sweatshirt? It's on me."

"Cool!"

Rick left to pack the case, while Eric sorted through the sweatshirt bin in the tasting room, which doubled as a gift shop. Sy walked around the small, slate-floored room. As he looked at the sweatshirts, wine stoppers, kitchen plaques, and corkscrews all stamped with the name Stony Kills Vineyard, it struck him that, for all his experience with wine, he'd never given much thought to the business of running a winery. He walked over to the far wall, where watercolors by a local artist were displayed.

"What do you think?" asked Sy, gesturing to a painting of the white, ridged mountains that Eric wanted to climb. There was a small card underneath, and a price tag. It was on sale for $300.

"I think you should buy a winery," said Eric, coming up for air wearing a green fleece with "A meal without wine is called breakfast" embroidered in gold. "Can I get this one?"

Sy laughed and nodded. He knew Marianne would disapprove, which was all the more reason to say yes.

"Do you like this painting?" he asked again.

Eric wandered over, pushing up the sleeves of the sweatshirt, which was several sizes too big. "Yeah. It looks just like the mountains."

"Would you like it for your room?"

Eric's eyes lit up. "That'd be so awesome!"

Rick came back a few moments later with the case, which he set by the door.

Sy indicated the painting. "I take it this is for sale?"

"Yes. That was done by Tigger Malouf, one of our local artists. He does great landscapes. I think he really captures the beauty and starkness of the Gunks."

"My friend here likes it a lot," said Sy, giving Eric's fleeced shoulders a squeeze. "We'll take it."

"What's the Gunks?" asked Eric, as Sy pulled out his checkbook and paid for his purchases.

"The mountains. They're really called the Shawangunk Ridge, but that's a bit of a mouthful."

"Did you ever think of naming your winery Gunk Vineyards?" Eric said, with a giggle.

"Only when I harvest really poor vintages," Rick said, laughing.

"Is it an Indian name?" asked Sy.

"Might be. So many names around here are. But the origins on this one are murky. Some say it is, but then others insist it derives from an early Dutch word meaning 'smoky air.' Either way, it's a great façade for rock climbing."

"Dad! I want to go!" chirped Eric.

"Maybe. We'll see," said Sy. He turned back to Rick. "How long have you been in business?"

"Let's see, I bought the property in 1984, and of course I had to buy grapes until mine were ready," said Rick, as he wrapped the painting in brown paper and cross-tied it with string. "My first vintage was 1994. I've been expanding steadily, and I turn a decent profit on about twelve thousand cases a year, average. That's with fifty acres of land and twenty acres of grapes. I can manage two kids in college, which is saying something, I guess." He snipped the string with a pocket knife and pushed the painting gently across the counter to Sy. "It'll never make me rich, but it does make me happy."

"How come it makes you so happy?" asked Eric.

"Well," said Rick thoughtfully, "it's a chance to express myself through the wines I make. I can show other people what I love and get them to love it, too. It's a creative process, but it doesn't require a talent in the traditional sense. Only passion and confidence in your own taste."

"And you get to do whatever you want?" asked Eric.

"It's all up to me. Nobody else tells me how to make my wines, what blends to try, what techniques to use, what color my labels should be," said Rick. "It's also a way to feel a connection to a particular place, to the land. And also to a particular time. The wine I make could only have been made with grapes grown on this land, at this point in the twenty-first century. That's what makes every bottle of wine special." He glanced at Sy. "I expect your dad knows what I'm talking about."

Sy cleared his throat and pointed at the clock, whose second hand was a bottle, with a tiny stream of wine that poured over each number as it passed. "We should go," he said.

"Here, grab one of these." Rick handed Sy a large, colorful tabloid. "Proof that we've landed on the map. Until now, we were the only major wine region in the country without our own magazine. It'll give you a better idea of what makes the Hudson Valley special. A little history, grape profiles, and features on some of the artisanal wineries I was telling you about, including us."

"Thanks. I look forward to it," said Sy, taking the magazine. "It was very kind of you to give us a private tour."

"No problem. Peter Blomgard is an old friend, and as they say, any friend of his . . ." Rick smiled at Eric's choice of sweatshirt. "You're wearing my favorite one, so you're definitely my friend. Maybe you'll come back up sometime and hike the Gunks with me. I'll show you the waterfall that gives the vineyard its name."

Eric's face broke into a broad grin. "Cool!"

Sy excused himself to use the bathroom, and when he returned, they loaded the wine and the painting into the trunk of the Lexus.

"I'm serious about climbing," Rick said to Sy as he closed the door after Eric. "Next time you guys have a free weekend, give me a call."

Sy shook the winemaker's hand and drove off. As the Gunks receded behind them, he glanced out of the corner of his eye at Eric, who was trying to read his sweatshirt upside down.

"Mom's gonna hate this," he crowed.

"I know. That's why I let you get it. Just to piss her off."

This struck Eric as completely hilarious and he threw back his head and cackled gleefully.

"Can we really come back and go climbing with Rick? He was cool."

"If you want. He seemed sincere in his offer."

Eric hunkered down in his seat, pressing his knees against the passenger seat back. "This is the most fun weekend we've ever had. It's like a mini-vacation. I'm glad you quit your job."

"Me, too." Sy smiled.

Eric yawned. "I mean it about buying a winery. You could afford it."

Sy caught Eric's eye in the rearview mirror. "What are you talking about?"

"I told you in the wine store. And then I could experiment with grapes myself. I like chemistry. I could have my own line of wine, maybe for kids with only a little bit of alcohol, like cough syrup, and I could do an anime label."

Buy a winery? What a crazy idea, thought Sy.

But as he drove through the winding back roads of Ulster County, and back onto Route 9W toward the city, Sy found he couldn't shake the idea. He recalled Rick Tague's words: "It's a creative process, but it doesn't require a talent in the traditional sense." Pippa would certainly approve. He could sell her paintings in the gift shop. Maybe he'd even commission her. Or she could design the labels. And maybe Eric could have his own line of nonalcoholic kiddie wine.

He was getting way ahead of himself. He knew nothing about winemaking, beyond what Rick Tague or any other guide had ever explicated on a tour. It was a pleasant pipe dream, but utterly impractical. It would be years before he'd be able to express himself through winemaking. He doubted he had enough years left.

"It's a nice idea," he said finally, "but I don't know the first thing about actually making wine. As much as I love to drink it."

There was no response, and when Sy looked into the rearview mirror, he saw that Eric had fallen asleep.

FIFTY-TWO

"SO YOU'VE COME ALL THE WAY DOWN to Atlanta for one day just to confess?" asked MaryLou Sampson.

The steadily deteriorating dam that had been holding back the flood of Annette's frustration gave way, and she burst into tears. Throwing herself into the arms of her mentor, she buried her head in the older woman's broad, soft bosom.

"Child, I have never seen you like this! Come and sit down."

MaryLou led Annette to a small table in the back of Sampson's, which, because it was open only for dinner, was quiet at one in the afternoon. Annette had arrived that morning and taken a cab straight there. Her return ticket was for the following morning. She didn't dare stay away from Parapluie any longer than that, but she had to see MaryLou. She hadn't realized how much she needed her mentor, until she'd seen the familiar face, with its wry smile and sharp, coal black eyes that missed nothing.

"I've ruined everything. I'm a failure," sobbed Annette.

"You stay there, I'll be right back."

MaryLou returned a moment later with a bottle of Jack Daniel's and a shot glass. She filled it and handed it to Annette.

"Take a good slug of that, and when you've calmed yourself, I want to know more about this little trick you pulled."

Annette did as she was told and set down the empty glass. The whiskey burned her throat in a purifying way. She wiped her eyes. "I'm sorry. I don't know what came over me."

"Opening a restaurant is a lot of pressure," said MaryLou. "If you're only now crying over it for the first time, I'm amazed you haven't had a heart attack."

Annette rested her head in her arms and stared at the scarred wood table. "I invited all the food and wine press, because he brought a priceless bottle of wine into the restaurant. I didn't ask his permission or warn him in advance. It wasn't my idea, and I guess I knew it was wrong, but it backfired in every possible way." Annette glanced sheepishly at MaryLou. "You'd never have tried a stunt like that."

MaryLou cocked her head to the side. "Annette, I'm no saint. I've pulled a few fast ones in my time. Though I have to admit, I don't think I'd have gone as far as ambushing somebody like that." She shrugged. "But I don't know, if I was desperate enough, maybe I would."

"Well, I learned my lesson," sniffed Annette.

"The real mistake you made was drawing their attention away from the food. You can't blame the press for doing exactly what you asked them to. They wrote about the wine, and it's likely they'd have done that even if it hadn't been a disaster. You had a secret agenda that you didn't share with them."

Annette hadn't thought of it that way. "Is there anything I can do to fix it?"

"Hire a publicist, for one thing. Didn't you learn anything at that fancy restaurant school?"

"You didn't have one. You were successful on the strength of your food and word of mouth."

MaryLou scowled. "And how do you think that happened? How do you think Caroline Wilbur found me? You think she just stopped in one day for a rack of ribs with a photographer trailing her heels? I had a press agent, child! Don't have her anymore, because I don't need her anymore. But you better believe I started off with one. She was friends with Miz Wilbur and that's how that all started."

"How did you afford it?"

MaryLou's eyes misted over momentarily. "My mama was a washerwoman, you know that. She saved her pennies. Not as many as Oseola McCarty, but there was a clutch of women in Mama's little community who saved up like that, trying to outdo each other. When I was starting out, I asked my mama for a loan. A publicist didn't cost nearly as much in those days, and not everyone was using them. But I knew I had a good story to tell, and I knew I needed help telling it. It cost me $500 to start, which was a lot back then, especially for me. I promised to pay my mama back, and I did, every cent and then some.

"But what's important is that you need to know how to ask for help. That's never been one of your strong points, if you don't mind my saying so. And you need to learn to take advice from the right people," MaryLou said pointedly. "Not from ex-lovers who got fancy ideas and are plotting for their own nefarious ends."

Annette pondered this advice while MaryLou walked to the bar and returned with a checkbook and a business card.

"If your grandma who made those fabulous fruit pastries were alive, she'd do this, but she isn't, so I will. I'm making an investment in your venture, and you're going to call this young lady, Jessica Whitbank. She used to work here in Atlanta, and now she's in New York. She's a smart cookie, she knows the restaurant business inside and out, and she'll get you on the right track. You tell her I told you to call." MaryLou wrote out a check and handed it over to Annette. "This'll get you started."

Annette stared at the check and her tears flowed anew. She shook her head. "Five thousand dollars?! MaryLou! I can't take this!"

"You should know better than to argue with me," said MaryLou.

"That's not why I came down here," protested Annette. "I don't want you to think—"

"I know it's not, and I don't think. And if this restaurant doesn't succeed, you'll open another one, somewhere else. I believe in you, Annette. So you made a mistake. I got lucky my first time out, but not everyone does. Cut yourself some slack."

Annette shook her head. "I just feel like somehow, with all the planning and everything I've done, I've gotten off on the wrong foot."

MaryLou folded her arms across her chest and appraised Annette. "Some people always look for shortcuts, and others feel it doesn't count unless they've sacrificed a limb. People like that create obstacles for themselves, even if they don't realize it. That's you, Annette. You like to make things hard for yourself."

MaryLou took Annette's hand in hers and squeezed it. "I know what you've been through. Don't make this restaurant about Roland. You might still meet another man, one who understands the commitment food service takes. Roland was the wrong person at the wrong time. But don't make opening a restaurant any harder than it already is by making it mean something that's only in your head and all wrapped up in your bruised ego."

Annette felt her breathing start to regulate. Maybe it was the whiskey; more likely, it was MaryLou, the only person whose straight talk she'd ever been able to accept. That was why she had booked herself a flight to Atlanta at one a.m. after returning home from work two nights ago. She needed absolution, not for the wrong she'd done Sy Hampton, but for the wrong she'd done herself. She hadn't realized how deeply she'd been blaming herself—her ambition, her ego—for losing Roland. But she supposed that the fault lay just as much with him. Musicians weren't exactly ego-free. It didn't mean she was unlovable. And if she did decide to devote herself entirely to her career—as, indeed, MaryLou had done—it was one thing to freely and consciously choose it, and quite another to sentence oneself to it as a punishment.

And how could Parapluie ever succeed if she was loading it with all that?

MaryLou threw a cook's apron at Annette.

"Prep with me now, and you can eat with the family at four. Then help out in back tonight."

It was a relief to be back in MaryLou's spacious kitchen, just another cook on the line, and Annette determined to pitch in in her own kitchen more. If Etienne didn't like it, that was too bad. By the time she bundled herself back into a taxi for the airport the following morning, she was exhausted, but she also felt cleansed somehow. As she settled into her seat on the plane, she fell almost immediately into a heavy sleep, with MaryLou's final words still echoing in her ear:

"Do it because you love it, not to prove a point. Because if you're doing it to show Roland you can get on without him, don't bother. He stopped watching a long time ago."

FIFTY-THREE

VALENTINA WALKED AROUND THE BLOCK four times before she got up the courage to ring Sy's doorbell. When she finally did, there was no answer.

Now what? She couldn't leave an $8,000 bottle of wine on the front steps. She'd just have to come back another time. It was very frustrating. After steeling herself to see him and practicing what she wanted to say, he wasn't even there. She sat down on the stoop to collect her thoughts, and was lost in imagining for the hundredth time what that evening at Parapluie must have been like, when a voice interrupted her reverie.

"You can't sit here, miss. It's private property."

Valentina looked up to see the woman who had turned her away last time. She jumped to her feet.

"I wanted to see Sy—um, Mr. Hampton."

The woman peered at her. "Didn't you come by once before?"

"Yes. I'm Valentina D'Ambrosio."

The woman looked at her blankly.

"I'm Miss Banks's assistant. He never mentioned me?" Valentina asked.

"No, I don't believe so."

"Oh," said Valentina, oddly disappointed.

"He isn't here. He's upstate with his son."

"I brought him something to . . . I wanted to cheer him up. I brought him a special bottle of wine." Valentina held out the bag.

"I can take that for him," said the woman.

There was no way Valentina was going to turn over the Pétrus to anybody but Sy. The woman must have caught Valentina's expression, because she added, "I'm his housekeeper. Claudine Johnson." She extended her hand, but Valentina was using both of hers to hold the bottle, so she just nodded.

"Why don't you come inside. You can leave it for him," suggested Claudine.

Valentina considered this. "I sort of wanted to talk to him personally," she said.

Claudine put the key in the lock and opened the door. "He's still not feeling up to seeing people. You can write him a note, and we'll leave it with the bottle on the dining room table. I promise, I'll make sure he sees it as soon as he gets home."

Valentina realized that even if she came back another time, she'd still have to get past Claudine. Maybe it was better this way. Even Vito would probably agree, under the circumstances. And she had to admit, she was relieved not to have to face Sy.

She followed Claudine into the house, which was beautiful, elegant, and empty. The kind of house Valentina only saw in movies or read about in glossy magazines. Rising up from the black-and-white-tiled foyer was a wide, curving staircase leading up to the second floor. The banisters and door frames were elaborately carved dark wood, and there was a breathtaking stained-glass chandelier above.

"Come into the kitchen," said Claudine, heading straight for the back of the house. "You can write your note at the desk."

Valentina followed her, marveling at the luxury of it all. "Sy lives here all by himself?"

"Except when his son is here. His wives decorated the place. Nice, huh?"

"You can say that again," said Valentina. "I've got three rooms in Bensonhurst."

Claudine laughed. "And I've got four in Astoria. That's life!"

The kitchen was huge—bigger than Valentina's entire apartment—with a granite-topped island in the middle, and a small desk, television, and easy chair in a little area to the side.

"It's very sweet of you to bring him some wine. He hasn't been himself since . . . since the accident."

"You make it sound like he got hurt," Valentina said nervously.

Claudine looked solemn for a moment. "He did. It hurt his

pride, that's for sure."

She indicated the small desk. Valentina sat and ran her fingers over the granite top that matched the island.

"I was his date. Except I wasn't. I chickened out at the last minute and sent my twin sister instead. I let him down. And I feel like if I'd been there, if it had been me, it might have all been different." She looked up at Claudine. "He still thinks it was me. He doesn't even know I have a sister. And he's mad at me, but he shouldn't be. Not for that anyway. I know he won't take my calls, so that's why I'm bringing him this wine."

Claudine looked at the bottle. "Pétrus, eh? That's an expensive one. How did you come by this?" she asked, narrowing her eyes suspiciously.

"Through a friend who's a wine expert. I can't say more than that."

Claudine sat in the easy chair and examined Valentina curiously. "Mr. Hampton asked you on a date to drink the wine and you didn't go?"

"I know. I feel terrible."

Claudine opened a drawer in the side of the desk. She pulled out a pad of white paper and set it in front of Valentina.

"He must like you a lot."

"I don't know why," said Valentina. "Am I anything like his wives?"

"Not at all. And that's a good thing." Claudine leaned back in her chair. "I've been with Mr. Hampton for twelve years now. He's a nice man. Very considerate, very sensitive. They didn't understand him, those two. The first one, Eric's mother, well, she's a first-class bitch, I don't mind telling you. Too bad, because Eric is a little sweetie." She looked thoughtfully at the ceiling. "The second Mrs. Hampton wasn't so bad, just a little airy-fairy, if you know what I mean. He needs someone with two feet planted on the ground." She eyed Valentina. "You seem pretty down to earth."

Valentina shook her head. "I'm not made for this kind of fancy life. I don't know anything about wine, for one thing."

"There's more to Mr. Hampton than wine." Claudine pulled herself up from the easy chair and began removing pots from cabinets. "And I don't know how much longer he's planning to keep up this lifestyle, now that he's retiring. I don't know whether he's even going to stay in the city."

Valentina looked up from her bag, where she was rummaging for her red pen. "He's retiring?"

Claudine paused and looked at her. "I figured you knew, since he hasn't been going to the office."

"Not me," said Valentina. "I got fired."

"Well, that's why. They don't need you anymore."

This was completely unexpected. Valentina was sure being fired was Sy's way of punishing her for the way Elisa behaved at the restaurant. But her job had simply been eliminated.

"What made him suddenly decide to retire?"

Claudine set the pots down. "This is just my two cents, but I'll tell you what I think. He's fifty-three, and he's lonely. When that wine bottle broke . . ." Claudine shook her head. "I think there are some people who could take a thing like that in stride. Sure, they'd be upset and angry, but they'd snap back. But for a person who's in a vulnerable time of life, that's the kind of thing that can put them right over the edge and they can't handle it. You know, he didn't come home for two days after it happened."

"Where did he go?" asked Valentina, shocked.

"Beats me. But let me tell you, he looked like hell when he got back. Like he hadn't slept or eaten in days. He's pulled himself together, but make no mistake"— Claudine wagged a finger at Valentina—"this has changed him."

Valentina was suddenly extremely grateful that Sy wasn't there. She needed time to absorb what Claudine was telling her. He was no longer a big private equity hotshot, and she wasn't a secretary anymore. They were just two people, both out of work, not sure where life was going to take them next. For the first time, it seemed as if they might have something in common.

She found her red roller point and pulled the notepad toward her. She had been struggling earlier that morning with what to say to Sy, but now the words flowed easily. They weren't the words she had planned on, but, thanks to Claudine, they were more likely to be the right ones.

She folded the note carefully, took some tape from the desk, and stuck it to the neck of the bottle. Claudine turned off the water in the large double sink where she was rinsing lettuce.

"Let's take that into the dining room," she said, drying her hands on a dish towel.

Valentina followed her back through the house, turning right, into the dining room just off the foyer. It was a dramatic room, all blue and peach, with a shiny mahogany table and shield-back chairs. She ran her hand over the smooth wood frame of the nearest chair.

"He must have lots of dinner parties in here."

"Not since he and Pippa split. It's a lovely room, isn't it? A shame it doesn't get more use. Here, why don't you set that down right here."

Valentina carefully placed the bottle on the end of the table nearest the door.

"You know, I caught him in here one night with the Lafite," said Claudine quietly. "I think he was about to open it and drink it himself."

Valentina gasped. "Why didn't he? It was never any use saving the wine for me!"

Claudine's eyes clouded over. "I talked him out of it. I thought he should make an occasion of it." She looked sadly at Valentina. "So, you see? We all played our parts. It was just one of those things."

"Yeah," said Valentina, looking at the Pétrus sitting by itself, the white notepaper flapping against the dark glass of the bottle. "Just one of those things."

FIFTY-FOUR

" '*IT WAS . . . JUST ONE OF THOSE THINGS! Just one of those crazy flings!
One of those bells that now and then rings, just one of those things!*' "
Tripp sang as he tossed tap shoes, dance briefs, kneepads, and other
items he no longer had use for out of his closet. The shoes, in particular, made a satisfying clatter as they landed in a pile in the
middle of the floor. It was amazing how much space he didn't realize he had, and all of it taken up with performing paraphernalia.

He'd been to a career-changing seminar at Actors' Equity, and
the possibilities were exhilarating. Five years ago—a month ago,
even—he'd have found such a gathering depressing, but as he
sorted his things into piles for Goodwill, the garbage, and the rag-
bag, he reflected on the possible futures open to him.

He could be a personal trainer or a massage therapist. Both of
those were body-oriented, natural choices for a dancer. He knew
an awful lot about muscle groups and fitness, and the healing element of massage appealed as well. The only downside was that
many dancers went those routes, and it wasn't so easy to get established with a good client list. Directing and choreographing held
some interest for him, but Tripp felt that divorcing the theater entirely was a healthier choice, at least at first. The other idea that had
taken hold was to become a food writer. He certainly knew the
restaurant industry, and the solid education his parents had insisted
on had made him a better than decent writer.

For so long, there had been nothing but theater. Tripp had only
the vaguest sense of the existence of other professions. Whenever
he met somebody who wasn't in the arts and asked the polite
"What do you do?" he was generally stymied by the answer, which
was usually some incomprehensible permutation of "I'm in quality
and standards, but it has an engineering component, which means
I'm always interfacing with new kinds of developing technologies."

Aside from the utilitarian task of waiting tables, other careers had no more entered Tripp's consciousness as viable options than did driving a team of Alaskan huskies. Although now that he thought of it, that didn't sound so bad. At least he knew what it meant.

He was being given a second chance. He was surprised at his own surprise that such an array of choices was available to him, although of course they always had been there. He'd just never noticed.

" '*Singin' in the rain! I'm singin' in the rain! What a glorious feeling, I'm happy again!*' " sang out Tripp as he opened and tried several five dollar umbrellas, none of which worked. He dumped them all in the trash, executed a pirouette just for fun, and landed on the pile of clothes.

Somewhere under him, his cell phone began to ring. Although he was still letting most of his calls go to voice mail, he was in such a good mood that he decided to answer it. Like a dog digging a hole for his bone, his hands sent socks flying for his own amusement, until he located the phone and untangled it from an old jock strap.

"Hello?"

"May I speak to Tripp Macgregor?"

"Speaking."

"This is Henry Lytle from Lytle-Sutel Casting, how are you?"

"Fine, thanks," said Tripp, trying to ignore the Pavlovian flutter his heart gave. Lytle-Sutel was the casting director for *A Chorus Line*. Tripp cleared his throat. "And you?"

"Good. Listen, one of the dancers in *A Chorus Line* has been injured in rehearsal and has to have surgery. He'll be out through the opening, probably longer. You gave a really strong audition, we were all very impressed, and if you haven't accepted something else in the meantime, we'd like to offer you the role."

Tripp slid off the pile of clothes onto the floor. He knew he had to say something, but a hundred thoughts had exploded into his head, the first of which was "I don't do this anymore." Which was followed almost immediately by "Oh yes, you do!"

"Um, which part is it . . . may I ask?" As if it mattered.

"Greg, the Upper East Side guy. I know you've done the role, so you shouldn't feel too far behind in the rehearsal process."

Greg? That was the role Michael had gotten! That meant it was Michael who had been injured.

Tripp was instantly filled with a combination of concern for Michael, satisfaction that he'd paid a price for his dishonesty, and elation at the opportunity.

He also felt like a complete fraud. If all it took was one phone call dangling a big, fat carrot to yank him right back into the world he'd rejected, then he had been deceiving himself.

A little voice inside his head reminded him that he didn't have to say yes. He could still say no and prove to himself that he really was ready to move on. Or he could tell Henry Lytle that he'd think about it and get back to him.

But why play games? In his heart of hearts, he knew he couldn't turn this down. He wasn't invalidating his future plans—he was justifying twenty-odd years of striving toward a single goal. There would be time for personal training, massage, food writing, or Alaskan huskies. He would do *A Chorus Line*, but he would not use it as a springboard to continue his career. It would be a culmination. He would choose the job because he wanted to do it, not because of where it might lead.

He would take this as the gift it was and move on.

"Yes. Of course. I'd love to do it!"

"That's great!" said Lytle. "Go to the studio tomorrow at ten a.m. They're rehearsing at Ripley-Grier on Eighth Avenue. They'll have your contract, your script and score, and all that good stuff. You'll have to fill out an I-9 as well as a W-4, so be sure to bring your driver's license and social security card, or your passport. "

"Right. This is . . . a real surprise. Thank you."

Lytle gave a little chuckle. "You know, just between us, there were two of you we were considering. And when we ran it past the producer, he said, 'Tripp Macgregor? Isn't he the waiter who dropped that famous wine? What a story! Let's get him.' "

Tripp froze, horrified. Had his dream just turned into a nightmare? Had they hired him simply to mock him?

"Um, they're not going to, um, use that as a publicity hook or anything, are they?" he stuttered.

"Lord, no, nothing like that!" exclaimed Lytle. "It just made him remember you. I think he was amused, because you're such a terrific dancer, and your name is Tripp. You know how these things work. One woman gets cast over another because she reminds the director of his high school girlfriend. But hey, don't knock it! Anything to make you stand out in this business, you know?"

"Right. Yes! Right," managed Tripp.

"Well, congratulations! See you opening night!"

Tripp flipped his phone shut and surveyed the wreckage from his closet. The piles would have to be reorganized. Clothes and shoes he'd need for rehearsal would be separated out from the Goodwill pile, some of which could still go. The world had shifted in an instant to include the one possibility he thought was closed to him forever.

And why? Because he'd dropped the world's most expensive bottle of wine.

He could add that to the twist that it was Michael who'd been injured. But the thing that struck Tripp as most ironic was that Broadway was only ready to welcome him when he had finally, genuinely, and with no regrets been willing to let it go. He could never have imagined that what the future held, after all, was his dream. And now he was no longer afraid of failing at it.

FIFTY-FIVE

ERIC TUMBLED INTO THE HOUSE with an exuberance Sy hadn't seen from him in years. He knew that the prospect of climbing the Shawangunk Mountains was what had Eric fired up, not the primer on winemaking, but the bottom line was the same. Sy had done something unexpected. He had provided his son with a day of excitement and promise, not to mention a little fresh air and a work of original art. For the first time in a long time, he had gotten it right, and he was finally beginning to understand where he had gone wrong.

There was a balance to be struck, an acknowledgment that Eric was still a child, but not a baby. It seemed so obvious, but as he drove his sleeping boy home, Sy realized that until today, Eric had frozen for him at the age of five—the age he was when he and Marianne had split up. Although a visitation schedule was established right from the start, the Eric who stayed in his mind between visits was always five. By the end of each weekend, he'd have adjusted to Eric at six, seven, or ten, but the damage was done in the first five minutes, when he'd hugged too hard, offered the wrong toy, chosen the wrong movie.

By showing up at St. Bernard's on foot without Bill or the car, he'd been a different father than the one Eric held in his own mind between visits, which had given Sy the opening he needed. Today's trip to Ulster County was a natural progression from that day, and Sy realized now that Eric had remained ten in his mind since their visit to the Guggenheim.

Even so, Sy experienced a strange flush of sadness and knew that it was a delayed reaction to seeing his child grow up. Eric had been maturing all along, but Sy had been too distracted to recognize it and make the necessary adjustments. As he watched an uncharacteristically voluble Eric unwrap the painting on the kitchen table and describe to Claudine the majesty of the mountain

range, its funny nickname, and the vineyard owner who'd offered
to take him climbing, Sy suddenly felt a fierce pride in his son, in
his interests, his energy, his person. Marianne was such a Mack
truck, and Sy had tired early on of fighting her, but the time had
come for him to have a stake in the boy's life, not just Wednesdays
and one weekend a month. Even if he couldn't see him more often
than that, he would be invested in a different way. Eric needed him,
and he needed Eric.

As he watched the flow of chatter between Eric and Claudine,
which used to annoy him but today warmed him, Claudine caught
his eye. "There's something for you in the dining room. On the
table," she said.

Sy was about to ask what it was when Eric pulled his sweatshirt
from around his waist, where he had tied it, and showed Claudine
the embroidered saying.

"You can't wear that!" she exclaimed. "They'll have your father
arrested!"

"I'll only wear it around the house."

"Well, you'd better leave it here. Your mother will have a cow if
she sees it!"

Sy left them arguing over the sweatshirt. He hoped Eric would
bring it to Marianne's—he'd decided to stop thinking of her house
as Eric's home. The thought of him wearing the sweatshirt instead
of the minimogul outfit made him smile, although Marianne
couldn't be blamed for the blazer and tie; that was entirely St.
Bernard's fault.

As soon as he entered the dining room, he saw the bottle and
his heart gave a tiny leap of delight.

Who on earth had brought him a bottle of 1961 Pétrus?

He walked slowly to the table, as if the bottle might be rigged
to explode, and carefully peeled off the white notepaper. He recognized the flowery red handwriting immediately.

One of the shield-backed chairs was pulled out a little way from
the table. He dropped into it and flipped open the note.

Dear Sy,

Please read this. There's something important I have to tell you.

That wasn't me with you at the restaurant on Saturday night. It was my twin sister, Elisa. I chickened out at the last minute and sent her instead. But when I saw the story in the paper, I realized I'd made a terrible mistake.

I lied to you, and I'm sorry. But I want you to know that I never would have left you standing there while I licked your wine off the floor. I would have made sure you were okay.

I probably should have turned down your invitation in the first place, and we could have just had lunch or something if you really wanted to get to know me better.

I hope you understand and don't think too badly of me.

Sincerely,
Valentina

P.S. I know you're wondering where I got the Pétrus. Let's just say that the person who should have paid for it did.

Sy let the paper fall on the table and stared, unseeing, at the bottle.

A twin sister? That was crazy! Was she telling the truth? How could he not have figured it out?

And yet, as he thought back on that night, he had been aware of something indefinably different about her. Her hair, for one thing, and she'd been wearing black, which he'd never seen her do before. There were a few things she had said that seemed evasive, but he'd put them down to nerves.

But now as the truth sank in, he felt almost giddy. He hadn't misjudged Valentina after all. Yes, she'd deceived him, but she'd done it because she hadn't felt worthy. She hadn't shown her true colors by licking wine mindlessly off the floor like a lemming, she'd shown them by trying not to hurt him. By sending her sister, she'd hoped to let him have his cake and eat it, too. He felt a tinge of anger rising up at the thought that she'd put one over on him, but mostly what he felt was a sweaty rush of relief.

He placed the wine on the breakfront. How would she have known to get a Pétrus—1961, no less? And, more important, how could she or anyone she knew afford such a bottle?

"The young woman who brought the wine . . . did you talk to her?" Sy asked, returning to the kitchen, where Claudine was plying Eric with homemade macaroni and cheese.

"Yes. She's very sweet, and she was very worried about you," said Claudine.

Eric looked up from his pasta. "What woman?"

"Oh, just . . . nobody."

"Come on, what's her name?" Eric pressed.

"Valentina," said Sy.

"Is she pretty?"

"I thought so," volunteered Claudine. "She told me she lives in Brooklyn."

"What else did she tell you?" asked Sy.

"Well," said Claudine, with a sideways glance at Eric, "it was very important to her that you read her note. I don't know what passed between you, but whatever it was, she wants to make it up to you."

"You should call her, Dad," said Eric, waving his fork energetically.

Sy pulled up a chair next to Eric's at the kitchen table. "We don't have anything in common, really."

"Why? Because she's from Brooklyn?" Eric asked.

Claudine laughed.

"It's not that," said Sy.

"Then what?"

Sy didn't have a good answer. The relief he'd felt upon reading Valentina's note had given way to the realization that just because she'd sent him a bottle of Pétrus, it didn't necessarily mean she had a continuing interest in him. She felt she'd done him wrong—and she had. It was an apology, not a promise.

That night, they watched *Howl's Moving Castle* on DVD, and when Eric fell asleep just before the closing credits, Sy carried him to his room, where the painting of the Gunks was resting against the wall. They'd hang it tomorrow.

Sy tucked Eric under his comforter and retired to his study, where he poured himself a glass of Graham's 1963 Vintage Port. The day had held more than its share of surprises, and he allowed himself to dream a little bit about what his new life might look like. It would have more quality time with Eric, that was certain. He wondered where Valentina might fit in.

He was aware of a shift in his feelings about her. The edge was off his obsession. He knew she had been as much of a fantasy as the Lafite. The Valentina he had expected to join him at Parapluie was, in the end, not so far removed from the erotic imaginings he had conjured when he first read her name on the memo from Human Resources. He'd tried to convince himself that his response was not purely sexual, that he had sensed something different or special about her, but the truth was, he had no reason to think they were suited to each other in any real or meaningful way. Moreover, she had never given him any encouragement. He had no idea what she really felt for him, aside from sympathy, and that was a relatively new development.

They had never had a future together, although now they did have a past. At the very least, he owed her some sort of resolution to the strange events that his hubris had subjected her to. With his expectations and fantasies stripped away, they might even find a connection. There was no real reason to think they would—but, by the same token, there was no longer any particular reason to think they wouldn't.

As he rose to turn off the light, the phone rang. He was feeling calmer and more sanguine than he had in days, so he answered it.

"It's Rick Tague. I hope it's not too late."

"No, not at all," said Sy, glancing at his watch. It was just ten o'clock.

"I had a phone call this evening from George Kirschenbaum,

who owns Cherrytree Cellars. Do you know it?"

"No."

"They're right near here, in Plattekill. They have the second oldest vineyards in the state after Benmarl. They're on page twenty-two of the magazine I gave you, if you want to read about them."

"And you think it's worth a visit?"

"George called to tell me that he's finally decided to sell. He hasn't been himself since his wife died, and the winery has gone downhill in the last few years. He's making a few discreet calls to see if anyone's interested before he puts it on the market. I'm sure somebody will snap it up, so I wanted to make sure you had a shot before it's gone."

"Had a shot?" asked Sy. He felt an odd tingle at the back of his neck.

"Eric said you were looking to buy a winery."

Sy sat on the arm of the chesterfield and brought the phone onto his lap. "Eric said that?"

"While you were in the bathroom. He said you'd left your business and were interested in a winery. This would be perfect because the vineyards are quality, and George's son, Laszlo, is willing to help out for another few years, so he could teach you the ropes. George can tell you their whole family history. It's fascinating."

"I'm sure it is," said Sy, trying to corral his racing thoughts.

"If you're interested, I should let him know right away. What do you think?"

"Yes, please do," said Sy, before he could stop himself. "That would be great."

"My pleasure."

Sy hung up and stared at the phone for what seemed like an eternity.

It couldn't hurt to look at the property, Sy reasoned. And why not a winery? It wasn't as if he had any other, better plans for the rest of his life, and it wasn't totally foreign. He certainly didn't need to make more money, but he knew he'd grow bored before long without something to do. Besides, what was it they said? The only way to make a small fortune in the wine business is to start with a large one. Maybe the best way to usher in this new phase of his life was to be a beginner again. To start something entirely new and give an arc to his remaining years that curved up instead of down.

He left his study and walked upstairs to Eric's room under the eaves. In sleep, Eric had his baby face again, and Sy leaned down and kissed the rounded cheek.

What a little scamp.

And yet, what better proof could there be that he loved his father? He was able to see right through to what Sy wanted—even if Sy wasn't entirely sure yet himself. That was, perhaps, the biggest surprise of the day.

FIFTY-SIX

"WOULD YOU CONSIDER FIRING your chef?" asked Jessica Whitbank.

Annette was seated in the nook with the publicist MaryLou had recommended, drinking coffee and eating hazelnut torte. It was ten o'clock in the morning, and Annette was grateful that Etienne hadn't chosen that moment to come in, uncharacteristically early, to work.

"Why would I want to do that? He's the best thing about the place."

"It always attracts attention when chefs move," explained Jessica. "And it might give the press a reason to come back. If you can snare someone really good, that is."

Annette groaned inwardly. Was this all a good publicist could come up with? Talk about throwing out the baby with the bathwater.

"Etienne has his quirks, but he's an excellent chef. People have been raving about the food, and we share a French-Canadian background that's reflected in the menu." Annette paused. "Besides, I couldn't afford anyone better known."

"Talk to me about this Canadian thing," said Jessica, leaning forward intently and brushing a rogue blond curl away from her eyes. "Have you invited the Canadian ambassador to the UN? Have you reached out to French and French-Canadian groups and set up an 'old home night' kind of event?"

Annette shook her head. "I hadn't thought of that."

Jessica made a note on her pad. "Good way to jump-start word of mouth. Let's talk about wine."

Let's not, thought Annette, but didn't say it.

"Do you serve Canadian ice wine?"

"Of course, but there's more to Canadian wine than Inniskillin. I feature several labels: Clos Saragnat, Colio Estate, Southbrook, among others."

Jessica scribbled some more notes.

"Can you show me where the bottle fell?" Jessica clocked the flicker of disgust that crossed Annette's face and quickly added, "I have an idea."

"It's right down there," said Annette, pointing to the stain, which was finally starting to fade and was no longer so distinguishable from other, newer spills.

"Good enough. We'll start a 'Spot the spot' campaign. Diners who can correctly pinpoint where the wine fell will get a free dessert. How does that sound?"

Cheesy, thought Annette. So this was how the professionals made lemonade.

"Can you give me a list of who's been here already? We won't get them back unless you fire the chef—do think about that—but I'll see who else I can reach out to. I'll also need a list of anyone you know connected in any way to decision makers. You know what I mean when I say decision makers, right?"

"People who are influential in their circles?"

"Yes, and beyond. The people who set the social barometer. How would you feel about writing up your personal history? I mean the stuff you were telling me on the phone about growing up on a fruit farm. We might be able to place it in a food trade as a bylined article. Or are there any trends you notice in the food industry? How about a piece about being mentored by MaryLou Sampson?"

"Um, sure, I suppose," said Annette, wondering when she'd possibly have time to write something up. Maybe some night between two and three in the morning.

Jessica must have read her thoughts, because she quickly added, "Don't worry. We could write it for you, although it would cost extra."

"I think for now we'd better stick to whatever's going to give me the biggest bang for my buck. I'm on a budget."

Jessica chewed the end of her pen and made a few more notes. "We should consider bringing the mountain to Mohammed."

"What do you mean?"

"Send food baskets to key media. What do you have that could be exported, say, as a cold lunch? We could send it in some nice Frenchy or French-Canadiany baskets if there is such a thing. Maybe put, like, a picture of a caribou on the top. Everyone likes free food, and there's no better way to get your point across than getting your product in front of them."

"I like that idea," said Annette. "Although if we're going to do that, I'd better not fire my chef."

Jessica blinked uncertainly. "Is that a joke?"

Annette tried hard not to roll her eyes. Really, she would have to speak to MaryLou.

"What do you like about the restaurant business?" asked Jessica, changing tactics. "I always thought it seemed like a hard job. Such long hours—you really have to devote your life to it, don't you?"

"Isn't that true of any job?"

Jessica shrugged. "I suppose, but food service is more demanding than most, isn't it?"

"Well," began Annette.

"So why do you love it? Do you . . . love it?"

And there it was. The question she hadn't dared ask herself. She could practically see it dancing on the tablecloth, given life and form out of the mouth of this flippant little PR chippie.

Did she love it, even if it didn't always love her back?

She loved the stress of it, the challenge of making plates of gourmet food materialize seemingly out of nowhere. She loved finding new recipes, new ingredients, and pairing foods, even if she didn't cook them herself. With a fleeting thought to Tripp, she realized that running a restaurant was not unlike producing a show. Food service was inherently theatrical, with the chef as the director and the staff performing their feats for a live audience while the clock ticks. And sometimes things went wrong—usually not as wrong as they had the night of the Lafite—but there was always some surprise. Con Ed might shut the power down during lunch service, or Etienne might run out of lentil soup, which takes three hours to make, in the middle of dinner. In Chicago, she'd had a waiter quit in the middle of dinner service, driven to distraction by a rowdy party of twelve. Dishes broke, toast points burned—toast was the hardest thing for any cook to master because it was so basic, easily forgotten in the rush to tend to the more difficult dishes. There were tantrums, drama, comedy, and applause. There was heartache and disappointment, too.

"Yes, I do love it," she said finally. "There's nothing else I'd rather do."

Annette folded her arms across her chest. She felt herself tearing up, and the last thing she wanted to do was cry in front of Jessica Whitbank. She'd probably suggest issuing a press release.

Annette realized that she had never articulated her feelings about her career before. She'd never had to. Nobody had ever asked, not even MaryLou. And despite what MaryLou said about starting over with a new restaurant or choosing another path if she failed, Annette was not giving up on Parapluie so fast.

After a moment, Jessica spoke. "We could try to guest you on Martha Stewart."

"Let's stick to what's possible," Annette said firmly. "I don't need to be a star, I just need my business to succeed. You've got five thousand dollars. There's no more where that came from. If you can't make something happen with that, then I'm on to the next idea."

She could see Jessica gauging her sincerity, and after a moment, the publicist nodded. "All right."

"If the restaurant business is a game, I want Parapluie to win it. I'm sure you know what I mean. Isn't public relations a game?"

Jessica smiled. "I suppose it is."

"And isn't it long hours and people saying no and slamming down the phone in your ear?"

"Oh, yes." Jessica nodded knowingly.

"But you do it anyway because you love it," said Annette.

Jessica looked mildly confused. "I enjoy it, but I wouldn't say I love it."

Annette sat back in the nook and looked at the Caillebotte,

where the well-dressed couple strolled in the rain, unperturbed by the obstacle it presented, intent on reaching their destination in the best shape they could manage. She looked back at Jessica.

"Then I'm sorry for you," she said. "Let's go back to those cold baskets."

FIFTY-SEVEN

"Now, you have to promise not to say anything mean," warned Valentina.

"I won't," said Trish. "You can trust me."

Valentina paced back into her bathroom and peered in the mirror, smoothing her hair back from her red velvet headband, and picking a stray pill from her pink and white candy-striped sweater. "Are you sure I look okay?"

Trish laughed. "You look like you always do. Like a big fucking pink and red heart."

"Thanks a lot," said Valentina, throwing a blush brush at Trish.

Trish bent down and picked it up, flicking the soft bristles against her palm. "I'm a little surprised you're gonna let him see where you live. Someone like that—he'll probably run screaming to the hills."

"I don't care," said Valentina. "I've got nothing more to hide from him. We been through that already, and the fact that he's willing to give me a second chance means I gotta do it right from the start. In other words, I'm not listening to you anymore!"

Valentina was teasing Trish, but they both knew that on some level she meant it. Before Trish could respond, the buzzer rang, and suddenly it was Trish who seemed nervous.

"Do I look okay? I've never met a billionaire before."

"He's not a billionaire, and you look like you, all blond frizz and cigarettes," said Valentina. She leaned on the buzzer. "Hello?"

"It's Sy Hampton."

"As if you know anyone else named Sy," snorted Trish.

Valentina released the buzzer and looked around her living room. She'd spent hours cleaning, making up the couch with the chenille throw that she used only when she was having company. The kitchen was tidy, and she'd finally gotten rid of the broken chair. She'd seen his house. He could see hers.

Valentina opened the door to Sy. She'd expected him to be dressed like he was at work, so she was surprised to see him wearing a striped polo shirt and jeans, with a leather jacket that was casual but still looked expensive. He looked tired, but he also seemed more relaxed than she'd ever seen him.

"Hi," she said.

"Hi."

"Come in."

Valentina held the door open for him.

"This is my friend Trish."

"Patricia Scarparelli," rasped Trish, holding out her hand.

Sy took it and gave it a firm shake. "It's nice to meet you." He glanced around the room. "This is cozy."

"Nothing like what you've got," said Valentina.

"But it's homey. It's warm," he said with a wistful smile.

"It's small," Valentina said.

"Yeah, but you know, size isn't everything," blurted Trish. They all looked at one another for a moment and then laughed.

"You might want to bring a scarf," said Sy to Valentina. "It's a bit chilly today, and we'll be outside."

"Yeah, okay."

As Valentina rummaged in the hall closet, she listened to Sy and Trish behind her.

"What do you do, Patricia?" asked Sy.

"Oh, I work at a salon."

"Really?" said Sy, interested. "I'm thinking of letting myself go gray. What do you think?"

Valentina turned around and watched Trish carefully. But she needn't have worried. Trish took the question as seriously as Valentina knew it had been intended.

"I think it'd look good on you. Is this close to your natural color?" she asked.

"Pretty close."

"It's not bad, but I actually think gray would be flattering."

His current dye job was so much better than the old one, but

Valentina thought Trish might be right. It was possible the gray would actually make him look younger, like he wasn't trying so hard. Valentina shrugged on her jacket and threw her scarf into her large red satchel.

"Okay, I'm ready."

Valentina locked the door behind them, and they all started down the hall. Sy went ahead, and Trish put a hand on Valentina's arm.

"He's nice," she whispered.

"I told you."

"Don't tell him I only work in a nail salon."

"I won't. But you're right about the gray."

They paused on the front steps as, below them, Sy held open the passenger door of a black Lexus. Valentina turned to Trish. "I feel better now that you've met him," she said under her breath.

"Me, too. And I'm sorry if I steered you wrong."

"You didn't, really." Valentina kissed Trish on the cheek. "I didn't know what I wanted. I've got a little better idea now."

She skipped down the steps and climbed into the Lexus, waving happily to Trish as it pulled away from the curb.

FIFTY-EIGHT

THE DRIVE UP TO PLATTEKILL with Valentina was as heady and scary for Sy as the first time he was alone in a car with a girl, when he was sixteen. For a while, they chatted warily about the weather, Trish, and Valentina's neighborhood. She told him more about her friend Vito, who she said was clearly gay, even though he was married with four kids. He'd apparently been the man with the scarf and the silk shirt waving at them in the restaurant, and from what Sy had seen, he was inclined to agree. Sy wondered briefly if Vito had found her the Pétrus, but he had resolved not to ask about the provenance of the wine.

"What's Sy short for?" Valentina asked after a while.

"It isn't," he quipped. "It's long for Sssssss." She laughed, as he'd hoped she would. "Seriously. My full name is Sy David Hampton."

"Did you ever think of going by David?"

"When I was little, my parents called me Davy, but I didn't like it. And my teachers always called me Sy, so that's what the kids called me at school."

"Where did you grow up?"

"Not far from where we're going. Poughkeepsie. On the other side of the river."

"I've never been up here before. I can't believe how country it feels, and it's so close to Manhattan," Valentina said, looking out the window. The sunlight was glinting off her hair, bringing out natural copper highlights that he realized her sister had enhanced. Sy wanted to reach out and stroke the hair he'd long dreamed of touching, but he didn't dare.

"Is it just you and your sister?"

Valentina shook her head. "We have two brothers, Vinnie and Dom. They're not twins, though." She glanced over at him. "I'm really sorry about the switch. It was a mistake."

Sy stared straight ahead as the glorious fall foliage whizzed by. "No, the mistake was mine. And I think that's all we really need to say about it." He pushed his hair off his forehead and cleared his throat. "There's a reason I asked you to come with me today. I mean, beyond your company. I want your advice."

"About what?" she asked, surprised.

"The winery we're visiting is for sale. I'm thinking of buying it."

"Really? You actually know how to make wine?"

"I have no idea," Sy replied. "I mean, I know technically how it's done, but I don't know the secrets of making good wine. The current owner's son is willing to teach me." He looked over at Valentina's green cat eyes, which had grown wide.

"I'm fifty-three. I know that must seem ancient to you, and you know what? It seems old to me, too. Every time I walk past a mirror, I'm surprised to see that I look different from what I remember. That doesn't bother me in itself. I've never cared much about how I look, except it reminds me that I'm changing. And I just . . . I'm tired of my life. And you . . ." He gripped the wheel harder. "You're so young and vibrant, cheerful and sexy. Down to earth. The city does things to a person, you know. I want more earth in my life. I know running a winery is hard work, probably harder than anything I've ever done, but I need to switch gears. I know it may seem like I'm running away from myself, but actually, I think it's more like coming home."

He chanced a glance back at her, and she was watching him, her brow furrowed, a serious expression on her face.

"I didn't grow up rich," he went on. "My dad worked in a hardware store, and my mom took care of me and worked part-time as a substitute teacher. It wasn't even like there were a lot of rich kids at my school and I felt I needed to be like them. I just got lucky. I rode into New York on the wave of the big mergers of the late 1980s and found myself in the right place, with the right skills, at the right time. I married women I loved but didn't like, and now I have a son whom I love deeply and whom I like more and more. It was actually his idea to buy a winery."

"He must be a pretty cool kid," said Valentina.

"Sorry. I didn't mean to go on like that. I just wanted you to know that I'm not really who you think."

"I'd already figured that out." Valentina leaned over and patted his arm. "But it's nice to have the details."

They turned into a long gravel driveway, past old, gnarled vines, heavy with ripe purple grapes, and pulled up in front of a semicircular arrangement of low stone buildings. Beyond a peeling painted sign that read "Cherrytree Cellars," the valley sprawled below them, rimmed with red-gold mountains.

Valentina stepped gingerly from the car, testing the ground as if she weren't sure it would hold her. "This is so beautiful," she breathed.

The door to a building on the left opened, and a small, stooped old man came out, accompanied by a younger, taller man, round-faced and balding. Both wore V-neck sweaters, jeans, and work boots.

"Hello," said the older man. "I am George Kirschenbaum." He spoke with a mellifluous Hungarian accent, the first-syllable stresses softened by years spent in the United States.

"Sy Hampton. And this is Valentina D'Ambrosio."

"Nice to meet you," said Valentina.

"This is my son, Laszlo."

They shook hands all around, and Laszlo said, "Let me show you the vineyards. Then we can speak with Dad inside afterward."

"I will wait for you in the tasting room," said George.

"How do you know Rick Tague?" asked Laszlo, as they crunched across the gravel toward the vineyard, leaving the old man behind.

"I don't know him well," said Sy, "but we have a mutual friend, and I was up at his place the other day."

"He's a good guy. President of our local wine association. And you're an investment banker?"

"Private equity. But I'm giving that up."

Laszlo smiled. "And you've never made wine before?"

Sy shook his head. "Rick says you'd be willing to stay on and teach me. I'm happy to be an apprentice."

They passed into the nearest row of vines, where two men were picking grapes.

"I have my own winery, not too far away," said Laszlo. "It's small, but we stay afloat. Frankly, I don't have the energy or the capital to take over this place. But I'm willing to supervise the winemaking here for a few more years. I have an assistant, Charlie Moke, who could work with you, too."

"You know," piped up Valentina suddenly, "I think I'll go in and sit with your father and let you two talk business."

"Did Rick tell you anything about our history here?" asked Laszlo as they watched her crunch back toward the house. Sy appreciated the way he discreetly ignored the obvious question of their relationship.

"A little."

"These vineyards date back to the early Huguenots. Around the same time, the Kirschenbaum family migrated from the Rhineland to Lake Balaton in Hungary and planted extensive vineyards there. When the Nazis came to power, they seized the vineyards, and my dad and his parents took a long walk across the border into Switzerland, with nothing but the clothes on their backs. Just like in *The Sound of Music.* But they'd been wise enough to store the family money in Swiss accounts, so when they were granted passage to the States, they vowed to start a vineyard here. There was a branch of the family here already, and in fact, my mother was actually my father's second cousin.

"They met and fell in love. By that time, my great-grandparents had bought this place and renamed it Cherrytree Cellars. Kirschenbaum means cherry tree in German, I don't know if you knew that. My dad took it over and ran it with my mom until she died. He doesn't have the heart to keep it up, and you can see it's falling into disrepair. In the good days, we harvested thirty acres. This year's crop is only ten. It's going to take a good five years to restore it to its former glory. But it can be done—the vines are first-class."

"What's your time frame?"

Laszlo looked squarely at Sy. "My father is almost ninety. He's tired. We'd like to sell the property as quickly and painlessly as possible. So if you really are interested, I'm sure we could work something out."

"And the house?"

"It's relatively new—built in 1924—but it needs fixing up. New plumbing and all that. It's part of the deal."

"Where will your father go?"

"He'll live with me in the summer and spend his winters in Florida. We own a condo down there."

"May I see the cellars?" Sy asked.

They walked back past the main building, where George and Valentina were waiting, and into a smaller one. They descended a flight of narrow stone steps and entered the chilly cellar, where a decorative plaque over the archway caught Sy's eye.

It gave the history of the settling of the Huguenots, and a date: 1787.

Suddenly, Sy knew exactly what he was going to do with the rest of his life. He would buy Cherrytree Cellars, and with vines that dated back to the time of Jefferson and Pichard, he would make wine. Unlike what he'd done with the Lafite, he wouldn't be trying to buy happiness, only a chance at it. He would learn, experiment, take risks. And should he ever have an exceptional vintage, he'd set aside one barrel and apply Pichard's trick of extended maceration. If Sy was lucky, before he died, he'd be able to create a wine as potentially great as Pichard's gold crescent Lafite, even if he never discovered Pichard's *chose secrète.* He would make his own time capsule and give back to the world of wine what he'd taken—and squandered.

They looked at the old, label-less bottles, some dating back to the 1950s and 1960s. Laszlo took two off the shelf to bring upstairs.

When they returned to the tasting room, George and Valentina were sitting at a round table, their heads close together. Valentina was nodding vigorously and wiping her eyes. She looked up as they came in, tears glinting on her cheeks.

"George has been telling me the family history and all about Amelia. Sy, they were married for sixty years!"

"Ours was a rare love," George said solemnly. "She was my star."

Valentina shook her head. "I never thought that was possible. My parents were so miserable, like everyone else I ever knew who was married." She looked at Laszlo. "What about you?"

"Chloe and I have been married for thirty-six years and we're very happy." Laszlo glanced from Sy to Valentina. "The key is finding the right person."

Sy cleared his throat. "Valentina, will you walk with me for a moment?"

She nodded and rose from the table. Laszlo set the two bottles from the cellar in front of his father. "Let's open these and see how they are. What do you think?"

"Yes, let's. If not now, when?" said George in his gentle voice.

Sy and Valentina left the Kirschenbaums and walked out beyond the circular driveway to the verge overlooking the vineyards and the majestic valley beyond. The sun was high in the sky, and the air was brisk and invigorating.

"What do you think?" asked Sy.

"If you really want to buy a winery, you should buy this one. The history of it . . . George and Amelia . . . I love their story."

"I am going to buy it," said Sy decisively. "I can sell the town house and just keep a small apartment in the city. I'll have to move up here to run the business and learn how to make wine."

"Oh. I hadn't thought of that," said Valentina. A frown involuntarily crossed her brow, but it was all the encouragement Sy needed.

"Valentina," Sy said, turning toward her, "do you want to help me? I mean as an assistant. We don't have to make any, you know, personal decisions, we can just keep getting to know each other and see what happens. But this is the second time it's my fault you're out of a job, and I want to make it up to you. You might like living out of the city for a bit. Don't feel you have to answer right away.

Take as long as you like."

"No." She shook her head. "I've made up my mind. Just like when you first asked me to drink the Lafite. You see, deep down I knew from the start that I wasn't going to go with you. This time, I know I am."

Sy took Valentina's hand in his and gave it a little squeeze. With her free hand, she smoothed back her thick, coppery hair and tilted her face toward his with a smile. It wasn't exactly what he'd dreamed about for so long, but it was a beginning. As the breeze tickled their necks, and the birds circled over the distant valley, they stood together, looking out at the undulating vineyards, breathing in the cool, grape-scented air.

FIFTY-NINE

THE WHITE-GOLD TUXEDOS SHIMMERED in Tripp's peripheral vision, as his turn came to round the wings and doff his top hat before joining the others in the line. He might have been imagining it, but it seemed to him the applause spiked a tiny bit when he took his bow.

He'd kept his promise to Shoshana. She was out there, along with his parents and his friend Margaret. He found himself picturing Sy Hampton in the audience, admiration for Tripp's talent paving the way for forgiveness. Tripp hoped Valentina had gotten past the housekeeper and that Hampton had accepted her apology. She was a sweet girl, and it was obvious that she cared. Tripp had been both surprised and touched that Annette had sent a congratulatory gift basket of dessert specialties from the restaurant, and he was genuinely pleased, in turn, to read on the card that her new publicist had managed to get her a small feature in *Food & Wine*. The world was righting itself.

The stage lights were blinding, as bright as the flashbulbs had been earlier when the dancers walked the red carpet on their way into the theater for opening night. But the lights didn't faze Tripp. He knew what they really were—rays of love from Jordan, who was watching over him in spirit, embracing him from above, letting him go.

Tripp kicked with the line, confidently and gracefully, practically levitating on the wave of communal energy. He felt a giddy joy and a deep sense of belonging, as his legs reached higher and higher, and, supported by the others, he landed firmly on his feet every time.

AUTHOR'S NOTE

THIS NOVEL WAS INSPIRED by an incident my husband, Josh, vaguely remembered hearing about: a waiter at the Four Seasons had dropped a ridiculously expensive bottle of wine dating back to the French Revolution. The bottle shattered and the wine spilled before anyone could taste it. But the part of the story that remained with me was the image of the assembled oenophiles throwing propriety out the window and themselves to the floor to slurp the wine from the carpet.

In the course of my research, which included attending several wine auctions, I learned more about the actual event that had captured my imagination. Suffice it to say that by the time the story reached my ears, it had fallen victim to a game of urban legend telephone. There was no waiter, the bottle didn't shatter (it was punctured), and only the maître d' got a taste, delicately dipping a finger into the lees and declaring the wine expired.

The accident occurred in April 1989, during one of the now famous "Margaux Dinners" at the Four Seasons. Wine collector William Sokolin was presenting a 1787 Château Margaux allegedly owned by Thomas Jefferson. He had the bottle on consignment and was hoping to resell it for a whopping $519,750, making it the most expensive bottle of wine on record. Most observers concurred that Sokolin himself knocked the bottle against a tray, and some suspected that he staged the accident when no buyers were forthcoming. In any case, he did collect the insurance money ($212,000) and sold the remains of the bottle at auction. Saddest to me, however, was the revelation that there was no mad communal dive to the floor to lick up the wine.

But the true story could not obscure the fantasy version—and, I should add, the utterly fictitious characters—that had taken root in my mind. I also felt that the loss would be more poignant if the wine were still viable. So while Nicolas de Pichard was a real historical figure, his experiment with extended maceration and *la chose secrète* was wishful thinking.

ABOUT THE AUTHOR

JOANNE SYDNEY LESSNER has written the book and lyrics to several musicals with her husband, composer/conductor Joshua Rosenblum, including the cult hit *Fermat's Last Tango*, which received its Off-Broadway premiere at the York Theatre Company. The Teatro da Trindade in Lisbon, Portugal, presented the European premiere and  subsequently gave the world premiere of their next musical, *Einstein's Dreams*, based on the celebrated novel by Alan Lightman. Ms. Lessner's plays include *Critical Mass*, which won the 2009 Heiress Productions Playwriting Competition and is slated for a New York production in the fall of 2010, and *Crossing Lines*, a finalist for the Eugene O'Neill Playwrights Conference. She is a regular contributing writer to *Opera News* and holds a BA in music, *summa cum laude*, from Yale University. Also active as a singer and actor, she has performed on and off Broadway. *Pandora's Bottle* is her first novel. Ms. Lessner was raised in the Hudson Valley and currently resides in New York City with her husband and two children.